Also by Eileen Brady
Saddled with Murder
Penned
Chained
Unleashed
Muzzled

Praise for Eileen Brady

Penned
The Fourth Kate Turner, DVM Mystery

"Animal lovers won't mind that the mystery solving takes a back seat to a wealth of fascinating pet lore, including how to clip a cockatoo's toenails and the proper method for tick removal."

—*Publishers Weekly*

"Veterinarian Brady imbues this page-turner with authentic details about a vet and the critters she treats."

—*Kirkus Reviews*

"The fourth book in the veterinary sleuth series by Eileen Brady, *Penned,* is a nice mix of cozy and semi-hardboiled elements, which is one of my favorite kinds of books to read. I am happy to say I was completely wrong about the killer's identity. *Penned* was a very enjoyable read on every level."

—*Mystery Scene Magazine*

Chained
The Third Kate Turner, DVM Mystery

"The discovery of the remains of Flynn Keegan, who everyone in Oak Falls, NY, assumed left for Hollywood after graduating from high school a decade earlier, propels Brady's well-crafted third Kate Turner mystery... As Kate's digging turns up more secrets and long-buried lies, she has too many suspects and too little evidence. But when a high school classmate of Flynn's is murdered, Kate knows she's both perilously close to the truth and in grave danger. Brady keeps the suspense high through the surprising ending."

—*Publishers Weekly*

"A client's chance encounter with a bone involves veterinarian Kate Turner in yet another murder case in the beautiful but apparently not so peaceful Hudson Valley town of Oak Falls... Brady's years of experience as a veterinarian supply plenty of amusing stories and helpful hints for animal owners while her complicated heroine investigates a tricky case."

—*Kirkus Reviews*

Unleashed
The Second Kate Turner, DVM Mystery

"Brady's sophomore effort is an appealing mix of murder and medicine. Kate is an amiable heroine with lots of spunk. Not willing to leave well enough alone, she joins the list of cozy amateur sleuths, such as Laura Childs's Theodosia Browning and Jane Cleland's Josie Prescott."

—*Library Journal*

"In Brady's amusing, well-plotted second Kate Turner mystery, the Oak Falls, NY, veterinarian investigates the death of Claire Birnham, whose Cairn terrier was treated at the local veterinary hospital. Claire appears to have committed suicide, but it begins to look like a case of foul play after various pet owners reveal details about the woman's life… Turner treats a pot-bellied pig and a smelly cocker spaniel, besides getting chased by a flock of geese. Readers will eagerly look forward to Kate's further adventures."

—*Publishers Weekly*

"Now that curiosity has killed the cat, will it kill the veterinarian?… Kate's second is a treat for animal lovers. The plethora of suspects keeps you guessing."

—*Kirkus Reviews*

Muzzled
The First Kate Turner, DVM Mystery

"Here is a novel written with exacting authority, along with a frolicking sense of humor about life, animals, and the lengths to which someone will go to right a wrong, all while still maintaining a solid sense of tension and suspense. I look forward to future mysteries featuring the charismatic Dr. Kate Turner…and I'm sure you will, too!"

—James Rollins, *New York Times* bestselling author

LAST BUT NOT LEASHED

LAST BUT NOT LEASHED

A DR. KATE VET MYSTERY

EILEEN BRADY

Poisoned Pen
PRESS

Published by Poisoned Pen Press, an imprint of Sourcebooks
P.O. Box 4410, Naperville, Illinois 60567-4410
(630) 961-3900
sourcebooks.com

Printed and bound in the United States of America.
KP 10 9 8 7 6 5 4 3 2 1

To my daughters, Amanda and Britt, who have brought love, joy, tears, and a welcome complexity into my life.

"*A well-trained dog will make no attempt to share your lunch. He will just make you feel guilty so that you can't enjoy it.*"
                                          —Helen Thompson

"*Even the tiniest poodle or Chihuahua is still a wolf at heart.*"
                                          —Dorothy Hinshaw

"*One cat just leads to another.*"
                                          —Ernest Hemingway

Chapter One

"KEANU. STOP KISSING ME."

Despite my pleas, Keanu drew closer, his soulful, dark eyes begging for more.

"You're being a bad, bad boy."

The friendly Labrador retriever mix, named after the famous actor, made a valiant effort to obey. I'd almost finished his final bandage change. The outside layer was lime-green vet wrap, and in about a minute I'd be done if my handsome patient would stop wiggling around. Keanu had cut his paw from catapulting himself in the air after a Frisbee; on descent, the athletic dog landed on a sharp wire fence but kept the disc firmly in his mouth.

Thanks to quick action by my staff at the Oak Falls Animal Hospital, the cut pad had healed nicely, but keeping a foot bandage dry in two feet of snow in New York's Hudson Valley presented a challenge.

"Okay, good-looking. We're done." With that, the dog stood up on the stainless steel table and looked around the treatment room. A bank of cages lined the far wall, punctuated by IV stands and infusion pumps. Most of our Christmas decorations were gone, but someone had left a card depicting Santa Claus as a water buffalo taped to the wall. Above the oxygen cage, perched on the highest point, sat our hospital cat, Mr. Katt, looking down in supreme feline disdain. A stealthy ninja, he sometimes jumped on our shoulders from on high with no warning.

My veterinary tech, Mari, waterproofed our work with some plastic wrap while I kept our star distracted.

"Ready?" I asked her.

"Ready, Doc," she replied.

The two of us lifted Keanu in our arms and gently placed him on the treatment room floor. We both received more doggie kisses for our work.

His thick tail kept whacking me in the knees as I walked him back to reception. As soon as he saw his family, the wags reached a crescendo. That tail felt like someone playing a drum solo on my legs.

The happy family reunion in our reception area quickly turned into chaos. Keanu jumped up on everyone, acting as though he hadn't seen them in years, instead of a mere twenty minutes. Trying to be heard above the ten-year-old twin boys' enthusiastic chatter, I reminded the adults to take the plastic covering off as soon as they got home, and to keep this new bandage clean and dry. Since dogs love to lick, Keanu had several types of anti-licking collars at home to wear, from stiff plastic to sturdy fabric.

"And no Frisbee playing until he's completely healed," I yelled as they walked out the door. "Promise?" At every bandage change I said the same thing, at the same time.

"Promise. Thanks, Dr. Kate. Happy almost New Year." We watched as the family of four piled into their SUV parked in front of our entrance, the mischievous twins sliding over to make room in the back for Keanu. Before the door slammed shut, I saw one of the boys hand the shiny black dog a bright red Frisbee.

My receptionist, Cindy, started laughing. "We should make up some 'No Frisbee' signs for those guys."

I sank into one of the reception chairs and asked, "Are we done for the morning?"

Mari slumped into the chair opposite me, her brown eyes glazed. "Please tell me we can eat lunch now. It's twelve thirty-two."

"Surprise." Cindy got up from her desk, purse and coat in hand. We watched as she flipped our office sign to CLOSED. Dangling her car keys in the air, she said, "Our next appointment isn't until two. The answering service is picking up our calls, so you both can relax. I've got to get to the bank and shop for some office supplies, but I'll be back to open up by one thirty."

The last time we'd had such a long lunch was when one of our house-call clients got murdered.

"Don't get into trouble while I'm gone." Cindy gave me a look like she'd read my mind. Then with a blazing white cheerleader smile she let herself out the front door, locked us in, and hurried over to her truck. Despite the wind, her hair remained undaunted, as unmoving as a steel helmet, stiff with spray.

We didn't wait around to watch her leave.

"This feels like I'm on vacation." Mari laughed as she hurried toward the employee break room to get her food.

"Don't jinx it," I said.

———

With so much extra time, I suggested we eat lunch at my place. It wasn't a long commute. One of the perks of the job, if you could call it that, was living in the attached converted garage apartment. It consisted of a bedroom alcove, a bathroom, small kitchen, living room, and not much more. With a student loan debt of over a hundred and fifty thousand dollars after graduating from Cornell University School of Veterinary Medicine, not having to pay rent made living in a converted garage more palatable.

My rescue dog, Buddy, barked and twirled with pleasure as we opened the apartment door. He loved company but also knew that Mari sometimes dropped delicious things on the floor that I allowed him to gobble up. Vacuuming up stray food was Buddy's contribution to housekeeping.

Usually when Mari comes into the apartment she says, "Looking good." This time she simply shook her head.

"I know. I know." The last week had been particularly frenzied. Piles of stuff were scattered all over the place. My boyfriend, Luke Gianetti, was finishing up his first semester in law school, living and working near the school, so I had no motivation to tidy up. At least that was my rationale. On the kitchen table, Mari found my list of things to do before he joined me for New Year's.

While munching on her sandwich, she eyeballed it.

The microwave pinged, signaling my canned soup was ready.

"You've got way too much on this list," she commented between bites.

"Welcome to my life." When I opened the microwave, I heard my soup bubbling. I'd punched in the wrong number of minutes and turned my tomato bisque into lava.

"No, that's not what I mean." She ripped open a bag of chips and started munching. "If your list is too long, it can be discouraging. Professional organizers say you should break your chores up into manageable units."

"Units?" I also misjudged the temperature of the blue ceramic soup bowl and yelled, "Ouch!" while racing for the kitchen table.

Mari noticed my dilemma but stayed focused on her advice. "Yes, units. That's what they call them, Kate. Like a math problem, I suppose."

"Okay." I blew on my soup a few times before trying it once more. "How do you know all this?"

She held a finger up to indicate a full mouth.

Seeing her occupied, I stole a couple of chips.

"Well, my sister-in-law, Barbara, signed up for this lecture series on home organization at the community center. I'm going with her tonight." Her dark eyebrows arched as she turned and asked, "Want to join us?"

I did a slow pan around the room. Stacks of stuff were everywhere, multiple single socks lay scattered on the floor in no discernable pattern, and dirty clothes draped over the furniture. After clearing my throat, I managed a sarcastic "You think I need to?"

"Hey, I've got a roomie to help me. You're all by yourself, plus half the time you work on the weekends, what with treatments and emergencies. I'm surprised it looks this good in here."

"Thanks." Mari always had my back. "I have to admit I've been feeling overwhelmed lately."

She finished off the last of the chips and crumpled the bag. "So, the lecture starts at six, followed by a short Q and A. It's over by eight. Why don't you meet us there? Count it toward your New Year's resolutions."

I was about to protest that I had too much to do but then realized that most nights I simply sacked out on the sofa with my dog, poured a glass of wine, and watched HGTV.

"Okay," I promised her. "It's a date."

Chapter Two

I GOT TO THE COMMUNITY CENTER A LITTLE LATE, thanks to a last-minute email from a client confused about his kitty's insulin dosage. I'd been to the center a few times, once to cheer on a client with a performing parrot. The large, paved lot next to the center, one of the newer buildings in town, was filled with cars tonight, forcing me to park at the far end.

Despite our recent December snowstorm, the main entrance was newly shoveled, with fresh sand spread about for added traction. Once inside the double glass doors, I followed the signs for the home-organizing lecture. The designated room proved easy to find and held a much larger audience than I expected. At the podium, a speaker discussed wood versus laminate cabinets. Mari had promised to save me a place, so once I caught a glimpse of her curly Afro in the front row, I attempted to join her. No such luck. The speaker paused, frowned at me, then pointed to the few empty seats near the back. I chose the closest aisle, slipped off my backpack and winter coat, and piled them on the seat next to me.

Behind me a man with a pink muffler around his neck scribbled in a pocket notebook.

The topic seemed to be drawers. I didn't know the speaker's name, but she'd dressed very professionally in a black pantsuit and white shirt. A striking green necklace made of large beads in differing shades drew attention to her attractive face. Her abundant brown hair with salon-bleached blond streaks was sleekly contained in a French braid. She radiated confidence.

As I tried to concentrate on her presentation, my body temperature went from comfortably warm to boiling hot. The room air smelled stuffy, full of people. Someone must have turned the heat up because my forehead quickly beaded up with sweat. In a hurry to leave my apartment, I'd neglected to layer, so I had nothing on under my heavy wool sweater except underwear. With sweat rolling down my back and sliding down my front, it became hard to concentrate on organizing your drawers.

While the lecturer continued discussing different drawer liner options, I scanned the room. Along the right wall was a beverage area. My salvation, in the form of a large iced-water dispenser, beckoned. As quietly as possible I stood up, reminding myself to grab a few extra napkins for damage control. Maybe I could casually stuff them down my bra?

"And we have a volunteer," the lecturer said loudly. "The blond woman in the back. Let's give her a hand."

I frantically searched for another blond but soon realized the applause was for me.

Dabbing delicately at my face with my sleeve, I

slowly walked down the center aisle and stood next to her.

"So tell us," the lecturer said, pausing and raising her palm toward me like I was a game show prize. "What is your name?"

"Kate," I answered.

"Tell us, Kate, what do you use to line your dresser drawers?"

Instead of making something up, I told the truth. "I'm not sure. Some kind of wrapping paper, I think? It was in the drawers when I moved in."

The look of disgust on her face could have earned an Academy Award. "You put your clean clothes on top of someone else's…used…drawer liner? Did you wipe it off first?"

This time I lied and said, "Yes."

I don't think she believed me. When I searched for a bit of sympathy from the audience, only Mari managed a smile.

The presenter paused dramatically, then sighed. "I think Kate here needs our help." A ripple of laughter rose from the mostly female audience, some of whom I recognized as my clients. I tried to slink away, but the organizer said, "Just a moment, Kate."

She took a step toward me, then picked something off my shoulder and held it up like a dead bug. "What is this?"

Trapped with the evidence dangling in front of me, I straightened my back, stared her in the eye, and replied in a loud voice, "Dog hair."

More peals of merriment from the audience. Someone with a braying laugh sounded particularly amused.

With a cluck of her tongue, she wrapped the fur in a Kleenex fished out of her jacket pocket and announced, "You, my dear, don't just need help; you need an intervention."

―――――――

"Well, that went well," Mari announced as the three of us drank decaf coffee and munched cookies in the lounge area after the lecture.

Her sister-in-law, Barbara, came to my defense. "I know it was just in fun, but Sookie Overmann could have been nicer to you." With her prominent over-bite, Barbara always reminded me of one of my rabbit patients.

"I'll exact my revenge by taking an extra cookie," I announced. Using a napkin, I placed a fat oatmeal raisin cookie in the center, put another on top, then folded the napkin over them both and stowed them in my backpack. "Talk about embarrassing."

One of my clients spotted us and came over. "I'm so sorry you got picked on tonight, Dr. Kate. But you aren't the only one. Sookie said something snotty to Larissa Jarris last week that had her in tears."

One by one other members of the audience stopped by, offering their condolences.

"This is definitely not the way to increase your clientele," Mari said. She pointed to a stack of business cards at a nearby table, then took an identical one out of her purse.

I read it out loud. "Overmann Organizing. Let a professional organize your home and your life."

For effect I tore it into confetti. "Guess I won't be needing this."

Just then the presenter herself, Sookie Overmann, slid past, gathered up her business cards, and, head held high, made for the exit. In her well-tailored black pantsuit, winter coat under her arm, she cut a much more formal presence than her audience members, most of whom wore jeans and sweatshirts. I wondered if she usually mingled with the crowd.

One of the audience members broke away from her friends, walked over, and said her goodbyes. After a brief conversation, Sookie continued toward the front exit doors.

"She may not have much of a bedside manner," Barbara remarked, "but she knows her stuff. I feel ready to tackle my husband's drawers."

Mari's explosive laugh turned a few heads.

Enjoying our night out, we sat and talked. Other participants also gathered in groups, taking advantage of this winter social event. After about twenty minutes the crowd began to thin. Barbara didn't seem in any hurry to leave. When Mari suggested they get going, she looked at her watch and said, "Just a little longer.

Steve is putting the kids to bed and promised to do the dishes. If he gets it all done, I'll consider it a miracle."

"Knowing my brother, I second that," Mari said.

Soon the room had emptied, leaving Mari, Barbara, and me alone in the lounge. A janitor in gray coveralls started emptying wastepaper baskets and straightening chairs.

"Time to go, I suppose," Barbara said.

Mari put on her coat and asked me if I wanted to walk out with them.

"I think I'll use the restroom. You go ahead." I picked up my belongings and thanked the women for inviting me. "Nice seeing you, Barbara."

"You, too."

Mari and her sister-in-law walked toward the front door. I took a quick look around, trying to remember where the bathrooms were.

"Can I help you?" the janitor called out.

"Yes. Where are the restrooms?"

"Straight down that hallway and to the right." He bent back down and picked up a spray bottle of cleaner.

"Thanks. I'll be quick."

"No hurry. Won't be closing up for another half an hour."

Hoping not to be the last to leave, I slipped my backpack over my shoulder and took off down the hall. Midway down, I caught a glimpse of a janitor in a gray utility jacket and a baseball cap. His back was to me as he slid a large, black garbage bag along the floor.

In my hurry, I must have taken a wrong turn because I ended up in front of the crafts room. I hadn't visited the community center in a while, and this late at night all the hallways looked the same. The bright overhead lighting was amplified in the white corridors. After another wrong turn, I doubled back and finally spotted the restroom signs.

The women's room appeared to be empty. A small armchair in the corner proved a convenient place for my coat. After washing up, I looked in the mirror. The overhead fluorescent lights cast twin gray shadows under my eyes, lending an unhealthy, yellowish gleam to my pale skin. Why did they always have the most unflattering lighting in public restrooms? At least my hair wasn't sticking straight up, crackling with static electricity.

After making a mental note to apply blush before I went out in public, I slipped on my coat. Thank goodness this night was over. Oh well; my staff would think my Q and A with Sookie was hysterical. I hoped I wouldn't bump into any more clients on the way out. A quick glance at my watch noted the time at eight forty-five.

I glanced around for the janitor to say good night but didn't see him. The lounge area, now empty, resembled a hotel lobby. My lone footsteps echoed loudly on the shiny floor tiles. Braced for the cold, I pushed open the glass doors and checked to make sure the walkway wasn't slippery.

Because I'd been late getting to the lecture, I'd been forced to park at the end of the parking lot. Now only two vehicles remained in the lot, each with a fresh dusting of snow. Closest was my beat-up Ford F-150 pickup, with the magnetic Oak Falls Animal Hospital signs on its front doors. Next to it sat a boxy new RAV4.

A bright motion detector light flicked on just before I got to the truck. Startled, I stared into the yellow beam, temporarily blinding myself. Bolted above what I guessed was a back door, it illuminated the walkway leading to this part of the parking lot. Glad for the extra light, although momentarily seeing glowing circles, I slid into the front seat, then dropped my backpack on the passenger seat. I started the engine and was about to leave when I noticed what looked like a pile of clothes next to the building. Bushes partially obstructed my view.

Even with the truck's high beams on, I still couldn't make out what it was. But if those clothes contained a human or an animal, they'd freeze to death tonight.

My guard up, I removed the pepper spray from the side pocket of my backpack. It was a gift from my Gramps, who made me promise to carry it with me at all times. As a fireman, then an arson investigator in New York City, he'd seen too many bad things happen to women. "Prepare for the worst, Katie," Gramps always said.

I got out of the truck and carefully approached the lump, not knowing what to expect. I called out, "Hello?

Are you all right?" Gradually, my mind translated what my eyes saw: legs protruding from a black pantsuit. An expensive dark wool coat crumpled in a heap.

Her upper body curled slightly, like a snail in the snow, Sookie Overmann lay motionless, cheek resting in a pool of frozen blood. Above her perfect French braid gaped a nasty head wound. Splattered with red and lying in the nearby bushes was the yellow-handled snow shovel that had bashed her head in.

Chapter Three

TIRED AND THIRSTY, WITH A HEADACHE THAT wouldn't quit, I sat in my truck next to Oak Falls Chief of Police Bobby Garcia's SUV, its emergency lights making day out of night. I was still parked in the community center parking lot about twenty feet from the crime-scene tape. After checking for a pulse, I'd called 911 and waited for help. That had been forty minutes ago.

Through the windshield I saw Sookie's legs sticking out of the bushes, but no house had fallen on this wicked witch.

Chief Garcia asked me to tell him everything I remembered. Anxious to repeat my story and get home, I began to explain but then backtracked to add more background and clarification about why I was at the lecture. A flood of words erupted, and I realized he didn't find them helpful.

"Gather your thoughts and I'll be right back."

Portable lights had been set up as photos were taken and evidence collected. Everyone worked efficiently. As more time passed I started to feel hungry, since I'd skipped dinner. After rooting around in my backpack, I remembered those oatmeal raisin cookies I'd taken while happily chatting with Mari and Barbara. It felt like years ago.

The sugar soon revived me, and I began to go over the evening in my mind, placing the events in a logical sequence, as I did when taking a patient history. That meant one emotional image needed to be pushed to the back—the sight of Sookie curled up dead in the fallen snow.

The police chief tapped on the hood of the truck and beckoned me to join him. With the temperature hovering around thirty-four degrees, he decided to take my statement inside his nice warm vehicle.

"We can postpone this if you'd like," he said. His jowly face showed concern.

I shook my head. "No, I'm fine. Better to tell it now while my memory is fresh."

In a conversational voice he explained the procedure to me. This was to be an audiotape only, so nodding or gesturing wouldn't convey any useful information.

"Understood. Should I start from when I left the restroom?"

A text message pinged on his phone. As he looked down at the screen he answered, "That should be sufficient for now."

Once ready, he turned off the heat so the blower noise wouldn't interfere with the recording. The chief held up the phone and began. After a slew of official declarations that included time, date, place, and case number, he cued me with a pointed index finger.

"This is the statement of witness Dr. Kate Turner, who discovered the victim."

I squinted a little. The chief had turned on the bright overhead dome light.

"Can you state your name for the record?"

That began my lengthy interview. After I went through my movements, step by step, the chief peppered me with questions. By the end, I could barely think.

At last, he turned off the phone and clicked the heat back on. "We might need to do this again at the station. I'll be in contact."

"Well, you know where I am." The Oak Falls Animal Hospital receptionist, Cindy, happened to be the chief's sister-in-law. A former head cheerleader at Oak Falls High School, Cindy had a perky exterior that softened her drill sergeant personality. She bossed us all around, and we let her. Not even the chief of police was immune.

When I opened the passenger side door and started to slide out, my pants stuck to the vinyl. No leather interiors for surveillance vehicles. "You sure I can go now?"

His head tilted up from his computer screen. "Yes. Want a police escort? It's no problem, but it might take a while to find someone."

I opened the door and inched off the tacky seat. "No thanks. I've got to get up early and work tomorrow. I'll be okay." The cold air blasted me in the face. For once, I welcomed it.

The chief called after me. "Sookie Overmann was

the victim of a vicious, angry attack tonight." Gray patches under his eyes made him appear older than he was. "You be careful out there, Doc."

———————

Not a single car passed me on the twenty-minute ride home. The dark trees cast no shadows; only the snow shone briefly in my headlights. By ten fifteen, I passed the hospital sign and with relief drove through the parking lot to the side entrance of my apartment. A large truck with an attached snowplow idled a few feet from my door. Plumes of exhaust billowed white in the freezing temperatures.

Then a giant holding a big wrench got out.

Over six feet tall and three hundred pounds plus, my neighbor, Pinky, cut a formidable figure. To the people who knew him, he was a pussycat. He waited as I climbed out of the truck.

"Heard the news on the police radio," he said. "Someone mentioned your name. Figured you'd be home late, so me and Princess waited for you."

An elderly poodle pressed her muzzle to the glass and barked.

"You working tonight?" I hoisted my backpack and locked the truck door.

"Yep." He shifted his weight. "One of the weekenders decided to drive up tomorrow, so I got to go plow him out."

Pinky ran two very popular businesses—winter

snowplowing, and summer yard work and cleanup. Many of his clients were second-home owners here in the Hudson Valley, as well as loyal locals. Cindy hired him to do both, and to keep the hospital grounds tidy all year.

His pampered poodle barked again.

"You're keeping Princess up past her bedtime."

Pinky looked upset for a second, before seeing my smile. "Oh. You're joking, Dr. Kate. You know she likes to keep me company when I plow."

"Of course she does."

Now slightly embarrassed, he flushed bright pink. I found myself relaxing. Our casual exchange helped to restore some normalcy to this lousy evening.

With a nod I wished him good night then added, "Don't work too hard."

He waited until I opened my door to say, "Sorry you found that dead lady."

Chapter Four

My morning alarm woke me out of a deep slumber. I'd finally fallen asleep at about two fifteen. That meant I had to function on less than five hours sleep. This day began shaping up as a multiple-cups-of-coffee day, starting now. After taking my dog, Buddy, out for his walk and eating a piece of leftover pizza for breakfast, I made two important phone calls—neither of which I looked forward to.

"What!"

So exclaimed the voice of my boyfriend, Luke, on hearing I'd discovered a body the night before.

"It's not like they think I did it," I retorted.

"I would hope not," he replied. "So, what happened?"

Spinning it the best way I could, I said, "She was lying on the ground, sort of hidden by the bushes, when I went out to the parking lot to get into the truck." That was the truth—a small, intensely edited version of it.

"Maybe she slipped on the ice?" he suggested.

With Luke immersed in his coursework, I didn't want to add to his anxiety, so I changed the subject. "Let's talk about a more pleasant subject. When are you coming home?"

"I'll be back on December twenty-ninth, provided

the Thruway isn't closed down. Did you make any New Year's plans for us yet?"

"Not really. How about watching the stars at your place sitting by a fire?"

"Perfect. I'll call my cousin Rosie and see if the crew can pack us a New Year's feast."

"With pie." I'm a sucker for a good piece of pie.

"Of course," he laughed. "I'd prefer to spend the first day of the New Year in bed with you, but we're invited to a brunch at my grandmother's house—and between my mom and my Nonna, there is no turning down this invite."

"Wouldn't dream of it." One of the things I liked about Luke was his big Italian family, and how close he felt to all of them. The Gianetti family ran a well-known diner just outside of town. Their delicious home-made baked goods were responsible for my tightening waistbands.

"Miss you, Kate. Got to run." He noisily blew me a kiss. "Don't get into any more trouble till I get home."

After we hung up, I took another sip of coffee. "Don't get into trouble" sounded like my new mantra.

The second phone call turned out to be a little trickier. That's because Gramps had raised me since I was an angry teenager after my dad wanted nothing to do with me. Gramps and I had been through a lot together. He always knew when something was up.

"Hey, Gramps. How are you doing this morning?" I smiled while I said it, hoping to make my words sound cheery.

He cleared his throat and said, "What's wrong?"

Busted. "Nothing."

"Katie. You never call me this early. Besides, I can hear it in your voice."

I immediately felt guilty. I'd wanted to spare him accidentally hearing about Sookie's death on the news. I should have left well enough alone.

After a pause, I told him all about the community center lecture and how I'd found a body in the parking lot.

"Of course you did," Gramps answered. "Why am I not surprised?"

Unfortunately, my Gramps knew this wasn't the first corpse I'd found. "It's not my fault," I protested, like a teenager missing curfew.

"Stop. You did the right thing." He coughed again. Gramps had lung damage from being a NYC firefighter for over twenty years. "Chief Garcia will have his hands full. The holiday season is a tough time to investigate a murder."

That stopped me short. "Who said it was a murder?"

"Please. Gimme a break." He chuckled into the phone so loudly that Buddy lifted his head from his dog bed.

For the second time that morning I said, "Well, I didn't do it."

"No, but someone did. And from the way you described that night to me, you are an extremely important witness."

"What do you mean?"

What Gramps noticed in my story changed everything. I checked my watch. In a few minutes I had to leave for work, but now I had an additional call to make. I wasn't happy. This third call threatened to pull me deeper into the mystery surrounding Sookie Overmann's death.

"May I please speak to Chief Garcia?" I asked the police operator. After she placed me on hold, I sat nervously tapping my foot.

"Garcia."

His voice sounded tired. Although we sometimes were at odds, his was a job I didn't envy. With a murder to investigate, there'd be no relaxing New Year's holiday for him.

"Chief, it's Dr. Turner. I've been going over what happened last night, and I may have left something out of my statement."

Something that sounded like a yawn preceded his question. "What did you leave out?"

"Did I tell you I spoke to the janitor?"

"Yes. We've already interviewed him. He confirmed your statement."

Now the chief sounded like I'd interrupted his nap.

"Did I tell you about seeing the other janitor cleaning one of the meeting rooms? All I saw was their back, so it slipped my mind."

"Where was this?" All hints of exhaustion vanished.

It proved difficult to explain exactly which room it

was. "On my way to the restroom, I looked to my left. There was a small meeting room. It was empty except for another janitor with a large, black garbage bag."

"Do you remember anything about this other janitor? Height? Build? Did you catch a look at his face or even his profile?" Garcia asked in an urgent way.

I reminded him the whole thing was over in four or five seconds. "I'm not even sure it was a man. Why not interview them yourself?" I asked.

"Because, Dr. Turner, the community center only employs one janitor. That second person you saw might be the murderer."

Chapter Five

Stunned by the chief's statement, I wondered what to do now. A full day of appointments lay ahead of me, but I felt like going back to bed and pulling the covers over my head. Buddy strolled over and sat at my feet. *Maybe there had been a mistake?* My impulsive night with the girls just kept getting worse.

Determined to put my conversation with Chief Garcia behind me, I left the apartment and walked through the connecting door to the animal hospital. As soon as she saw me, Mari came over to give me a hug.

"We just heard. How awful." Mari picked up her coffee then added, "Are you okay?"

I nodded my head.

The rest of the staff gathered around, full of questions I wasn't allowed to discuss. "Sorry, guys. The only things I'm allowed to talk about from last night's meeting are drawers."

Cindy turned to Mari, disappointment on her face. "I can't believe you didn't invite me to go with you last night."

Our technician didn't miss a beat. "Why would you need to go to an organizing lecture? You could have taught the class."

No longer annoyed, Cindy said, "You have a point."

Both of us knew that Cindy wasn't simply organized; she was über organized, which we both appreciated, since it made our work much easier.

"You know," Mari said while cleaning the countertop, "I learned quite a bit last night. Too bad the lecture series had to end that way."

No doubt Sookie Overmann agreed with her.

———————

The only visible part of my first patient was his rear end. Somehow the fuzzy little poodle-mix dog wedged his body under his owner's arm in an attempt to become invisible.

"White coat syndrome," I joked. "You can bark, but you cannot hide."

The owner smiled at me. She looked familiar.

"I'm glad you've got your sense of humor back, Dr. Kate, after last night," she said.

No wonder her face seemed familiar. Now I realized she'd been one of the clients who spoke to me after the lecture. This was going to be tricky.

"Mrs. Kotvik. Nice to see you again."

Mari stood in front of her, trying to figure out how to extricate the patient. "Grover is hiding, I see."

"It's okay. Let him think he's invisible for a while."

The owner gave her dog's rump a soothing pat. "It's the other end that's the problem. Loose tooth."

"Let's see. Your pet is twelve, so a loose tooth is not out of the ordinary. How long has it been like that?" The last time Grover had been seen at the hospital was three years earlier. At that exam, Doc Anderson noted severe dental disease and a mild heart murmur.

"Oh, it's been loose for about two weeks. I keep waiting for it to fall out but…"

"Well, let's take a look, shall we?" After a few false starts we slid Grover out of his hiding spot and placed him onto the stainless steel exam table.

Mrs. Kotvik chatted away while I tried to examine her dog's mouth. Sure enough, dangling and moving with each pant of his tongue, the upper right canine tooth held on against all odds. Grover didn't help by growling and refusing to let me open his mouth. After I listened to his heart, I graded the murmur a three out of six.

I removed my stethoscope and caught the end of a sentence.

"…her assistant finish the lectures?"

"I'm sorry. What did you say?"

"I said I wonder if Sookie's assistant will finish out the lectures?" Mrs. Kotvik tilted her head, and darned if the dog didn't do the same thing.

Mari handed me a new exam glove. "Sookie had an assistant?"

"Certainly. Her name's Elaine Armstet. She wasn't there last night, or at least not the whole night."

Curiosity won and I asked, "Was Elaine supposed to stay for the whole lecture?"

"Normally she does," my client answered. "At least she did the last two times. Generally, she helped set up everything—the mike, the display table—then she would take everything down after it was over. The drawer lecture was the third in the series. I was a little disappointed Sookie didn't show us any samples, but she did give us several websites to go to."

On hearing her name again, my mouth dried up.

"Strange to think she's gone, just like that." Mrs. Kotvik snapped her fingers.

In the snap of a finger.

Unfortunately, I knew how fragile life could be. My mom and brother went out for ice cream when I was fifteen and, thanks to a drunk driver, never came back.

Mari ended our awkward silence. "Dr. Kate, do you want me to take Grover to the treatment area?"

"Is that all right with you, Mrs. Kotvik? We need to take that tooth out before he swallows it."

"Will it hurt?" Her lips puckered up in a grimace.

I shook my head. "I doubt it. But I'd also like to take some blood samples since his heart murmur has gotten significantly worse. The infection in his gums might have entered the bloodstream and affected the heart valves."

"Whatever you say, Dr. Kate." Mrs. Kotvik sat down in the exam room chair and extracted her cell phone.

Mari carried Grover, following me out of the exam room and across the hallway to the treatment area. The little dog knew something was up.

"Weird that this client was at the organizing lecture last night, don't you think?"

I thought so, too, but kept that to myself.

Grover sat on the treatment table and shot us a pathetic look. It didn't work. We could see the tooth dangling from a thin piece of tissue.

"What's holding that tooth in there?" Mari asked.

"Sheer stubbornness."

Grover stayed surprisingly cooperative through the blood draw and even gave us a voluntary urine sample, just missing Mari's sleeve. However, he jerked his neck away whenever I tried to open his mouth. I shone my penlight and with the help of a tongue depressor got a good look at the loose tooth and his gums.

"Okay," I told Mari, "let me get some gauze. There shouldn't be much bleeding. And don't worry about being bitten. That's the only tooth this guy has left."

Mari distracted him while I gave a sharp tug. It was over in two seconds.

"Soft food for you, dude, but I suspect that's what you've been eating most of your life." The gum around that remaining tooth was swollen and red from long-standing gingival disease.

When I returned Grover to his owner I discussed the relationship between dental disease and heart disease. "I'm sending him home with some antibiotics to treat that gingivitis," I told her, "and Cindy will give you the name of a veterinary cardiologist. I strongly recommend an echocardiogram for this guy. As far as his lab tests go, we should have his results tomorrow or the day after. Cindy will contact you."

Happy to be leaving, Grover started yowling a doggy song.

As we walked to the reception area, Mrs. Kotvik tried to grill me about Sookie's murder. Mari countered by wondering what the community center would do now.

"I just saw an email regarding that," our client said. She stuffed Grover into a pet carryall and plopped him on Cindy's desk. "They've asked Elaine, Sookie's assistant, to finish the course, but she hasn't decided. There are three more weeks left in the series."

"I suppose that makes sense. It must be a money-maker for them." Grover started sniffing a vase of flowers on Cindy's desk. Mari intervened before he could flip it over.

Mrs. Kotvik rummaged around in her purse for her credit card while Cindy waited. She continued chatting. "I hope Elaine does step into Sookie's shoes. Next week is organizing your closets."

———

After Grover's owner left, I asked Cindy when she'd made her appointment.

"Two days ago, I think. I've been trying to get her to come in for a while, but she swore that tooth would fall out on its own."

"So. Not this morning."

"Nope."

"Good." The idea of people booking veterinary exams with me simply to talk about Sookie's death gave me the creeps.

After finishing morning appointments, I sat at the computer in my office brushing some potato chip crumbs off the keyboard. As usual I was multitasking, eating lunch while catching up with client emails.

Cindy poked her head in my office doorway, opened her mouth to say something, paused, then thought better of it.

"I'll clean up the crumbs."

"That's perfectly all right," she said, not meaning it at all. "I wanted to tell you I snuck an extra house call in this afternoon. Mari's got them arranged by location, so there isn't that much extra driving time. Sorry."

With my left hand I fished a random chip off my lap. "No problem. What is it?"

"A cat that's not eating."

"For how long?"

"Two days. The owner locked the cat in a home office, but he can't catch it to bring it in."

"All right. Make sure we have an extra cat carrier in the truck, in case we have to bring the kitty into the hospital." Our office always tried to make accommodations for our clients, especially the elderly and anyone in a bind. We'd even been known to drop off medicine for owners stuck at home.

Cindy lingered then added, "That appointment I

squeezed in is at Sookie Overmann's place. The husband, Glenn, called an hour ago, frantic."

Discovering his wife's body then going to his house
the next day?

"I don't know about this, Cindy. Are you sure he
wants me to come over?" First Mrs. Kotvik, now Glenn
Overmann. Two people connected with last night. A
coincidence? I wasn't a fan.

"So...what do you want to do? The cat is sick."

My watch alarm beeped to remind me lunch was over.
"Keep them on the schedule. Encourage him to try to get
the cat in a carrier and come into the office if he can."

"Okay." She turned to go, already moving on to the
next problem to solve.

"Wait. Do you know if Mari is ready?"

"She said in about half an hour. I'll text you when the
truck is loaded."

As Cindy walked away, Mr. Katt swished his fluffy
body past her legs. Seeing my lap was empty, he took
that as an invitation. He enjoys potato chips, almost as
much as I do.

With an effortless leap he settled himself comfortably in place. He looked up at me with guileless cat
eyes. "Go ahead," I told him.

While Mr. Katt meticulously cleaned up my crunchy
crumbs with his pink tongue, I decided to google
Sookie Overmann.

Like most entrepreneurs, Sookie had a professional-
looking website, linked to her Facebook page. I clicked

on the bio, skipping over the early stuff and concentrating on recent postings. What I learned surprised me. Besides the organizing work, she also ran a successful estate and auction firm and had an MBA from NYU, and tens of thousands of followers. Other links led to some short YouTube cleaning videos and an active Instagram account.

After a brief look, I backtracked and clicked on her photos.

They were labeled and organized, and very impressive. Along with a gorgeous picture of a young Sookie holding up a diploma were several dramatic wedding photos in which her blandly handsome husband, Glenn, played a supporting role. Most often seen in profile, his chin jutted out at a movie star angle. At the top of the page grouped under "portfolio" were multiple photos of shelves, pantries, and closets, etc., plus a blatant ad for her organizing and consultation services.

The rest of the day, spent doing house calls, passed quickly. Several cases needed follow-ups, which I detailed in my notes to Cindy, who received a slew of texts from me with details on callbacks for our patients. However, being busy didn't lessen my dread of our last appointment—visiting Sookie Overmann's home. It felt creepy, like I was standing on her grave.

"Do you think her house will be really, really organized?" my technician asked.

"Don't be morbid," I scolded.

"Just curious." Sensing no response from me, she went back to our hospital laptop screen.

We rode in silence for a while. Snowplows had been out all night, sanding the roads in anticipation of freezing temperatures. The winter sun started to set, which meant we'd be driving back in the dark.

"Mari, I'm really not sure we should do this," I confessed. "What would Chief Garcia say if he knew? This has to be some kind of conflict-of-interest sort of thing."

Busy at the computer, she didn't look up. "You won't be alone—you've got me. This is a professional call, and you're the only house-call veterinarian in about fifty miles."

Of course she was right. It was all about the sick cat that the husband couldn't catch. But I also entertained the strong possibility that Glenn was lying to us.

Chapter Six

I SLOWED DOWN AS THE TRAFFIC LIGHT AT THE crossroads turned yellow. When I applied the brakes, the back tires slipped a bit. The GPS said we'd be at the Overmanns' place in ten minutes.

"Icy," Mari muttered.

"The temperature is dropping. I hope this won't take too long."

Mari glanced out the passenger side window at the banks of snow lining the shoulder.

"Well, at least promise me you won't say anything about his wife's murder."

This time my technician looked up and grinned. "I promise."

We both felt the tires slip once again when I gently applied the gas. "The driving is getting a little iffy."

"I just thought of something," Mari said, closing the laptop. "I bet Glenn Overmann is Chief Garcia's number one suspect. You know what they say—if it isn't the butler, it's the husband."

We were headed to an area of traditional farmhouses, many with orchards and barns. But unlike most of their neighbors, the Overmanns lived in a new home in a small modern complex set back from the road.

"I remember when the developer petitioned the town to build these," Mari told me. "The property is just outside Oak Falls town limits; otherwise they wouldn't have gotten approval. Our historical society is still annoyed."

We turned in at the sign. Maplewood Estates.

"This used to be a cow pasture back when I was a kid. Here—make a left." Mari checked our GPS map for the address. "It's the third one down. Ninety-four Woodland Drive. The kitty's name is Babykins." Mari texted the client to say we had arrived.

Dark clouds had been rolling in all afternoon, promising more snow. We parked the truck directly in front of the bluestone walkway. I slipped my stethoscope off the rearview mirror and picked up my medical supplies bag.

"Ready?"

"Yep." As soon as we got out of the truck, we noticed the dropping temperature.

"Hope we don't get sleet." Two rows of juniper hedges lined the walkway, their gray-green spiky branches rising out of the snow.

"You're from the animal hospital?" Glenn opened the door wide for us, and Mari and I walked into bedlam.

In his wedding photos, Glenn appeared clean-cut, nice-looking, and perfectly groomed. The man in front of us sported a couple of days' beard stubble that hid his chin and upper lip and a forest of uncombed hair. I didn't recognize this version of Glenn.

He led us past the living room. Noticing our astonished looks, Glenn said, "Sorry about the mess. My wife died two days ago."

Mari stared at me. We said, "Sorry for your loss" at the same time.

"This must be a terrible time for you," I added.

"Terrible. I can't concentrate. We were divorcing, you know, but still living together until we sold the house. Sookie divided up the place into zones. I got the living room and half of the dining room. She got the bedroom and the office. We shared the kitchen."

Which explained a lot. Rumpled sheets and blankets took up most of the living room sofa. A portable rolling clothes hanger, the kind you usually see in laundry rooms, held men's clothes. Some pants had slipped off hangers and fallen on the floor. An empty pizza box sat on the coffee table, the last remaining piece stuck in a circle of grease. The room smelled like pizza and body odor.

Though astonished that he revealed so much personal information to strangers, I kept my expression neutral.

Mari got right to the point. "Can we see the cat? Cindy, our receptionist, said Babykins wasn't eating."

"That's right, Doctor. Can you follow me?" He set out ahead of us down a wide carpeted hallway. The walls, painted a creamy white, complemented the silvery carpet. Muted silver light fixtures mounted flush to the ceiling marched in a straight line.

"I'm the veterinary technician. This is the doctor." Mari gestured toward me, but by then Glenn Overmann had turned away.

We stopped in front of a room with a professional sign mounted on the door. Sookie's logo, a pair of interlocking *O*s, said OVERMANN ORGANIZING.

"Babykins is in there. Do you mind if I don't come in? It's too stressful right now." Before waiting for an answer, he retreated back to the living room.

"Time to play my favorite game. Find the cat."

"I think Glenn still thinks I'm the doctor," Mari said.

"No matter. Let's get this done. You go in first; then I'll slip in fast behind you and close the door." I checked to make sure I had my stethoscope and placed the cat carrier out of sight in the hallway. Nothing spooks most kitties like seeing the cat carrier.

On the count of three, we snuck inside.

Any doubts about Sookie Overmann teaching organizational skills vanished when we turned on the light. This office was efficient yet comfortable, her desktop blissfully uncluttered by tangles of wires and wasted space. A comfortable chair and soft indirect lighting defined a more casual area, while the many open and closed shelves made putting things back in their place seem easy.

"Wow." Mari seemed as shocked as I was.

Then I saw the built-in cat bed and feeding station. This woman had been good at her job. But if cleanliness is next to godliness, I needed an exorcism.

"Kate," Mari whispered, "there's Babykins. Look in the cat bed. She's hunkered down under the shelf."

In a slow and quiet movement, I turned my head and saw Babykins trying to blend with her bed like a chameleon. It proved impossible since her pillow was hot pink.

"Let's sit and talk for a moment. Get her used to us."

I got down to the cat's level. She didn't move.

"I don't think she's going anywhere." Without a warning, I plucked Babykins out of her safety spot. When I lifted the skin up behind her neck, it didn't slide back down, a clear sign of dehydration.

"Mari, can you go speak to Glenn and get a bit more history for me?" I asked. "And tell Mr. Overmann I recommend admitting his cat for a workup."

"Will do." Mari snuck out while I continued my exam. Babykins was an elegant Abyssinian cat with a beautiful spotted coat. For this normally friendly and active breed, she acted far too quiet.

While waiting for Mari to return, Babykins securely in my lap, I took a closer look around. On one wall hung multiple framed diplomas. One of those mock *Time* magazine covers in a similar frame sat on her desk. A pair of French doors led to an outside bluestone patio with its own gate. It made me wonder if Sookie saw clients here in her home, using this private side entrance.

While I was trying to read the book titles on her bookcase, Mari came back in, the cat carrier hidden behind her back. "Not much of a history, except she's not eating. He said Babykins preferred his wife, but the lack of appetite started the day before the murder. He also thinks she's vomited a few times."

"Got it. We'll sort it out at the hospital." Uncharacteristically for a cat, Babykins didn't protest getting into the carrier.

As we prepared to leave, Mari asked, "What's your impression of Glenn?"

"I didn't have any chance to form an impression." Bending down, I checked the cage lock and the bolts that held the carrier in place to make sure they were secure. "Except that he's a secret slob."

My technician had a pensive look on her face. "You know what I think of Glenn? He's extremely talkative."

"Chief Garcia will like that."

She opened the office door. "I don't think so. His thoughts jump from topic to topic for no reason. During my questions about his cat, I had to keep stopping him from going off on tangents. Maybe it's the shock of losing his wife?"

"Maybe."

We walked down the hallway, Mari leading the way, the thick carpet muffling our footsteps. When we approached the living room, I heard Glenn speaking loudly on his cell phone to someone. Mari gestured me to stop and raised a finger to her lips.

"Yes," Glenn said. "Yes, you heard me right. I said I'm happy that bitch is dead."

"Guess he's not as shocked as you think," I whispered to Mari as we tiptoed back down the hallway.

Chapter Seven

On the way back to the animal hospital, Babykins meowed a medley of her top hits.

"Should we bother to tell the chief what Glenn Overmann said?" Mari reached behind her to try to comfort and quiet the pretty Abyssinian cat. "He could be referring to some other dead bitch."

"Right." My sarcasm level rated a ten out of ten.

"Okay. I'll tell Cindy, and she can mention it to the chief and ask if he needs to talk to us."

"A little convoluted, don't you think?" The slippery road demanded my attention as the light faded.

Seemingly happy about her scheme, she continued. "And since I was closest to him, I should be the one who reports it. You're only the backup witness."

"This isn't *Law & Order*, you know."

A truck zipped past us, going at least fifteen miles over the speed limit. I'd hate to be nearby when he stepped on his brakes—spinouts being pretty common on these icy roads. Black ice, the kind that blended into the road, made me a believer of steady and slow.

After pulling safely into our parking lot, I said a silent thanks to Pinky. Once again, the parking lot had been plowed and sanded. He'd credited us with saving his dog's life, and ever since he'd tried to make it up to us—and to me in particular. Thanks to his dedication and close proximity, our clients and staff only needed to worry about the roads leading to the hospital.

"Long day," I said after turning off the truck. The cabin smelled like potato chips and cat. My head ached and my eyes felt itchy. The level of concentration needed to safely drive in icy conditions was surprising and tiring.

Mari brought Babykins and the laptop into the treatment room while I followed with my backpack and the rest of our gear. Once inside I asked, "Can you set her up for a complete blood panel with enzymes? And let's hang a cage card that says 'save urine, monitor appetite, note any vomiting, and weigh daily.'" I stuck my finger through the bars of the cage and scratched her chin.

"Will do."

The sound of Cindy's footsteps came down the hallway, but I wasn't ready to discuss our afternoon yet. "I'm going to zip into the office and check pending lab results and client email. I'll be right back." I made it to my office in time for a few moments of quiet. A cold water bottle from the mini-fridge felt wonderful pressed against my eyes. Knowing you can get dehydrated in winter, I twisted the top off and took a drink.

Feeling better, I scrolled through my emails and noticed a message from Glenn Overmann. It posted twenty-five minutes ago, while we were still in the truck coming back from his place.

Once I started reading, I frowned, not sure why Glenn had sent such a bizarre email. After mentioning that Babykins might be traumatized because he and his wife were fighting so loudly, he stated that Sookie had ordered him out of her study in front of the cat. He was certain their behavior frightened the kitty. He then freely confessed to getting drunk and throwing his wife's favorite vase against a wall, and the vase shattering all over the floor. His question—could Babykins have eaten glass from the broken vase after he passed out?

My quick and brief reply said it was highly unlikely, but I'd take an X-ray. Glass fragments are radiopaque and can easily be visualized in a standard X-ray. Since anything is possible, we'd know soon enough, but most cats are particular about their food. I doubted one would gobble up glass. There are those rare felines who get hung up on sucking fuzzy blankets, nibbling plastic bags, munching underwear, or eating anything that has a food or funky smell on it. Veterinary treatment ranged from behavior modification all the way up to kitty Prozac.

I texted Cindy and told her to add an X-ray to Babykins's workup and to present an estimate to the owner. But the more I thought about it, the odder Glenn's email seemed—almost as though he wanted to be a suspect in Sookie's murder. Why admit to a stranger that you had anger management issues and a drinking problem? Most people want to be seen in the best light, but Glenn wasn't one of them—quite the opposite.

And it felt deliberate.

It turns out that Glenn's email went first to the Oak Falls Animal Hospital general mailbox. Cindy had read it before me.

A quick knock on the office door and Cindy stuck her head in. "Did you read his email?"

"Unfortunately." It was interesting that she didn't have to clarify who sent the email. We both knew Glenn was a problem.

She stood in the doorway and tapped a foot. "This guy is either incredibly dumb, or he's got a secret agenda," my receptionist said.

That about covered the entire spectrum of guilt or innocence. "I hate to dump another problem on you, but should we tell the chief?"

"Should we? No idea. I'll call him around lunchtime—off the record for now. But I suggest we only contact Glenn Overmann by email or text. Paper trail, paper trail."

"Agreed. Can you deal with him? Luke and I are planning on enjoying his winter break from school, and I'd prefer no distractions."

"Ah, young love," my friend commented. "I remember it well."

Our patient, Babykins, did not swallow glass. Instead, her tests indicated a mild case of pancreatitis. She'd have to be medicated and watched carefully for the next few days. Glenn's reply to my news was to ask if we could please board his kitty in the hospital for treatment.

Funeral arrangements were occupying his time, as relatives, students, and friends made plans to attend. People would be in and out of the house at all hours. Babykins, in his opinion, would be better off under our care.

I enthusiastically agreed.

After inserting an intravenous line and administering her medication, Mari and I gave Babykins extra attention, coaxing her to purr and to eat a tiny bit of her special diet.

After the staff left, I made my way through the quiet building, checking door and window locks, and closing the blinds. With the hospital alarm set, I opened the connecting door into my apartment.

Once inside I knew I couldn't put a deep cleaning off any longer. I was determined to whip my surroundings into shape for the New Year. First, I changed out of my uniform and into my sweats. You have to be comfortable when you clean. Next, I gathered all my dirty clothes together, sorted them, and started a wash. Taking a hint from Sookie, I divided my place into Four Zones—kitchen, bedroom alcove, living room, and bathroom. I had to admit—it felt a lot less intimidating. Since my to-do list still lay on the kitchen table, that was the logical place to start.

With spray cleaner held high, I squirted one spritz into the sink before Cindy called.

"Want to meet at Judy's? I've got some juicy tidbits to share, but not on the phone. In person, only." She muffled the receiver for a bit then added, "Come on. You deserve a treat."

Let's see. Stay here and clean, or eat a homemade

brownie with hot fudge and whipped cream while listening to gossip. Tough decision.

"Be there in fifteen minutes," I told her.

True to my word, fifteen minutes later I walked into Judy's Café, a hangout for locals as well as weekenders. The clapboard-clad building had been in her family for generations, right on picturesque Main Street of Oak Falls. Judy's menu relied on homemade soups and sandwiches, as well as a mean bowl of chili. Depending on her mood, she sometimes baked scones and muffins. I was a fan of her brownie special. Two brownies, drizzled in hot fudge, topped with whipped cream under a shower of bananas or strawberries—or if you asked nicely, both—to share, of course.

The restaurant's square oak tables were comfortably worn from years of use. In the back near the restroom, a community bulletin board advertised everything from milking goats to reading individual auras with photographs. Cindy caught my eye and waved from a table in the far corner. As I passed by the register, Judy asked me if I wanted the brownie special because she had only one serving left. I gave her a thumbs-up.

"Hope you don't mind, but I texted Mari to join us," Cindy said, a cup of tea in front of her.

"Good idea." Bearing that in mind, I took the chair closest to the wall, so Mari didn't have to climb over me. "Did you order?"

"You're looking at it." I only saw a cup of tea.

"Ahh, come on, Cindy. Order some carbs, please?"

As if on cue Judy, the owner, arrived with my order. The sliced strawberries made the high caloric delight appear deceptively innocent.

Right behind Judy, Mari made her way to our table.

"Hey, Mari," Judy said. "Didn't realize you'd be joining them. Dr. Kate got the last special. Want an extra plate and fork?"

"Perfect. And a glass of milk, please."

My technician practically vibrated with excitement. In fact, she immediately whispered, "This had better be good."

Cindy took a good long look around the café, making sure we couldn't be overheard. She leaned in and said, "Unofficially speaking, the chief might want to take statements from you both and might ask for a copy of that email Glenn sent you, although that request is a little iffy." She emphasized each "might."

"Okay." So far, I'd heard nothing new.

A knowing smile promised more. "Glenn and Sookie separated about one week ago, but no formal papers were signed. They also didn't update their wills. Glenn implied to his estate lawyer they were talking about reconciling, which is a pile of horse poop according to Sookie's assistant, Elaine." Cindy took a slow sip from her tea. "With Sookie's death, Glenn inherits everything— the home, the auction house and its assets, her business bank accounts, the corporation, everything."

"Big motive for Glenn to kill her." I used the break in the conversation as a cue to stop eating, hoping Mari would finish our shared plate.

"Yeah, but here's where it gets interesting. Elaine got a call from one of her auction house employees. He'd been scheduled to deliver a living room table and chairs. Everything was paid for. Sookie always had him buy gas for the delivery truck with a business debit card, but when he tried to use it, the card was denied."

Mari dug into the brownie again, an underwhelmed expression on her face. "So? Don't credit and debit cards automatically get canceled when someone dies?"

"Nope." Again, that knowing smile appeared on our receptionist's face.

"Which means...what?" I asked Cindy.

"Sookie withdrew all the money from the personal, joint, and business bank accounts. She left a five-dollar balance in each. The chief suspects the victim was fixing to disappear."

"Wow. Did her husband know?" Mari put her fork down into a wisp of whipped cream.

"He does now. She took everything—all the savings and investment accounts, plus she maxed out the cash advances on their credit cards. For all intents and purposes, Glenn is now broke. He's got to hire a forensic accountant to trace his own money."

"Why did she do it?" I asked my friends.

Our guesses ranged from spite to running away with a secret lover to the Witness Protection Program. One thing I was sure of. Sookie was an organizer, attentive to details.

There must have been a plan.

Until someone slammed a snow shovel into her head.

Chapter Eight

AFTER RETURNING FROM THE MEETING AT JUDY'S, I was tempted to postpone my chores again, but restless with questions and fueled by chocolate, I went back to cleaning.

While scrubbing the glass stovetop, I recalled the day I moved in.

I'd quit my stressful job on Long Island and desperately needed a change. An unusual veterinary help-wanted ad caught my eye. On an impulse Doc Anderson, the owner of Oak Falls Animal Hospital, who rarely took a vacation, had decided to accompany his only sister, a cancer survivor, on a world cruise. The decision meant he needed someone to run his practice for a year. After speaking on the phone and checking my references, he hired me to start in one week.

Being from New York, I knew the Hudson Valley area but had never been to Oak Falls. One thing that clinched the deal was the use of a free apartment. With no rent to deal with, I could accelerate my student loan payments. So, sight unseen, I accepted.

After his wife's death, Doc Anderson had renovated the animal hospital garage to create a studio apartment.

It had a haphazard feel to it. Nothing disguised the fact I lived in an old garage.

It was a short one-year commitment. After the world cruise ended, Doc Anderson would be back, and I'd be out.

Over the months of living here I'd hung a few paintings, bought some comfy blankets and sheets, but the place still screamed "temporary housing!" My budget couldn't stretch to do more. Student debt for vet school hovered around one hundred fifty thousand, and that payment alone took a chunk out of my paycheck.

Once my year was finished, who knew? Luke's family ran a busy diner here in Oak Falls. Most of his close family lived nearby, with one sister out in LA. My Gramps lived in Brooklyn, while my father and stepmother owned a house on Long Island. When law school ended and Luke passed his bar exam, we'd have some tough decisions to make. I wanted to stay somewhere in New York, close to Gramps.

Would we plan that future as a couple or go our separate ways?

The approaching New Year forced me to think about the future, whether I wanted to or not.

Two hours later, I'd completed cleaning Zone 1. The kitchen gleamed and the pantry made sense. I poured myself a cold glass of white wine to celebrate and sank into the sofa. After one sip, my cell phone rang.

"It's nine thirty. Are you sitting on the sofa with a glass of wine?"

"Luke. That's the kind of thing crazy stalkers say." A part of me felt annoyed that I was so predictable. Of course, he was right on all accounts.

He laughed. "You work hard. I work hard. Tonight, nine thirty is our private happy hour. No dress codes allowed."

Luke chatted away, bringing me up-to-date on his roommate Alden's invitation to spend a few days in NYC law libraries.

"Is your roommate with you?" The two law students had a habit of studying late into the night.

"Nope." Luke made a melodramatic sigh. "I'm jealous. He's with his girlfriend."

I shifted my weight and pulled the blanket up higher. "You'll see me soon."

"Can't wait. Good news is I've almost finished my research. The paper's still far from written, but now I've got a lot more to work with." He lowered his voice. "I didn't realize how wealthy Alden's family is. We're staying at his parents' building on Park Avenue. Lucky guy, his grandfather's a retired judge, and his mother made partner in a high-powered law firm."

"He's only lucky if he needs legal help," I joked. Personally, I thought the attention and love given by a grandparent to a grandchild were more important than what they did for a living. My Gramps was a perfect example.

"Are you kidding me? A judge in the family can smooth your way."

Jumping to another subject, we began planning a day trip, and then I mentioned cleaning the kitchen.

"Cleaning a kitchen is an endless job. All through high school I peeled potatoes, cut vegetables, and bused dirty plates at the diner." Luke made a low groan. "Everyone in my family ended up scrubbing that kitchen at one time or another. I'm finished with that crap for good."

He sounded as if he meant it.

"Well, I'm cleaning the whole apartment in a systematic way." Buddy nudged my knee. I reached down to pet him.

"Hmm," he said. "Is this the influence of that organizing class?"

Trying to compose my answer, I took another sip of wine. "Yes, I suppose so. I did use one of her suggestions, and it worked quite well."

Then came the question I dreaded.

"What ever happened with that investigation into her death?"

For the sake of romantic bliss, I didn't want to talk murder. However, since Luke used to work for Chief Garcia as a police officer, I figured he'd quickly find out. "It was murder," I admitted. "The prime suspect is her husband." I left out the "of course" since I didn't want to appear cynical.

"Are your clients telling you who they think did it?"

"Of course. But the husband…" How could I explain

this to Luke? "Glenn Overmann has revealed details of his marriage, personal details—like fighting, throwing things, getting drunk, committing acts of domestic violence in the past. And he did it in writing!"

No reply on the other end of the call.

"Luke?"

After a moment I heard, "Sorry. I was answering a text."

"Did you hear what I said?" I felt myself transferring my frustration onto Luke.

"Calm down," he answered in a soothing voice. "What does this have to do with us? Chief Garcia will arrest someone soon, I'm sure."

If there's anything I hate, it's someone telling me to calm down. This wasn't the romantic phone call I'd envisioned. With a final sip I finished my wine. Luke talked on about himself and more law school experiences, and I listened.

Five minutes after Luke hung up, my phone rang again.

"Glenn's got an alibi. Do you believe it?" Mari sounded annoyed. She thought he had no class dissing his wife so soon after her death. Her opinion? He killed Sookie.

As I listened, I began putting my cleaning supplies away in their newly designated spots. A noisy dog yawn interrupted our conversation. Time to walk Buddy and go to sleep.

"Mari. That info you told me about Glenn Overmann

having an alibi. That came from a reputable source, right?"

"Of course. I heard it from the cashier at Circle K."

Much as I appreciated the collective wisdom of our local Circle K, I put that factoid on hold. What I couldn't get out of my head was the awkwardness between Luke and me. A disconnect. For the first time, I realized we were on two different tracks, at two very different points in our lives.

Being apart only emphasized it.

I curled up on the sofa and wrapped myself in a plaid blanket. My life from fifteen on had been difficult. After losing my mom and brother, my surgeon father immediately started a second family. Every adolescent step I took was fueled with anger toward him until I went to veterinary school. Once I began my classes, I never looked back.

It was as though I'd gone through a long, dark tunnel and had come out on the other side. I loved my job. For the first time I had begun to put down roots, in Oak Falls.

People recognized me. I looked forward to settling down, buying a home, maybe starting a family. Luke, on the other hand, had settled down at eighteen with his high school sweetheart, Dina, and become an Oak Falls police officer to make ends meet. He'd been engaged and dumped, then reengaged to Dina over the years, all the while living in Oak Falls. His life seemed settled. But he'd wanted more. Things started to change with his acceptance into a prestigious law school. He began to hang out with his roommate, Alden, and a gang of trust-fund kids. The fellow who never wanted to leave his hometown talked about moving to Chicago, or getting a job with a big-time law firm in California, or maybe clerking for a Supreme Court justice. He'd reinvented himself, and he liked it.

I also had a feeling Luke still had a few wild oats to sow.

And I wasn't going to be anybody's oat.

Chapter Nine

OVERNIGHT, THE WIND MUST HAVE KICKED UP, because a branch or something landed briefly on the roof, then skittered away. Strong gusts of wind were a fact of life in the Hudson Valley. My watchdog, Buddy, lay snoozing in his dog bed, so I threw the covers over my head and went back to sleep.

Then, for the second time something woke me up. How long had I been asleep? As that foggy feeling left, I realized Buddy was awake and barking, staring at the front door. My clock read five in the morning. Still a little groggy, I got out of bed and looked out the window. The motion detector light above the door glowed in the dark. It illuminated the walkway and the thermometer, which registered thirty-one degrees Fahrenheit. Except for the hospital truck, the parking lot stood empty and quiet. There'd been no new snow. What had tripped the spotlight sensor?

At my feet Buddy danced around, giving quick little yips, eager for his morning walk. I didn't share his enthusiasm. My alarm was set for six thirty. The universe owed me one hour and thirty minutes of additional sleep. I let the curtain drop, hoping my dog would forget about everything and go back to sleep.

Buddy stared up at me, brown eyes alert, and barked again. If I thought I could get away with telling him to wait, he made it clear by his body language that this wasn't an option.

I pulled boots and a jacket over my pajamas. Still half asleep, I slipped Buddy's paws into his new snow booties, ribbed on the bottom for better traction. He hated getting his feet wet.

When I stepped outside, icy air frosted my nose and lungs. With his muzzle down to the ground, Buddy cheerfully trotted over to his favorite maple tree in the fenced side yard and proceeded to do his business. Usually he scurries back inside, but this morning he sniffed the air, gave me a worried look, and whined.

"Let's go," I told him, turning my back to open the door. To my astonishment, he took off across the empty parking lot toward the dumpster and stopped near the shrubbery on the property line.

"Come on, Buddy," I called. "It's freezing out."

His head turned toward my voice, but the rescued King Charles spaniel stood his ground. Since he was normally a very obedient dog, this behavior meant something was up. Periodically he'd been distracted by a squirrel, or a dead bird, or a meet-up with one of the neighborhood cats. But I couldn't imagine anything or anyone hanging around in this weather. As I moved closer to him, I saw a red plaid blanket at the base of the dumpster. Buddy pawed at the ground, whining louder. Flashbacks of finding Sookie's body in the snow put me on alert.

I hesitated. Cindy said she'd once found the body of an elderly dog, lovingly placed in a cardboard box, near this same dumpster—a bullet wound in the middle of its forehead.

"That's how some people put their pet to sleep. We've got a lot of folks up here who hunt," she'd explained.

Words failed me. I hoped this wasn't one of those.

It wasn't. Inside the blanket lay a dog, barely breathing.

Buddy followed me as I hoisted the dog in my arms and ran back inside my apartment.

"Stay," I told him, then opened the connecting door to the hospital, turned off the alarm, and hurried into the treatment area. A quick feel of the inside of his mouth told me hypothermia was the first issue. White teeth signaled a young dog. I got out the surgical warming blanket and plugged it in. Unwrapping the old plaid blanket revealed a gray pit bull with multiple cuts and bite wounds on his trunk and legs and belly.

His heart rate was slow but the rhythm steady. When I covered him with the warm blanket, his eyelids moved. Although working by myself, I took the opportunity to pull some blood and inserted a catheter in his front leg—solo skills I mastered while working the late-night shift in a busy emergency clinic.

I hooked him up to a temporary, slow-warmed saline drip until I knew if he had any underlying health issues. His temperature gradually climbed from ninety-seven to an almost normal one hundred degrees. By that time, the clock read five forty-five.

Our in-house lab machines would soon give me a complete blood count as well as kidney and liver functions. Meanwhile, I knew my early-rising tech would be up having breakfast.

"Mari," I said when she answered her cell after three rings.

"Kate. Everything okay?" Her voice sounded worried, all kinds of horrific things probably going through her mind.

"I'm fine," I replied. "Someone abandoned a dog outside by the dumpster. He's all chewed up but still alive. I was hoping you might come in a little early so we can finish working him up before appointments start."

A palpable sigh of relief was followed by "No problem. I'll get there as soon as I can."

While I waited for preliminary results, I sat down on the floor in front of his cage. "Good boy," I told him, words most dogs know and respond to. Stroking the short silvery-gray fur on his head, I noted the amateurish cropped ears. Another flutter of his eyelids made me hopeful he would wake up. "Good dog," I whispered over and over to the pit bull. "Good dog."

By the time Mari got to the animal hospital, my pit bull had lifted his head up. His temperature had returned to almost normal, and his pupils were responsive. I placed a water bowl and a small amount of canned food in front of him. He gobbled everything up.

Mari came bearing gifts. She walked toward me, two

large takeout cups of coffee in her hands. "Thought you could use this," she said. With a practiced glance, she checked out the dog in the hospital cage. "So this is our mystery patient. Looks better than I thought he would."

I stood up, my back protesting as I stretched out my shoulders. "You should have seen him earlier. He perked right up, though."

"How on earth did you find him?"

"Buddy woke me up at five a.m. Someone must have dropped him off right around that time. They were gone by the time we found him."

"You know you're still in your pajamas."

"Totally forgot." I rubbed my face with my hands. "Can you watch him for a bit? I need a shower and some kind of breakfast."

"Here you are." She reached into a brown paper bag on the countertop. "I bought some breakfast sandwiches for us when I picked up the coffee."

The egg, cheese, and bacon smell made me ravenous. I gave her a high-five. "You're the best. If he starts to crash, call me. We can do a complete exam when I get back."

"Okay. I think Mr. Pitt over there wants a taste of my breakfast." She pointed to the cage and our new patient, who eyed Mari's food.

"Sure. But only food, no fingers."

About a half hour later I'd showered, fed Buddy, thrown on a pair of clean scrubs, and slicked my limp hair into a ponytail. Anything else would have to wait. Armed with a tube of lip balm and some sugar-free gum, I hurried back through the connecting door into the hospital.

I found Mari humming to herself as she checked our surgical packs and took out some bandage material.

"You look better," she told me.

"So does he." Our mystery patient was sitting up in the cage, fully alert, a bewildered look on his face.

"Let's get him out and have him walk around." Mari took a leash from our stash and opened the cage door, while I went to get a leather muzzle, just in case.

She slipped the lead over the dog's head without any problem. "No collar," she said. "There was one, though. I can see the imprint on his neck."

With a little coaxing, the big gray dog got to his feet and gingerly stepped out onto the hospital floor. His head hung down, eyes focused on the floor. Then his body started to quiver.

"Let's get him up on the table. I want to get a good look at him. But first put that muzzle on. We have no idea what we're dealing with here." Safety always came first when handling animals—safety for the animal as well as the handler. I'd had a veterinarian friend lose an ear during an exam when a passive German shepherd mix dog suddenly turned on him.

We both lifted the dog onto the treatment table. Pit bulls are dense dogs, with a lot of weight packed onto their compact bodies. I could feel and see right away this guy was underweight.

"Holy mackerel," Mari said, getting a good look at the multiple bite wounds. "Did a coyote attack him?"

I stood directly in front of the dog. His light green eyes looked into mine. There was no sign of aggression—only sad acceptance of whatever pain he thought was coming.

"No coyote did this. Only a human could be so cruel."

Mari's eyes met mine.

"This guy was used for dogfights."

With our patient stable, I went into my office and called Dierdra, our contact at the local no-kill shelter.

"Hi, Dr. Kate. What can I do for you this early in the morning?"

I explained what I knew about the pit bull I'd found, complete with an update on his physical description and status.

Dierdra said, "Sorry. You've called us at a bad time. Animal control brought us twenty-nine dogs and ten cats confiscated from an animal hoarder last Friday. We're packed. I'm really sorry."

Early in my veterinary career I'd dealt with an animal hoarder. She'd meant well but ended up doing more harm than good—to herself and to the animals she tried to help.

"No problem. I can keep him here for now. He's going to need medical care anyway for his wounds, and close monitoring of his kidney and liver function."

Another apology from Dierdra was followed by an enthusiastic question. "Wait. Aren't you a certified foster parent? I remember when you adopted…"

"Buddy?" My King Charles had been a rescue dog from a show breeder. "I'd be happy to foster Mr. Pitt."

"Mr. Pitt?"

"You know Mari—she's already given him a name. Now we have a Mr. Pitt and a Mr. Katt. If you want I'll go on your website and fill out all the forms and a lost-dog search, too." The shelter was very efficient, trying to make adoption and fostering as simple as possible. All animals' information, Q & A, and photos were updated regularly.

"Perfect. Anything else you can tell me?"

Unfortunately I could. "I suspect he's been used in dogfights. Maybe a bait dog."

"Poor guy. At least he's in good hands now."

By the time Cindy arrived, Mari and I were caught up with our lab tests and I had sent emails out to all my pending cases. At this point I was running on multiple cups of coffee. I anticipated taking a nosedive around five thirty, after the last client left.

A sweet meow from Babykins Overmann indicated the Abyssinian cat was much improved. Rubbing on the cage doors, she asked for some loving. I went over and scratched her under the chin.

"Kate," Cindy sort of whispered to me. "Look at that."

My gaze followed hers. To my surprise, Mr. Katt sat in front of Mr. Pitt. The big gray dog wagged his tail as he gazed back at our fluffy hospital cat. Mr. Katt was a great judge of dog temperaments. As we watched, our tabby strolled back and forth in front of our new arrival, gradually getting closer, until he rubbed on the front of the cage door. The pit bull stuck out a pink tongue and the two touched noses.

"That's a good sign," I told her.

Cindy smiled. "He seems like a lover, not a fighter."

My eyes took in the massive head covered with scars and scabs. "I agree. He wouldn't fight. That's what got him into trouble."

Chapter Ten

SHARP FANGS BARED AND LIP CURLED UP, MY PATIENT didn't hide his willingness to bite down hard on me. Brown eyes with huge dark pupils stared into mine—furious and ready to lunge. Then, with no warning, he catapulted himself at my face.

"Stop that, you naughty boy," his owner told the eight-pound Chihuahua, pulling him back against her chest. His skinny stick legs scrambled about like eggs in a pan, but to no avail. Mother Nature had put the heart of a lion into the body of a mouse.

As always, I didn't take it personally. Little Man and his owner, Daffy, were two of my oldest and most favorite clients. Often dressed in costumes, the pair never ceased to entertain us and feed us. But first we had to tame the beast.

Our house-call routine was as choreographed as a competition dance number. Mari distracted our grumpy Chihuahua with her keys, dangling them above his bulging eyes and translucent ears. Meanwhile, I silently snuck up behind him and lassoed his nose with a homemade gauze muzzle. Safe from his bite, we proceeded to torture him by cutting his toenails.

I suspected that Little Man also put on a show for

us. During each house call, he forcefully defended his home and family from the creature in the white coat. He had every right to expect success. We, the invaders, always left eventually, defeated by the power of the Chihuahua.

"Just the nail trim today?"

"Yes. Thank you so much," Daffy said when we finished and returned her fur baby into her arms. "Come sit down and have some tea or coffee. I've got your favorite cookies, Mari."

We ignored the random halfhearted growls from our patient and sat down at the kitchen table. It was almost New Year's and, as always, Daffy and Little Man were dressed in appropriate costumes.

Simply for fun, we'd bet on how they'd be dressed, and Mari lost. I figured Father Time, but my assistant went for the baby-in-a-diaper look, which made me cringe. How our client tailored a robe to fit a Chihuahua was genius. A retired teacher who never married, Daphne had been given the nickname Daffy by her family because of her delightful eccentricities. She indulged her creative side by sewing costumes for theater productions, Halloween parties, and pets, and knit copious numbers of mufflers and gloves for needy charities. To my mind, she deserved her bit of fun.

"Nice decorations," Mari added, after peeking into the living room. I'd caught glimpses of holiday hats strung across the window, and silver streamers hanging from an overhead light when we'd first come in.

Daffy placed a large plate of assorted cookies and pastries on the kitchen table. The aroma of butter and cinnamon spiked my appetite. "Wait, you have to see the full effect." She took off down a hallway, carrying Little Man under her arm like the French carry a baguette.

"What do you think the full effect is?" I questioned my technician.

"No idea." Her hand snaked out and took a large chocolate chip cookie from the display.

"No diapers, please," I whispered. "I don't want to see either of them in a diaper."

A banging noise made us turn our heads. Out of the dark hallway came a large metal scythe pointed toward us. It looked very realistic. A bit too realistic.

I stood up and backed away.

"Ta-da!" With one hand under the Chihuahua and the other hand on the large scythe, Daffy stood hunched over, a long white wig on her head. Little Man had been transformed into Baby Time, with the infamous diaper held on by a strap over one shoulder. Across his owner's chest draped a sash announcing the beginning of a new year. "Father Time waits for no man or dog. Prepare!"

Of course we both clapped and admired her handiwork. I'd expected a rubberized blade on the scythe, but instead it was a nasty-looking piece of sheet metal cut into that characteristic New Year's curve.

"That looks dangerous." Mari pointed to the blade, light bouncing off its shiny surface.

Daffy disagreed. "I've got a plastic sheath that slips over it," she insisted. "The high school shop teacher, Dan Belson, made it for me a few years ago. I can't have anyone cut themselves at the New Year's party."

Daffy? Going to a party? Although she often played bridge and went to gardening club meetings, I'd never pictured Daffy going partying.

"What party?" Mari always focused on the main issue.

The question hung in the air.

"Judy's Last-Minute Costumes-Optional New Year's Eve Blast-Off Party."

Mari and I exchanged looks.

"Why didn't…" Mari began but was cut off by Daffy.

"Judy just decided this morning that everyone needed to give this year a big send-off. It starts at ten and goes till who knows when." Our client took a moment to laugh at her rhyme. Even Little Man appeared pleased.

"Where is it going to be held?" I asked.

"The old hay barn on Miller Road," she said, giggling a bit. "Be there or be square—*dancing*." This time Mari joined in the laughter.

After accepting a parting gift of cookies, we passed through Daffy's front yard and opened the picket fence gate. Once inside the truck cab, Mari began furiously texting. She and Cindy prided themselves on knowing what was going on in our community. A major slipup like this wounded their pride.

I didn't get what all the fuss was about.

"Where now?" Our receptionist/office manager booked all the house-call appointments, working them around regular hospital hours. Often, they were rescheduled or updated by text.

"Just a sec." Mari's fingers flew at a ridiculously swift speed.

Watching her repetitive movements, I bet that twenty years from now doctors would be treating plenty of arthritic thumbs.

With no address to input into the GPS, I turned on my blinker and pulled to the curb a few doors down from Daffy's house. Heat started to flow from the F-150's vents, quickly warming the cab. A wave of drowsiness, fueled by the food and the warmth, took over. I glanced off to the left, through my driver's side window. All was silent except for the click of text messages.

In the distance, the blue-toned mountains glowed, peaks painted winter white. Small ice crystals trapped in the drifts of snow caught the light, twinkling like fallen stars. I'd read that millions of years ago, glaciers had carved out the Hudson Valley. Its beauty had inspired scores of artists over the years, many drawn to Oak Falls and nearby Woodstock.

"Kate."

My reverie interrupted, I turned to Mari, who wore a triumphant expression on her face.

"This is going to be fab," she said. "Last time Judy threw a party, she almost burned the town down."

That night after checking on Mr. Pitt, I called Luke.

"Hi Kate," he said in a rush. "I'm about to leave in a few minutes. What's up?"

In the background I heard loud laughing. "Okay. I'll make this quick. Judy is having a party at the old hay barn on Miller Road on New Year's Eve. Do you want to go?"

"Judy's Café Judy? Sure."

I heard a muffled voice in the background. It sounded like Luke had placed his hand over the speaker.

"Are you at a party?" I asked.

He sounded a bit defensive when he said, "It's just a few of our classmates and some friends they dragged along. We're celebrating finally having some free time."

The only conclusion I could draw was that he didn't want to spend that free time with me.

He must have noticed my silence. "You there?"

"Yes." I swallowed the hard lump in my throat and said the first thing that popped into my brain. "Any idea where this hay barn is?"

That elicited a chuckle from Luke.

Annoyed, I asked, "What's so funny about a barn full of hay?"

"Because that specific hay barn is infamous. In high school we used to call it the make-hay barn, if you get my drift."

"Yep. Got it." From my vet experience I also knew hay barns could be dusty, drafty, and dirty.

"Sorry." Someone in the distance called Luke's name—a female someone. "Have to go. Miss you."

"Miss you too." I waited, debating what to say next. "Luke, I..."

The loud dial tone cut me off.

I felt miserable after my conversation, so I figured I'd check on someone who had my personal misery beat.

"Mr. Pitt," I said as I turned on the lights, "you've got a visitor."

Buddy looked around, then tentatively approached the large run we'd assigned to our newest patient. I didn't expect any aggression, but I prepared for it. Instead, Mr. Pitt greeted the much smaller dog like the dog pal I hoped he'd be.

After watching the playful body language between the two dogs, I brought out a treat. "Sit." I held the treat up for the pit bull to see. He immediately sat.

Buddy watched the other dog chomp his treat and sat without being asked. Wagging tails made me hope for the best. I tried a very brief nose-to-nose visit. That culminated in a definite down-on-the-front-legs invitation to play from Buddy.

"Okay. Let's try this."

Attaching a strong lead with a nose loop to Mr. Pitt, I opened the cage door. He walked out and waited by my side. Someone had taught him good dog manners. How had he ended up in a dogfight ring?

Had he gotten lost like so many dogs, or been stolen?

After the two dogs did their business in the snow, I took them both back into my apartment. I made sure there was no food on the floor to argue about. Then I brought out the two spare dog beds often used by Mari's Rottweilers and showed them to Mr. Pitt. He gladly lay down on my command, rolling on his back and grunting with pleasure. Next to the bed I placed a ragged stuffed moose toy. He delicately picked it up and held it in his mouth.

Too restless to go to sleep, I curled up on the sofa with a hot cup of tea and turned on HGTV.

When my cell phone rang, I gladly answered the familiar number. My Gramps always had a way of making me feel better.

"Hey, Gramps," I said.

"Hey, sweetie," he answered, his breathing harsh. "Watching *House Hunters*?"

"Of course." We sometimes bet on which house would be chosen.

Gramps could always read my moods by my voice. In the background I heard noises, like dishes going into a sink.

"We can talk another time if you're busy," I told him.

"Katie," Gramps said, "there's nothing in the world more important than talking to you."

Determined not to burden him with my dumb problems, I started out by talking about Mr. Pitt. Gramps knew a bit about dogfighting, having once investigated a fire set to destroy fighting evidence.

"There used to be quite a lot of backroom-type gambling and dogfighting in New Jersey and Lower Manhattan," he commented. "But thanks to arrests and publicity from animal rights groups, those numbers are way down."

"Gramps," I began, "I think someone rescued him, then brought him as close to the animal hospital as they could without being caught on camera. Whoever it was woke me up by throwing something up onto the roof."

The phone went silent while he thought. "It must be someone who's familiar with you or the animal hospital and your routine."

The pit bull gently snored, the fuzzy brown moose firmly in his mouth. "Whoever did it saved his life."

"Agreed. But I don't think that is the only thing on your mind."

Reluctantly, I gave him an edited version of my current relationship or lack of relationship with Luke. After going on and on without any comment from him, I stopped and waited for his response.

"Keep working on yourself," he cryptically said. "When you're happy, you'll know if he makes you happy."

Mulling over our conversation, I went back to the *House Hunters* episode. As I drifted off on the sofa, I dreamed Luke and I were participants on the program trying to choose between three houses. We kept arguing and changing our minds and arguing again, until the producer kicked us off the show.

When I woke up just before dawn, I found Buddy snoring on the couch next to me and Mr. Pitt sound asleep, his head resting on my foot.

Chapter Eleven

"WELL, LOOK WHO'S HERE," MARI EXCLAIMED AS SHE bent down to say hello to Mr. Pitt. "Nice collar." He rewarded her with a slow wagging tail. I stood with him in the treatment room trying to decide whether I really needed another cup of coffee.

"Gray fur is very popular and goes with anything," she joked. "He's styling now."

I'd picked out a patterned turquoise dog collar from the many collars and leashes donated by clients. The animal hospital, in turn, pays it forward by providing these items to anyone in need.

Cindy walked in and stopped dead when she saw the big dog. "Is he going to be all right?" she asked, temporarily stunned by all his wounds.

"He should be. Mari, let's check him for a microchip. Use the universal scanner."

Cindy reached into the pocket of her jacket and pulled out a mini bone. Pitt's eyes immediately snapped to attention, and he sat like a champ.

"Good boy," the receptionist said, giving him a pat on his lumpy head. He stood up and watched Mari approach with the chip scanner in her hand. His back legs quivered.

"You're okay," I told Pitt and scratched his chest.

"Anything I need to do?" Cindy often ran down owners of lost dogs through their implanted microchips.

We were interrupted by a shout from Mari, who'd checked between Pitt's shoulder blades. "Bingo. We have a manufacturer and their phone number." Cindy jotted down the info. Because different chip manufacturers have different databases, it was important to be able to read the data correctly. Once we tracked down Pitt's owners, one part of his past would be revealed. We'd coordinate with the fostering program at the shelter to make sure he wasn't returned to a dangerous situation. With any luck, we'd found his family.

With both Buddy and Mr. Pitt snoozing in their beds, I brought my lunch back into the hospital and joined Mari and Cindy in the employee lounge. They were mid-chat about Judy and her unexpected New Year's Eve bash.

"When I spoke to her a while ago, she said it's a pop-up party—like a pop-up restaurant, only better."

"Pop-up meaning spur of the moment?" I asked, taking a tentative bite of my microwaved burrito. Instead of being "surface of the sun" hot, it had barely reached warm. My relationship with our office microwave was like Goldilocks and the Three Bears, either too hot or too cold. Only rarely did it turn out just right.

"It means temporary." Cindy confirmed the meaning of pop-up. "Judy has so many chef friends with pop-up restaurants, she figured why not a pop-up party instead?"

Mari held up a family-sized chip bag and offered it to us. Cindy frowned at her choice and went back to her salad. I begged off, knowing that I couldn't eat only one chip. One chip led to one hundred chips. I blamed the addictive crunch and the salt.

"How do you eat like that and never gain weight?" Cindy was constantly on a diet of one sort or another. Mari, on the other hand, ate enormous amounts of food and snacks, yet never gained a pound.

"Fast metabolism," our technician answered. "My sister's the same way." She went over to the refrigerator, rooted around, and came out with a doughnut.

"You're killing me here," I told her. "The truth is we all have to work with the genetic cards we've been dealt. One size doesn't fit all."

Cindy finished her food and put the empty plastic container back into her lunch bag. "Knowing your weaknesses really helps. At least it's helpful to me."

"I agree. But chocolate and pie always make me feel happy."

"You don't have to eat the whole pie and all the chocolate," Cindy said. "Portion control is important."

I'd bought some mandarin oranges at the grocery store, and scrounged around for them in the fridge's fruit bin. With the burrito long gone, I began to peel one, the tangy smell of citrus driving the hospital smells away.

"Listen guys," I began, "being healthy should be our ultimate goal. All you have to do is look at the wide range of dog body types to get an idea of the power of genetics.

The greyhound is an example of a doggy ectomorph, a dog who stays slim under all sorts of circumstances. Contrast that to a chow or a pug. There's no point in a pug being upset because she's got a pudgy neck or body. She's got no choice. People love all the shapes and sizes of dogs. It's only with our fellow humans that we are so judgmental and critical in unproductive ways."

Cindy eyed me and asked, "Something bothering you, Kate?"

"Yep. My scrub pants are getting tight."

Between appointments Mari met me in the hallway and whispered, "Do you want to go with us to the lecture at the community center tonight?"

"What?"

"The organizing series. Sookie's assistant will be giving the class. It's on closets."

I hadn't intended on ever listening to another organizing lecture, but at the moment my closet was so stuffed full of clothes I never wore that I could barely hang anything up.

"Okay. I'm in."

"We'll pick you up at five thirty. Lecture starts at six. And be aware that I am not letting you out of my sight. No discovering any more bodies for you." She gave me a thumbs-up, brushing past on her way to reception.

An unwelcome image of feet sticking out beneath a snowy branch briefly grabbed hold and wouldn't let go.

I gritted my teeth and went back to work.

Chapter Twelve

MARI ARRIVED PROMPTLY AT FIVE THIRTY AS THE darkness thickened and claimed the night sky. She and Barbara happily chatted away in her SUV, but my stomach began to protest going back to the scene of the crime. To derail those thoughts, I asked Barbara what she knew about Sookie's assistant, Elaine.

"She's so sweet. A little timid at first, but once she gets going, that vanishes. Sookie let her speak a bit at the first lecture, and her suggestions sounded very practical." Barbara half-turned toward me. I sat in the back seat next to two huge bags of dog food. "You'll like her, I'm sure."

"Are you okay back there?" Mari wondered.

"Sure." What could I say? I was crammed against the window, the forty-pound bags taking up two of the three seat belts. With the funky smell of dog kibble ripe in my nose, I hoped my clothes wouldn't reek when I got out of the car.

"Anyway," Barbara continued, "I guess she and Sookie were best friends. This death has been very difficult for her. Very difficult."

I saw the lights of the community center up ahead.

"Sookie's husband, Glenn, probably killed her, you

know," confided Mari to her sister-in-law. "For the money."

"Love or money," Barbara replied. "The two biggest motives for killing anybody, at least in the mystery novels I read."

We pulled into the parking lot, which was rapidly filling up with minivans and SUVs. If Glenn Overmann had knocked off his wife, I thought, I'd bet he'd combined those two motives into one—killing for the love of money.

He must have been pretty pissed off to find all the cupboards bare.

I'd carefully dressed in layers, but tonight the auditorium felt chilly. While Barbara and Mari discussed renovating her bathroom, I glanced to my left and studied the crowd. Again, the majority of attendees were women, with a few husbands or boyfriends trapped into coming along. When I turned to my right, I saw someone two rows behind staring back at me.

"Dr. Kate? What are you doing here?" The man who spoke was tall, muscular, and dressed in black leather. A Harley jacket lay draped over the seat next to him. I recognized him immediately, and he definitely didn't fit the category of boyfriend or husband.

"Same as you. Learning to organize my closet, I hope." My client and friend, Henry James, otherwise known as the Baking Biker, was a proud cat daddy and a minor celebrity in town. His teacher parents had gifted him a famous literary name, but he'd never fit into their upper-middle-class mold. After their deaths and while dealing with a midlife crisis, he'd started baking to relieve his stress. To everyone's surprise, it turned into a successful cottage industry. After an article featuring him was published in the *New York Times*, he became even more in demand.

"I see Mari is here with you. I can tell by the hair."

My friend's gorgeous Afro was exuberant with life compared to my flat blond strands. "Mari," I called out, "look who's here tonight."

Someone loudly tapped on the microphone, a rapping noise echoing in the room. The lecture was about to begin.

"Henry, see you at break." My technician blew him a kiss. Their parents had been next-door neighbors, and she'd known him since she was a baby. In his late teens, Henry joined the Hells Angels. He messed up and eventually ended up in prison; Mari and her family wrote and visited him frequently, a kindness he never forgot.

"Good evening." An older woman I recognized as one of the volunteers from the senior center tapped the mic again, making the audio screech. "Good evening. I'm so happy to introduce our speaker for tonight and for the remaining three lectures in this series. Although a tragedy has struck here"—she paused as if waiting for everyone to settle down—"I'm certain dear Sookie would want us to continue."

A smattering of applause broke out.

"Elaine will be sharing her tips and suggestions for taming your closets. We are so grateful and happy to introduce tonight's speaker, Elaine Armstet."

The woman who stepped up to the podium had soft brown hair and a pleasant round face. She'd dressed in a business suit, like Sookie had, but where Sookie looked sharp and professional, Elaine resembled a distracted middle school teacher on the first day of class.

"Tonight we'll be discussing closets," Elaine began, her voice tentative.

I strained a bit to hear her as she spoke into a microphone perched on a stand.

"Louder," yelled someone in the room.

The volunteer suggested she take the mic off the stand and hold it, which helped quite a bit. As Elaine warmed to the subject of hangers, her voice gained in authority. One of the things she said had never occurred to me.

"Be warned that if you have pets, their fur will cling to velvet-finished hangers—and those hangers might transfer that fur onto your clothes."

A murmur of whispered voices moved through the room. Fancy plush hangers had been tempting me for a while, but now they didn't sound like such a great idea.

As the evening progressed, I found myself jotting down a few notes and even laughing as Elaine told us some funny closet stories. She'd made the evening informative and fun without putting anyone or anything down.

The enthusiastic round of applause at the end of the evening was well deserved.

In a repeat of the prior meeting, we once again congregated in the reception area, drinking decaf coffee and eating cookies. I noticed Elaine close by, surrounded by fans, busily chatting away. The lecture had ended precisely on time.

Henry came by, and he and Mari began to talk.

"She did a great job, don't you think?" Barbara had also been taking notes during the presentation. "I'm going to make my husband go back into the closet and put up more shelves."

A stifled laugh came from Henry's direction.

Picturing my own stuffed closet, I vowed to myself to clean it out. The four of us were chattering away about multiple pants hangers when someone yelled in a loud voice.

"Elaine, half of tonight's speaker payment is mine. Cough it up."

Everyone turned to see Glenn Overmann, red-faced and hair askew, striding toward Sookie's assistant. He looked annoyed, ready for a fight.

To her credit, Elaine didn't flinch. The thought crossed my mind that she had seen him like this before.

"That was the agreement," he continued, but this time he pointed his finger in her face. "You split any fee you got through Sookie fifty-fifty. Did they pay you yet?"

Henry James walked over and said, "Is he bothering you, Miss Elaine?" He towered over both of them.

Elaine quickly said, "No. It's just a slight disagreement between friends. Thanks for checking."

Henry gave Glenn a scowl and then rejoined our group. We all heard Elaine say, "Let's talk about this in private."

They walked toward the glassed double-door entrance, with Glenn leading the way. After stepping into the space between the two sets of doors, and in full view of everyone in the lobby, the two began to argue. Their voices were muffled, but we got the gist of the conversation.

Glenn's gestures became more and more violent. He lifted his arms with balled fists and punched the air. Elaine glanced behind her, noticing the rapt audience staring at them. She said something that made Glenn look too. Elaine grabbed his arm and they both exited, making a quick left into the parking lot.

"That was awkward," Mari commented.

Her sister-in-law poured herself more tea and reached for another cookie. "It's about money, of course. It's the root of all evil, so they say."

"Personally, I think *lack* of money often forces bad decisions." Several people I knew had made terrible choices for the sake of money.

"Or wanting to prove yourself," Henry said. "Being macho."

"Well," Mari added, "I'll bet losing his wife and all his money has been difficult for Glenn to adjust to. Although it doesn't excuse his obnoxious behavior."

"Rumor is he killed his wife." The Biking Baker

noticed a fresh batch of cookies and gave them a professional once-over.

I waited for Mari to mention the Circle K clerk's alibi report, but she remained admirably silent.

Conversation soon turned back to closets. I listened but kept my eye on the double glass doors.

Henry mentioned that he loved the velvet hanger tip.

"Elaine is so sweet," Barbara said. "She helped me organize my pictures and store them in the cloud. We also made some photo books using a company on the Internet."

"I was thinking of doing that, too," our only male voice commented.

Mari's sister-in-law continued to praise our lecturer. "I think she's just as good as Sookie, but infinitely easier to work with."

My eyes stayed focused on those glass doors.

Elaine appeared suddenly on the front entrance sidewalk, unsteady on her feet. She pulled at the outside door, before leaning against the entry wall.

I jumped up and ran toward her. Blood matted her hair and a few drops trickled down her forehead.

"Let's get her into a chair," I told the other women, who sprang to the rescue.

Several people helped Elaine into the lobby, settling her into a large armchair. Meanwhile, Henry rushed past us and flung open the outer doors. Mari followed him outside.

It was obvious Elaine had suffered a head trauma. You could see a bloody clump of hair sticking up.

I called 911 and requested EMTs for a head wound. Another woman, who identified herself as an RN, took Elaine's vitals and briefly questioned her.

"Can you tell us what happened, Elaine?" She dabbed some of the blood off with a moistened tissue.

A puzzled look came over our lecturer's face. "I'm not sure. I think I hit my head on something."

Her voice sounded tentative.

Using the light on my phone, I checked her pupillary response. They were reactive and the same size.

"Elaine," the nurse said, "we're going to let the EMT crew deal with that wound on your head." She held up her hand. "How many fingers do you see?"

"Four. Please, I'm fine, I think." She moved to stand up then sank back down. "A little dizzy, perhaps."

We heard the sirens wailing from far away coming toward the community center. In less than five minutes two emergency vehicles rolled in, parking directly in front of the entry doors, bright lights glaring.

As the EMTs hurried over, I rejoined Barbara. We all watched the emergency crew huddle around the victim. More movement at the front door revealed Mari and Henry coming back in.

"Did you see anything?" I whispered to them.

"Nothing. But there's a faint trail of blood from the parking lot to the front door."

In ten minutes, the EMTs had Elaine on a stretcher

with a temporary dressing on her wound. Someone handed back her purse and coat, and then the EMTs whisked her to the hospital.

"I'm taking off, too, before the cops get here," Henry said as he slipped on his leather jacket. "Better if they don't see me and start asking questions."

"All three of us are your alibi," Mari reminded him.

Henry kissed her on the forehead. "Sometimes that don't matter."

Everyone began talking, not sure if they should stick around. Barbara had to get back to her family.

I wondered where Glenn had gone. I could very easily see him getting angry enough to push Elaine, watch her fall, then walk away.

If that was tonight's scenario, it made Glenn Overmann look guilty as hell.

Chapter Thirteen

New Year's Eve was looming, and I hoped to see Luke soon. Today was December thirtieth. Luke planned to leave New York City sometime that morning and be here in Oak Falls by noon. I was more nervous than I thought I'd be.

Any hopes for a peaceful day shattered before my first cup of coffee. An early morning emergency showed up at the animal hospital that quickly threatened to derail my day. A goofy golden retriever named Gonzo with a face full of porcupine quills needed attention fast. All of his rubbing and pawing at his eyes and nose were breaking off quills and making things worse for both of us. We put him under light anesthesia and began to remove them.

Appointments were scheduled to start in twenty minutes, and I needed every one of those minutes. Under his silky blond coat lurked hidden quills we had to find by touch. The champagne chilling in my fridge to toast the New Year with Luke seemed light-years away.

As Mari pitched in, Cindy wandered over and began asking me questions about some pending lab results for a client on the phone. I felt as though I couldn't cram one more thought into my brain.

"Let's get those broken ones around his eyes," I told Mari.

"Don't forget to save all of them," Cindy reminded me. Whenever a dog came in loaded with quills she told everyone the same thing. A local artist had first dibs on any quills we retrieved for use in her homemade jewelry.

Seeing how busy we were, Cindy told the client on hold she'd call him back around lunchtime.

"How did it go with Babykins this morning?" I asked Cindy while my hemostats clamped onto another quill. I didn't realize she had left the room.

My voice must have carried halfway down the hallway because in a moment she reappeared by my elbow.

"Babykins Overmann?" I reminded her. "She was released from the hospital."

Cindy raised her eyebrows in a way that said *I'm getting to it*. "After Mari told me about his public fight with Elaine, I was prepared for a little excitement, but Glenn came in and did his Mr. Charming act."

"I didn't know he had a Mr. Charming act." One more smooth pull deposited another quill onto our pile. "That's surprising. He didn't complain about the bill? Throw something at you?"

Cindy again raised an eyebrow. "Everyone knows the chief of police is my brother-in-law. He'd have to be crazy to start up with me."

"Did he have any questions?" I'd already emailed him information about his pet's mild pancreatitis. Usually I try to speak to the owner in person, but Mari and I were deep in quill removal when he showed up to take his kitty home.

Cindy smoothed her hair back. "Not really. I gave him your list of instructions and email. He didn't say much, just that Babykins was going to stay with one of Sookie's friends for the immediate future."

"Perhaps that's better." A quick check confirmed that almost all the quills in the face and neck were out. I moved farther down to search Gonzo's front paws.

"Agreed."

"His cat is doing well now," I continued, prodding the pads of the golden retriever's feet. "But someone needs to keep a close eye on her eating and make sure she gets her medications. Pancreatitis is a serious disease. Does this friend know Babykins well?"

"She's their cat sitter and adores that little Abyssinian."

Cindy looked over my shoulder as I discovered two last quills lurking in long golden fur.

"That's it. Let's clean up his nose and put pressure on whatever is still bleeding." I took another look around the muzzle, neck, and chin to make sure I didn't miss anything. Early this morning on his off-leash walk, Gonzo had smelled the delightful odor of a large rodent and couldn't resist sticking his sensitive nose into trouble. Judging from the size of the quills, he'd encountered a full-grown porcupine with thousands of quills, one who knew just how to get away from a persistent dog.

Mari and I monitored him, making sure his recovery from anesthesia was a smooth one. Most people don't realize that veterinarians and doctors use many of the same anesthetic drugs. Before we let him up, we'd already finished an inch-by-inch search of his entire body, nose to tail, to make sure we didn't miss any stray quills—but just to be sure we did it again. Veterinary literature documented cases where sharp quills migrated from the skin and, in rare cases, penetrated deep into the body, even piercing the diaphragm.

While I watched his recovery from anesthesia and removed his endotracheal tube, Mari went to the fridge and brought back my water thermos for me and an energy drink for herself.

"Bet you're looking forward to seeing Luke," she said, handing me the water. "Did you tell him about the New Year's party?"

"Yep." I gulped down the liquid to avoid saying anything else.

Mari took the hint and moved to another subject. She frowned and randomly hypothesized about Glenn Overmann. "Do you think Elaine fell in the parking lot because he pushed her?"

Happy to talk about something else, I said the thought had crossed my mind. "Elaine says she doesn't remember what happened."

"That may be," Mari replied. "Or perhaps she's covering for him out of some misplaced loyalty to her friend Sookie?"

Fully awake now, Gonzo sat up, his tail wagging as if nothing at all had happened.

A strange thought came to me. What if this over-blown animosity between Elaine and Glenn was camouflage for something else? What if the two were closer than anybody suspected?

On my break I took Mr. Pitt and Buddy for their walks. The parking lot on our side of the building was empty except for the hospital truck. Mr. Pitt proudly trotted around with Buddy's discarded moose toy hanging from his mouth. In the weak sunlight, I noticed the two dogs kept their eyes on each other and, of course, had to sniff each other's business.

Once that bonding experience passed, we all went back inside. I offered them individual treats then checked Mr. Pitt's wounds. Already responding to the cleaning and antibiotics, his lesions looked much better. With any luck through the microchip information, we'd soon find his owner.

My lunch break over, I left both dogs busily chewing their toys from the comfort of their doggy beds.

I checked my messages again. Nothing from Luke.

I'd just walked into my office when I received a text from Cindy to meet her in reception. She'd tracked down the phone number listed on Mr. Pitt's microchip and called the company, with mixed results.

Cindy made notes into the office computer as she explained. I listened and looked out the front window hoping to see Luke's car pull in.

"Mr. Pitt's chip is registered, but the contact

information is out-of-date. Someone named Bill Phillips is the owner. Mr. Pitt's name at that time was Mighty Mouse. Phillips no longer lives at the given address, and the home number is disconnected. We can send him a letter, but if the forwarding address order has expired, we'll have to get a bit more creative."

Her news disappointed me. By implanting a microchip, veterinarians make it easier for lost pets to be returned home. Unfortunately, busy owners often forget to update their current addresses with their chip company, or they enter a local landline as an emergency number instead of a cell phone. And if the pet gets rehomed, someone needs to alert the chip registry.

"At least we have a name and an old address. That's a start," she continued.

With many years of experience behind her, I knew the search for Mr. Pitt's people was safe with Cindy.

"Maybe we should send an email out to all our clients reminding them to keep their microchip information current," I suggested. "They can add it to their New Year's resolutions."

Cindy looked up from her desk. "Good idea. I'll send a mass email, and add a general description of Mr. Pitt. We'll post something on social media, too."

More and more, social media provided a very effective way of reaching a large number of people. In this case, we would hold back pictures and descriptions of Mr. Pitt's distinguishing marking, a lightning-bolt-shaped white patch on his chest. We wouldn't hand him over to just anyone.

"Your next appointment is in a half hour," Cindy told me after getting up and pulling out a file drawer. "Sorry, but you are completely booked until six."

"Thanks for the warning." I took off for the employee lounge in search of my midday cup of coffee. Cindy began cleaning and straightening up reception in anticipation of the afternoon rush.

"Fancy meeting you here," Mari said when I opened the employee lounge door. She lay on our worn green sofa, her shoes dangling in midair.

Doc Anderson had installed the sofa so staff members or relief vets could take a quick nap or simply get off their feet. I'd used it many times for just that purpose.

"We've got about twenty-five minutes until appointments start," I informed her, surreptitiously checking my messages.

Still nothing from Luke.

The smell of freshly brewed coffee lured me over to the countertop machine. Everyone on staff had their own mug. Mine was a gift from Gramps that said "Keep On Truckin'," a joke about the beat-up Ford F-150 I drove. Mari drank from hers, customized with pictures of her two huge rottweilers, otherwise known as her "babies."

Mari grunted and stretched her arms out above her head. "So, what time is Luke getting here?"

Mug in hand, I sat opposite her. "As soon as I know I'll tell you." The tone of my voice must have signaled something because my friend sat right up and asked, "What's wrong?"

My awful habit of holding everything inside warned me not to share too much, even with a friend. With my eyes lowered I murmured, "Luke hasn't been very attentive lately. I know it's silly on my part, but I feel ignored."

"You saw him last when?"

"Christmas morning. He was still asleep when I left to join Gramps out on Long Island for Christmas dinner. Luke stayed here, celebrating with his family. By the time I got back, he'd left to meet up with his law school roommate. They're both writing an extra research project."

Mari rubbed her temples. "Relationships are a bitch. When they go wrong, they take your whole world along with them."

That's exactly right, I thought. I made the leap to share the worst. "Christmas Eve I sort of gave him an ultimatum. Commit to our relationship or walk."

Her dark eyes filled with sympathy. "Sometimes ultimatums work. More often they don't."

"That's what I'm afraid of," I confessed.

That ultimatum meant two choices—staying together or breaking up. I just wasn't sure which outcome scared me the most.

When it was time to send our quill patient home, the enthusiastic golden retriever greeted his owner with yips, wags, and a doggy smile. Yes, dogs sometimes imitate human grins. They curl their upper lip almost like a modified snarl and show their teeth. It's funny and endearing at the same time.

"You had me worried, you goofball," his owner said while she scratched his wiggling back.

Mari and I enjoyed the sheer delight of Gonzo's joy for a moment before we got down to business.

"I'm afraid after the memory of this episode fades away, Gonzo will be curious again," I began, "so don't let him wander up where the porcupine dens are. We also need you to use your fingertips and check all around his neck and head and legs for quills that might have burrowed under the skin." I showed her the easiest way with the tips of my fingers.

We watched as she repeated my gestures.

"Perfect. If you find one, call the office right away."

The owner patted Gonzo's head and looked first at Mari, then me. A little bit hesitantly she confessed. "I saw both of you at the community center, for the organizing classes, the night Sookie…died. Can I ask you something? I moved here from the city to get away from violence. Oak Falls is so picturesque. But I checked, and there've been other murders here. Is there some kind of weird curse in the Hudson Valley I don't know about?"

Mari spoke up before I could muster an answer. "Having a murder at the community center is very unusual. Sookie's death might end up being a domestic abuse case, so I don't think you have anything to worry about."

"Good. I love it here. Also, I was thinking of hiring her assistant, Elaine, to help get my house organized, and I wanted to make sure she wasn't a killer or something."

My technician whooped out a nervous laugh.

Gonzo gave a sharp bark indicating he was ready to leave.

I also plastered a grin on my face but said nothing. I knew Glenn Overmann was a wild card, impulsive, potentially violent, and possibly the person who killed his wife, either in a fit of rage or with cold calculation. But Sookie's assistant, Elaine Armstet? I didn't know enough about her to have any kind of opinion.

Maybe I should remedy that.

Chapter Fourteen

THE HOSPITAL USUALLY CLOSED BETWEEN FIVE thirty and six p.m., but it was closer to seven by the time I returned to my apartment. Several clients came in with candy and other sweets to wish us Happy New Year. A rush of emails kept me at the computer longer than usual. Still no news from Luke, although I knew from experience there were areas of spotty reception on the long drive into town. After showering, I changed, then sat on the sofa wearing my new sweater, waiting for a text that didn't come. The last update from Luke had arrived at three thirty. He said he might have to wait until rush hour was over to start the two-and-a-half-hour drive from New York City.

After that, only silence.

Both Mr. Pitt and Buddy kept looking at me, sensing my distress. Finally I thought, *Screw it. I'm not going to sit around and wait for him to show up. Let him find me.*

Changing my new clothes out for jeans and a red flannel shirt, I threw on a heavy coat and ventured out into the cold. A strong breeze blew, swirling a mist of old snow on the ground. After firing up the truck, I started into town heading for Judy's Café, only to be stopped by the glow of the low fuel light. Luckily, the Circle K was close by.

After I started the pump and locked the nozzle, I dashed inside to pick up some Kleenex and a bag of dog treats. A teenaged boy, his scraggly blond hair hanging on his shoulders, pushed open the door just as I reached for it. We almost banged into each other. I noticed the tips of his hair were dyed bright pink.

"Sorry," the fellow said and stepped back to let me in.

Then as I passed, his eyes startled—out of fear or recognition. He quickly looked down, before slipping out the door. Through the glass I saw him get into a beat-up black truck with a dented front fender. He didn't look familiar to me. *What was that odd reaction all about?*

Dismissing the thought, I strolled to the back of the store and checked out the pet section. This Circle K was more like a mini supermarket, stocked with a supply of frozen foods and ice cream for impulse shoppers.

I resisted the potato chips and virtuously stuck to the dog treats and tissues. When I got to the counter, the cashier greeted me by name. The employee name tag pinned to her chest read Posey.

"Evening, Dr. Kate. Is that all tonight?" Her tight reddish-purple curls clung to her skull like a cap.

"Do I know you?" I asked, embarrassed that she might be a client I didn't recognize.

"Not directly," she said. "I know Mari. I've seen your picture on her Facebook page."

"Well, that explains it." My staff was constantly posting all kinds of things on social media. Deep-set hazel eyes eyed me up and down. *Judging me in some way?*

"So, how's it going?" I asked, wondering how an older woman like her, probably in her early forties, ended up being a late-night employee at Circle K.

"Same old." She rang up my purchases and asked me if I needed a bag.

"No, I'm good. I've got my backpack in the truck."

Posey handed me the items and asked, "Are the treats for that pit bull you found? Mari told me he was awfully beat-up. Sometimes I really hate people."

I silently agreed. "Good news is he's recovering really well. We're trying to find his owner now."

She leaned on the countertop and pointed to a bulletin board mounted near the door. "Mari told me she'll bring in the Found poster as soon as Cindy makes it up."

"Good." This cashier appeared to know a lot about our office. Could Posey be Mari's Circle K source about Glenn Overmann's alibi?

A quick look around confirmed we were alone, so I had nothing to lose by asking a few questions. "Tell me, Posey. Do you believe Sookie's murderer is still loose?"

That elicited a sly smile followed by a flood of conjecture. "You know, it is disgraceful Chief Garcia hasn't arrested that husband of hers."

"Glenn?"

"Of course, Glenn. Do you know how many times the police were called out to their place? Plenty! Problem is no charges were ever filed. Either one or the other always withdrew their accusations."

The thought occurred to me that the Circle K, with all glass windows in the front, sat at the intersection of the two main roads in town. Police get thirsty and hungry while on duty, and this Circle K was open 24/7. I noticed a romance novel, spine side up, open on the counter under the locked cigarette case. This woman must have stood behind the counter many a long night. Maybe a little banter or gossip between her and the customers made the shift go faster.

Posey just became much more interesting.

"So did Glenn or Sookie usually call the police?" I'd assumed there'd be some domestic violence history from the way Glenn behaved. The clerk immediately confirmed my suspicions.

"Both of them!" Posey licked her lips then continued. "They called so often that the cops felt it was a big waste of their time. Why one of them didn't move out of the house I can't say, except neither wanted to give the other the satisfaction."

Bright headlights of a car flashed as it turned in and stopped next to a gas pump. Another customer. I might not have Posey all to myself for long. There was something else I desperately wanted to know.

I lowered my voice. "Is it true Glenn has an alibi for the night of the murder?"

The cashier leaned in and whispered, "That's what I heard."

The door flung open, letting in a cold blast of air.

A man in a ski hat wearing a blue plaid muffler around his neck and across his mouth walked in. Paying us no attention, he strolled into the snack aisle.

Mimicking Posey now, I leaned in and asked, "Who told you Glenn had an alibi?"

"Wyatt. Glenn's boyfriend."

Glenn has a boyfriend? Holding my purchases close, I exited out to the parking lot, then stopped under the red neon OPEN sign. Who could have anticipated this twist in what was becoming a more and more complicated case? I'd entertained the possibility that Elaine and Glenn might have been involved at one point, but not this.

Police Chief Garcia must know all about the domestic violence accusations between Sookie and Glenn. Does he know about their extramarital activity too?

Standing on the sidewalk, I noticed Muffler Man used his shoulder to open the door, and with his back turned he headed toward his CRV. With the coast clear, I snuck back inside before the door completely closed. How could I miss the perfect opportunity to find out more about this toxic couple?

Posey looked up at me, a question in her eye. Noticing the sign behind her, I said, "I forgot to buy my lotto tickets."

"Sure." We stared at each other. "NY Lotto? Powerball? Mega Millions?"

"All of them," I stammered.

"Quick picks?"

"Yep. I'm feeling lucky tonight. Two of each." Although I rarely played games of chance, I figured it was a cheap price to pay for questioning Posey.

"Here you are." She handed me the tickets after I paid.

"You know," I began, "what you said about Glenn cheating on Sookie with that guy, Wyatt—?"

The cashier didn't need prompting. "Wyatt Cressan? Well, Sookie was no angel either. I've seen her in town with local guys. She's been in here bunches of times, usually late at night, all lovey-dovey with this older dude from the city. Gray hair. Sort of pudgy."

"Hmm." Raising my eyebrows, I didn't have to feign interest.

"Drove a big silver Mercedes sedan, last time I saw them together. Expensive-looking gold watch on his wrist, too."

Her powers of observation amazed me; then I realized how boring her job must be, stuck behind the counter all night. No wonder she kept a mental catalog of the people she saw. "Posey, you remember so many details about people," I told her. "Are you an artist?"

She smiled widely, exposing a large chip on her front tooth. "No. I've got a bunch of jobs, but I'm trying to be a writer. See?" From under the counter, she pulled out an old-fashioned but still popular notebook. I'd used them myself in grade school. The black-and-white-speckled cover of the composition book appeared well worn, the wide-lined pages thickened from use.

"Are you writing about your experiences here at Circle K?"

"That's what everyone around here thinks. But I'll tell you a secret." Her forehead wrinkled, eyes squinted with concentration. "I'm writing an Edwardian vampire romance/mystery. With aliens." A knowing smile bathed her tired face. "Got to write what sells."

I nodded, not knowing what to say.

Posey leaned in again, lowering her voice. "But I'm not counting on my book to make me rich. Knowledge is power."

"You're going back to school?"

That provoked a high-pitched laugh. "No way," she said, still chuckling. "You see, if you know something you're not supposed to know, that gives you power. Power you can turn into cash."

The doorbell jingled as another customer entered the store.

I stuffed my lottery tickets into my coat pocket and said goodbye. Someone else pulled up as I made my way toward the truck. Cold air stung my face. What Posey said disturbed me. *Power you can turn into cash?* It sounded an awful lot like blackmail.

Backing out of the parking lot, I debated continuing to Judy's Café. But if anyone else knew the dirt on Glenn and Sookie, it would be the owner and manager of the most popular coffee place in town.

By the time I reached the town of Oak Falls, most of the tourists were heading home or out to the many nearby restaurants and bars. There were several tables empty plus a few seats available at Judy's counter. I chose the counter, sat down, then wondered how to bring up the delicate subject of Sookie and Glenn's love lives over a bowl of soup. Before I got a chance to order, another woman sat down next to me, and nodded a hello.

Like so many people in town, she looked vaguely familiar. This presented a problem because I always remembered the animals I examined, but I didn't always recognize their owners.

"Hi, Dr. Kate," the middle-aged blond said. "I took your advice and added green beans to Midnight's food, and she's already lost two pounds."

That brief statement made it easy. Midnight was an overweight setter mix I'd seen only a few weeks ago. A happy, energetic dog, she'd packed on some winter inactivity weight. In my mind I visualized her medical record. Midnight Heally.

"I'm so happy, Ms. Heally."

"Please, call me Irene."

Our brief conversation was interrupted by the appearance of the restaurant owner, Judy, visibly tired after her long day. "What can I get for you tonight, Dr. Kate?" Her elbows rested across the stone countertop.

"Bowl of veggie soup and a blueberry scone," I answered.

"Irene?"

"Hot tea and a shortbread cookie. I'm waiting for my son to meet me. His truck is in the shop." She fussed a little with her napkin after Judy disappeared into the kitchen.

I unbuttoned my coat and placed it on the other empty seat to the left of me. Irene kept smoothing her napkin with her fingers. Something preoccupied her. I took my phone out and checked my messages.

Nothing from Luke.

Frustrated, I decided to text him but was stopped by a question from Irene.

"Dr. Kate..." Irene hesitantly turned toward me. "I'm not sure how to ask this, but...you found Sookie's body, correct?"

Whatever I thought Irene was going to ask me, this wasn't it. "Yes," I replied and put my phone in my pocket, not sure where our conversation was going.

She lowered her head and spoke into the napkin. "Do you think she suffered?"

That was a tough question. *How could anyone really know?*

"I heard Chief Garcia say in an interview that Sookie probably became unconscious after the first blow to the head."

Irene's eyes became misty. She sighed and said, "That's a blessing. I'm so glad she didn't suffer."

Of course that's not what the chief said, but I let it go.

The kitchen door swung open and Judy approached with my soup and Irene's tea. Her eyes darted from one of us to the other, but she simply put down our orders and went back to the kitchen. Sometimes restaurants acted as confessionals or therapy sessions for folks. Judy had probably heard more than her share of life's stories. I suppose servers are like bartenders, only with food.

The steamy soup smelled of carrots and a hint of ginger. After the tentative first sip, I blew on the next spoonful to cool it down. Irene did the same with her steaming tea.

"Did you know Sookie well?" I asked. It felt comradely, perched at the counter together, blowing on our hot liquids.

"We saw each other at yoga twice a week for over a year," Irene said. "Usually after class we'd go to the juice bar in the gym and talk. I knew she and Glenn had issues, but I never thought he'd kill her."

She spoke as if it were a fact.

Once again, I tried the soup. Much better. "Glenn hasn't been charged with any crime," I said between sips.

"Well, who else could it be? Not her rich boyfriend. And certainly not Wyatt—he's too sweet." Irene loosened her coat and appeared more than ready to continue our talk. "Although Wyatt did once joke that he tried to stab Sookie in the heart but couldn't find it."

From the frankness of her banter I guessed that she must have assumed I knew all about the couple's lifestyle choices.

My scone magically appeared, as did Irene's cookie.

Still hungry, I broke off a piece and buttered it. "Irene, maybe you can answer this question. What did Sookie see in someone like Glenn?"

With half a shortbread cookie in her hand she answered, "He's one of those guys you either hate or you love. He's very emotional and opinionated about everything, super charming when he wants to be, and always about to hit it rich. It's exciting to be with him. Did you know his eyes are greenish, and he has the thickest black eyelashes…"

That didn't sound much like the Glenn I'd met. However, now that I thought about it, I never got that close to him. His back had been turned to us during our house call. He mistook Mari for the veterinarian, and we'd missed each other when he picked up Babykins. I'd read his outrageous emails and seen him in wedding photos. All I remembered was his strongly backlit profile.

Irene described him quite differently. *Fondly*.

"By the way. What exactly does Glenn do for a living?"

A laugh-like snort erupted from my countertop companion. "Sorry. It's just something Sookie wondered about, too. Glenn does a number of things—all of them self-employed. He speculates in the stock market, does some day-trading. In college, he got his real estate license and sold time-shares. That's where they met, by the way. Whenever you speak to him, either everything is the greatest or his investments have tanked. No moderation. It drove Sookie crazy, which was another reason she had decided to file for a divorce. Their life was like a soap opera."

"What about Sookie's boyfriends?"

"Well," Irene said somewhat defensively, "she needed some joy in her life, and I guess Morris, the guy from the city, was a lot of fun. Of course he's married, but I think Morris and his wife have some kind of under-standing—at least that's what Sookie implied."

Fighting to remember who was with whom, I swal-lowed the last bit of soup. Irene went quiet, weighing whether to tell me anything more. Finally, she leaned over and added one final tidbit. "Don't tell anyone, but that's why I wasn't surprised to find out Sookie took all their money. She rescued Glenn financially so many times; believe me, she deserved it all—especially her Apple stock."

"Stock?"

"I'm not sure how true it was, but she bragged quite often about her personal financial portfolio. In college, I think, they both invested in Apple stock early on. She—kept her shares, but Glenn sold his the first time the market went down. Some great financial consultant he is." Irene chuckled. "Sookie told me after it split, the value skyrocketed, and…"

The restaurant door opened and a voice called out, "Hey, Mom."

Irene put her cup down. "Lucky, come over here and meet my friend."

Swallowing the last of my scone, I turned to find myself staring into sky-blue eyes that widened in surprise at seeing me. The neon pink tips of his dirty-blond hair stuck out from under his wool cap.

"Meet Dr. Kate, Midnight's veterinarian. My son, Lucky."

It all clicked into place. This was the boy who'd looked so afraid when we briefly passed each other at the Circle K.

"Hi, Lucky. Nice meeting you," I said.

After Irene and Lucky left, Judy came over, a cup of coffee in her hand. "Nice kid," she said. "But he should be called Unlucky, from what I hear."

Of medium height, and a bit thin, the boy was memorable more for his hair than anything else. "I'm curious. Why would you say that?"

"He's a senior in high school, but a few months ago he got himself suspended for a week. The story is he snuck into school late one weekend with a bunch of his friends."

That sounded odd. "What did they do?"

"Nothing much. Played basketball in the gym. Got into the equipment locker and took a bunch of stuff out. They didn't steal anything, but those boys did leave a mess. Of course, before they entered the school, they disabled the alarm system and turned off the cameras. However, one of them couldn't resist taking pictures on his phone and sending them to his girlfriend."

"Okay, that wasn't a good idea."

"The girlfriend made it worse. She forwarded the photos to a bunch of people on a multiple message that included her mother."

"Who notified the school?"

"No one is sure."

"Did they all get into trouble?" The reckless behavior of teenagers was no surprise to me.

"No. Everybody in the photos wore masks except Lucky, who was eating a bag of onion rings at the time and looking straight into the camera. The kid refused to rat anyone else out, so the principal made an example of him. Like I said, unlucky. He barely made it to graduation."

"Unlucky Lucky."

A few customers stood up and made for the door, wishing Judy good night. After they left, Judy continued her story. "It's always something with Lucky. If he goes down to the quarry, bees swarm him. When he parked his truck on the street in the city a few weeks ago, it got hit. Stuff like that."

What must it be like to be a teenager named Lucky, who brought bad luck with him everywhere? I felt sorry for him, but it still didn't explain his odd reaction to me outside the Circle K. As if he were frightened. The sudden ping of a text message made me dig into my pants pocket for my phone.

SORRY. JUST GOT IN 2 TOWN. LOUSY TRIP.
I'M BEAT.
SEE YOU IN THE MORNING XXX

I stared at the message. Judy asked, "Bad news?"

"No." I put the phone back in my pocket. "Luke just got into town." I made my voice sound enthusiastic. "I'll see him tomorrow."

"Of course you will. Tomorrow is New Year's Eve. You're both coming to the party, right?" Judy questioned, her tiredness temporarily forgotten.

Reaching for my credit card, I tried to match her enthusiasm. "Absolutely. We are so excited!"

A few minutes later, after paying my tab, I walked to the truck waiting patiently outside for me. As I stepped off the curb, my foot broke through the snow to sink into a puddle of dirty, icy slush. It was the perfect ending to a perfectly disappointing day.

Maybe Lucky and I have a few things in common.

Chapter Fifteen

New Year's Eve night, and my anxiety levels rose. Alone in my apartment, I felt on edge, like I was back in high school, not a twenty-seven-year-old professional woman. Clammy hands betrayed my nervousness, so I poured myself a large glass of white wine—perhaps not the best decision. *What do novelists call it? Liquid courage?*

I shouldn't be so worried about seeing Luke again, but I sensed something was wrong. My hope had been to get together early and perhaps skip the New Year's Eve party altogether. I'd envisioned us alone by a crackling fire, easing back into our relationship. However, when we finally spoke, I discovered other arrangements had been made.

Luke's family's diner, closed New Year's Eve and New Year's Day, had offered to donate their leftover baked goods to the party, along with loaning Judy serving trays and catering items. Luke's cousins expected him to help them organize and transport the deliveries out to the hay barn. He'd also been roped into being a designated driver, so now we had to hang around and chauffeur whichever of his family or friends needed a ride until the party ended.

At least we'd have some time alone tonight, I thought, as once again I sat on the living room sofa in my new clothes, waiting. I'd impulsively bought a pale blush skirt, with a sparkly fine mesh overlay. Quite unlike anything I usually wore—like a princess. *What was I thinking?*

When the doorbell rang, Buddy started barking. I'd kenneled Mr. Pitt, since I wasn't sure how he'd be with strangers, but I heard his deep bark faintly resonating through the apartment's connecting wall.

With a welcoming smile on my face, I opened the door wide—only to have a brassy blond-haired girl push past me, yelling, "Where's the can?"

I pointed behind me. She sprinted off, zipped inside, and slammed the bathroom door.

Luke appeared silhouetted in the doorway, dark wavy hair slightly mussed. The crooked grin that always got to me was missing. Instead, he stomped his feet on the doormat.

"Kate," he apologized, "I'm sorry about my cousin. Some kind of stomach issue, I think." Cold air blew against my legs and arms before he partially shut the door, leaving it ajar as though poised to run.

Not the romantic moment I'd hoped for.

Buddy, meanwhile, gave Luke a greeting befitting a king, yipped with joy, twirled around, and licked his hand slavishly like a traitor. Luke, in turn, ruffled Buddy's coat and said, "Who's a good boy?" My dog's tail thumped rhythmically against the door.

We heard a noise coming from the bathroom, sort of a thunk, then the door opened, and Luke's cousin walked out. Slamming the door, she dramatically said, "I'd wait a while before going in there, if you know what I mean."

Luke laughed and the girl joined in. About five two, dressed in tight leather pants, with a sparkly low-cut blouse showing under her coat, this was a pretty cousin I'd never met.

"Rainbow, I'd like you to meet Kate."

The four-inch heels on her black leather boots created a slight wobble in her walk.

"Hi there," I said, noting her gold nose ring. She looked about eighteen or nineteen at the most. "Luke's got so many cousins it's hard to keep them straight. Now, what side of the family are you from?"

She giggled. "My mom is Luke's mom's first cousin. Soooo, I'm a second cousin. There are a bunch of us."

Great. Could you date your second cousin?

Rainbow took a measured look at my converted garage studio, then gave a little wave to catch my attention. "Uh, Karen. You coming with us to the party?"

"My name is Kate, not Karen." *Was I going with them?* Obviously, she was riding along with us. When I glared at Luke, he shrugged his shoulders as if it weren't up to him.

Rainbow watched the two of us through her fake eyelashes. "Whatever." She giggled again as if she'd said something funny. Rainbow appeared to have started the party without us.

"I guess we're all going together." Luke conveniently sat on the sofa, continuing to rub Buddy's floppy ears. "Are you ready, Kate?"

"Luke, can you help me walk to the car?" Rainbow tiptoed over and pulled Luke to his feet. "I almost slipped coming in here. Remember?"

"Of course," he answered. "Kate, I'll be right back."

"Take your time." My voice dripped with sarcasm, but the effect became lost in a flurry of yips.

After that little scene my mood shifted from nervous anticipation to confusion, then anger. Mostly anger. Although I knew I shouldn't, I poured myself another large glass of wine.

Midway through my drink, Luke returned.

"Listen, Kate," he said as he walked toward me. "I apologize for bringing Rainbow. She missed her ride, and my grandmother insisted she go with me instead of calling an Uber."

Blaming your grandmother? That was low. On the other hand, I suppose it could be true. With a flourish I finished my wine, picked up my coat, and magnanimously declared, "That's fine. Could happen to anyone."

"Honey, I've missed you," he said, moving in closer to give me a lingering kiss. "Let's not let this spoil our evening. We've got a whole new year ahead of us."

A loud flurry of honks from the parking lot interrupted any plans I'd had of kissing him back.

With my arm clutching his, we made our way to Luke's SUV. I expected to sit next to him in the passenger seat, but nope. Little Miss Rainbow sat there and didn't budge. With another cute wave she pointed to the back seat. Something told me I was in for a bumpy night.

The Hay Barn Gallery was exactly that, but much more. Its former life as the tallest barn in the county became reinvigorated after it caught the eye of computer software millionaire Jacob Zolvechek while he visited the Hudson Valley with his Icelandic artist girlfriend, Signe. Although the gallery was conceived as a performance art space for his sweetie's massive kinetic sculptures, he poured money into it. After his lawyer petitioned the town for a variance, they raised the roof even higher. Luke told me an intricate catwalk and pulley system allowed three-hundred-sixty-degree visualization of the Alexander Calder–like sculptures.

After his girlfriend publicly dumped him, Zolvechek sold the property to a nonprofit organization that worked with local artists. They painted the barn a classic red with white trim. Multiple signs advertising the Hay Barn Gallery and Studios directed us to a large, paved parking lot surrounded by farmland. An architect designed the inside of the barn to be configured in many different ways. It could even serve as a theater.

Cars, trucks, and even several RVs jammed the parking lot. I guessed half the town decided to party.

The New Year's Eve party was already slamming when we arrived at twenty minutes past ten. While we looked for a parking spot, I felt the music vibrate the car windows. The funky smell of marijuana perfumed the outside air. Walking toward the entrance, we dodged clusters of smokers. One offered Rainbow a hit, which she happily accepted.

Although Luke and I entered hand in hand, Rainbow and another friend swept him away for "just a minute." An emergency had cropped up with a young relative, who needed Luke's advice.

"Can't it wait?" I asked him. "We just got here."

Rainbow tugged at his arm. "I'll be right back."

He left me standing alone next to the front door as it opened and shut, admitting more smoke and more partygoers. I moved toward the wall to avoid being trampled.

To pass the time, I plucked a brochure from a Plexiglas wall organizer and scanned its contents. This interesting space displayed paintings, mixed media, sculpture, sketches, and glasswork. Judy had wisely moved all the artwork out of danger. Only the small tags identifying titles, artists' names, and prices remained attached to the walls, creating a disjointed checkered pattern. The warm air buzzed with conversation, music, and the heavy smell of marijuana.

"Are you looking for something in particular?" asked a deep voice directly behind me.

Startled, I said, "No." When I turned to explain, my

eyes met the black eyes of a stranger. A sketch of him—tall with a fit runner's build and shoulder-length dark blond hair—was listed for sale in the Hay Barn Gallery catalog.

"Oh. Are you an artist's model? There's a picture of you…"

He laughed, showing a glint of white teeth. "Not really. Although when I can't afford a model, I sketch myself."

More people came through the door, skirting around us to join the crowd. Feeling slightly dizzy, I searched the room expecting Luke to have returned by now.

"You must be getting hot," the stranger said. "May I?"

Before I could reply, he gently slipped my wool coat off my shoulders, saying, "Follow me. I'll show you where we're storing the coats."

He reached out his hand and without really thinking, I took it. He expertly picked our way through packs of enthusiastic dancers, their arms flailing and hips swaying, until we broke through to the other side of the room. A mix of small bistro-type tables lined the walls. Hanging from the rafters were four industrial-sized electric heaters, their coils glowing bright red. Thanks to the wine and the heat, I felt pleasantly relaxed. Sure enough, several rows of portable racks already stuffed with coats stood tucked into an alcove adjacent to the unisex bathrooms.

"I'll hang it up," I told him, taking back my only good

coat, and placing it on a purple plastic hanger. "Are you helping Judy with the party?"

The stranger smiled and said yes. "We've got a rowdy crowd tonight of musicians, artists, and people who are plain tired of being cooped up this winter."

Due to the heat radiating from above, I soon went from warm to hot in the cramped space—then hotter.

I fanned myself with my hand.

We both leaned against the wall. He explained that several local artists who showed their work here had helped Judy safely stow the sculptures and other artwork in the storeroom. "We began setting up the temporary wall panels early this morning," he explained. "Tomorrow we're meeting at three in the afternoon to put it all back together again." A shout went up from the crowd as the eclectic DJ played "Y.M.C.A." Young and old began to laugh as they tried to become letters in this perennial favorite. The crowd appeared to be enthusiastically celebrating the imminent demise of the old year. Several men and a few women took off their shirts, swinging them over their heads like lassos.

My choice of a hand-knit sweater, lovely as it was, quickly became way too hot. Thankfully I'd worn a silk camisole under it. A couple danced past, the man with a sweaty bare torso, the woman dressed in a short skirt and red bra.

With the sweater secured to my coat, I decided it was time to introduce myself to Judy's pal. "Thanks for helping me. I'm Kate."

"I know exactly who you are." He bent down so

I could hear him above the noise. "You're Dr. Kate Turner, friend to animals, and fierce pursuer of justice. I admire you."

A deep blush flushed my face at that unexpected compliment. "And you are?"

"Colin Riley." He paused as though thinking, before adding, "Poor purveyor of poetry and paint."

He expected me to be charmed. My Gramps would say that Colin had the Irish gift of the blarney— someone whose words could effortlessly persuade, charm, and often deceive. Tonight, I chose to find him charming.

Some passersby inched past, engulfing us in a cloud of pungent smoke.

I shifted away and kept searching for Luke in the crowd.

"Smoke your weed outside, guys," Colin said, "but thanks for sharing."

Their answer was lost as the crowd shouted again. Through a momentary break in the dancing bodies, I noticed my client Daffy, dressed as Father Time, with that long scythe flung over her shoulder. Just as quickly, she vanished. The cashier from Circle K passed by, sedately dancing the cha-cha all by herself.

Friends and acquaintances moved back and forth like shadows in mirrors. The world felt woozy. Colin moved closer, making way for a large man dressed as a clown. Someone else wearing a hooded black cape and Freddy Krueger mask shoved past. *Why the Halloween get-up?* I wondered.

The music pulsed and moved like something alive. After the song ended, everyone clapped. "Change of pace, guys," the DJ said. Then the sweet notes of a violin began a familiar melody. "Colin," I said, "thanks for everything. You don't have to stay here and babysit me. I'm sure you have a million things to do."

"Yes," he replied. "Millions and millions of things to do."

For the second time that night he held out his hand to me. "Shall we dance instead?"

Colin was a wonderful dancer, the kind of partner who makes you look better than you are. It helped that the DJ played a slow, old song about a Tennessee waltz. We glided and twirled as one, my skirt sparkling as it moved to the smooth country rhythm. It reminded me of waltzing in the living room with my Gramps, who insisted on giving his shy granddaughter home dancing lessons. He'd taught me all the traditional and silly party moves I'd needed.

"Having fun?" Colin whispered as he pulled me closer.

I leaned my head back for a moment, the steps flowing naturally, unbidden. "My Gramps taught me how to waltz," I confided, as we drifted along. "It's been so long since I danced."

"Dancing is good for the soul." With that he slowed a bit, his strong arm pressed flat against the small of my back. Our dance had a languid, dreamlike quality to it.

He lowered me in a classic dip just as the song ended. Other nearby couples who had already stopped politely applauded. A silly burst of unexpected happiness glowed in my chest. Nothing existed but the…

"Kate?" Luke's surprised, slightly annoyed voice brought me back to reality. Colin gently guided me up before twirling me one last time. He ignored Luke. Still holding my hand he said, "It was a pleasure to dance with you, Kate. Please thank your Gramps for me."

Before I could introduce him to Luke, Colin lightly kissed the back of my hand and walked into the crowd.

My absentee boyfriend stared through the dancers. "Who was that?"

Before I could answer, Luke draped his arm over my shoulder. I blocked it by bending down to adjust my shoe strap.

"That's Colin," I said as I straightened back up. "He's helping Judy with the party."

"Hmmm." Once again his eyes roved in Colin's direction.

"Why don't we get a drink?" I suggested. I'd noticed an informal bar set up near the entrance, so Luke followed me, saying hi to several friends as we moved along. I was dying for some water. My throat itched, unaccustomed to smoke.

Judy had told everyone to BYOB, and the long table was littered with a wild assortment of alcoholic and nonalcoholic beverages. At the far end, large stainless bowls held mounds of chips, popcorn, and other snacks.

Sandwiched in between were plates holding cookies and sweets for those who developed the munchies.

"Shoot," I said as I looked around. "Your wine is still in the back seat of the car."

"Nope. That's why I disappeared." Luke reached toward the back of the bottles and pulled out a cold bottle of expensive pinot gris wine. "I bought it for you," he said. "Happy almost New Year."

This was a nice surprise. Too bad I didn't feel like drinking it.

"May I pour you a glass? Plastic okay?"

"Absolutely." The afterglow from my waltz with Colin slowly faded. Life returned to normal. Several clients busy pouring drinks acknowledged me with good wishes for the upcoming year. Before I forgot, I fished a bottle of water from a tub full of ice.

After Luke handed me my drink, he poured a half glass for himself. "This is only for our toast," he said, reminding me of his designated driver status. Holding our glasses awkwardly in front of us, we attempted to find a place to sit down.

Another familiar face broke through the crowd and headed for the snack table. Elaine glanced about uncertainly while a woman companion chatted away.

"I'll be right back." I handed Luke my glass and made my way toward Sookie's assistant.

Her face broke into a smile as she greeted me. With her brown hair bundled up in a high topknot, there was no evidence of any head wound.

"So good to see you," I began. "I was worried about you. How are you feeling?"

The older woman beside her chimed in. "Elaine is a trouper. She insisted on coming here tonight, but the doctor said no alcohol."

Elaine smiled sweetly and held up a bottle of water. "That's okay. I'm not much of a drinker, anyway."

I held up my own bottle of water and returned her smile. "You didn't have to stay in the hospital, did you?" For someone with a head injury, she appeared to be doing well.

Again, the woman accompanying her spoke for Elaine. "Nope. Just a mild concussion and five stitches."

"The nurse insisted on shaving the area around the cut. That's why my hair is up, to cover the bald spot." Elaine pointed to her head. "A bit of a nuisance, really."

That's an understatement, I thought. "May I ask if you remember what happened? After I helped you into the lobby, my friends ran outside to the parking lot, but they didn't see anyone."

Elaine appeared puzzled for a moment before answering. "The doctor thinks I slipped in the parking lot and hit my head on someone's side mirror. A woman who was at the community center that night called the chief of police to report blood on her car." She turned to her friend. "I knew I shouldn't have worn those heels that night."

My mind paged back to Glenn and Elaine arguing in the lobby, Glenn still in an overcoat and Elaine dressed in her suit and a pair of modest black heels.

"She's not allowed to drive for another day either," her friend added. "In fact, if you'll excuse us, I think we'll get something to snack on and then sit down."

Elaine briefly held her hand to her forehead and added, "If I don't see you again, Happy New Year."

"Happy New Year," I answered.

Elaine took her friend's arm and melted into the crowd.

"Who was that?" Luke asked as we searched for a place to sit. Multiple tables were jammed into a corner of the room. We sat at an empty one that looked out onto the dance floor.

"A friend," I told him. "I wanted to wish her a Happy New Year."

"I poured just enough for myself for one toast." Luke held up his plastic cup. "To a fantastic New Year."

Not the kind of toast I expected, but I raised my glass to his and repeated it, "To a fantastic New Year."

I took a long sip of the wine he'd brought. It tasted delicious. This drink officially put me over my self-imposed limit, but I wasn't driving tonight. When I glanced toward my boyfriend, all I saw was his back. In spite of everything, my toe tapped to the music.

Luke took my hand and asked. "So, the person you were speaking with was—?"

"I thought you knew everyone in town," I chided.

"Obviously not." Mimicking Colin, he kissed my hand. It didn't feel the same.

Surprised and upset with that thought, I took another sip of wine. "That's Elaine Armstet, Sookie Overmann's assistant." I watched him put that news into focus. "Sookie is the woman who was murdered."

"Right. Then Elaine either fell down, or was pushed in the community center parking lot, ending up with a head wound. My sisters updated me on all the local gossip last night at dinner," he admitted.

A glint of something drew my eye up to the rafter crosswalks. It looked like Judy handing streamers to a young man.

Luke continued. "My grandmother thinks Sookie's husband is responsible."

"That's certainly a possibility," I said, taking my hand away from his to smooth back my hair. "Problem is, Elaine has no memory of what happened."

Luke cleared his throat before he answered, "That's convenient."

Absence can put a strain on a relationship. As Luke chatted away about his professors, fellow students, and obtuse points of law, I found my attention drifting. Most likely he felt the same when I shared a medical case with him. One of the first people I'd met in Oak Falls, Luke at that time was in an on-and-off relationship with his high school sweetheart. I'd rekindled an affair with an old college buddy. We became platonic friends. Luke got in the habit of dropping by my place with Chinese food after his classes. We bonded over egg rolls and murder. What started off as a friendship evolved into something more. But our dynamics changed once more when he moved away for law school.

There was a strong possibility our relationship had run its course.

"Stay here. I'll be right back," Luke said as he stood up. "Do you want me to see if there's any more of our wine left?"

"Sure," I replied automatically.

Most of the people around us were talking and laughing and seemed to be enjoying themselves. I knew Luke knew how to dance. He'd told me his girl cousins and sisters practiced their dancing with him. That didn't mean he liked to dance.

When the song ended, I noticed Mari across the room, busily chatting away. They'd pushed two tables together and had ten or more people crowded around. After a moment the music started up again, and dancing partygoers flooded back into the space, obscuring my view. I glanced at my watch. Eleven fifteen. That's past my normal bedtime. In a little less than an hour I'd wish all of us a wonderful New Year. Maybe my wish would come true.

Another slow love song floated in the air. I closed my eyes.

"Alone again?" Colin's voice asked.

"Only for a moment," I answered, keeping my eyes closed.

His warm breath whispered in my ear. "If you were here with me, we'd dance all night."

When I opened my eyes, he was sitting next to me.

Once again, I found myself in Colin's arms, dancing away. Had he been observing me from afar, moving in when Luke left? People watched as we glided smoothly around the dance floor. My dance partner let our synchronous movements speak for him. I felt like I'd been dropped into a romance novel, the handsome stranger flirting with the pale blond heroine.

Except I wasn't a big believer in that kind of romance.

When I gazed at Colin, I couldn't help but notice how much he enjoyed the attention of the crowd. Our circles became wider and wider, his turns and twirls more intricate. More and more partygoers stepped away, leaving the dance floor to us. I began to feel dizzy again, but his arms held me tight. After a final twirl, he firmly grasped my waist and began to lift me into the air.

Like in a movie.

But I wasn't that girl.

I moved his hands from my waist, half expecting to fall to the floor. Instead, he caught me, and together we inched down to a graceful bow.

Luke glared at us from the sideline. Colin paid him no mind, simply said, "Thank you again, Kate."

"What's going on here?" my boyfriend asked, his face flushed and furious. "You're making a spectacle of yourself. You're with me, not him."

"Well, you weren't around, now, were you?" I hissed. Luke and I often argued, but never in public like this. We returned to our chairs and sat in silence, until he took a long breath and tapped his fingers on the tabletop.

"Look. We haven't spent much time together lately. I'd hoped tonight would go much better than this." The anger seeped away from him like air from a torn balloon. He turned away, but I saw the hurt look in his eyes.

"Luke," I told him, "Colin saw me sitting alone and asked me to dance. That's all. We're at a party," I reminded him. "People are here to have fun."

Unasked questions about our relationship hovered in the air.

But none would be answered because Mari came over, dragging a familiar-looking teenaged boy with her. The tips of his hair glowed a shocking purple.

"Hi, Luke. Kate." Her cheerful smile quickly changed to a wary look after she looked at Luke, then me. "This is Lucky. He's been helping Judy tonight." She turned to the boy, whose eyes stayed fixed on the floor. "He's too shy to ask you, but he'd like to volunteer at the animal hospital one Saturday. Lucky here wants to be a veterinarian."

This entire exchange couldn't have happened at a worse time, but it wasn't Mari's fault—or the boy's. "I've met Lucky," I told her. "Let me speak to Cindy, and we'll see what we can do," I answered with as much enthusiasm as I could muster.

His eyes lifted, an eager smile brightening his face. "Thank you, Dr. Kate."

The boy turned, thanked Mari, and excused himself.

"I hope you don't mind," my assistant said. "He came over to our table and was so worried about our pit bull patient. I told him you thought his wounds would heal up just fine."

That made me think of the first time I'd seen this boy. He was leaving the Circle K and nearly ran into me. For unknown reasons he acted surprised and frightened to see me. His mom was a client. She'd mentioned her son went to the city and banged up his car.

Could this boy be the Good Samaritan who left Mr. Pitt by our dumpster?

Perhaps his New Jersey friends took him to an illegal dogfight. Did he take pictures with his phone? If animal-lover Lucky had rescued or stolen one of the promoter's injured dogs, he might be in trouble.

A dangerous, unlucky pile of trouble.

Chapter Sixteen

As the evening continued, I spotted Glenn Overmann hanging out at the bar. Dressed as he was in expensive Ivy League clothes, with his hair freshly groomed, I saw for the first time what had attracted Sookie. A handsome, thin man I didn't recognize stood by his side.

Several songs played and finished, but Luke didn't ask me to dance. We joined Mari and Judy's table, but after listening to us girls chattering away for fifteen minutes, my date became bored and excused himself.

"What's going on with you two?" Mari asked in a low voice.

"It's hard to pick up a relationship where you left off," I answered. "We probably should have celebrated alone at his place."

"So, Kate, I see you've met Colin." Judy had a funny expression on her face. I wondered if she'd heard Mari's whispered question. I know she'd seen Colin and me dancing.

My faithful friend immediately changed the subject. "What's going to happen at midnight?"

Judy began to explain the night's finale. "We're going to turn the heaters off now, so nobody throws confetti onto the coils. I'll make my announcement. Next the overhead lights go out and blue spotlights come on." She pointed to the barn's towering roof, its rafters bathed in shadows. "Unlike the ball at Times Square, our disco ball will be pulled up and should hit the middle rafter at midnight. That releases an explosion of confetti and streamers, which will rain down as you all scream 'Happy New Year!' At least that's what's supposed to happen. We'll continue the party for another hour, then start throwing everyone out."

"Got it," Mari said, trying unsuccessfully to stifle a big yawn. "I hope I last until midnight."

"See you next year." Judy rose and stretched. "Gotta go. I'm part of the fire warden crew. We banned all sparklers, but you never know."

"Happy New Year, Judy," Mari and I cried out in unison. "Great party."

After she left, I leaned over to Mari. "Can I hitch a ride home with you?"

"Trouble in lovebird land?" She yawned again. "Of course. I drive right past the animal hospital on my way home. But do you mind leaving soon after midnight?"

"Not at all."

The music started up again, a popular Taylor Swift tune. I spotted Luke having an animated conversation with his golden blond cousin, Rainbow. In her right hand was a sparkly fairy wand, which she playfully tapped several times on his chest.

People were coupling up as the countdown came

closer. No one really wanted to greet the New Year alone.

"I love this song, but I'm too pooped to get up," Mari said, leaning back in her chair. "I should have taken a nap this afternoon."

A pack of Mari's friends joined us, eager to celebrate at the stroke of midnight.

My watch confirmed we had seven minutes to go. Luke must have noticed the time because he cut off his conversation with Rainbow and walked toward me. Once he sat down he leaned his head toward mine.

"Kate, I'm sorry…"

"It's okay," I interrupted him, not in the mood to discuss our relationship while both of us felt exhausted and grumpy. "I'm going to hitch a ride home with Mari. Let's both get a good night's sleep and talk tomorrow."

I turned away so I wouldn't see his face.

The music stopped. Judy's voice took its place, followed by a screechy feedback noise and tap, tap, tap on the microphone. "Hi, everyone. Can you hear me?"

Most people nearby yelled, "Yes, Judy."

"It's almost time to ring out the old year and welcome a brand-new one. I'm glad we got to celebrate together here at the Hay Barn Gallery. Thanks to all my wonderful helpers who made tonight happen." She blew a kiss to the audience. "Okay. We're getting close."

An eager silence came over the crowd.

"Now. Keep your eye on the disco ball."

All the indoor lights blacked out. Three blue

spotlights switched on, illuminating a basketball-sized ball composed of tiny, mirrored surfaces. It fragmented the light back into the crowd, flashes of blue, red, and silver pulled from the colors in the bystanders.

"Here we go," Judy shouted. "Ten, nine, eight…" The ball began to rise. People joined in the counting. "Seven, six, five, four…"

I planned to give Luke a quick kiss, then arrange with Mari to leave.

"Three, two, one!" The disco ball reached the rafter, sparkling in the lavender-blue glow of all three spotlights.

"Happy New Year!" Judy shouted. The crowd went wild, screaming and kissing and screaming some more. Confetti, glitter, and streamers drifted down. The spotlights made crazy circles around the room, illuminating kissing faces and twisting bodies in momentary flashes of light. Horns blew. People jumped in the air, fingers stretched wide to catch the glittering confetti as it lazily floated away.

Luke and I stared at each other.

Then something large wrapped in streamers and glitter hurtled down and crashed headfirst into an empty table. Shatterproof glass crumpled onto the floor.

A body.

Chapter Seventeen

A WOMAN SCREAMED, HER SHRIEK DROWNED OUT BY the crowd. Horns still blew, couples still kissed. For a moment, I thought this was part of the New Year's show until blood began to trickle onto the confetti-strewn floor.

Luke pushed his way toward the body. I followed close behind. Since he was a former police officer, his emergency training automatically kicked in. With his right hand, he reached out and pressed two fingers on the person's exposed neck—a neck twisted into an impossible angle. Glass crunched under Luke's shoes.

The spotlights kept moving, blue lights now illuminating a horrible sight.

A gradual change in the revelers' noise signaled something was wrong. The celebratory sounds became patchy. Nearby faces reflected disbelief, horror. Luke cautioned the crowd to back away as he dialed 911 on his cell phone.

In the garish light, the body looked like a grotesque child's toy, arms hanging over the tabletop. Head embedded in the glass. Someone began to cry.

The body was that of a woman. I recognized the dress, the tightly curled red-purple hair. She'd been dancing the cha-cha only an hour ago.

Posey, the chatty clerk at the local Circle K, had fallen from the Hay Barn Gallery catwalk to her death. *An accident? A suicide?*

Or murder?

Although Judy made an announcement for everyone to stay put, many of the crowd took off, not wanting to start their New Year with a police interrogation. When Police Chief Bobby Garcia arrived, he quickly closed the back exit, designating his rookie to make a list of all the remaining partygoers. Many clustered in silent groups, watching the first responders like motorists gawking at a car wreck. Others formed a slow-moving line that snaked toward the front door. Luke walked toward one of the officers. Unsure what to do, I headed back to our table, looking for Mari. The festive tables, strewn with silly hats and empty glasses, didn't know that the party was over.

My last conversation with Posey played in my brain on an endless loop. Another movement high above caught my eye, but this time law enforcement looked back. Several officers moved slowly on the catwalks and rafters above the crowd, tiny as leftover Christmas elves. Judy, appearing pale and shocked, sat in a corner with the chief, shaking her head and pointing to the soaring ceiling.

Mari broke through the crowd. Her shoulders slumped with exhaustion.

"Time to go?" I asked.

"More than time to go." She answered. Her eyes darted in the direction of the body, then back again. "Let's get our coats."

When we reached the alcove containing the coat-racks, I noticed a police officer stationed outside the restrooms. Although he seemed vaguely familiar, he didn't speak to either of us. As I slipped my coat on, I remembered how Colin had appeared at my side, debonair, on the prowl. Strange how he'd suddenly disappeared just before midnight. Maybe he, like me, had come with a date.

We wove our way around a makeshift barricade toward the front door. The long line I'd observed began to move faster. Mari and I stood silently, waiting our turn.

Two police officers sat at a table, each with a laptop, entering names. Another person in plainclothes took a passport-style picture. It felt very formal, very impersonal. After adding our names to the list and pausing for our pictures, Mari and I headed out to her truck. The icy night air tasted good after the stuffy air inside. I noticed my throat felt dry and scratchy.

We trudged along, trying to avoid patches of ice.

"Kate." I heard Luke call and turned around.

When he reached me, I hugged him closely, resting my head on his chest.

"Are you okay?" he asked, concern in his eyes and in his voice.

"Yes." There wasn't time to tell him how I really felt.

"I've got to drive a few more people home than I thought. Rainbow can hardly walk, and my sister is too shaky to drive."

Behind him, a small group of somber faces stared back at me.

This was the Luke I knew. Someone strong. Good in an emergency. Responsible.

"Fine. Go." I gently kissed him. "Talk to you tomorrow. Happy New Year."

Mari drove slowly, concentrating on the dark road in front of us. All I could think about was the friendly woman at Circle K, doing a thankless job, optimistically writing her book. *What did she call it—an Edwardian romance, with a sci-fi subplot?* She hadn't seemed the least bit suicidal when I'd last spoken to her, but then you never knew.

"What was she doing up in the rafters?" Mari suddenly asked. "This doesn't make any sense."

The SUV's headlights illuminated a deer standing by the side of the road. Its eyes glinted a goblin green.

"I agree." I turned my head to search for any others. "Be careful," I cautioned as I noticed a small herd of deer about twenty feet away, staring at us.

The SUV slowed down, tires crunching in the gritty snow. A flash of the high beams bathed the scenery in icy-blue light. "There's a meadow over on your side that the deer all like to hang out in. We'll be past it in a few minutes."

Mari was like a living GPS with narration here in the Hudson Valley, where she'd lived all her life. The only sign of stress was her hands tightly gripping the steering wheel, knuckles a bony white.

"Did you know her?" I asked.

"Enough to say hi and chat. Posey worked part-time at that Circle K for at least the better part of five years—usually the night shift."

"She was on the night shift when I last spoke to her. I'd stopped for gas and decided to go inside for something. We started talking, and she mentioned Mr. Pitt and Cindy and you and offered to put up a poster for us."

"Yeah."

After that we didn't speak at all until Mari pulled up at my apartment door.

"I'll wait until I'm sure you're inside with the door locked." The SUV idled a little high, and exhaust flowed back inside the cab when I held open the door.

"Happy New Year?" I asked her.

"I certainly hope so," she answered. "Can't get much worse than this, can it?"

When I woke up the next day, my head pounded and my throat burned. Buddy licked my hand in sympathy. I remembered taking both dogs for a late walk before I crashed for the night. Although I wanted to go back to sleep, they needed to go out. As I opened my eyes, the room appeared to lazily spin until the memory of Posey's broken body brought me to my senses.

The phone rang. I'd slept until just before eleven. Caller ID forced me to sit up in bed. Regardless of how I felt, I had to pretend to be bright and alert and happy for my Gramps.

"Happy New Year," I answered in someone else's gravelly voice.

"Happy New Year, honey," he answered. "You sound like you just crawled out of a dumpster. I take it you enjoyed yourself at Judy's party?"

My Gramps and Cindy were Facebook pals. From the lilt in his voice, he hadn't heard about our bloody midnight surprise.

Yeah, I wanted to say. *Judy knocked them dead.*

"Let me get some water," I told him as I dangled my feet over the side of the bed, trying to make the room stop spinning. "There was a lot of smoke in the air last night. My throat is scratchy."

Former fireman Gramps expressed his dismay. "Wasn't the party held in a hay barn? That's a complete violation of every fire code I can think of."

"No hay in the barn anymore," I rasped before grabbing a water bottle off the nightstand. "It's an art gallery." I eagerly gulped down the tepid water. "Sorry. A bunch of people were smoking weed near me."

"Everyone's gone a little crazy now that our state made it legal." Gramps gave a slight cough, a reminder of the smoke damage to his own lungs he'd suffered over his years of service. "I even smelled some pot here last night."

"What?" Gramps lived in an assisted living community.

"Katie, you'd be surprised at all the CBD and hemp oil around here. Plenty of seniors use medical marijuana and all kinds of drugs for pain or anxiety. Plus alcohol. Lots of drinking, of course, to lubricate our old joints."

While he spoke, I got up and pressed the button on my coffee maker. The best smell in the universe started wafting from the kitchen. I'd filled up the refrigerator, anticipating Luke stopping by, so for once I had plenty of yogurt, fruit, and eggs. My stomach signaled that coffee and yogurt was all it could manage.

"Are you there?" Gramps asked, concerned because I hadn't said anything.

"Yes." After another gulp of water, my voice sounded more normal. "Listen, can I call you back? I've got to walk Buddy and our pit bull. They've got their legs crossed." I watched Buddy trot up to my side, eager to start his doggy new year.

Gramps laughed and said, "I know how that feels. Call me later?"

"Will do. Happy New Year, Gramps."

"Happy New Year to you too, Katie."

My Gramps was the only person left who called me Katie. The hospital staff all called me Kate. My father called me Katherine. My mom and brother had called me Katie.

Sad thoughts overwhelmed me—not the way to start a new year.

I threw my coat over my pajamas, slipped on a pair of boots, and let the dogs out into the dog run. The parking lot was deserted. Only a few cars passed by on the road in front of the hospital on this brand-new January first.

As the dogs chased each other over the crusted snow, a familiar snowplow pulled into the long driveway next door. Pinky gave two taps on the horn by way of a greeting. I hadn't noticed him at Judy's party. He must have been working last night, since the front of the plow was caked with snow and gravel. I waved before he disappeared into his oversized garage.

"Come on, boys," I called out. "Let's get inside."

With a couple of weak yips, the dogs waited for me to open the door. Inside they kept up their playing. I admired their energy. Crawling back into bed sounded like a better option.

Then the ping of a text message changed everything.

It was Cindy, wishing me a Happy New Year—and giving me a heads-up that her brother-in-law, also known as the Oak Falls chief of police, was going to be contacting me soon.

I had a suspicion Chief Garcia wasn't going to offer me a Zoom meeting.

Steam swirled around in my tiny bathroom as I tried to get mind and body up to speed. I'd taken ibuprofen for my wine headache, and after the second cup of coffee I felt somewhat human again. Drying myself off, I noticed the message light on my cell signaled a voice mail. While I'd been washing my hair to get the funky smell out, the chief of police's office had reached out.

Someone had scheduled an interview between me and Chief Garcia without asking. I had ten minutes to get down to the station. Problem was the police station was twenty-five minutes away. Since I didn't want to start the New Year with a speeding ticket, I called the police station back and told the truth: I just got out of the shower and couldn't get there for at least a half an hour to forty-five minutes. She tersely accepted my terms.

No doubt I'd pay for that.

Before I left, I checked to make sure the animals all had extra food in case I got arrested or detained. My hair finally felt dry, which was good because otherwise it would freeze when I stepped outside. I texted Cindy back and wished her a Happy New Year. My phone chimed with another text message on my walk out to the parking lot.

Probably Gramps, I thought while I opened the driver's-side door. I hoped he hadn't seen any of the newer Oak Falls Facebook posts about last night. The truck roared to life after a few false starts. I put on the heat, hoping not to freeze from the initial blast of cold air. My teeth chattered and my phone pinged again. Since I never text while driving, I figured I'd check it now, before heading over to the police station. I revved the engine a bit, trying to speed up the warm air.

The message was from Luke.

Already running late, I decided to wait and call him later. As I drove, I took deep breaths, trying to focus my energy for my interrogation. For some absurd reason, I felt a little guilty for Posey's death, as if I knew a secret. Which I didn't. A crimp in my neurological wiring often made me feel guilty for things I had no control over. It was the same reason I felt uneasy when a police car pulled alongside me at a light.

I took it slow. All the people who normally sanded and salted the roads were home enjoying the holiday.

Arriving at the police station, I figured delaying my appearance another few minutes wouldn't hurt, so I dialed Luke's number.

"Good morning," he answered, sounding a lot more alert than me. "How's your head feeling?"

"Not too bad," I lied. "Chief Garcia has summoned me to the police station for an unknown reason. I don't think he's hosting a New Year's Day brunch."

"Crap." I heard voices in the background. "That's actually what I was going to do. Remind you of my family brunch this afternoon. Listen," he continued. "When are you meeting him?"

"Now." The engine's temp now in the normal range, I turned the heat to low. Warm air continued to spew out of the vents.

"I'll meet you there," he declared. "Hopefully, I

can speed up your interview. Then afterward you can follow me back to my grandmother's place."

I started to protest that I didn't need his help, but he cut me off. "This is nonnegotiable. Meet you at the station."

He'd hung up on me. As I opened the truck door, I checked the time—about eleven minutes late. The Oak Falls chief of police's demeanor toward me in the past ran the gamut from gracious to grumpy. Maybe Luke's presence and friendship with Chief Garcia would smooth things over.

When I pushed open the door of our Oak Falls Police Station, I found a mostly empty reception area. Since there was no sense in explaining why I was late, I simply told the receptionist my name and who I was there to see. She, in turn, looked royally pissed off about spending New Year's Day at work.

"He's busy at the moment. Take a seat. I'll tell him you're here," she said curtly. Clearly this middle-aged person with the side-buzzed hair wanted to be anywhere but here.

I didn't blame her. I felt exactly the same way.

An older man slumped in a corner chair, sort of propped against the wall, snoring away. I wondered if he was waiting for a ride. Since there was nothing to read, I busied myself on Facebook, where floods of good wishes had been posted to the Oak Falls Animal Hospital page. I knew Cindy took care of most of the social media postings, but since I had time, I decided to answer as many as possible.

Someone with familiar shoulders appeared silhou-etted at the door.

Luke wore a new coat, much smarter than the famil-iar ski jacket he usually wore. This coat was three-quarter-length, made of wool dyed a dark gray—very unlike his regular student gear.

"Hi, Gigi," he said to the receptionist. "Sorry Garcia roped you into this."

With a grin, the previously dour receptionist rose and gave Luke a big hug. "When did you get into town?" she said. "Are you a lawyer yet?"

After the quick embrace she jerked her head in my direction. "Dr. Kate's over there."

"Happy New Year," he told her. "Ask Garcia for a raise."

She punched him on the arm, squinted her eyes at us, and went back to her paperwork.

Luke looked a lot better than I felt. I felt frazzled while he looked as though he'd had nine hours of bliss-ful, uninterrupted sleep.

He turned away from the reception desk, stood in front of me for a long moment, then leaned down and kissed my nose. "Great way to start the New Year," he commented, and sat down in the chair next to me.

I put away my phone. Last night's awkwardness intruded again.

Before we could speak, Gigi interrupted. "The chief will see you now, Dr. Kate."

With a feeling of dread, I stood up.

"I'm going in with you. After all, we were together the whole night." Luke's eyes stared into mine, giving me a signal. One I wasn't sure I should follow.

I opened the reinforced steel door of Chief Garcia's office. His initial staid look changed when he saw Luke follow me in.

"Good morning, Dr. Kate. Luke."

I could see from his expression he'd been taken by surprise.

"Luke, it's great to see you. But I'd like you to wait outside while…"

It took guts to interrupt the chief, but my boyfriend did it smoothly and confidently. "Chief, Kate and I were together all last night at Judy's party. I figured it would be easier to interview us both at the same time. Between the liquor and whatever the Angus brothers were smoking last night…well, you know." He turned and squeezed my shoulder. "Together we might remember everything a bit clearer. I'm sure you understand."

The chief laughed, and Luke joined in. I didn't. Luke was a designated driver last night. He didn't really drink anything, except a swallow of white wine during our toast. Plus, I barely saw him the whole night.

Was I supplying him an alibi?

The two men soon became sidetracked with memories of previous New Year's Eves. Bobby was older than Luke, but I knew they'd worked together as law enforcement officers and played in the same softball league.

Didn't that qualify as some kind of prejudice for the witness? But then I wasn't the one becoming a lawyer.

While they continued to chat about the good old times when Luke was a member of the Oak Falls police force, I took out my phone. I felt guilty I hadn't called Gramps back, but my dismay didn't last long. Two new texts waited for me. In terse language Gramps implied I'd spent New Year's with a corpse. Which technically was correct.

I texted back *everything's fine* and that I'd explain later.

Chief Garcia noticed me on my phone and decided to cut reminiscences short. "Well, good to catch up with you, Luke, but we're here to discuss something much more serious. You're both witnesses to a death. Now let's do this one the right way, one at a time."

Luke was banished to the waiting room while the chief went over my movements from the time I entered the Hay Barn Gallery. I explained that Colin, who was helping Judy, guided me to the coatrack. Although several people passed by, I didn't remember any details— except for the guy dressed like Freddy Krueger.

"Not a problem," the chief said. "Jim always dresses like Freddy Krueger."

The early evening played out a little hazy in my memory, due to the wine and smoke, but the minutes leading up to midnight and Posey's death were more straightforward.

"She came hurtling down," I told him, "headfirst,

and crashed into a table. Luke checked for a pulse and several people called 911."

"Did either of you go near the victim, other than to check the body for signs of life?"

"No," I said truthfully. "It was obvious that her neck had been broken. Several of us made a ring and kept the crowd away until you arrived."

"Did you interact with the victim at any time during the evening?"

"No," I told him. "When Luke and I were sitting at our table, I saw her briefly as she passed by. She was dancing the cha-cha."

"Do you remember who she was dancing with?" Chief Garcia's pen hovered over his notebook in anticipation.

In an effort to remember, I closed my eyes. For the life of me nothing came to mind. After a moment of reflection, I shook my head. "I'm sorry but...wait...she was dancing alone. I only saw her for a couple of seconds," I volunteered. "The Hay Barn was unbelievably crowded and noisy. And hot."

The chief put down his pen. "So I've heard. Do you know anyone who had a grievance against the victim?"

"Not really. I only met her once," I said. "I stopped to pump gas and went inside Circle K to buy some dog treats. As I checked out, we chatted, mostly about dogs." My thoughts skipped over that encounter, editing it for submission to the chief. *Would he be interested in her gossip about Sookie? Writing a romance during working hours? Vampires?*

Before I could add anything, the chief said, "Thanks for your statement. If you remember anything important, please call the office."

He stood up and escorted me out. Luke sat in the waiting room, checking his phone, looking up when I walked toward him.

"Oh, Dr. Kate," the chief added, "can I reach you today at the hospital?"

My mouth opened but nothing came out.

"She'll be with me, Chief," Luke stated, a bit more emphatically than necessary. "It's New Year's Day. The animal hospital is closed." With a big grin he looped my arm around his. "We're going spend the day working our way through some of our New Year's resolutions."

I waited until we reached the parking lot before pulling my arm away from his.

"What the heck did that mean?" I asked. "Working our way through some of our resolutions. What New Year's resolutions?"

"Calm down. They're probably watching us," he said.

As I was about to tell him not to tell me to calm down, he walked around to the driver's side of my car and kissed me hard on the lips.

"Follow me," he said, getting into his car.

Fuming at this game played for the benefit of the chief, I drove behind Luke, a million questions on my mind.

What happened to spending the day together? Or *any* time together? He'd mentioned brunch with his family before, but now it seemed like an afterthought. My heart pounded against my chest.

The familiar winding roads helped me calm down. *Don't start the new year off mad,* I told myself. *Make the most of what you have. Life is short. Just ask Sookie and Posey.*

Luke turned into the wide driveway first, while I waited for a break in traffic. By the time I parked, he'd already started to interact with his relatives. Another cousin with his wife and three kids was unloading their car when I pulled up. I vaguely remembered meeting them before.

We all walked together into his grandmother's home on the same property as the diner. They'd built away from the road and into the trees, close enough for emergencies, but hidden away for privacy. Several additions over the years had expanded the original stone building. On the oldest section, thick green ivy crawled almost to the roof, its gnarled stems twisted with age.

Children screamed and yelled with pent-up energy. Family members greeted each other, eager to catch up on family news. Watching everyone laughing and smiling, I felt my remaining anger cool. It was Luke's family, not mine, but for a while I could pretend.

Once I was inside, a feeling of familiarity wrapped around me. His grandmother's home and furnishings never changed–very old-world Italian. A marble bust of someone sat on a stand in the hall. With all the children and grandchildren running around I couldn't believe that Caesar or Plato or whoever it was hadn't been shattered to pieces.

Recordings featuring Italian tenors played vigorously in the background as we headed toward the dining room. A throng of people who resembled each other were gathered around the table chatting away, smiles on their faces. At the head of the table, dressed in black, was the matriarch of the family, Grandma Gianetti.

Grandma. Nonna. Hers was the brain behind it all.

"Dr. Turner," she said, formal as always. "Wonderful to see you. Thank you for joining us today." Despite the festivities, she wore black as a sign of mourning for her husband who had passed away many years ago.

"Come. Sit." She patted the seat next to her.

Two huge tables had been set up running against the wall, acting as a buffet. I recognized some of the diner employees, also relatives, as they efficiently brought out trays of food. The room smelled of aromatic herbs like rosemary and oregano, punctuated by roasted garlic.

"Sit down, everyone," Grandma Gianetti called out in a surprisingly loud voice, raising her hands in greeting. Around her neck she wore a ribbon of lace, fastened with an antique cameo. The crowd of family moved toward the table. The scene became a little raucous, with babies being passed to aunties, toddlers trying to grab food, and older children doing laps around the huge mahogany table. Most of the teenagers surreptitiously stared down at their phones.

I loved it. It felt like life itself pulsing around me.

Luke appeared at my side, with two plates piled high. "Got you most of your favorites," he said. Then in a feat of magic, he pulled a small dessert plate from behind his back. It held a perfect piece of cranberry pecan pie.

"Just in case you wanted dessert." The smile in his eyes reflected the smile on his face.

"Good boy," Grandma Gianetti said, her sharp eyes watching us. *"Mangia. Mangia."*

I loved pie, and Luke knew it. *Was this an apology for last night?*

The next half hour raced by as everyone talked and laughed between stuffing their faces. I noticed Rainbow sat farther down the table on the side opposite us, wrapped like an octopus around a cute guy. Nobody seemed to care.

Grandma Gianetti took a spoon and tapped her wineglass. Gradually the noise stopped as they waited for her New Year's Day toast.

She raised her glass of red wine in the air. "This last year has been hard for all of us," she began, "but I want you to concentrate on the future. When my dear husband, God rest his soul, bought this piece of land, I called him a fool. But he had a vision—and that's what I want each of you to have. A vision. Make your vision come true."

Rising slowly from her chair at the head of the table, she lifted her glass again.

"*Coraggio*," she said in Italian. "Courage to you all and *Buon Anno*—Happy New Year!"

We stood up, raised our glasses, and pledged to be brave in this fresh New Year.

I'd fallen in love with Luke's family almost as much as I'd fallen in love with him. Maybe our relationship ultimately wouldn't work out, but I realized the uselessness of worrying about it now. *Enjoy the day.*

I was counting blueberries in a blueberry pie with a three-year-old when Luke pulled me aside.

"Sorry about last night," he began.

We ventured outside, detouring into his grandmother's kitchen garden, protected from the winter storms by a large greenhouse. Basil grew abundantly toward the overhead grow lights, oblivious of the season. I recognized a vigorous clump of Swiss chard filling a terra-cotta pot.

"Mint," Luke said, lifting the trailing stems next to us seeking to escape. He took my hand, the smell of the mint and damp earth on our skin.

"What happened last night isn't the way to start a new year," he said. "It makes you think about your own mortality."

We walked for a while, stopping to admire a rose in bloom.

"Did you know Posey?" I asked Luke.

"No," he said. "I vaguely remember her ringing me up at Circle K a few times, but I don't think I ever had a conversation with her."

We stood in silence, his hand in mine.

I wondered how many times a day her clients bothered to talk to her. So often people behind the counter or credit card terminal are anonymous in our hurry-up culture. Working her shift day after day—people running in, and out—filling their gas tanks and driving away. The Circle K, and the woman in it, a momentary memory.

"Did you know her?" Luke asked me.

I reached down to smell a miniature rose tangled in the plantings. We started heading back to the dining room. I still hadn't answered his question.

We'd been two lonely, single women in a Circle K, briefly talking about their lives, dogs, books. Dreams. Would a man understand that quick female bond?

Some children playing hide-and-seek noisily searched for each other behind the heavy curtains as we entered the dining room. I paused at the table filled with people sharing stories. I thought back to that night at Circle K, Posey, wearing her cheap corporate jacket, harshly lit by overhead fluorescent lights. Only a name tag identified her. When I'd approached the register, she'd stuffed her notebooks out of sight under the locked cigarette display. *Who was she? A woman working the night shift—not because she wanted to, but because she had to? Did she have a family? Who mourned her today?*

If she were alive right now, would she be eating lunch alone on the first day of the New Year?

Luke had asked if I knew Posey. *What should I tell him?*

I whispered my answer in his ear. "I only met Posey once. That's not enough time to really know anyone."

Chapter Eighteen

THE NEW YEAR THAT STARTED SO TERRIBLY CONTINued making our lives miserable in the next few days. A frozen pipe burst on an outside wall of my garage apartment, making a piece of Sheetrock bulge out of the wall like a tumor. Cindy's car was rear-ended at a stop sign. The sudden jolt gave her a bad case of whiplash with a pounding headache. And since bad things come in threes, I'd ended up driving home alone from Luke's family's New Year's brunch, with no real explanation on his part. I was tired of trying to interpret his mixed signals.

On the third of January, Mari and I were in the truck driving back to the office when the low fuel light popped on. We were particularly tired, having had to spend part of our time on a farm call, trying to trap and examine a stray cat that wandered into a client's barn.

Other than an advanced state of pregnancy, the kitty seemed fine when we caught her. Just to be sure, I'd drawn some blood to test for FIV, the feline immunosuppressive virus and feline leukemia virus. After a detour through the goat and sheep pens to say hi to my old friend, Billy the Goat, Mari and I smelled a little gamey.

The closest gas station was Circle K—the same Circle K Posey had worked in. With the weather hovering below freezing, I made sure to park at a pump close to the store's entrance.

My assistant unbuckled her seat belt. "Want anything?" she asked.

"I'm not sure." The memory of Posey behind the counter came to mind. I wondered how the other employees were coping with her death. "Wait up. I'll go with you."

Leaving the truck gassing up, I wiped the bottom of my boots in the snow. Protected by the overhang from the flurries just starting to fall, we ducked inside. The door handle felt uncomfortably cold in my hand.

Two people stood behind the cash register—a young boy, who looked just out of high school, and an older man with a swarthy complexion and deep frown on his face. They were in the middle of a conversation.

"I'll stay with you for the first two hours," the man said. "After that, you're on your own." His restless fingers straightened up the display of single-serving jerky in front of him. "Text me if you have any computer problems. Otherwise, I'll review your shift with you tomorrow."

I wondered if this was Posey's replacement. The kid looked scared to death. Making my way over to the endcap display of candy and snacks, I pretended to mull over the selection. In reality, I blatantly eavesdropped. Neither clerk bothered to watch me.

The older man's phone chimed. He muttered what sounded like a curse, then sent a text, the same angry frown frozen on his face. Trying hard not make a wrong move, the kid started fidgeting, eyes wide. I thought he might faint.

Abruptly the man I assumed was a manager asked the kid, "Did you bring a book or something, like I told you?"

"Yes, sir." The boy's face blanched. "I have a textbook with me."

"Make sure you bring it home with you every night." It was obvious the manager didn't relish small talk. "These yours?" He'd fished out a stack of notebooks from under the cigarette display, with black-and-white marbled covers. They looked like the ones that Posey had written in.

"No, sir." His voice trembled. "I don't know whose they are."

The manager's dark eyes alighted on me for a second, then moved on. "I'm tired of you employees leaving your stuff all over the place. Keeping a clean work space is part of this job. " With a sharp stride he abandoned the register, scooping up random items left on the countertop behind him. A wrinkled newspaper, two half-empty soda bottles, several random potato chips—all of them went into a white plastic bag. The manager took a moment to open one of the notebooks. After he glanced down at the page his face changed, some hint of emotion before it tightened back down. He stuffed all three notebooks into the garbage bag.

"I'll be right back," he told the kid. Without waiting to put on his coat, he marched out the door. Meanwhile, Mari came up the aisle with some food items on her way to check out.

"Meet you in the truck," I told her, pulling my hood up over my head. I opened the glass exit doors and noticed the manager tossing the white plastic bag into the dumpster.

I needed to retrieve that bag.

As casually as possible, I hurried down the walkway next to the building. A moment later, the man returned, still frowning. Acknowledging my existence with a brisk nod, he passed by.

Aware there might be cameras on me. I pulled out a tissue and pretended to blow my nose. Kleenex in hand, I made for the dumpster. Nonchalantly, I raised the lid and threw the tissue in while fishing out the white plastic bag, which, thankfully, rested on top of a used but closed pizza box. Sliding it out of sight under my coat, I walked back to the truck and opened the driver's door, covering my movements. With the plastic bag now safely out of sight in the back seat, I exited, finished gassing up, and paid with the hospital credit card.

The snowflakes coming down turned fluffy, the kind of snow that piles up in drifts and in your hair. Mari still hadn't come out of the Circle K. I started the engine and took a deep breath. I didn't think it was a crime to lift something from a dumpster, but I wasn't sure. Even if it was against the law, I couldn't let Posey's words be thrown away with the trash.

Mari appeared at the passenger side window and yanked the door open. She had a paper bag in her hands, which she placed on her lap. I recognized the colorful potato chip logo sitting at the top.

"Sorry it took so long," she said, popping the bag along the seam and retrieving a chip. "The cashier was new and he messed something up. They had to void the first receipt and ring me up again. That manager didn't look real happy about it."

It was a short drive to the animal hospital. Mari continued to chat away between bites. Most of her conversation had to do with Posey's death. She passed along the town gossip, which ran rampant. Someone said Posey had overdosed with pills and booze on the previous New Year's Eve. Others said she'd always been a little odd. No known family members, or next of kin survived her. A high school friend set up a GoFundMe page for funeral expenses. The coroner had officially ruled her death a suicide.

So what did I hope to gain by reading Posey's stories? Mari kept up her banter, and I kept quiet.

With the snow falling faster and my eyes focused on the road, a memory of my conversation with Posey lingered in my thoughts. I'd asked what she was writing. She surprised me with her answer—some kind of Edwardian, sci-fi vampire novel. Not stories about the people she saw on her night shift. Then I remembered her final words.

Knowledge is power. And power means money.

I had wondered then if that meant blackmail; I wondered still.

When we turned into the hospital parking lot, I realized Cindy had left. Only Mari's SUV was parked at the back entrance, at least an inch of snow covering the hood and luggage rack. A familiar vehicle waited outside my door, engine running.

Mari glanced over at Luke getting out of his car and said, "I can finish up." She zipped up the hospital laptop case. "Go on. Take your time. You've got a visitor."

The snowflakes floated around us like tufts of down. When I lifted my lips toward his, he kissed me on the cheek. My stomach gave a thud.

"Listen, Kate. I'm leaving town today. I wanted to tell you in person." His dark eyes avoided mine.

I wish I could say I was surprised, but I wasn't. Something had changed since he'd left for school—and it wasn't me.

"You know," he began, "you're a wonderful person."

Part of me felt like interrupting, to make the cutting of the ties between us as quick as possible. Layers of snowflakes dotted our coats as he explained. He'd met someone at school. They were only friends, but...

That's when I tuned him out. I'd heard this story before, and the ending never got any better. A bright red truck rumbled past on the nearby road.

"It's not you, it's me," he added, as sincere as a stab in the heart.

Of course it's you! I wanted to yell at him. We'd been dancing around this relationship for a while. It had never been easy. Something always got in the way. Maybe that was the point.

He took my hand and held it close to his chest. "You okay?"

"I'm fine," I lied as always. "You better get going before the roads ice up."

"Friends?" he asked, the charm in his crooked smile still tugging away.

"Of course." I took my hand back, turned my back to him, and headed for my door. Halfway down the walkway I paused. It took an effort to glance back and pretend it didn't hurt so much. "Have a safe trip," I called out and waved goodbye.

My eye caught a glimpse of Mari staring at us through the hospital window.

A snowflake landed on my eyelash. Luke waved back before opening his car door. Through the movement of the windshield wipers I saw his shoulders relax with relief. Our awkward discussion had gone well, much better than he'd anticipated.

So civilized on both our parts.

One final wave goodbye was all I could muster. Eager whines and yips behind my apartment door reminded me that Mr. Pitt and Buddy waited inside, joyously eager to see me. Only their loving eyes would see my tears.

Chapter Nineteen

"Sometimes I just hate men." Cindy angrily picked at the salad she'd brought for lunch. "Good ones are getting harder to find."

I agreed. My food choice for lunch had hit a new low—a pint of fudge ripple ice cream and a diet soda. Both of my coworkers watched sympathetically as I tried to eat my way to a little happiness. We all knew that never worked, but it sure tasted good.

We were sitting in the employee break room, with about a half hour left before Mari and I had to leave for our house-call appointments. Cindy and Mari chatted about a new crochet technique, so my focus waned. Most people in town knew Luke and I were seeing each other. I'd have to prepare myself for their well-meaning questions.

Most of all I dreaded explaining to Gramps that we'd split up. My track record with guys wasn't very good. I wish I could simply say, "Luke's up on the roof and won't come down."

"Kate?"

Mari's voice interrupted my thoughts. "Sorry, wasn't paying attention. What's up?"

"Why don't you come with us to the organizing

lecture tonight? It's about laundry." My assistant flashed a big smile at Cindy and me as if she had tickets to a rock concert. How could Mari get so enthusiastic about dirty clothes? Then I realized her show of eagerness was probably for my benefit. "Sure. Sounds great," I lied. Keeping busy the next few days might help my frame of mind.

After a quick glance at the wall clock, Cindy told us, "Time to get back to work." She closed the plastic lid and put her remaining salad in the fridge.

"I'll be right back," Mari told us. "I need to check the truck's supplies. I think we were running low on a few things." All our coats hung on a wooden coatrack. She slipped hers on and walked toward the side door.

Thanks to my diet soda/ice cream lunch, I felt sluggish and on a sugar high at the same time. I made a mental note to stop at the grocery store after work and buy something healthy—also an extra pint of ice cream in case of the blues.

From behind me I heard Cindy say, "Don't blame yourself, Kate. Luke's a great guy in every respect except one."

I was pretty certain she'd now tell me about that one exception.

Sure enough, she came and stood in front of me. "Luke can't commit to a relationship. Look at his history with Dina. All through high school and college they were on and off so many times I lost track."

Her soft blue eyes studied me. I bit my lip and said,

"I get it. We are in different places. But that doesn't make it hurt any less."

"I know. But here's a friendly warning. Your ex might decide to come back. In fact, I'd say it's a strong possibility."

Funny, I'd thought about that same possibility ever since he'd waved goodbye in the parking lot. And I'd made a decision.

"Don't worry, Cindy. There's nothing for him to come back to."

The last part of the afternoon was sheer fun, thanks in part to having a "puppy" break. Two wiggly, fluffy, and irresistible golden retriever puppies needed their second round of shots and their sharp little toenails trimmed. A brother and sister, at this age they enthusiastically loved everything and everyone.

The owner, Sarah, had lost her fourteen-year-old golden to cancer a few months ago. "I needed some time to grieve," she explained. "But the house felt so lonely without a dog. Then a friend told me her neighbor's golden had given birth." She paused to bend down and ruffle one of the puppies' soft fuzz. "Anyway, as soon as I saw them I melted. Now I've got twice as much fun."

As she spoke, a pink tongue decided to lick my nose. With the male puppy tucked under my arm I listened to his heart, checked him for an over- or underbite, and ran my hands along his ribs and abdomen. Next I placed him on the makeshift exam table and had Mari hold him for the rest of the exam. The shot record the owner showed me noted that both puppies had been wormed by the breeder.

"I think their stool is a little stinky," Sarah added. "But I'm trying to housebreak them, and that means pooping in the snow."

"So, you've got lots of poopsicles out back?" Mari asked.

Sarah laughed. "Easier to pick up."

"Don't worry about bringing in a stool sample." I picked up the nearest puppy. "I'll go directly to the source." Although the pups looked healthy, they could be harboring anything from coccidia to roundworms to giardia. All are commonly found where groups of dogs are housed. If I didn't find anything under the microscope, more sophisticated tests were now available.

After giving the vaccinations, which they didn't seem to feel, we stayed for another fifteen minutes, to make sure there were no rare allergic reactions. With our stool samples securely labeled and safe in our portable lab cooler, I took one last smell of sweet puppy fur—and was rewarded with a final puppy-breath lick.

Chapter Twenty

After feeding the dogs and changing my clothes, I started out for the community center lecture. As yet I hadn't had a moment to read anything in Posey's notebooks. While driving, I mulled over what Daffy had told us. My conduit to the chief was through Cindy—coincidentally the chief's sister-in-law. If Daffy was correct and Posey was murdered, then surely the two deaths were tied to each other?

The parking lot was half-filled, leaving a spot close to the entrance free. This time I'd left early, in part so I could speak to some of the other audience members. To my surprise, Henry James pulled his massive black truck into the row just behind me.

"Hey, Dr. Kate," he said as I got out of my much smaller F-150. "Wait up."

Dressed in black biker leathers, Henry was the last person you'd expect to find at a lecture on laundry. The Baking Biker brand of cupcakes and other goodies earned him a comfortable living. Never apologetic, Henry was comfortable showing his feminine side. Since he was built like a brick, I assumed nobody made rude comments about it.

"Let's hope there's no excitement tonight," he

laughed, taking my arm as we walked across a patch of ice. "Although the unusual does seem to follow you."

"That's what Mari says."

We walked through the lobby/reception area and followed the signs to our lecture. Inside the conference room, people had begun claiming their seats. The sound system was more than adequate, but many preferred to be up close to the speaker.

"Let's sit here," I told Henry. We moved into the tenth row from the front and began laying our coats and mufflers on the chairs.

Henry slipped off his lined leather coat and carefully draped it over the back of the aisle seat. His short-sleeved black T-shirt revealed full-sleeve tattoos on both arms. I counted at least three skulls. "How many seats do we need?"

"Ahh, it's you and me, Mari and her sister-in law, and maybe Cindy. So that's five." Between my backpack, coat, and muffler and Henry's stuff, we easily covered five seats.

On the stage Elaine began setting up. One of the staff volunteers rolled a large whiteboard out from behind the curtain. In the small balcony overhang, I noticed cameras being set up. Had all the lectures been videotaped? An irritating scraping noise continued as multiple examples of laundry baskets and hampers were lined up next to the podium. I wanted a chance to speak to our lecturer alone, but now wasn't the time.

"Let's get some coffee," Henry suggested. "I'd hate to fall asleep and snore during the lecture."

"Me, too."

Together we headed to the lobby.

Several women milled around in pairs or clusters, the level of excited chatter making the room come alive. Henry took off for coffee, while I scoped out the scene. As I walked toward a small table, two clients approached me. As usual, my dismal recollection of names betrayed me, although I remembered their animals as soon as they began to speak to me.

"I'm so excited," the woman in the green hat said. "What do you think will happen tonight?" Her eyes glittered.

"Don't be morbid," replied the client, who owned a spaniel mix.

"What do you think, Dr. Kate?" the woman persisted. "Anyone going to die tonight?" The outrageous statement set off a nervous giggle.

Before I could answer, her friend said, "You've been bingeing too much Netflix."

Henry interrupted, handing me a coffee. "Hello, ladies. Ready to learn how to sort your undies?" That set off a round of belly laughs, which I'm sure Henry counted on. "See you inside," he said while taking my elbow. We rapidly moved toward an empty table in the far corner.

Over my shoulder I noticed the two women whispering and staring at our backs. Maybe showing up here with Henry would spark romance rumors that would leave Luke's absence in the dust. The nicest thing about a small town is everyone knows you—and the worst thing is everyone knows all about you.

"Hey, guys," Mari called out behind us. "Did you save us seats?"

"Of course." Henry high-fived Mari and nodded a greeting for her sister-in-law, Barbara.

A loud chime sounded.

"I think it's about to start." Most of the other participants began moving toward the auditorium. After a final gulp, I placed my coffee mug on the provided tray and followed my friends inside.

As before, one of the community center's staff introduced the presenter. At the beginning of the lecture, Elaine seemed a bit timid, but she soon warmed to her subject. Although not as dramatic as Sookie, she did provide us with an overview of tonight's topic—a well-structured presentation on the ins and outs of laundry, including a history lesson about fabrics and the difficulty of drying heavy wool garments in the winter.

"That's another reason why most people smelled back then," Mari whispered in my ear.

I turned to see if Henry had heard us, but instead of looking at the stage he was staring toward the back of the room. As Elaine held up a sample of lye soap, I subtly leaned over to see what had engaged his interest. Against the wall, arms crossed, stood a man who appeared quite out of place in rural Oak Falls. He was dressed in a long dark coat, black pants, and a suit jacket; his eyes remained hidden behind tinted sunglasses.

Henry nudged me and pointed to the left. Sure enough, a second guy leaned against the other wall. Same glasses. Same stance.

The man on the left caught us staring at him. Probably noting Henry's size and the glare on his face, he signaled his pal and the two quickly left. Elaine paused, noticing the movement in the back of the room, then smoothly returned to pre-wash sorting methods.

During our fifteen-minute break I asked Henry what he thought that was all about.

"No idea." He kept his eyes on Elaine busy speaking to an elderly woman with a cane. When the break ended, we both checked out the waiting area and conference room, but the men had vanished.

"FBI?" I asked Henry as I scooted past him to my seat.

"I doubt it," he answered. "Those guys looked like thugs to me." He rubbed his shiny shaved head and frowned. "Something's up."

Back in our seats, with Mari to my left and Henry on the aisle to my right, I pondered what the appearance of the "thugs" meant. The only thing I could come up with was they were either looking for someone or watching someone in the room. I didn't think they wanted laundry tips.

Elaine continued her review of fabrics, and how to best clean each type. Since my clothes ranged from poly-blend scrubs to jeans or sweats, I concentrated on the speaker. Dressed in a dark brown pantsuit with a cream silk shirt, Elaine likely hoped to model her clothes after her former boss. But where Sookie was sharp, Elaine proved dull. Sookie challenged while Elaine consoled. The odds of her being successful in this competitive, often personality-driven field seemed slim.

Then she surprised me.

"People wonder why I teach organizational skills," she began. "What's so important about putting your laundry away?"

A few audience members lifted their heads up from their notes.

"For many people the state of their home can contribute to their state of mind. Before I met Sookie, God rest her soul, I'd fallen into a deep hole. I'd become a secret hoarder. First my possessions took over one room, then another. All these things were crowding me out of my own best life."

The women in front of me began to nod in agreement. Elaine was reaching them on a level Sookie never had, a direct emotional level.

"My mind became cluttered too, with impulsive thoughts," Elaine continued. "Acquiring things made me feel better, but it became a beast that had to be fed. Sookie encouraged me to seek help; she taught me techniques to help me join the world again. Now, each week, I invite friends over—and I don't have to scramble to clean or stuff anything into the closet." She stopped and smiled at the crowd. "Our lives are complicated enough. Being organized can become a bright spot in your day and give you the gift of peace of mind."

Next to me Mari had a broad smile on her face. You could feel a change of energy in the room.

"So let's make that pile of laundry your bitch!" Elaine shouted to the crowd.

Everyone around us jumped up and cheered.

Despite her mousy exterior, Elaine had the makings of a star.

After the lecture ended, Henry insisted that the four of us leave immediately while there were plenty of people still around. First, he escorted Mari and Barbara, and then he walked me to my truck.

"I'm following you home, and don't argue with me," he said.

Something about those two thugs, as he called them, had spooked him. And Henry didn't spook easily.

As we stood in front of my truck, I noticed another odd thing. Irene Heally, a client of mine, stood by what I presumed was her car. She didn't get in but kept glancing around the parking lot. As I stared, something moved inside her car. Someone appeared to be wedged up against the dashboard down out of sight. Before I could warn her, a hand snaked up to grasp the seat back, followed by a familiar head of hair. Meanwhile the puzzled expression remained on the mother's face until she opened the car door.

Her son, Lucky, the kid with the multicolored hair tips, had been cowering from view in the community center parking lot, the same Lucky who wanted to volunteer at our animal hospital. Also the same person who was so interested in how Mr. Pitt was doing.

I started placing the random things I knew about him together. He'd gone down to New Jersey to see friends. His mother said her son's car was in the shop from an accident. The boy had to hitch rides from his mom. Maybe he saw someone go into the community center lecture series, someone he never wanted to see again.

Could those two thugs be looking for him?

Chapter Twenty-One

THAT MORNING MARI AND I BARELY HAD TIME TO say hello before our day started with a bang, or rather a slice. A Samoyed dog was brought in with a severely lacerated pad, blood spurting from an injured artery. Snowbell had slipped her leash and taken off, romping and rolling in the field next to their house. When the owner caught up with her pet, she saw bloody footprints. They'd tried to put a bandage on it at home, but Snowbell quickly disposed of it. The couple burst into the waiting room in a rush of white fur speckled with blood. Gory paw prints painted our tile floor, while the husband appeared to be sick to his stomach.

With her reception area looking like the set of a slasher movie, Cindy took charge. First she paged us. Next she pulled some vet wrap out of her desk drawer. Thus armed, when Mari and I arrived, she commanded the greenish-faced client to sit down and tossed the wrap to me.

Vet wrap is an adhesive bandage that adheres to itself and is a dream product. Within minutes, we had a temporary pressure bandage on, enough to slow the bleeding until we could assess the damage.

After working in an animal hospital for twenty years,

Cindy had an iron stomach, nerves of steel, and could charm a frightened cat from a tree. We left her in charge of cleanup and carried a wiggly Snowbell into the treatment area.

Bloody incidents are common in veterinary medicine. You can tell a human to hold still and put pressure on a bleeding wound. Most of the time they comply. Try telling that to a dog with a lacerated tail or ear, who insists on wagging or shaking the injured part. Many a veterinary hospital employee has had to scrub blood off the walls, woodwork, and sometimes the ceiling.

Snowbell had been to see us only a month ago. Because she was a healthy, spayed three-year-old with fluffy white fur, we were confident the stitches in her pad would heal quickly—as long as she had limited exercise and cage rest for the next ten days.

"Are we having some kind of special on cut pads?" Mari joked.

With Snowbell snoozing peacefully under light anesthesia, and a hemostat securely stopping any blood flow, I proceeded to clean the wound and begin suturing. "Neat trick using the fluorescent pink nylon," Mari said, jotting down the number of stitches in the surgical record. "Who taught you that?"

"One of the first patients I ever sutured." I remembered it vividly even now. "I was just out of vet school and needed to stitch up a pad wound on a black toy poodle. Not thinking, I reached for the black suture material."

Mari laughed. "So when it came time to remove them you had to play find-the-suture?"

"Yep. In front of the owner, who visibly winced each time I tugged on them. Finally, one of the surgeons at the practice took pity on me. He slipped on some magnifying glasses and quickly removed them all."

We carried Snowbell from surgery over to the treatment table. Mari clipped her nails; then we wrapped the wound. After covering her bandage in a towel and waterproof wrap, we rinsed the remaining blood off her white fur.

"Anyway," I continued the story as I cleaned her muzzle, "that's when the surgeon gave me two pieces of advice. Always count your sutures and mark them in the chart, and buy fluorescent pink suture material. It's hard to miss, so long as none of your patients are pink."

Our Samoyed began waking up, so we did the rest of the drying in her recovery cage and gave her an injection of a long-acting antibiotic. As the pièce de résistance, we slipped the dreaded cone over her head and anchored it to her collar. However, it was a kinder, softer variation of the rigid plastic ones so infamous among pet owners. Many a cone-headed patient with limited visibility has goosed its owner or knocked things off coffee tables. Luckily, we now have a variety of types to choose from.

"Let's make sure we send her home with the bandage care handout. Also put her on my callback list for tonight. I want to make sure she doesn't yank out those sutures." Every working veterinarian has dealt with at least one surgical patient who ripped out every stitch within the first twenty-four hours. Teeth make a surprisingly easy job of it.

Mari said, "When I had stitches a couple of years ago, nobody called me to see how I was doing."

"Tell me about it," I answered. "I bet they didn't clip your nails, either."

Snowbell was post-op and sitting up when I went out and spoke to the owners. The reception area smelled like grapefruit or lemons and gleamed, immaculately clean. Cindy, however, quickly noticed my white coat was not and skillfully handed me a new one in mid-sentence. The clients barely noticed as tears welled up in the wife's eyes, and they both thanked all of us profusely. Sometimes it takes an emergency to remind all involved how quickly the gift of life can be taken away.

Of course, all that gore didn't put us off our lunch. While Cindy arranged for Snowbell's release later in the day, Mari had half a pizza warming in the microwave.

For lunch I heated up some soup and enjoyed one of those Christmas pears a thoughtful client dropped off. Cindy picked at yet another salad and peeled a banana.

We had brought our chairs out and formed a semicircle in front of Snowbell, now awake and plotting her escape. No one wanted a repeat of this morning. With all of us keeping an eye on her, it limited her chance of success.

"Maybe we should introduce her to Keanu," Mari joked. "They could compare stitches."

Once settled in we began to chat. I noticed both my friends made a concerted effort at first not to ask me any personal questions. That didn't last long.

"So what was that all about last night, with you and Henry James?" Mari paused for a moment before chomping on a slice of stuffed pizza.

Cindy's head rose from contemplating her lettuce. "What? You and Henry?" Her voice took on a disapproving tone.

"Easy now, mother hen," Mari answered, the remainder of the slice poised in the air. "We were all at the organizing meeting learning about dirty clothes."

"Two words," our receptionist said. "Wash them."

I laughed. Mari and Cindy could bicker over any topic under the sun.

"Henry got all protective because he saw two guys dressed in black in the back of the auditorium. Tough guys, according to him," I said, "which is ironic because Henry looks pretty tough himself."

Cindy frowned at something, maybe our crazy story.

"Mari didn't see them," I continued. "They looked like gangsters, or actors playing gangsters. Maybe they went to the wrong meeting?" As I explained my take on the strange sighting, even I thought it sounded pretty odd.

"Two guys, you said?" Cindy asked.

"Yep. Wearing long dark coats and sunglasses. Inside the building at night!"

The hard snap of the lid of her plastic container startled Snowbell. All eyes turned to Cindy, who shifted in her seat like a child who has a secret.

Mari squinted her eyes. "You know something about this, don't you?"

"Maybe." She pursed her lips as if making a decision. "All right. I may have heard about some weekenders who have bodyguards. They bought that huge estate on the mountain that belonged to the Vanderbilt family. Near the Tibetan Buddhist monastery."

"What were bodyguards doing at a lecture on organizing your laundry?" Mari sounded astonished. I knew if she had millions of dollars, she'd never do a load of laundry again for the rest of her life.

I felt the same way—but to infinity and back.

Snowbell gave a grunt and lay back down in her cage. Damned if she knew either.

"They're not just for him, but also for his wife. Whenever she goes out, she's got these two, ah, gentlemen with her. Daffy told me this is his second wife. She starred in some indie movie when she was seventeen. French. Gorgeous girl. Former model."

"Is there anything that happens around here that Daffy doesn't know?" Mari shoved her final bite of pizza into her mouth.

I poured another cup of coffee and tried to recall the members of the audience without much success. I'd spent the entire night talking to Henry and the rest of our group and observing Elaine on stage.

Finished eating, Mari asked, "Do these mystery people have a name?"

"Gambino. Mr. and Mrs. Arthur Gambino."

"That's a famous name," I said. "Are they related to the…"

"No idea."

Cindy had abruptly cut off my question, which more or less confirmed the answer. Most people recognized that name. In the 1960s and '70s, Carlo Gambino was rumored to be the organized crime boss of New York City.

Cindy finished her lunch first and scurried abruptly back to her desk in reception. Mari was sure she'd escaped because she didn't want to get in trouble with her brother-in-law, Police Chief Garcia. She juggled a delicate balance between what her sister told her in gossipy confidence, and what she felt comfortable sharing with us. As her friends, we were under no such constraints.

"This requires some well-placed phone calls." Mari began cleaning up. Soon the treatment room smelled like pizza and disinfectant.

I stood up and stretched. "Don't forget to keep me in the loop."

"It still doesn't explain why that kid Lucky was hiding in his mom's car," she said. "That's plain odd."

"He might have something to do with Mr. Pitt showing up here," I theorized. "Maybe he stole the dog away from the dogfight promoters."

My assistant's eyes widened. "They're prosecuting people for running those things. Putting them in prison. Do you think those guys…?"

"Might be looking for him?" I finished her thought. "If they're looking for Lucky, that means they're also looking for Mr. Pitt. The kid would be a witness, and that sweet pit bull he took would be evidence."

As soon as I had a chance, I took Cindy aside. "Any idea when that kid is coming in for an interview? Did he schedule a time he wanted to volunteer?"

My barrage of questions made her suspicious, of course.

"You mean Lucky Heally? Why do you ask?"

Cindy had an inquisitive nature. She liked to gather as many facts as she could about the world and its occupants. My problem? I didn't want to cause a ruckus where there wasn't a reason.

"If he does a good job, we might want to start training him as another veterinary assistant. You know how busy it is in the summertime. Tony is going to college full-time now, so he won't be available for kennel work."

As at most veterinary hospitals in New York, our appointments increase in summer, when people aren't fighting inclement weather. Summer is when we often take on additional staff. Of course, that's not the only reason I wanted to talk to Lucky, but I kept that to myself.

"You've got a good point," she said. "Winter won't last forever."

Winter won't last forever.

Cindy's words described my current dilemma. Parts of my life felt frozen in an endless winter. To move forward, I had to melt the ice.

After work I slipped into my old routine. The dogs and I got comfy on the sofa. My baggy sweats, soft as velvet, felt cozy and familiar. While sipping my wine, I picked up my cell and…almost called Luke. That's a habit I'll need to get over, I thought. So instead, I called my Gramps.

Often when I phoned Gramps, there was lots of background noise when he answered. An active senior and widower, he kept a busy schedule in his independent living home. From the many poker parties to his several lady friends, Gramps didn't let his COPD from his fireman days stop him. This time, however, when I called I had his complete attention.

Try as I may, I can't keep a secret from Gramps. As soon as I spoke to him and he heard the tone in my voice, he suspected something might be wrong.

"I'm guessing this has something to do with Luke," he said. "You haven't mentioned him at all recently."

With a big sigh I confided, "We broke up. For good."

"You can't force someone to love you, Katie," he said. "You deserve so much better. We all deserve better than that."

"I know."

His voice gentle, he told me about a happily married couple who'd each gone through two divorces before they found each other. "Of course I'm not suggesting that for you," he said with a chuckle. "But I think the number of available men you meet a day is pretty small. Perhaps you should widen your field."

Was Gramps suggesting a dating service? That shocked me.

"Gramps, I don't have time for any of that. I'm working too hard." Didn't he realize I was the only vet at Oak Falls Animal Hospital? Between the house calls and hospital appointments and surgeries, I barely had any personal time.

Laughter met my question. "That's precisely what I'm getting at. You've devoted yourself to your work. Have you given any thought to what you will do when Doc Anderson gets back?"

That stopped me. Periodically I remembered I only had a one-year employment contract with Oak Falls Animal Hospital. When Doc Anderson returned from his round-the-world cruise, he would reclaim his business, and that would be that.

"Well, I guess I should think about it," I admitted. "If I make a decision, you'll be the first to know."

"Anything else happening up there in the Hudson Valley?"

Gramps usually kept an eye on me through my Facebook page, which I rarely posted on, and Cindy's page. She and Gramps were avid Facebook friends. Our busy receptionist posted all the hospital news on several social media sites. Her own page was crammed with photos and messages. I still was reluctant to share too many personal things on the Internet.

"Did the chief arrest anyone for Sookie's murder?" he asked.

"Uhh…"

"Have you spoken to your father since Christmas?"

That, I could answer. "We've emailed a couple of times. It's a start."

"Good. Listen, Katie. You may never have a close relationship with him, but after I'm gone, he and his children—your half brother and sister—will be the only family you have left."

Great, I thought after we hung up.

Something else not to look forward to.

Chapter Twenty-Two

I'D BEEN AVOIDING THE OAK FALLS DINER, OWNED and run by Luke's family, but a sudden desire for something sweet overcame my reluctance. My talk with Gramps only accelerated the need. At first I intended to just order takeout but decided to face the possibility of meeting one of his cousins head on.

When I arrived at eight, the parking lot was half full. I sat in a booth at the far end of the dining room. The waitress who took my order was a stranger—so far, so good. Taking a quick glance around, I saw that no one seemed familiar. With that last hurtle cleared, I started to relax. Blessed anonymity.

Then it happened.

The swinging doors to the kitchen opened. Out came Rainbow, Luke's kissing cousin from New Year's, her arms wrapped around a guy with streaky blond-ish hair. After an X-rated kiss, he headed back inside. Rainbow strode out, only to yell, "Hi, Kate."

Everyone in the diner turned to look at us.

She walked over with that strange tiptoed, extremely high-heeled boots stride and plopped herself opposite me. "How's it going?" she asked. A big wad of gum miraculously appeared in her mouth. Her orange-blond hair almost glowed in the dark.

"Great," I told her. "Yourself?"

"Oh, it could be better. I took this semester off to travel," she explained. "But that's not going to happen. No money. Can't hang around here anymore. I've got a three-year plan in place."

That surprised me. "Rainbow, how old are you?"

"I'm eighteen. I'll be nineteen in November." Then she added proudly, "I'm a Scorpio."

The server briefly interrupted our chat by bringing my decaf coffee and slice of chocolate walnut pie— with a scoop of ice cream on the side. She placed a fork and spoon in front of each of us.

Rainbow leaned back against the red plastic booth and gave me a side eye. "Drowning your sorrows?" she asked.

"As a matter of fact, yes."

"Well, good for you. Get it out of your system and then jump in again. 'Onward and upward' is my motto. 'Get more than you give.'" Rainbow lifted her fork and snuck a chunk of pie.

The couple behind us got up and started to leave. My eye followed them out the door. There were plenty of empty booths now. Most of the customers left meditating over their food were singles.

Since Rainbow appeared in no hurry to leave, I asked her what her major was. I expected theater or communications, not mathematics.

"Yep. Mathematics. Statistics. Algorithms. I've been coding since middle school." She delicately dipped her spoon in my melting ice cream. "I see numbers in everything. Just born this way. A shrink told my mom it's like Asperger's syndrome."

"That's fascinating," I told her truthfully. "Do you plan on teaching math?"

My suggestion elicited a snort-laugh. "Are you crazy? I'm going to create an app and sell it. Start a statistical analysis company and then sell that too. Independently wealthy is what I'm aiming for, like Musk. I wish I'd been born a dude." Her bravura turned serious. "My mom worked dead-end jobs most of her life and wasted herself on dumb-ass guys. Did you know she's not even sure who my father is?"

"I'm so sorry…"

"Don't be sorry for me," Rainbow lashed out. "Feel sorry for my mom, and her dead high school friend."

"What do…?"

Again she interrupted me. "Her friend, Posey. Nosey Posey. The one who took a high dive from the rafters on New Year's Eve."

Before I could question her, Rainbow abruptly stood up and disappeared into the restaurant kitchen. I waited for a while but suspected she'd exited out the back door. I had a feeling this girl confronted problems by running away—not a sustainable choice. As for her possible Asperger's diagnosis—I wasn't a medical doctor, but I did observe her abrupt language, clumsy walk, and fascination with computers and numbers. And, so far, I'd seen her physically involved with at least three guys since New Year's, which was worrisome.

Gramps always told me you never knew what strangers were dealing with on a personal level, so give them the benefit of the doubt. Rainbow hid her problems from view behind those false eyelashes. As usual, Gramps was right.

Someone else hid her problems from view, I thought. Maybe there also was more to Posey's story than anyone thought.

A progression of nightmares interrupted my sleep that night. Every hour I woke up with the vision of Posey falling from the sky and Rainbow laughing. Over and over that brief memory played in my brain...until I realized something at around four a.m.

I'd seen no voluntary movement as Posey dropped to her death. No last-minute scream. No arm or leg movements. Maybe she'd been unconscious when she fell or was pushed.

Or perhaps Posey was already dead.

In the morning, I felt my lack of sleep. I walked and fed the dogs, showered, and dressed in a sort of stupor. Figuring coffee would jolt me awake, I headed for the employee lounge and the luscious smell of vanilla almond mocha.

"Hey, Kate." Mari greeted me while pouring a cup of coffee. "Can I get you one?"

"Definitely." I sank into one of our lounge chairs, desperately wanting to go back to sleep. The worn corduroy upholstery welcomed me into its folds.

When I looked up and gratefully took my coffee from Mari's hand, she commented, "Rough night?"

The coffee tasted bitter and hot and perfect. I took another sip before answering her question. "I got to sleep fine. But then every hour I woke up from this nightmare I couldn't shake."

"I'm sorry. Maybe you can sneak in a nap at lunch."

Mari often took catnaps, sometimes as short as ten or fifteen minutes. Napping simply made me more tired.

Another sip and the caffeine began to work. "Just keep it coming. Did you happen to look at the appointment schedule for today?"

She glanced down at her phone. "It's not too bad. I think we're done by five-ish."

The clicking of heels along the hallway signaled Cindy was about to join us.

With a quick gulp I finished my first cup and made a beeline to our coffee station.

"Good morning, everyone," Cindy said in her cheerleader voice. "How are you this morning?"

"Tired," I said. An individually wrapped biscotti on the countertop by the side of the coffee machine caught my eye. "Can I have this?"

"Sure," Mari said. "A client dropped a bunch of them off for us yesterday."

Cindy watched me go back to my chair. Her sympathetic look assumed, I think, my exhaustion had something to do with my love life.

"Well, I started my day cleaning up puppy poo," Mari volunteered. "Can't wait until I can house-train those little beasties."

"Sounds like everyone has been busy." Our receptionist smiled at us like a kindergarten teacher does at her pupils. "Kate, Lucky Heally dropped in to schedule an interview. Do you have time now?"

At the moment I didn't even want to talk to myself.

"Please? That would be one less item on my to-do list," her voice pleaded.

With effort I pulled myself out of the chair, hoisted my coffee, and replied, "Okay. Give me five minutes to prepare and then escort him to my office."

"Will do. Mari, let's go over the house calls for today so you can inventory the truck." Cindy didn't wait for an answer but instead hurried out the door and down the hallway.

"And so it begins." Mari tossed me a smile and shook her curls into place.

Precisely five minutes later, Cindy knocked on my office door. I'd tried to jot down a list of questions but hadn't gotten past writing the number one. Trailing behind was the boy I'd seen hiding in his mother's car.

"Dr. Kate, this is Lucky Heally. He just graduated from high school and is entering community college this semester. Can you speak to him about volunteering and the vet assistant position?"

"Nice to officially meet you, Lucky." Today the tips of his hair were a subdued shade of purple.

"Dr. Kate. Pleasure to meet you."

Lucky's voice wobbled a bit on the word "pleasure." He'd suddenly become very formal, perhaps courtesy of his mother's coaching.

"Why don't you sit down and tell me about yourself?" I gestured to the chair in front of my desk.

Once sitting, Lucky stared at me, physically growing more nervous by the second. A tiny twitch contracted over his eyebrow. The poor kid seemed intimidated. I took pity on him and started the conversation myself.

"So, have you always lived here in Oak Falls?"

"Yes. I mean no. Uh, we moved here from New Jersey when I was a kid. When I was ten."

After that jumbled response, he seemed to relax a bit.

"You graduated from…"

"High school."

Boy, this was like trying to pull teeth from a shark. I jumped to the main topic. "Why do you want to work at an animal hospital, Lucky?"

His blue eyes rose up to look into mine. "I love animals. All animals. And to help them when they are sick, or hurt, seems like the best job in the world." His shy smile betrayed a caring heart.

"I'll tell you a secret," I replied. "It *is* the best job in the world."

Before I could ask him anything else, he said, "How is that gray pit bull doing? Will he be okay?"

Taking a gamble I asked, "Did you leave him out by the dumpster? Tell me the truth. I won't get mad at you."

His face flushed red. "Yes."

I leaned closer. "Can you tell me what happened?"

His story was simple and direct. He'd gone down to New Jersey to meet up with friends to celebrate their graduations. They'd gone out as a group, but somehow Lucky got separated, instead ending up with some friends of friends. These guys were older, edgier, and suggested they go gambling. With one too many beers in him, poor Lucky followed the crowd. Someone pushed him into the passenger seat of his own car and drove it to a warehouse. Two of the boys played craps and the other dragged him into a back room to watch an illegal dogfight. Lucky sobered up quickly when he saw the poor gray pit bull that wouldn't fight back.

After the fight was over, Lucky snuck into the back to find the bait dog lying still in the ring. He wrapped him up in his jacket, slipped out an unlocked back door, and loaded him into his car. One of the promoters noticed and started yelling. Panicked and scared, Lucky backed his car into a Porsche convertible, before taking off. The poor kid headed for home, driving up the interstate uncertain what to do.

"My mom mentioned how kind you were with our

dog, Dr. Kate, so I figured you'd take care of him. That he'd be safe with you. I stayed that morning until I saw you open your door."

Those shining bright eyes stared at me with total faith.

"You're right. He's safe with us," I told him. "Lucky, you did a very brave thing." I left out the part about backing into an expensive sports car.

His upper lip quivered. "Yeah, well I might be in trouble. I'm not sure, but I think one of the guys from the dogfight was at Mom's meeting the other night. I'm afraid they're looking for me."

Lucky left with my assurance that I wouldn't tell his mom, and that I'd keep Mr. Pitt safe from harm. I wasn't sure how practical the first promise was, but I was rock sure about the second.

After much thought, I texted Mari.

"What's up?" she said after opening the office door and poking her head through.

"We've got a situation," I began.

"Don't we always?" she replied with a laugh. "Something to do with unlucky Lucky, I suppose?"

Nodding my head, I leaned back in my office chair and gave her the condensed version of how we ended up with Mr. Pitt.

"Poor kid," she said. "Do you think those guys have anything to do with dogfights? I thought Cindy said they were bodyguards?"

I'd wondered about that, too, and come up with a tentative conclusion. "I think the best thing is for you to take Mr. Pitt to your place." Mari owned two gigantic Rottweilers, Lucy and Desi, both schooled in Schutzhund, which includes protection and attack commands. In addition, her home was right around the corner from Chief Garcia and Cindy—not somewhat isolated like the animal hospital.

"No can do," Mari reminded me. "I've got Lucy and the puppies. There is no way she's allowing a strange male dog into the house. But I'll be happy to loan you Desi if you like."

Desi weighed almost a hundred pounds, most of which was muscle. Mari had trained and showed him very successfully, and now the five-year-old routinely accompanied her on hikes and camping trips. The alarm system and his presence in the hospital would give me an additional feeling of security when I was by myself.

"Deal," I told her. "I need you to tell me something."

"Sure."

"What are his on guard and attack commands?"

I wanted to be prepared for the worst.

Chapter Twenty-Three

MORNING LIGHT STREAMED IN THROUGH THE GAP IN my living room curtains. Today, I had the luxury of sleeping in. Our house-call appointments started at ten, so Mari and I didn't have to rush around to get on the road. I texted Cindy I'd been in soon.

I checked my emails on the office computer, and then Mari and I were on the road again.

Throughout the previous evening, I'd heard the rumble of heavy machinery on the main highway. When I pulled the truck out of our parking lot, I found the roads clear and newly graveled, with dirty snow shoulders piled up higher on both sides. Since the weather hadn't warmed up much, the nearby fields stayed hidden under snow-covered blankets that stretched up to the National Forest tree line. We were on our way to see another of my favorite clients. Although my patient today was one of her rescue dogs, the animal I hoped to see was her adopted mustang, Lobo.

"Our turn is coming up soon," Mari reminded me.

Her voice pulled me out of myself. My thoughts had drifted off to murder, and vengeance, as the tall pine trees slid darkly past.

A sign pointing to Maple Grove Farm came quickly

into view, so I slowed down and put my turn signal on. I remembered her steep driveway and shifted into low gear. Sure enough, the tires dug into the semi-frozen soil. As the truck climbed a rise, we spun gravel as we approached the crest.

Suddenly an SUV crested the hill and headed right toward us. I immediately honked my horn, then moved over onto the right shoulder. The driver casually waved as they sped by.

"That was a bit close," I commented. The farm's driveway width was comfortable for one and a half vehicles, tight for two.

Mari turned in her seat to watch the SUV disappear down the hill. "I think that was Elaine. A sign on the side of the car said OVERMANN ORGANIZING. Wonder what she's doing here?"

I drove back onto the road and continued up the hill. The driveway soon opened onto a large clearing with flat grazing fields on both sides. One of the older properties just outside of Oak Falls, the picture-perfect farmhouse featured a wraparound porch. Smoke rose from the chimney and dispersed over the nearby corral and faded red barn.

Originally from New York City, Ashley and her partner bought and ran the farm as an animal refuge, taking in a slew of rescue dogs, cats, horses, and assorted other creatures. We were here today to recheck a shaggy dog that had won my unofficial Oak Falls Animal Hospital award for the stinkiest ears in the Hudson Valley.

A quick glance at the front pastures showed burros, goats, and one horse casually munching hay from a rack, flicking it every which way, some landing on the back of a nearby goat. Large rubber mats covered the ground on both sides of the hay manger, to cut down on mixing the feed with gravel and dirt. There was no sign of the mustang, Lobo.

When we pulled up in front of the farmhouse, Ashley opened the door and a flood of barking dogs poured out to greet us. I immediately spotted Tommy, our patient. His ears hung normally, and I didn't notice a smell. *So far so good*, I thought.

A wild chorus of yips and yaps escorted us inside. The farmhouse interior revealed a recent remodel that appeared tasteful and expensive.

"So glad you could stop by," Ashley said as she lowered herself onto a kitchen chair. "This boot is so cumbersome. I only go out now if I have to." She leaned down and adjusted the strap on her orthopedic device.

"How's the ankle doing?" I asked, taking a seat at the table. Tommy came over for a pet and head rub.

"Well," she sighed, "I've got another two weeks to go before my next recheck. Then let's hope it comes off permanently."

While she was talking, I had been sniffing my patient's ears. Mari noticed and dug out the veterinary otoscope. With a little help from my assistant, I examined each ear, careful to change out the plastic cover between ears.

"I'm impressed," I told Ashley as I palpated the dog's lymph nodes and listened to his heart. "Mixed ear infections like his, with yeast and bacteria, are difficult to clear up. Getting the ear canal pH back into normal ranges in floppy ears like he has takes dedication."

A big smile lit her face. "I've been stuck inside since I last saw you, so Tommy benefited from that regimen you prescribed."

On hearing his name, my patient loped over to his owner.

Handing the equipment to Mari, I removed my exam gloves and dumped them into a bag for disposal. A quick soapy hand wash, and we were done.

The aroma of freshly brewed coffee wafting from the coffee maker smelled delicious. "Would you like some?" Ashley asked.

"Don't get up," Mari said. "We can help ourselves."

"I just made it a few minutes ago for Elaine, but she had to run."

With cup in hand, Mari sat down. "I thought that was her on the driveway. Are you using her services?"

A glance at the kitchen showed a well-ordered space, but I knew, from my many house calls, that different parts of houses present different challenges for people. The kitchen might be clean, but the garage could be a disaster.

"Originally I hired Sookie, to redesign my laundry area. We had a meeting, and I put down a deposit. After she passed away, I contacted Elaine. She's been very helpful, full of fresh ideas. I'm making accommodations in case of another injury since I am super clumsy."

"That's prudent." With my coffee still too hot to drink I said, "Has Elaine taken over Sookie's business, now?"

"We discussed that. She's been having a difficult time with Glenn Overmann. Seems he wants to sell the remaining business and whatever assets are left. Elaine is focusing on completing Sookie's projects, so their customers aren't left with half-finished jobs, but Glenn is trying to prevent that. Elaine offered to split any profits, but he just keeps screaming and threatening her. The poor girl tries to hide it, but she's frazzled, trying to please everyone. I think she could use a friend."

Mari and I looked at each other. "She did a great job the other night at the community center," I told our client.

"The center appreciated her finishing off the series." Ashley hesitated. "Maybe you can tell me why Glenn isn't under arrest?"

Her question was one I'd asked myself. "The police need some solid evidence. Forensics didn't uncover much, I heard."

"Weren't there cameras in the parking lot?" Her voice sounded exasperated.

This time Mari answered. "The only one working was right at the front entrance, and those images came out blurry."

"Did you know he threatened to kill her before—and

kill her cat? I know because Glenn called Sookie while we were working. I heard him. She put him on speakerphone."

That didn't surprise me, given his previous violent outbursts. "Has anyone reported this to the police?"

Ashley became visibly upset. "As soon as they found Sookie's body I called the department. Someone took down my statement, and I haven't heard anything since." Worried by the tone of their owner's voice, the dogs rallied around her.

Mari stretched out her hand and patted Ashley's arm. "You've done all you could. I'm sure law enforcement is doing their part."

Ashley's eyes blazed. "Well, they better hurry up. Elaine told me today she's afraid he's going to kill her next."

An uneasy feeling overwhelmed me after we said goodbye to Ashley. Mari sat next to me in the truck, uncharacteristically subdued. The real threat of more violence both disturbed and frustrated me. What steps had the police made to stop it?

"Look." Mari pointed toward the pasture.

Lobo the mustang stood at the fence accompanied by Sweet Pea, his best horse buddy. I suspected he recognized the sight and sound of our truck. For the formerly aloof gelding to approach on his own was a huge leap of faith.

"I'll be right back," I told my assistant, checking to make sure there were some apple treats in my coat pocket.

Speaking softly, I moved toward the fence, apple treat in the palm of my hand. Sweet Pea whinnied a welcome, while Lobo shifted his feet.

I scratched their long noses as the two nibbled the treats from my fingers. Voluntarily waiting at the fence for me showed enormous progress toward trusting humans for the formerly wild mustang. Lobo was settling in.

Progress often felt like one step forward and two steps back, I thought. Maybe it was time to change that choreography.

Daylight was fading when we finished up and Cindy and Mari left the office. Frustrated and not wanting to sit alone in the apartment, I went into town to do some shopping, but mostly to get out of the house. The wind began to blow strong gusts against the truck. With each impact I felt the wheels slip a little. I decided I wasn't in the mood to fight with Mother Nature. Instead, I turned into an empty parking space near Judy's Café. An early dinner of soup and some date nut bread sounded perfect. Maybe buy something for tomorrow's lunch. I hoped the weather would ease up by the time I finished.

As soon as I stepped out of the truck the wind slammed into me. I yanked at my hood, clutching it with one hand, and lowered my head to keep the wind out of my eyes. My destination wasn't too far away. The snow swirled up against the storefronts as I reached for the café door.

Someone else reached out at the same time, pulling the door open for me.

"Thanks," I muttered, my hood half over my eyes.

"Kate?" a voice from behind me said. "Is that you?"

Once I got my bearings, I turned toward the familiar voice. "Colin?"

"Let's get in out of the wind," he said, taking my elbow. We were standing in the entryway, blocking a middle-aged couple from leaving. Only a few steps away, an empty table overlooking the street beckoned. "Are you meeting someone?" Colin asked, glancing around the room.

"Nope. Just felt like soup." The difference in temperature inside the café was astonishing. My muffler felt like it was strangling me in the heat.

"Come join me." Still holding my elbow, he guided me to the empty table, pulling out the nearest chair for me.

This was the first time I'd seen Colin in the daylight. At the New Year's Eve party the lighting had been diffuse, sometimes downright dim. It didn't matter. I stared up at the sculptural planes of his face, marveling at its beauty.

"Everything okay?" he asked as he slid his coat off and hung it over the back of the chair. He wore a slouchy blue cable knit sweater over a white T-shirt. A pale streak of yellow paint decorated the side of his hand.

"Fine. I'm glad to be out of that wind." I sat down,

conscious of my ancient sweatshirt worn over baggy jeans. I hadn't intended to meet anyone, hadn't planned stopping to eat. My blond hair was frizzled from the hood of my coat. The only beauty aid I had on me was a plain unscented lip balm.

Colin appeared oblivious to me, intent on scanning the menu.

When our server approached, we both asked about the specials.

"Let me check," he said before scurrying away without taking our drink order. Judy's employees took a casual approach to their jobs.

"So nice to see you again," Colin said. "I was going stir-crazy in my studio. Had to get out to keep my sanity."

I didn't think Colin could get more handsome until he smiled.

"I know how that feels. My apartment is attached to the hospital. It's convenient, but you feel like you're always at work. Sometimes I need to get away, too."

The server interrupted us. He read off the specials from a scrap of paper.

"I'll have the mushroom barley soup and a toasted slice of date nut bread." I'd been thinking about that combination and had my taste buds set on it.

"Sounds great," Colin said. "I'll have the same, with a pot of Earl Grey tea. Two cups, please."

A trio of pedestrians walking in front of the café picture window clutched at their knit hats to prevent them from blowing away. A discarded receipt soared above the parked cars, twisting and floating in the wind.

Colin stared out at the street. "This sort of weather is a huge distraction to me when I work. There are constant random bursts of noise as things get knocked over. Glass panes rattle. Snow slides off the roof."

"Unexpected noise," I said. "It startles you when you're trying to concentrate."

"Exactly." We smiled at each other. The server set down our orders.

"Do you want me to pour the tea?" Colin asked.

"Sure."

Colin poured a little in my cup, the amber liquid fragrant with bergamot oil. "Has it brewed long enough?"

"Perfect," I answered.

We sat companionably, periodically commenting on the date bread or the soup. Judy's casual ambience, the old oak tables full of dings, the local consignment art pieces on the walls all made for a relaxing experience. Plus the homemade food was delicious.

"Do you keep to a schedule when you're working?" I asked him.

"That depends on the type of project I'm doing. If it involves a live model, the answer is yes. But usually, for my large pieces I work all kinds of hours." Colin took a bite of date bread and washed it down with tea. "That's how I ended up here. I'd just finished a section, realized I was starving, and decided to take a break. What about you?"

"My hours are pretty rigid. Our appointment schedule is handled by our receptionist. It's Monday through Friday, eight thirty to five thirty then every other Saturday until noon. After work, I stay and check my hospital email and do callbacks." Almost finished with my soup, I slowed down, savoring the flavorful tea. "Because of the weather we got off early today, which is a rare occurrence."

The couple behind me stood up to leave. I squished closer to the table to give them room.

"Sounds like you don't get much time away," Colin said. "Winter makes that feeling of isolation worse. It's different if you could get out and ski or hike. But uncertain weather such as this forces you to stay inside and stare at the walls."

An older man walked past the window clutching his coat, buffeted by the wind.

"I've got a friend, Jeremy," I told him, "who is on a yacht in the Caribbean right now, soaking up the sunshine."

Colin smiled a lazy smile. "Lucky man."

"He's rich. Family money. The only person I know with a trust fund. I can't imagine what it must be like to be able to fly on a whim to Paris or London. Or spend a week in Peru."

"That lucky bastard probably doesn't appreciate it, wallowing in money his whole life." He leaned back into his chair and stared out the window. "Freedom from worry, freedom from having to work for a living.

Being able to produce the art you want to, not the art that will sell. Most of us don't get that kind of break from the Fates."

"Tell me about it. A big chunk of my paycheck goes to student debt."

"Same here." Colin took my hand and held it to his chest. "We shouldn't complain, though. We're young, healthy, and love our jobs. How many people can say that?" He gave the tips of my fingers a quick kiss, released them, and added, "If only the sun would come out."

A commotion at the front door drew our attention. A man was speaking loudly to Judy, who stood at the counter drying her hands with a striped dish towel. When she turned away, he strode over to the community billboard and pinned up a notice. I got a good look at his face. Glenn Overmann appeared angry, as usual.

"Everybody," he announced in a loud voice, "check out my flyer. I'm offering a twenty-thousand-dollar reward for the recovery of my stolen assets portfolio. Details are posted at tracksookiesheist.com."

With his hair sticking up and his entire face covered with stubble, he bore no resemblance to the handsome groom in the romantic wedding pictures on Sookie's website. I wondered if anyone had taken those photos down from the Internet.

His eyes scanned the customers, briefly stopping on me before moving on. Without warning he shouted, "A piece of advice, guys. Don't tell anyone your passwords, especially your soul-sucking spouse!"

Hearing the noise, Judy stuck her head out through the swinging doors, a wooden spoon clutched in her hand, but by then Glenn had reached the exit.

"I'm going, I'm going." A quick blast of frigid air and he was gone.

After some murmurs and comments, most people went back to their meals. Pot of coffee in hand, Judy walked around making sure everyone was happy. When she got to us, she said, "More hot water, Colin?"

"Sure, Judy. Thanks."

"Be right back. Enjoying your meal, Dr. Kate?"

"Very much so. The soup is great." She smiled back at me before turning away toward the wait station—but did I see a trace of a wink?

"What was all that yelling about?" Colin asked.

"That's Glenn Overmann. His wife, Sookie, was murdered not long ago." I started to explain but was interrupted.

"Dr. Kate. You should investigate that theft," Judy returned, removing the cover of the teapot and refreshing it with more boiling water. "Might as well solve Sookie's murder, too. The cops seem stalled or something."

All eyes now on me, I felt a mild blush begin. "All that is best left to the professionals," I said.

Colin's interest had been piqued because he asked Judy what she meant. Judy went on to give a summary of some of the cases I'd helped Chief Garcia solve.

"Then one time Kate was face-to-face with…"

"Enough, please," I implored Judy. "Give me a break."

She raised one eyebrow as if to question me then said, "Sure. I need to go back to work anyway. Just think about it. It sounds tempting. Twenty thousand bucks."

"Okay. Thanks." I poured another cup of tea. "That was embarrassing," I told Colin.

"Don't think anything of it." He waited for me to finish, then poured another cup of his own. "Do you know the number of people who've asked me to paint pictures of their dogs, or children, or want me to give them an estimate on painting the walls in their guest bedroom? It's better to tell them you can't take on any new projects at this time."

"I've got a problem saying no to people."

"Ah." Colin took the last morsel of his date nut bread and popped it into his mouth. "Many women have that problem. Society expects you to be helpful. To nurture."

"Exactly."

He stood up and began putting on his coat. "Well, this has been lovely, but I, unfortunately, need to get back to work. It's been a pleasure, Kate. If I don't see you before I leave town next week, have a fascinating life."

"Where are you going?" I asked.

"To Helsinki, for an exhibition. Bye, now." When he draped his muffler around his neck, it fell into professional-looking folds. He made a stop at the counter, laughed at something Judy said, and paid the bill.

I stared out the window for a while, thinking about

the twenty-thousand-dollar reward. When I passed by the counter, Judy brought her cup of coffee over, ready for a little chat.

"Handsome guy, isn't he?" she began. "But not the settling down kind. At least not yet." She slid the bill over toward me. Colin had paid only for his meal. "I've seen that guy with every available woman in town, and some unavailable very married ones."

"He's an artist," I said as if that excused or explained his lifestyle.

"We're all artists of our own lives," Judy commented.

I placed my credit card in front of her. "Yes, but I have a feeling Colin wants to produce a masterpiece."

Chapter Twenty-Four

ONCE I GOT HOME, MY MIND KEPT COMING BACK TO Glenn's reward offer. Twenty-thousand dollars would pay down some student loan principal, with money left over for a vacation. I'd never been to Helsinki.

Sitting down at my computer, I quickly found Glenn's website explaining the stock and bond and mixed investments portfolio he was looking for. At first glance it seemed hopeless. Whoever stole his computer files and passwords could simply sell off everything or transfer them to another brokerage, likely outside the U.S. Surely some forensic computer guys were hot on the trail? I learned from reading about a Russian ransom group's hack of an American company that a trail is always left, even if payment is made in elusive Bitcoin.

My doorbell rang, prompting both dogs to start barking. Buddy ran over to the door first, with Mr. Pitt hesitantly standing behind him.

"Hey, it's me," yelled a familiar voice.

Buddy immediately started wagging his tail, and even Mr. Pitt appeared less fearful. I opened the door to see Mari standing outside, her rottie, Desi, looking out the window of her massive SUV.

"I've been texting you, but you haven't answered," she said. "Come on, Buddy, Mr. Pitt. Let's go potty."

Right outside my door is a fenced-in dog walk area. Mari shooed them through the gate and then let Desi out. Her dog immediately walked over and touched noses with Buddy, one of his favorite dog friends. Mr. Pitt hung back, the hackles on his shoulders and back standing up.

"It's okay, everyone. Desi, sit." Digging into her pocket, Mari gave a dog treat to Buddy, one to Desi, and then called Mr. Pitt over. Reluctantly, he moved closer, nibbling the treat from her hand. "Good boy," Mari told Desi. "Good boys," she said to the other dogs.

I noticed a tiny wag of the pit bull's tail. "Didn't you tell me this introduction signals everything is good?"

"That's right." She let Desi into the fenced area. "Go play, guys."

First two dogs, then three began to romp, encouraged by some interesting dog toys Mari brought. "They seem to get along fine," I said. "Oh, let me look at my phone." I dug it out of my pants pocket and sure enough, I'd run out of charge and not noticed. "Maybe I need a new battery." The wind stirred up the fresh snow, dispersing it into a fine mist.

"I'm freezing. You bring them in, and I'll get Desi's stuff from my truck." Mari raised the tailgate with her key fob and took off.

"Inside," I called out. I lifted the lock on the gate and quickly opened my front door. Desi glanced at Mari but followed his buddies inside.

Half an hour later, Mari and I sat in my living room surrounded by snoring dogs. All three showed brachycephalic characteristics, meaning shortened muzzles—the better to snore and snort and drool.

"That's quite a racket," Mari commented to me. She lay stretched out on my sofa, feet perched on the coffee table.

"I'm used to it now." I'd plugged my phone into its charger when we came inside. After a few minutes I popped up to check it was taking the charge. "Amazing how much time we devote to our phones."

"True." She reached over for her mug of tea. "I've saved about a thousand pictures of the dogs. I'm convinced that's what's taking up all my cellular memory."

"Hey," I said, settling back to my place on the couch. "Did I tell you I ran into that guy from the New Year's party? Colin?"

She immediately sat up. "Tell me everything."

"Not much to tell. We ran into each other at Judy's, and had dinner together."

"Nice."

"Well don't make too much of it, because he's leaving for Finland soon."

"Finland?"

"He's showing at a gallery in Helsinki. And I know what your next question is." Our eyes locked as I tried to figure out what she was thinking.

"So, I'm thinking…"

"Did he hit on me? Right?" My friend dissolved in giggles.

One of the dogs moaned and rolled over.

"The answer is no, although Judy implied he'd dated half the town. Maybe I should consider it an insult?"

"He already tried at the dance, and you shot him down."

"Right."

"Did he mention Posey's suicide?" With a sigh she leaned back into the sofa.

"Not over supper. But something odd happened while we were eating. Glenn Overmann came in and made a big deal about offering a twenty-thousand-dollar reward for helping find the money that Sookie embezzled. We should ask Cindy if the police have any leads."

Mari stood up and stretched. "I did ask her. Glenn is still their primary suspect. They're busy trying to find some proof. As far as his money—Cindy said the guys who trace missing financial portfolios are swamped with cases. They've got malware and international hackers holding companies for ransom to deal with. No one is treating Glenn's case as a priority."

"So he's offering his own reward. That makes sense." I slid the big bag of dog food Mari gave me across the floor and into the pantry.

"Here's his food bowl and water bowl." The water bowl resembled a stainless steel mixing bowl. "Desi drinks a lot of water."

I saw the big dog lift his massive head up on hearing his name.

"Kate, you should try to find Glenn's portfolio. I know you could use the reward money."

My enthusiasm didn't match Mari's. "Nope. This is way above my level of computer skills. You're talking moving in and out of secure databases. I'm not even sure it's legal."

"If he hires you, he's got to supply his accounts and passwords to you. Right? You probably won't be the only one trying, though." That look of concentration on her face was one I knew well. "Maybe you should pair up with someone? You follow the real-life paper trails, and the computer geek does the online stuff."

Thinking about someone else's problem did help push my own into the background. Maybe I could...

"Know any computer guy who might be interested?" Mari took her empty cup and put it in the kitchen sink. "There's got to be a guy around who can do it."

That phrase kept moving around in my head. Computer guy. Then I got it.

"I do know a computer geek who might be up for it," I told her. "But she's a gal."

At first Mari thought I was joking, but I reminded her that first impressions are often wrong. As for assuming every computer geek is male, well, that doesn't hold true anymore. Coding schools and education programs were changing that.

After Mari left to take care of her mommy dog and puppies, I headed to the one place I thought I'd find Rainbow. Or find people who might know where she was.

This time when I pushed open the door to the Oak Falls Diner, I didn't care who saw me.

A table with a view of the kitchen was what I wanted. A few were available, one much more private and pushed against a wall.

"Hi, Doc. What can I get you?" One of Luke's cousins who worked part-time as a server came over to take my order. "Pie?"

She knew me well. "No, I'm cutting back on the pie a bit. I'll have the fresh fruit plate and decaf coffee and the dinner special on the blackboard, to go."

"Good choice."

As she started to leave I said, "Do you know if Rainbow's around? I need to ask her a quick question."

"Oh, that one. Yeah. She's working in the back today." In one fluid motion she turned and snagged the decaf carafe and a mug from the serving station. "We're not that busy, yet. I'll see if she can come out."

For the next few minutes, I tried to plan what to say. From what I gathered, she wasn't staying in town for long. I needn't have worried. Rainbow had only one question.

"How much?"

"He's offering twenty thousand dollars," I repeated.

She rolled her eyes, a habit I was becoming familiar with. "No. How much is our split? I might end up doing all the work, you know."

"You've got a point." How would we be able to figure this out? I didn't want to have to keep track of my hours, or meetings, or phone calls.

Rainbow stared at me. She still wore those fake eyelashes. "I could probably do this solo. Why do I need you?"

Good question. I was beginning to wonder that myself. However, Rainbow answered her own question without prompting.

"It's, like, why am I working in the kitchen instead of out here?" A mischievous look betrayed how young she was despite the makeup and flashy clothes. "They would have fired me already except I'm family. I suppose I'm sort of a smart aleck. And impatient." She fidgeted with the salt and pepper. "I get fired a lot."

"I don't," I said. "I'm persistent, and capable of listening for a long time." I threw that in because Rainbow already appeared distracted. "I'll gather all sorts of information about Sookie—who she hung out with—and see if she left any clues to follow."

"That's chill," Rainbow said, staring out the window. "When do you want to start?"

The girl lined the salt and pepper up. "Tomorrow night. Your place."

Like it or not, I had a partner.

After I returned to my apartment I played with the dogs, put them through basic obedience commands, and straightened up a bit. All the while I kept wondering why the heck I thought I could help find Glenn's money. I suppose I like a challenge.

Once the boys settled down onto their dog beds, I settled in with my personal laptop and went directly to

the tracksookiesheist website. At least ten other inquiries had been posted, all of which were directed to the
information section. On that page was a bare-bones
coming-and-going timeline of Sookie's final weeks.
Serious inquiries would be answered and required the
signing of a confidentiality agreement. At that point, an
extensive file would be made available.

Not sure whether to proceed, I called Gramps.

I didn't expect him to start laughing.

"Sorry, Katie," he said as he pulled himself together.
"But wasn't our last conversation about you not having
enough free time? Now you want to jump into an
investigation?"

Hearing this from his point of view, I began to cringe.

My silence made him back off a bit, worried he'd
hurt my feelings. "You took me by surprise, Katie. Tell
me you don't have to pay to do any of the investigating?"

"No, there are no fees involved." I wasn't sure about
any expenses, but didn't want to muddy our conversation with too many facts.

He continued questioning me. "You can quit
anytime?"

"Anytime."

"So basically you're trying to win twenty thousand
dollars by solving the mystery of the vanishing money.
Along with other random strangers who are running
their own separate investigations?"

"Right." I decided not to mention solving Sookie's
murder, too.

As if he could read my mind, Gramps cautioned, "Don't go trying to solve that woman's murder, now. Leave that crime to the police."

Since he couldn't see me, I crossed my fingers and told a little fib. "That's the plan."

"If I can help, let me know," he told me. "But don't take any chances, you hear me? You are irreplaceable, Katie. Totally irreplaceable to me."

"I think it's a great idea," Cindy said as soon as she heard. "I'll tell you anything I can."

"You don't think it's crazy?" I'd called her after speaking to Gramps, probably for a little validation.

"Heck, no. The chief mentioned Glenn's reward offer yesterday to my sister. Glenn's got no money to hire private investigators. He's got legal issues to settle before he can sell the condo." Cindy paused for a breath. "It still doesn't make me feel sorry for him."

Mari's response when I called her was much more specific. "I know you're pretty good with our computer, but I'm not sure about this level of expertise." In the background a television blared.

I'd expected this from her. "There are tons of websites that help with all kinds of fraud."

"Wait a minute. Let me turn this down," she said. Immediately the background noise leveled off. "Okay, that's better. I wish I had time to help, but six puppies are a handful."

"That's all right. I'm going to try to work with someone on this—a computer hacker, and a mathematical genius to boot. If we're successful we'll split the reward." I thought Mari would be happy, but instead she sounded skeptical.

"Who is it?"

"Ahhh, it's Rainbow. You know, Luke's cousin? She came to the New Year's party."

"Rainbow?" Mari repeated. "Tight skirt, tall boots, and flirty. False eyelashes?"

I made my voice sound upbeat. "Yep. That's her."

"So, Kate, who told you that girl was a computer genius?"

"She did."

After fending off more questions, I started to do some preliminary fact-gathering. To keep track of my thoughts, I pulled out a small whiteboard from storage and propped it up on the sideboard table. Armed with multicolored dry erase markers, I started in.

Why did Sookie take her husband's assets? There were a couple of obvious answers. She wanted all the money and also some revenge on her husband. According to Daffy, Sookie made the bulk of the money during their marriage. There was a hint that Glenn was living off his wife.

Knowing Glenn the way she did, Sookie knew he'd be coming after her with everything he had. There must have been an escape plan in place. Was she running alone, or with someone? In this computerized world, how could she truly disappear?

I got up, stretched out on the sofa, and thought it through. An FBI agent had once told me disappearing is harder than you think, especially if you lug a lot of personal stuff along with you. Sookie was smart. She would have known that.

Which still didn't tell me why she was murdered.

All that thinking must have worn me out because I fell asleep, only to be awakened by soft whines.

Three pairs of doggy eyes were staring at me. A quick glance at my watch told me why. The trio thought I'd forgotten the before-bed bathroom break. Standing in front of me, Desi towered over the crew with thick shoulders and a massive head. Having Desi gave me an added level of security but also served to remind me that if someone wanted to steal Mr. Pitt, I might need it.

Chapter Twenty-Five

THE NEXT MORNING, I WATCHED AS ALL THREE DOGS once again romped around and did their business. Mr. Pitt interacted with Desi as nicely as he played with Buddy, a far smaller dog. When I called, he immediately responded. I scratched his silver head, noticing how well he was healing from his wounds, both physical and emotional. I only wished Cindy and the shelter had had more success in tracking down his owner. An alert had also gone out to veterinarians in New York, New Jersey, and Staten Island, along with notices on social media.

With the animals taken care of and busy playing with their toys, I showered, pulled on my scrubs, and "commuted" to work.

After coffee, my first half hour was always the same: checking lab reports and emailing or calling clients. When Cindy stuck her head in, I assumed she wanted to go over today's schedule. Instead, she shut the door, sat in the chair opposite my desk, and waited for me to finish my call.

"Something up?" My rapidly cooling coffee sitting next to the computer beckoned. I hated to drink it when it got cold and had that floating layer of who-knows-what on it.

"Did you start your snooping yet?" Cindy's enthusiasm for the reward money far outpaced mine.

"Only brainstorming at the moment," I told her. "This is much more complicated than I thought."

Cindy agreed then added, "My sister confided something to me last night that Bobby let slip. Since it has to do with missing money, I wanted to share it. However, it doesn't seem to have anything to do with Sookie."

"You never know. What is it?"

She leaned in closer even though we were alone in the office. "You know that new guy in town, Mr. Gambino?"

That surprised me. I took a long sip of coffee and answered, "What about him?"

"He's missing a large quantity of Bitcoin. Someone ripped him off. Bobby heard a rumor that he's got experts going through his business computers here and at his other homes, trying to find out what happened."

"How much is a large quantity of Bitcoin?"

"Forty million dollars' worth. Give or take a million."

My understanding of Bitcoin hovered around zero percent. Not only that, but I couldn't see any way it might pertain to Sookie—except it was missing money. I knew there were many different electronic currencies, but that was about the extent of my knowledge. I made a note to mention the theft to Rainbow and started work.

Waiting in exam room one was an older couple with a middle-aged mixed-breed poodle, whose patchy coat and round belly signaled a problem.

Mari had triaged these clients, taking a preliminary history as well as recording the female dog's vitals.

The owners had brought Licorice in because of shedding and a thinning coat.

"I don't know why she isn't better," the wife told us. "She's on a daily supplement for a thicker, healthier coat, and we bathe her with an all-natural shampoo. Is it stress? Because we wait on her hand and foot." Both owners took a moment to pet their dog, her pink zirconia-jeweled collar sparkling under the exam room lights.

Going over Mari's notes, I said, "Is Licorice taking any other medicines or supplements? Maybe for itching?"

They both looked puzzled. "No, she's not particularly itchy, although her skin seems dry."

Sometimes owners gave their dogs over-the-counter medications with an anti-inflammatory in them. Inappropriate steroid use had to be ruled out as a cause of what I suspected might be Licorice's problem.

"What about eating or drinking more water?" In the notes, the owners denied seeing that.

"Well, she's gaining a little weight, but aren't we all?" The husband patted his own belly. His wife didn't seem amused.

Trying to unmask symptoms in animals sometimes goes astray because owners misinterpret signs or multiple people feed or water the pet. "How many times do you refill her water each day?"

"Twice," said the husband. "Maybe two or three times," the wife said almost simultaneously.

Licorice was drinking a lot. Now we were uncovering an important symptom. "Do you both routinely feed and water Licorice?"

They answered, "Yes."

"And are you keeping track of who does what?"

They looked at each other. "Well, not really," the wife said. "I like to keep food in her bowl all day, in case she's hungry."

"Me too," her husband echoed.

"I'm suspecting that Licorice has an endocrine problem that is responsible for her thinning coat. Often there is a cluster of symptoms, from the potbelly and darkening of her skin to drinking and urinating more. It's called Cushing's syndrome, or Cushing's disease. Mari will give you a pamphlet and some information to take home."

The husband cleared his throat. "How serious is it?"

My patient looked up at her owner, sensing his concern.

"It is manageable. But before we get too far ahead of ourselves, I need to confirm her diagnosis with some lab tests."

"Do we have to leave her?" Fear reflected back at me from their voices and their faces.

I shook my head. "We can draw the preliminary labs today, and then go from there. If they are suggestive of Cushing's, we'll need to determine which of the two types she has, adrenal or pituitary. Those tests will require her to stay here at the hospital for timed blood tests. You'll drop her off in the morning and pick her up at night. Once we have our test results, we can go over a treatment plan."

Licorice's owners stared blankly at me. I'd given them a lot to digest.

"What's an adrenal gland?" the husband asked. His wife glared at him, not wanting to feel embarrassed in front of me.

"Good question," I said. "Before I went to vet school, I didn't know much about them either. They are small endocrine glands that are located on top of each kidney and produce different hormones, including cortisol and adrenaline. I think Licorice is producing too much cortisol."

Although they both nodded, I suspected the information and medical language had overwhelmed them—and most likely frightened them.

Licorice lay down on the exam table, bored with all the talk.

"Here's the important thing," I said. "You've taken the first step to helping her. You brought her to the veterinarian."

While writing up the exam notes on Licorice and my treatment recommendations, I couldn't get the image of the couple's faces from my mind. I'd seen those blank looks before. Clients often want simple answers, not understanding the complexities of the medical issue their pet is dealing with. It's frustrating to all involved. How can I expect a pet owner to understand in twenty minutes a medical issue it took me four years of veterinary school to learn?

Chapter Twenty-Six

WHILE I WAS BETWEEN CLIENTS, I CHECKED MY phone messages and saw something odd. Rainbow had texted me to meet her for about fifteen or twenty minutes during my lunch. She included an address and urged me to tell no one.

I'd seen how impulsively my math whiz acquaintance behaved sometimes and already regretted tying myself to her.

"I've got to run a quick errand at lunchtime, around twelve thirty," I told Cindy. "Any problem?"

She glanced down at her computer, squinted at the screen then picked up her reading glasses. Slightly vain, Cindy hated to admit she needed reading glasses at the age of forty-five. Once finished, she whipped them off and tucked them out of sight. "That should be fine. Our first appointment isn't until one fifteen. It's a new client, so Mari will be taking their history. Make sure you're back by one thirty."

"No problem." I figured that would be enough time to gently ease Rainbow off team Kate, if necessary.

When 12:20 rolled around, I practically galloped out of the office, plugged the meeting address into the GPS, and took off. Mari was going to walk the dogs for me and enjoy some playtime with her own dog, Desi.

The address was in town, slightly past Main Street but still in the business/tourist area of Oak Falls. When the GPS told me I'd arrived at my destination, I eased into a parking space and jumped out of the car. To my surprise, I stood in front of the Overmann Organizing office. A second, smaller sign read ORGANIZATION, DESIGN, AND LIFE STRATEGIES. After visiting Sookie's house, I'd assumed she worked out of her home office. Obviously, she booked enough jobs to rent a separate space.

Maybe Rainbow had a motive to her madness.

A chime dinged when I opened the door. Painted in fashionable shades of gray, silver, and white, the reception area radiated clean and fresh. Multiple fitted cabinets, many with opaque glass doors, surrounded the welcome desk. Stainless steel blended with painted surfaces, pulled together by industrial black-and-white photographs and line drawings of closets, kitchens, and offices. The computer on the desk displayed no tangled cords or ugly plugs in outlets to trip on or distract.

A door at the end of the waiting area opened and Elaine appeared. "Dr. Kate, what a pleasant surprise. Your friend Rainbow told me you might stop by for some help with your bedroom closet." Her pleasant demeanor, calm and relaxed, welcomed me under the false pretenses cooked up by Rainbow. I felt guilty. What did Rainbow have in mind?

"Kate, I told Elaine you didn't have much time today. Why don't you guys talk? I've got to check on one of my online classes."

"Sure." Rainbow had obviously set this up so I would distract Elaine. Getting with the program I replied, "Sounds good. Can I tell you a little bit about my closet issues?"

Elaine smiled. "Sure, follow me." We both glanced back at Rainbow, who had pulled a sleek tablet from her large purse and was busy scrolling.

Once inside, Elaine closed the door and sat down at a wide expanse of clean desktop, something I never seemed to achieve.

"Now. How can I help?" Elaine must have pressed something because a thin computer screen rose up from the glass.

Distracted, I said, "That's neat. How did you do that?"

"Sookie ordered this desk from Norway, I believe. A lesson she taught me was that it's a mistake not to be familiar with international designs." Elaine positioned her fingers at the keyboard, ready to take notes. "Now, can you tell me the worst thing about your closet?"

Once I got started, it was easy explaining to Elaine how much I loathed my jam-packed, disorganized closet. We started talking about summer versus winter clothes, my work clothes, mostly scrubs, and what would make my life easier. We were deep in a discussion on how to prune down the contents when there was a knock on the door.

"Sorry to bother you," Rainbow said. "But, Kate, you told me to watch your time. I think you're wanted back at the clinic."

A glance at my watch confirmed that I needed to leave. "This was so helpful, Elaine," I said sincerely. "Can we continue at another time? Do you have my email?"

"Yes, and I'll type up a summary and email that and a suggestion list for you. I'm so happy I can return the kindness you showed when I fell in the parking lot. That was so upsetting."

"Kate," interrupted Rainbow, her social skills definitely lacking.

"Got to run," I told an embarrassed-looking Elaine. "I'll talk to you soon."

My accomplice and I walked out the door. Rainbow strolled next to me, chatting about school and classes. She continued until we got to my truck when she said, "I'll follow you."

Her ride was a beat-up Toyota Corolla sedan. Someone had tried to camouflage a rusted dent with flat black spray paint.

I started the F-150's engine and backed out of the parking spot. The office was only about ten minutes away, but we needed to watch the clock. Just enough time for me to quiz Rainbow on what the heck she was doing at Elaine's office.

We'd barely pulled in next to the animal hospital when Rainbow flung open her car door and started to do a little dance in the parking lot.

For the life of me I couldn't figure out what she was so stoked about. "Are you celebrating something?" I asked as I climbed down from the truck. "What was that all about, by the way?"

"I got it. I got it," Rainbow sang and continued dancing to her own music.

"Hey, hey," I said, waving my hands. "What did you get?"

"The files. I copied all the files off the reception terminal."

Her laughter horrified me.

"You copied Elaine's files without her permission?" My voice began to rise.

Rainbow rolled her eyes. "No, I copied Sookie's files. That business was Sookie's until someone whammed her in the noggin. Glenn Overmann is Sookie's next of kin, since they're still legally married, so technically the files are his. And we are working for him, once we signed that confidentiality agreement."

"We haven't signed it yet. It has to be notarized, Rainbow." What the heck did she just do?

"Technicalities. We're getting a jump start on everyone." She looked at me and must have noticed the look of horror on my face. "Listen. Don't worry. I'll call Glenn. I'm only going to load the flash drive on my tablet. This has nothing to do with you."

Somehow I didn't think a jury would believe her.

"Go, go." She shooed me with her hands. "You're going to be late. See you tonight. Make sure you order takeout for dinner—your treat." With those words, she slid back into her car and roared out of the parking lot.

Numb, I watched her pull into oncoming traffic without looking. A puff of black smoke backfired out of her exhaust pipe.

What the heck have I gotten into?

Sure enough, Mari had begun my one fifteen appointment. I had my coat on and was waiting in my office when she told me they were ready.

"Any issues or concerns?" I asked her as we walked to the exam room.

"No. They need to get a rabies shot for their pet's dog license."

"Well, that should be easy," I said with relief. My nerves were still jangling from dealing with Rainbow.

"You'd think so," Mari said, "but they don't believe in vaccines."

═══════

The rest of the day passed quickly, although my afternoon appointments ran late due to an unexpected bladder stone surgical emergency. I'd only just gotten into my apartment when my doorbell rang. Immediately a chorus of barking eclipsed anything I could say. "It's all right, guys," I told the dogs. "Desi, stand off." Mari told me to always specifically address Desi when strangers were involved. The big rottweiler needed to know his alarm status. I pushed the curtain away from the window then opened the door.

"Hi, Rainbow," I said. "Glad you could make it." When I stepped aside all the canines surrounded her.

"Doggies!" she cried out and crouched down to greet each one individually. That went on for quite a while until I said, "Let's go inside."

Seeing her with the dogs reminded me of how petite a person she was. Probably only five foot one or two, she made up for it by wearing platform boots or stiletto heels. How she could walk in those things, I didn't know.

"Let's go inside, babies," Rainbow told the dogs, who swept into my house, three tails wagging their approval. Over her shoulders hung two large purse/messenger bags. A stylish gray coat worn over dark boots kept her warm. Gone were the spangles and heavy makeup except for the ever-present false eyelashes.

"Where can I work?" she asked, wading through the excited dogs. "Kitchen table?"

"Sure." My official office was inside the hospital, but since this definitely was not hospital business, I wanted to keep her away from it. "I'll work over here, on the coffee table."

Rainbow took a quick glance at my whiteboard, full of different colored arrows and names with question marks hovering over the letters. Most of the time I wrote random ideas that occurred to me. Sort of brainstorming by markers.

"Do you need anything?" I asked.

In the kitchen, Rainbow was making herself at home. She'd divested herself of coat and bags. A new-looking laptop computer rested on the kitchen table, with two other tablets and several additional devices unknown to me. She'd brought her own extension cords and swiftly connected them all up, like a spider unfurling its legs.

"What'cha got to eat?" Rainbow didn't look up, intent on something on the screen.

"Not too much." The dogs were busy munching their food, but my cupboards looked a little naked.

"Let's get takeout. Chinese is good. I'll have tofu moo shu with extra pancakes, and a side of stir-fried broccoli. I'm mostly vegan."

I stood there thinking about my order when she blurted out, "Hurry up and call it in. I'm starving."

This must have been why Rainbow was always being fired. If she spoke to a boss like that, she'd be toast.

Meanwhile, Desi had finished his food and, after a long stretch, walked over to Rainbow and lay down at her feet with a grunt.

So much for a collaborative relationship. Since I had the restaurant's phone number on speed dial, I placed our takeout order. The last time I'd eaten Chinese food was here in the apartment with Luke, when things were good between us. Associating takeout with Luke was another habit I needed to let go of.

"When will it be ready?"

I started, for a second forgetting Rainbow was here.

"Twenty minutes."

"Why don't you get going? In case it's ready early."

There was something about her eagerness to get rid of me I didn't like. "I've got a better idea," I told her. "Why don't you pick it up, Rainbow, since you're in such a big hurry?" The truth was I'd suddenly realized I didn't want her to be alone in my apartment, not after the hack she performed on Sookie's computer. Her answer to my request was unexpected.

"Now you're catching on."

Surprisingly, we worked well together. I suggested we track both women who passed away, Sookie and Posey. I did all the phone interviews and hard-copy checking involving the actual person, their habits, friends, interests, and work. Rainbow worked on their electronic presence. Then we tried to piece together what they did in the last four weeks of their lives. Anything unusual got put on the whiteboard.

My sources were mostly Daffy and Cindy, Posey's coworkers; Sookie's assistant, Elaine; and any of Sookie's clients who would talk to me.

Tackling Posey's life was pretty straightforward. She lived modestly and worked several part-time jobs including her shift at Circle K. Her home was a second-floor apartment in a large family home, a one-room studio outfitted with a hotplate and small refrigerator. One shared stairwell led to the driveway, so the landlord often saw his tenant. Posey's lease was a strict one: no pets, no loud music after ten p.m., and a host of petty restrictions. The upside was cheap rent. One of her coworkers mentioned she thought Posey seemed particularly excited the week before her death, but no one else I spoke to noticed anything unusual.

Her landlord said she paid her rent on time.

Sookie, on the other hand, lived a more chaotic existence. Everyone described her endless battles with Glenn. He wouldn't agree to the terms of the divorce. He constantly verbally and physically harassed her. No one had anything good to say about her ex, and most believed he killed her. Everyone seemed to know about the boyfriend in the city whose first name might be Morris, but that didn't help much.

"Sookie was full of life," Daffy said during our phone call. "Being with her was invigorating. There were always new projects, new ideas she was working on. She was a creative force of nature."

Others weren't so kind. One of her former clients expressed annoyance about a project that dragged on, even after paying in full for an overhaul of her kitchen cabinets. Another commented on Sookie's design, complaining that although it was innovative, it wasn't practical for her or her family. The Oak Falls Community Center, on the other hand, had been thrilled with how professional her lectures were and had decided to offer her another seminar on the topic of her choice. It seemed as though you either loved her or hated her.

I was waiting for several people to call me back when I realized I'd forgotten one important source.

"Excuse me, Rainbow. Can I ask you something?" I'd stood next to her for a few minutes hoping she'd stop, but she hadn't looked up from her monitors or acknowledged me.

"What?" Her voice sounded annoyed.

"Do you think your mom would talk to me about Posey?" I figured a friend could give me some background info on the Circle K clerk.

"What day is it?" Rainbow asked.

"It's Tuesday."

The girl looked up at the ceiling for a moment then answered, "Go ahead and call her. Casino nights are Wednesday and Saturday."

"Your mom works at a casino?"

Her laugh didn't sound funny. "If you call gambling with money you don't have 'working,' then yes, she works at every casino within a hundred-mile radius." She scribbled a number down on a piece of paper. "Her name's Linda."

I felt odd calling while Rainbow sat nearby so I diplomatically moved as far away as I could and dialed the number. In about five rings a woman gruffly answered.

Once I explained who I was she became much more friendly. Unfortunately, I also noticed Rainbow's mom was slurring her words.

"Posey should have talked to me," Linda said, her voice choking with emotion. "Suicide like that is a horrible thing. Thank God I wasn't there."

No, I thought. *But your daughter was.*

"Did you have any idea she was depressed?" I asked.

There was the sound of someone lighting a cigarette, and then Linda answered, "Posey was always depressed about one thing or another. It all boiled down to no money and a crappy job. I kept telling her to come to the casino with me, but lottery tickets were her big deal. Every week Posey played lotto, Powerball, Mega Millions, and Scratch Off."

"How much did she win on those?"

"Like a buck here, a buck there. Go for broke, I used to tell her."

"So nothing much out of the ordinary the last few weeks?"

"Naaah." Linda paused to take a drag of her cigarette. "Well, she had taken my advice and prettied herself up a bit. We were having lunch, and she told me she took my advice and went for broke."

"Went for broke about what?"

"She never said."

Were those the words of someone contemplating suicide? I asked Rainbow's mom what she thought.

"Truthfully," she said, "I don't know. She tried to off herself before, and I didn't see that one either. Drew up a secret will that time and gave me everything." Linda paused to blow her nose. "Last time I saw Posey she seemed pretty happy. She'd even bought me a present for New Year's, a fancy china cup for my tea. It's covered with forget-me-nots."

I listened to her sobs and said, "I'm so sorry, so sorry you lost your friend," until the crying stopped.

After receiving a text, Rainbow abruptly left, saying she had to meet someone. I wasn't that sorry to see her go. The dogs and I got ready for bed, the icy night air on their walk making the heated apartment that much more enjoyable. I telephoned my Gramps and asked him what he thought of Linda's recollections of her friend Posey.

Gramps thought for a while before replying. "I'm no expert, but I've read that some people who decide on suicide actually appear happier, or euphoric, before they die. Psychologists think it's because they are at peace with the decision and are looking forward to ending their lives. Giving away possessions, cleaning their homes, writing a suicide note are all part of their letting go. Then there are others who kill themselves with little warning. Perhaps impulsively."

His words hit home. One of the members of my veterinary class had committed suicide. Supposedly she had planned everything out. Only a few details about her death were released, but she'd given some textbooks away, and even gifted her expensive stethoscope to her former lab partner.

Another one of our class jumped to his death after failing Topographical Anatomy. Not many people know that veterinarians have a high rate of suicide.

"As much as we try," Gramps said, "we can't see into another's heart. Were Posey's friends surprised by her suicide?"

"Not really," I answered. "The only thing that

surprised them was the method, and how public it was."

"So you're seeing if there is some kind of connection between the organizing woman's death…"

"Sookie Overmann."

"Sookie's death, and the death of Posey, who worked at Circle K, right?"

"Right."

"Didn't you mention Posey was writing a book?"

"Yes." I took a moment to remind him how I'd scooped the notebooks containing her historical mystery out of the dumpster.

Gramps coughed a bit, then asked, "Did they help at all?"

I was embarrassed to admit I hadn't read them yet.

"Well, I suggest you start."

Chapter Twenty-Seven

AFTER I HUNG UP WITH GRAMPS I SAT ON THE SOFA, snoring dogs all around me, and opened the first notebook from the stack of three I'd rescued from the garbage. The emotional wear and tear of the last week had taken up so much of my time that Posey's books had been overlooked. A quick look at the inside cover pages revealed they were numbered. I brewed a pot of tea and started reading.

Now, I normally don't have much time for reading anything but veterinary-related magazines and articles. An Edwardian Age vampire mystery with aliens was new to me. I wasn't even sure what the Edwardian Age meant so I looked it up. The Edwardian Age referred to the time period after the death of Queen Victoria to the death of King Edward, or the start of World War One. There seemed to be differing opinions on it. That was close enough for me. My knowledge of British history was murky at best.

Before I continued, I fluffed my pillow and drew a blanket over my legs and feet. The first notebook was titled *The Search for Answers*. It began with the story of a young woman betrayed by those around her, mostly the men. Alone and penniless, she takes a menial job in the castle of the local duke. It wasn't much of a stretch to assume the fictional Pansy was modeled after the author, Posey, except for the physical description. She wrote:

She was a tall girl with lusty bouncing bosoms and luxuriously long red-blond curls; men couldn't keep their ravaging eyes in their pants when she skipped past. Many a boy longed for the touch of her elegant hand on their sobbing chests.

"Lusty bouncing bosoms?" This was quite a change from my veterinary textbooks. If Posey patterned her heroine after herself, she'd created an idealized vision. And why not? An author can create anything in their fictional world. After jotting down the Posey/Pansy connection in my notes, I kept on reading.

At the duke's palace, the servant watches everything and everyone around her. Basically, she snoops. She tells of a grand lady who impulsively discards a gold charm by throwing it across the room. Almost instantly regretting her action, she makes her servants hunt for the piece of jewelry on their hands and knees for hours. Pansy, the servant, finds the charm and hides it in a tear in her apron hem. Soon other small items disappear in the castle, unnoticed among the piles of excess.

The fictional Pansy didn't feel taking the charm was stealing.

Small items purloined from the palace, the lovely servant girl believed, were her rightful due. Shining jewels and gold, her birthright.

I paused. It might be a good idea to see if any petty thefts happened at Circle K or at any of Posey's other jobs. I recognized that pattern of thinking you're actually entitled to take things from work. But why did Posey use the word "birthright"?

Twenty minutes later during a royal banquet, I dozed off. After two sleepy nose-dives into the notebook binding, I gave up and crawled into bed.

That night I dreamt of Posey. In my dream she rode triumphant on the back of a gilded snake, slithering into people's homes at night, stealing their trinkets as they slept.

The next morning before work I skipped to the second notebook titled *True Love Blooms*. This introduced the duke's children's tutor, who morphs into a sexy vampire each night. Pansy immediately falls for him, but their love must remain a secret. Her new lover promises to bring her wealth and eternal life. Together they begin to plot against the duke—and enjoy a number of sexual encounters in unusual places.

His vampire love flowed across her porcelain globes like peanut butter on jelly.

Posey certainly had a vivid imagination.

———

In the truck on our way to the first house call, I described the plot, so far, of Posey's book to Mari.

"It sounds like a romance," she commented, while booting up the laptop. "Those are really popular. Some women love to read about a strong man sweeping them off their feet."

"I'd be happy to find a guy who sweeps the house," I joked.

"Do you think Posey modeled her characters from real people? Gee, I hope I'm not in it as the girl buying dog food and wine at midnight." She glanced over at me, her dark eyes shining. "Yes, it really happened and, no, I don't want to talk about it."

"Well, if you were buying dog food late at night at the Circle K, then I was the one always buying ice cream."

Mari opened the laptop and said, "I think reading fiction takes you away from your own life and inserts you into someone else's for a while. Why not have a gorgeous guy groveling at your feet? Or do outrageous things and never get caught?"

A broken tree branch stuck out into the lane. I dodged it and continued on. "I suppose you've got a point there. Pretending to be a princess or a pirate is fun. Sometimes you need to step out of the real world into a make-believe universe that only you control."

"Yeah, it's fun. As long as you don't get the two confused," Mari said.

Following the GPS with its haughty British accent, I drove the truck slowly up the many hills behind town. I downshifted as the inclines became steeper, although plenty of gravel and sand kept the road from being slippery.

"Where are we going?" I asked Mari.

"Not sure. It's a new client," she answered, once again looking at the computer screen. "Owner is Chloe Ramboulle. She's got a French bulldog with some kind of orthopedic problem—let's see…limping on the front leg."

"All right." The road made a sharp turn. We kept climbing. The amount of snow in the woods had increased to almost three feet with accumulation building the higher we went. Tall pines lined the shoulders, effectively blocking most of the patchy sunshine. Shadows fell across the graveled surface of the road, darkening the spaces between the trees. It felt terribly gloomy.

We'd almost crested the top when the GPS told us to make a left turn in five hundred feet. Mari called out when she spotted the driveway, almost hidden from view.

"This looks pretty new," she commented as we followed a paved, wide road that led to a tall iron gate. The property had hi-tech security fencing stretching deep into the woods. A camera light mounted on the empty gatehouse suddenly glowed green. I pushed the buzzer and waited.

"Can I help you?" a voice asked.

"Yes. I'm Dr. Kate Turner from the Oak Falls Animal Hospital, with my veterinary assistant, Mari. We've got a one o'clock appointment with Chloe Ramboulle and her French bulldog." I was hoping my pronunciation of her name sounded authentic enough. My frightening tenth-grade French teacher had drilled the importance of a correct accent into our class.

An electronic crackling noise emanated from the call box. After another burst of static, the voice came back. "Proceed to the main house. Someone will meet you."

I waited for the gate to open. Dealing with a house-keeper or caretaker wasn't unusual. Quite a few wealthy people made their homes in the Hudson Valley. Several clients of mine had elaborate security systems, especially the part-time residents. Mari had a friend who acted as a caretaker for five clients who spent most of their time in New York City or California. Making sure her customers' pipes didn't freeze was a major concern.

Dense stands of pine and white aspen lined the road, but the farther up we went, the more the forest had been thinned out. A last steep hill had the F-150 struggling, but once we reached the top, everything leveled off, revealing a vast hidden meadow with a magnificent view of the mountains and reservoir.

"Wow." Mari looked off to the right and left, while I kept my eyes on the road. An innovative home came into view, constructed of steel and glass. Very modern in design, some of its huge windows soared two stories high. The house was an architectural gem, hidden away from view.

Mari put it succinctly: "Big bucks. Really big bucks."

I concurred.

Someone waved from the front of the house. I flicked my headlights on and off and headed toward whoever was greeting us.

When we drew closer, I saw two people, one of whom looked familiar but not in a good way. Dressed all in black including a black overcoat was a clone of one of the "thugs" at the community center lecture.

Running toward us, her designer coat billowing behind, was a beautiful young woman clutching a fawn-colored French bulldog. Her red-gold curls fanned out in long tendrils behind her. Tears glistened on flawless cheeks.

She reminded me of the beautiful servant in Posey's book.

We barely came to a stop before she walked up to the driver's side window and tapped on the glass.

I opened the door, narrowly missing hitting her.

"Are you Dr. Kate?" Her voice was warm, like melted honey, with a faint accent.

"Yes, I am. And this is my assistant, Mari."

Her luminous hazel eyes locked on mine. "I'm afraid my sweet baby is in horrible pain." The French bulldog wiggled in her arms, before turning to lick her owner's face.

"Why don't we go inside and I'll examine…"

"Baby. He's only ten months old, and I can't stand it to think he's hurting." Tears welled up again as she placed her other hand over her heart.

A bit dramatic, I thought, though her emotions appeared genuine. The story Cindy told us of weekenders who needed bodyguards came to mind. Could this be them?

Meanwhile, Mari walked around the front of the truck, carrying our equipment. I lifted my doctor's bag from behind the driver's seat and asked, "Should we follow you?"

After a moment of confusion, our client abruptly turned and walked toward the house. All the while, the man in black stared. Chloe made no attempt to introduce him to us.

Saying the home represented "big bucks" had been an understatement. The inside resembled a magazine ad, clean and modern, with many unique built-ins that probably housed electronic equipment. We marched past a sleek steel fireplace, flames burning through glimmering stones. I counted at least four leather sofas before noticing a professional-style bar in a corner. The views from the many windows were all extraordinary.

"I thought you could do your exam in here," she said, motioning to a door off a hallway. It turned out to be a laundry room with a granite slab work island. I'd never seen a laundry room with three washing machines and four separate dryers. The only colors in the space were black and white and stainless steel.

A run of custom metal countertops added to the industrial look of the space.

Mari pried Baby from Chloe's arms and secured him

on the tabletop. A quick exam revealed all vitals normal and no immediate problems, but his symptoms were orthopedic. There was only one thing to do.

"Let's watch him walk," I told my assistant.

Mari lifted the dog off the countertop, gently bent over, and placed the Frenchie on all four feet. For a moment he stared up at us, perhaps wondering why he was on the ground.

"Can you call him over to you?" I asked the owner. "But please don't pick him up yet."

Chloe nodded and said, "Baby. Come here, *chéri.*"

The dog's comical pointed ears flickered, and he tried to scamper across the floor to his owner. After a few steps he lifted his left front paw up, hesitated, and attempted to walk again.

Chloe immediately ran over and scooped him up into her arms.

Mari and I looked at each other.

"Let's put Baby down again," Mari asked. "Dr. Kate needs to see him walk around for a while."

"Oh, *mais oui.*" Chloe gently placed the dog down, then backed a few feet away. Tears had already begun to well in her lovely eyes.

The dog didn't move.

"Do you have any treats he likes?" There was nothing like bribing a dog to get it to do what you want.

Her hands dug into the pockets of her dress. An outstretched palm revealed a clump of freeze-dried treats. The Frenchie sniffed the air and immediately became more animated. In fact, he paced back and forth in front of Chloe and even briefly stood up on his hind legs. Only a slight limp or hesitancy remained.

Mari lifted him back up onto the table. I spent several minutes palpating both front legs from the shoulder joint through the elbow and down to his toes. It was when I explored the puppy's front pads and nails that I found an anomaly. A small black pebble had wedged itself between two of his pads, tucked under a thick fold of tissue. Normally, a dog could bite or lick something like that out, but I suspected a combination of the bulldog's anatomy and the stone's location made that impossible.

Using my fingers, I gently rolled it up and out. The skin where the pebble had rested looked a bit irritated. I showed it to the owner, explaining that she needed to check the site twice a day. My opinion at this point was it didn't need any medication. Baby's walking should improve and the area return to normal color in a few days.

"Please call me if you have any concerns, or if it begins to look worse." I handed Chloe my card. "You can take a photo of his pad and send it to us, too."

"Thank you so much," she said, smothering her dog with kisses. "I looked at Baby's foot, Bruno and Aldo looked, but we didn't find anything."

Bruno and Aldo? I wondered if those were the names of the two men I saw at the community center. As if on cue, someone knocked at the door.

"*Entrez*," Chloe told them.

The man who poked his head in was not the man on guard at the front door.

"Everything okay?" His eyes darted back and forth, from Mari to me and back again.

"Aldo," Chloe said, "this is Dr. Kate, the veterinarian I called. She found a rock in Baby's foot."

His disbelieving eyes swiveled to stare into mine. "I didn't see nothin' yesterday."

"It took a while for me to notice it," I answered, showing him the dark pebble. "Baby couldn't reach it himself."

Aldo stared at me suspiciously, as if I'd inserted the stone into the dog's pad.

"I'm so happy," Chloe cried out, twirling around the room with Baby hugged to her chest. "Merci beaucoup."

Aldo relaxed a bit then said, "She's French," as if that explained everything.

I stripped off my exam gloves and waited for Mari to open our medical waste bag. "Do you have somewhere I can wash my hands?"

"Sure, Doc," the man said. "Follow me."

While following him down the hallway I took note of the powerful shoulders, short thick neck under his golf shirt, and slightly bowlegged walk. Someone who lifted weights, possibly used steroid—a lot of bulk without much refinement.

We passed an office, its door slightly ajar, and several other rooms before he stopped. "Here's the powder room." Out of habit, it seemed, he took a quick look up and down the hallway.

The powder room was easily twice the size of my full bathroom at home. It even had a separate mir-rored area with a chair. After washing my hands and splashing some water on my face, I dried myself with a luxuriously soft towel and opened the door.

Aldo stood outside, his arms clasped in front of him.

"Thank you for waiting," I politely fibbed. "I'm not sure I could find my way back."

"No problem." He looked up and down the hall-way again then turned and headed back to the laundry room.

He opened the door to raucous laughter. Mari had her phone out and was showing Chloe something on the screen.

"We're looking at the video I took of the puppies," my assistant explained.

"Aldo, come look," Chloe said.

The last thing I expected a bodyguard to do was to look at a puppy video, but that's exactly what he did. Maybe checking to make sure Chloe wasn't lying?

"Are those rottweilers?" Aldo asked.

"Absolutely. AKC-registered. Both their parents are also Schutzhund certified."

"Those guard dogs?" he questioned.

"That's right. Trained to protect and defend on com-mand. My male weighs a little over one hundred pounds."

Aldo stared at the screen and said, "Very impressive. But I'll take a shotgun over a dog any day."

An awkward silence sprang up between us. Chloe broke the tension by changing the subject.

"Dr. Kate delivered all these puppies on Christmas Eve. She saved the last pup that was stuck." Chloe clapped her hands enthusiastically. "I could talk about animals all day. Please—can you stay for a quick *café*? Or tea?"

Before I could answer, Mari checked her watch then said to me, "Maybe fifteen minutes? We're a bit ahead of schedule."

"A coffee sounds wonderful," I answered back.

Under the watchful eye of Aldo, Mari and I followed Chloe, who led us past more living rooms into the kitchen. A party of twenty or more could easily be served in what resembled another commercial space. Our hostess warmly greeted an older woman standing by the stove stirring a simmering pot. "Madame Merchad, can you please brew some *café* for us? This is Dr. Kate and her associate, Mari. They found a stone in Baby's foot and now he's cured! See!"

The woman laughed as the dog came running over to her. "*Mon petit chou!* Everything is good now?"

Chloe indicated we should sit at a large round table in the dining alcove with a view of the mountains. As we waited for the coffee, Chloe began asking questions about what it was like being a veterinarian in the United States.

"When I was a girl in France," she said, "I wanted to be a veterinarian or an actress." She smiled and I noticed a slightly indented side tooth, unlike the perfect

American smiles in so many actors. The tiny imperfection made her endearing.

Mari interrupted and asked, "How did you end up here?"

"My husband, Arthur, works in New York City, but we love to spend time in the country. We both ski and hike." She stared out the window with a smile. "I'm also starting work on a theater production in the city."

We were interrupted by the delivery of a pot of coffee, steamed milk, and some small chocolate biscuits. "I take my coffee the French way. Café au lait." Chloe filled her cup halfway with coffee, then topped it with the steamed milk.

Baby, the French bulldog, began to scratch at his owner's leg and yipped a few times. Chloe leaned over to pet the dog, her long Renaissance hair cascading to the floor.

Had Posey used Chloe's appearance as an inspiration for her own heroine? The more I studied the pale skin and classical profile of the actress, the more I believed she had.

"Is he telling you something?" Mari asked.

"Definitely." Chloe smiled. "Aldo," she called out. The bodyguard, who'd been leaning against the doorway, came over. "Can you please take Baby out for his walk? And make sure there isn't any gravel."

"Yes, ma'am," he said. "Is the leash by the back door?"

"I think so." Chloe watched as Aldo picked up the young dog. "Make sure you go potty," she ordered the dog, now resting in Aldo's arms.

Her eyes watched him leave. As soon as the body-guard left her demeanor changed. "*Alors*. Now we are alone. Finally. I never get to invite friends to the house. I feel like a prisoner."

"Why is that?" Mari asked.

She craned her neck to make sure Aldo was out of sight. "Because of the theft of those stupid coins. Security thinks one of the people I hired took my husband's ledger with the secret numbers in it."

That sounded confusing—like a child's story. "What do you mean, Chloe?"

"The key to the invisible wallets floating on the Internet. He wrote the numbers of his Bitcoins in a green leather ledger. Don't ask me to explain it because I can't. Sometimes Arthur carried it with him. Sometimes he'd stick it in a drawer."

"Who do they think stole the ledger?"

She thought about my question. "The only strangers here were Sookie and her crew. The day she finished, we had to put everything back in the closet, and her helper started bringing in all the shoes and clothes, and my husband's office was unlocked… And—the security people couldn't prove anything because the alarm cameras on this side of the house were being repositioned and reset. I told my husband not to trust that security company. Some of them looked at me strangely—as though I were meat."

Her explanation sounded jumbled, but I understood. "They questioned everyone. They tried to prove

Sookie's crew might be untrustworthy but…well, that's when everything became *merde*."

Which was a more elegant way of saying everything went to shit.

I wondered how much Chloe knew about Sookie's death. My unspoken question was quickly answered.

"Now Sookie has been murdered. And her helper committed suicide, and I think it's all my fault." Our French friend's lower lip trembled.

"Do you remember the helper's name?" I asked.

"It was a flower. Daisy, or Lily or…"

Mari interrupted. "Posey?"

"Yes." Chloe pointed her finger at my assistant.

The sound of scampering dog feet interrupted our conversation. Baby had returned from his walk.

And so had Aldo.

Chloe and Baby personally escorted us to our truck and enthusiastically waved goodbye until we were out of sight.

As I drove down the road, my thoughts went back to the Bitcoin theft. Could Sookie and Posey have had anything to do with it? I didn't know much about virtual money, but I knew someone who did.

"By the way, while you were washing up, Chloe told me she hates staying home with the bodyguards." Mari opened the laptop but didn't enter anything. "She's got another week before rehearsals start. That's why she attended the community center lecture. She's been bored out of her mind."

I thought for a moment. "So, her bodyguards were at the community center to protect her, not to find Lucky?"

"So she says. When the bodyguards spotted Henry James in the audience, they forced her to leave early." Mari continued, "Chloe told me she'd never met Elaine, only Sookie and Posey."

That was in line with what Elaine had said. Sookie kept the big jobs for herself and farmed the smaller projects to her assistant. Posey was the hired help. "Was Chloe satisfied with the closet design?"

"She loved it. The whole experience was fantastic. In fact, she planned to send three or four of her friends to Sookie."

We reached the iron double gate. Sensors on each side allowed the panels to slowly swing open from the middle. A quick turn onto the road and we set off for the animal hospital. I felt a huge sense of relief getting away from those foreboding gates.

I'd briefly felt trapped too. Just like Chloe.

Chapter Twenty-Eight

As soon as we walked into the office, Cindy pounced on us.

"So, what was it like?" she asked. "A friend of mine said they brought a huge crew in from New York City to work on that house. It's probably worth several million dollars, or even more." With a quick move, she picked up the bag of medical waste we'd generated and followed Mari and me into the treatment room.

"Did you know I used to go camping up there in that meadow? Gorgeous spot. Mostly used for grazing because it was terrible in the winter. The wind is fierce on the mountaintop," Cindy added.

"I guess we lucked out," I told her. "The sun was shining, and winds were fairly mild. You could see an entire panorama of mountain ranges and the whole reservoir."

Mari jumped in. "The house was fabulous. Inside it was all glass and stainless steel, and very modern, but not impersonal. Cool, clean lines. I wanted to dump all my stuff and start all over again."

Cindy threw back her head and laughed. "I know that feeling. Sometimes I could include the hubby in that stuff."

Getting back to the reason for our visit, I said, "Easy

house call. Their Frenchie puppy had a pebble wedged up under his front pad. You couldn't see it. I had to run my fingers around everything to find it. He wasn't even chewing at it."

"Well," Cindy said, "I had some free time, so I did a little social media background check on our new clients. Very interesting."

Oh, no, I thought. No wonder celebrities build houses in meadows on top of mountains. Celebrities balance their lives on a double-edged sword. They love the worldwide attention that fame brings, but they say goodbye to any privacy.

Mari eagerly asked, "What did you find out?"

"So, the husband is Arthur Gambino. He's a self-made multimillionaire, one of those Wall Street guys who invests in start-ups and cutting-edge technology. He's a workaholic but supposedly super charismatic. His stockholders adore him."

"What about Chloe?" During the short time I was with her, she impressed me with her bubbly personality and emotional nature.

"Ah," Cindy said. "Chloe is an altogether different person. Her family is one of the wealthiest in France. Private schools. Governesses."

"Go on," I said.

"She was on a school trip to Rome, when a French filmmaker saw her."

"How old was she?"

"Only sixteen. He spirited her away from her school

group and did a screen test with no one's permission—except for Chloe's."

"She went all the way to Italy to be cast in a French movie?"

Cindy shook her head. "Strange, isn't it? Anyway, the movie opened the Cannes Film Festival. Arthur Gambino was in the audience. He says he fell in love immediately. There's a fifteen-year difference in their ages."

"How old was she?"

"By the time the movie came out, she was eighteen, almost nineteen."

"So they waited…"

"About six months. Supposedly, she told her parents on her birthday she was going out shopping. Instead, she met Arthur. They were married on his yacht in the South of France by a justice of the peace."

"Very romantic," Mari told everyone. "I'd like to be swept off my feet and married on a yacht."

"Grow up," Cindy abruptly said. "Fairy tales are just that."

To avert an argument I asked, "Anything else about Chloe?"

"She's been cast in a Broadway play. It's only for a limited run, and she starts rehearsals soon. After that, it's off to Hollywood to shoot a major studio production."

From the lingo Cindy was using, I assumed she was directly quoting her source. "Anything else?"

"The people who've worked with her say she's sweet, unsophisticated, sort of a wild child. One director said she's maddening to work with, while another said making a movie with her was blissful."

"Nice," Mari said. "I guess."

"Her husband is crazy in love with her and very protective," Cindy quoted. "She had a stalker, and there's also been a kidnapping threat."

More and more details fell into place. No one was chasing Lucky. Gangsters hadn't moved into town. Glenn Overmann most likely killed his wife. And Posey? The police say she committed suicide.

Was it a coincidence that Chloe's husband thought these two local women may have stolen his Bitcoin? Two women who now were dead?

It felt like one coincidence too many.

That night I mentioned to Rainbow the Bitcoin theft from Arthur Gambino.

"That's more like it," said Rainbow, her eyes gleaming. "I assume this theft involved a substantial amount of money?"

"Forty million dollars, give or take a couple of million." At least that was the figure Mari had said.

"I'm sure there's an army of hackers and FBI people looking for that. The finder's fee's got to be at least a million plus."

"I read somewhere it's hard but not impossible to trace Bitcoin."

My statement provoked a snort from Rainbow. "That's what law enforcement would like embezzlers and drug dealers to believe. It all depends on how the money is being moved and stored. Whoever stole that ledger with the deposit codes could easily move the Bitcoin from one electronic wallet to another, then perhaps to Switzerland or the Bahamas."

This new world of electronic money confused me. "Is it true some investor forgot their Bitcoin numbers and can't retrieve their money? Or is that an urban legend?"

"No, it's true," Rainbow answered. She looked up from her computer. "This guy lost his password to open up his Bitcoin wallet. That's where you store your funds," she explained. "Personally, I don't like random computer-generated passwords. They're the worst. I think your password should mean something to you. At least then there's a chance of remembering it if you need to."

"We're getting off track here," I told Rainbow. "Our job is to find out what Sookie did with Glenn's money so we can claim the reward."

"Oh, that. I've found some of it, but so have two other guys, or so they claim on one of the hacking bulletin boards. It's sort of odd, though." Rainbow turned her monitor so I could see it. A complicated spreadsheet took up the entire screen. "It looks like Sookie began separating Glenn's assets from hers at least two months ago. New York is a fair and equitable distribution divorce state, not a community property state. Their finances weren't that entwined anyway. Sookie had a prenuptial agreement and most of the money." Rainbow pointed to several columns before swiftly scrolling through a few pages to point out more statistics. "You can see where she created a separate account here"—she pointed to the screen—"then moved some assets into a diverse portfolio, and did some trading," she scrolled away again, "over there."

Keeping track of the numbers and different pages was giving me a headache. Her system complicated rather than simplified. "Can you use less technical words and explain this to me?"

Rainbow rolled her eyes, which obviously was her thing. "All right. I think Glenn put up this reward not to recover his assets but to take Sookie's."

Chapter Twenty-Nine

After Rainbow left, hauling her laptops with her, my mind switched to a more pressing matter—something to snack on. The fridge held leftovers from our Chinese takeout binge, so I consolidated all the little cardboard boxes and settled in. After learning of other hackers making headway, whatever hopes I entertained of earning half of Glenn's twenty-thousand-dollar reward money rapidly faded away.

I sat alone at the kitchen table, takeout containers littering the ancient Formica top. In the distance, the sounds of trucks and maintenance machinery clattered away. A gap in the living room curtains revealed only darkness.

At nighttime, now, I often thought about Luke. Did I make the right decision? Should we try to go back to being friends again? Even picking up the chopsticks reminded me of all the times Luke and I ate together at this table. As friends we were pretty good, but lousy with everything else at the end. To avoid mentally reliving our relationship second by second, I decided to continue immersing myself in someone else's problems.

The stack of Posey's notebooks beckoned, so I picked up where I'd left off. Skipping past more sexy scenes between the tutor/vampire and the servant, I went back to her story.

Inside the castle the servant, Pansy, begins scheming with the tutor/sexy vampire to steal gold from the duke. It was hinted that somehow Pansy was related to royalty and deserving of a portion of the duke's wealth. The details on how the servant fit into this wealthy family remained foggy. Pansy meets a sorceress in the village who smuggles her inside a hidden room in the castle.

Unbeknownst to the sorceress, Pansy searched for the key to the golden coins. Her quest was righteous for she knew the duke and his kin to be black-hearted thieves.

Not sure where this story was heading, I kept reading. Then the plot slowed while Pansy and the tutor got it on for six pages. I skipped through the pulsing this and the throbbing that.

When the sorceress discovers Pansy wants to steal the duke's gold, she insists on taking half for herself. This leads the servant to smite the sorceress in a fit of anger.

I paused and put the notebook down. Could "smite" be a euphemism for bashing someone's head in with a snow shovel?

As Posey's story continued, I found it hard to separate fact from fiction. Did she weave Sookie's death into her fictional tale of the servant and the vampire?

Getting to sleep that night took a while. Dreams that turned into nightmares jarred me awake. A woman stalked my sleep, a woman who looked like a combination of Posey and Chloe. Regardless of which human form the apparition took, she always carried a broken snow shovel in her bloody hands.

I'd finished taking care of the dogs and put on my scrubs when unexpected visitors interrupted my morning routine. Even before the doorbell rang, early warning system Buddy growled, and then Desi began to bark.

A quick look outside led me to quiet the dogs and give Desi the okay command.

"Good morning," Cindy said, walking in and heading straight for my kitchen table. "I brought us some chocolate croissants."

Having breakfast with my receptionist wasn't the surprise. It was her brother-in-law, Oak Falls Chief of Police Bobby Garcia, strolling into my home that was the wild card.

"Dr. Kate," the chief said pleasantly, as though we often met this way.

"Chief." As an excuse to get out of his way, I picked up a small bag of dog treats and made a big fuss over giving them to the eager dogs.

My eyes darted back and forth between Cindy and the chief. I was about to ask if I were in some kind of trouble when Cindy ordered everyone to come and sit down.

Handcuffs usually didn't come with pastry.

"Sorry for the surprise, Kate," Cindy began, removing three croissants from the oven.

"That's okay." The smell of coffee brewing perked me right up. How did Cindy get everything done so fast?

"Bobby has something he needs to talk to you about." Cindy glared at her brother-in-law, who wisely averted her glance.

"You might want to stop trying to land that twenty-thousand-dollar reward Glenn Overmann has put up."

Although I'd already come to that same conclusion, I asked him why.

"Let's just say," he said as his eyes met Cindy's, "it's doubtful he will be able to pay up."

That interested me. I asked, "Is Glenn Overmann a person of interest in Sookie's murder?"

The chief smiled and replied, "I don't believe I said that."

"No," I smiled back. "I don't believe you did."

We paused to drink our coffee and munch on the croissants. Cindy asked me if anything interesting had happened lately.

"No, not in particular."

This time the chief gave Cindy a side look.

What the heck is going on here? Knowing that eventually someone would say something, I went back to enjoying my breakfast.

It was Cindy who broke first. "Mari told me about one of your house calls that was a bit unusual. Up on the mountain?"

"Oh. Well, this French bulldog puppy…"

"I don't want to hear about the puppy," the chief blurted out, impatient with this charade. "Tell me about the people, and what Gambino's wife, Chloe, said about the Bitcoin theft."

"Are you investigating their Bitcoin theft? Aren't those types of crimes investigated by the FBI?"

His face began to redden, like boiling shellfish.

Cindy came to the rescue. "Just tell Bobby what Mari told me."

Since I suppose my job was verifying Mari's account of her conversation with Chloe, I dutifully recounted our visit, from the very beginning to driving away from the property.

"For the record, Chloe Ramboulle is a very sweet person."

"This has simply been an informal conversation among friends over breakfast," the chief said, clearing his throat.

"Yes, sir," I replied. Personally, I thought that was funny, but it didn't get a laugh.

A quick look at her watch prompted Cindy to say, "Time to go to work. Thanks for the ride, Bobby."

"You're welcome, Cindy." Bobby picked up his coat and made straight for the door. As an afterthought, he said, "Dr. Kate, have a nice day and stay safe."

After he left, I asked Cindy, "What the heck was that all about?"

"Probably nothing. I'm not at liberty to say anything

more." A quick blot to her lips, followed by a sweep of a rosy-colored lipstick and she said, "Let's get to work."

I followed her into the hospital more confused than ever.

When I was about halfway finished with my morning appointments, Cindy texted me. I'd been entering some notes into a record, waiting for Mari to triage the next patient.

A FRIEND OF YOURS WANTS TO SAY HI

Not sure who it could be, I budgeted a quick five minutes to talk and made my way to the reception area. The thought occurred to me it might be Luke. Instead, Cindy was in the midst of an animated conversation with a different attractive man—Colin.

"What brings you here?" I asked him, conscious of my baggy white coat and makeup-less face.

He stepped over and landed a peck on my cheek. "Two things. I'm rehoming an iguana. It's not mine. I sort of inherited it with my rental studio. Anyway, I gave Cindy a flyer to put up on the bulletin board."

Cindy waved a brightly colored picture of an iguana before diplomatically excusing herself.

"What's the second thing?" I asked him.

"I wanted to say a proper goodbye. I'm leaving for Finland next week." He pushed a long strand of hair behind his ear.

"That's right. Helsinki," was my lame answer. *Too bad* kept running through my mind. *It's too bad you're not staying longer.*

Colin gazed at me as though expecting something. "Okay. Please thank Cindy for putting up that flyer. Take care, Kate."

He began to move toward the door, but I called after him. "Wait. Maybe we can do lunch before you go?"

"How about dinner tomorrow? Seven thirty? At Bella Italia. I'll meet you there." Before I could react, he pulled on his hat and walked out the office exit to his car.

The empty reception area was still, only the sound of the fading door chime interrupting the silence.

I wasn't sure how it happened, but I guess I had a date with Colin.

Mari squealed when Cindy told her my dating news during lunch. "He is sooo good-looking. Romantic, too."

"He's leaving next week for Europe," I added. "There is no way I'm beginning anything with him. Would you?"

Our receptionist instantly replied, "Are you kidding me? If I were twenty years younger and not married, sure I would. Why not? You only live one life."

They both watched me while they ate their lunches. This time, I nibbled at a veggie salad, in penance for all the ice cream and pie I'd been indulging in.

"Coffee anyone?"

"Of course," I answered. My coffee consumption had steadily risen since I started drinking it as an undergraduate. At some point, I probably would need to cut back. Some point in the far distant future.

"Well, I'm sorry to see such a charming guy leave. Maybe he'll be back someday." Cindy took another discreet bite from her whole grain chicken and avocado wrap. "Why Finland?"

My fork speared a cherry tomato. "Something to do with a gallery showing, I think."

Balancing three cups, Mari came back. "Watch out, it's hot," she cautioned and handed me my mug. Cindy reached out and snagged hers.

"So what were you talking about?" Mari asked as she sat down.

"Colin. Going to Helsinki."

She shook her head. "I never understood how artists and musicians can afford to go to all these exotic places. Most of the ones I know don't make a lot of money."

"This trip was arranged through his agent, I believe. Colin's paintings are being shown in a gallery in Helsinki."

Leaning back in her chair, Mari said, "When did you meet him? New Year's Eve? That seems so long ago, doesn't it? Cindy, are the police any closer to finding Sookie's killer?"

I kept quiet.

"Cindy? You must know something? Kate, make her tell us."

"Yeah, Cindy," I sided with my assistant. "Surely you know something?" I didn't share her scaring me to death this morning with her brother-in-law.

Our receptionist pressed on the side of her face with the palm of her hand—a sure sign she was about to talk. "This is completely unofficial, and you can't discuss this with anyone. Agreed?"

"Agreed." We eagerly huddled closer.

"The police department is announcing this afternoon that Glenn Overmann is a person of interest in his wife's death—and that said person has retained legal counsel"

Mari slammed her hand on her knee. "I knew it. I didn't like that guy at all."

"I thought he had an alibi?" I asked Cindy.

"Nope. His sister gave the police some story about him being with her. The chief has been interviewing everyone who attended that lecture, and two women say they saw Glenn smoking a cigarette in the parking lot. Over by the back door."

"Where the camera was broken."

"Right. Both witnesses independently identified him from pictures."

"So his sister was lying? What a relief to have this murder solved," I told them. "All along it was a case of domestic violence."

"Now all we need is to find Mr. Pitt's owner and our lives will be mystery-free."

"Oh," Cindy said. "That reminds me. I've got

Lucky coming in for some training tomorrow. We're starting with cleaning, doing inventory, and shadowing you, Mari."

"Good. Did Tony decide not to come back to work this spring?" She got up from her seat and threw her trash in the bin.

"Yes. He's a full-time college student now. I'm glad Tony is sticking to his studies, but I'm sorry to lose him. I think he worked here all four years of high school. But I'm happy to say he promised to drop by at Spring Break."

"Oh, goody." Mari didn't sound enthused.

Mari's sarcastic tone amused me. Since I'd started work at Oak Falls Animal Hospital, she and Tony were always arguing about something or other.

Gramps called me while I was eating my dinner in front of the television surrounded by dogs pretending to be starving.

"So, how's your search for the lost money going, Katie?" he asked. "Don't go spending it until you get it."

"Don't worry. That's not going to happen." I explained that some other hackers beat us to it, not to mention Glenn was probably going to be arrested for Sookie's murder.

"I'm not surprised. The husband or boyfriend is always a suspect until proven innocent."

"Aren't you supposed to be innocent until proven guilty?" When I put a piece of chicken in my mouth, the dogs followed my every movement.

"Of course. That is the foundation of our judicial system. But when you're investigating a murder, anyone you interview might be guilty and lying to you. I've seen killers cry their eyes out in front of the camera, begging for the return of their loved one—whom they've murdered."

"Don't those guys usually try to hide the body?"

The phone went silent. I could visualize my Gramps sitting back in his reclining chair and thinking. "That's right. Most of my police buddies immediately suspected foul play when women disappeared and left their phones and purses behind. The last person to see them usually is the boyfriend or husband."

I turned my back to avoid the dogs. Their pleading eyes resembled those pictures of children begging in the streets.

"Glenn Overmann never pretended to be sorry over his wife's death," I told him. "He always seemed more concerned about her money. A very unpleasant man."

After clearing his throat, Gramps said, "Murderers come in all flavors. Take care out there, Katie. Concentrate on the animals."

I'd just about finished my chicken and rice when Buddy gave a sad little sigh, which made me feel super guilty. Carefully, I fished three remaining pieces of chicken out of my bowl. "Okay," I said to the dogs, "you each get a piece for being so good."

Between the three of them, a chorus of lips smacking and tails wagging accompanied their treat. Although I was the human, I'd caved in after a coordinated effort spearheaded by the dogs.

I'd lost count, but I thought that upped the score to Dogs 3, Human 0.

Before I went to sleep, I set out my clothes for tomorrow's dinner with Colin. I didn't want to dress formally because that might signal that I considered this a date. Which I didn't. On the other hand, the last time he saw me I was wearing scrubs and a mildly furry white doctor's coat.

To raise the bar on my part wouldn't require much.

Chapter Thirty

THANKS TO A LAST-MINUTE EMERGENCY I WAS RUN-
ning about twenty minutes late for my dinner with
Colin. Cindy texted him, using the number off the
iguana rehoming flyer, and he responded "No worries."

The Bella Italia restaurant was one of the many
chef-driven kitchens in the Hudson Valley. Coming
from an Italian background, the chef was part of the
popular farm-to-table movement. The bounty of New
York State, which includes artisanal cheeses, organic
fruits and vegetables, and so much more, was show-
cased each night. New dishes were the rule, and the
menu changed daily.

I'd never been there—a special-occasion kind of
place—so I was looking forward to our dinner. As an
added bonus, I'd be looking at Colin instead of dogs.

Once I was inside, my eyes quickly adjusted to the
subdued lighting. The greeter's podium stood empty.
The dining room looked about three-quarters full. I
quickly spotted Colin sitting at a window table, two
servers hovering over him, drinking in his every word.
What must it be like to be so charismatic?

White tablecloths gleamed with silverware and
fresh flowers in glass vases. The walls were painted a

warm cream. Paintings of the Italian landscape hung throughout the room. The sound of a fountain added to the ambience.

I strode across the room. "Hi, Colin. Sorry I'm late."

He stood up and came around to pull out my chair. "Never apologize for doing such noble work. Besides," he said, wading between the servers, "these two ladies have kept me well occupied."

A man in a suit scurried past us toward the entrance. As soon as he appeared, both servers suddenly became very professional, one asking for our drinks order, while the other drifted toward another couple seated a few tables away.

"I've been here a few times," he said, picking up the menu. "The homemade ravioli are particularly good."

I opened the menu, saw the prices, and immediately said, "Let's split the tab, shall we?"

"Of course," he said. "My agent texted me this morning that I've sold a painting, so this is a celebratory indulgence."

We chatted for a while. Colin was easy to talk to, full of funny anecdotes and little stories. My glass of white wine was ice cold. He drank red.

"Did you ever go through with your idea of capturing that reward money?" Colin asked.

"That's right. We were in Judy's when Glenn came in and announced his reward for the return of his money."

"Yes," Colin said. "A little melodramatic, that."

The server brought us a warm breadbasket with two

dishes of olive oil mixed with herbs and a drizzle of balsamic vinegar. Everything smelled delicious, and I was famished.

Between bites, I explained that Rainbow and I had begun looking at Sookie's financials, but most likely would quit since Glenn had become a person of interest in her murder.

"Someone told me it was on the local news yesterday." He broke off a piece of bread and swished it in the oil. "What exactly does that mean, anyway? Person of interest."

"My boyfriend…my ex-boyfriend said it means someone who might be connected to a crime but isn't legally charged with anything." Luke and I had discussed this topic over Chinese food not that long ago.

"The fellow you were with on New Year's? The one who kept abandoning you?" Colin lifted his glass to his lips. "Are you happier now that he's gone?"

I raised my glass to his. "I'm working on it."

We laughed and talked over our dinners. I told him about Gramps and veterinary school, while he talked about growing up in the Midwest and getting an art scholarship to Cooper Union in the East Village of Manhattan. We shared the burden of having student loans, although as a veterinarian, my future income was more secure than his. I described meeting my actress client, Chloe, and briefly mentioned their Bitcoin theft.

He launched into a funny story about customs and taking a high school class online in Barcelona.

"How did you manage to travel so much?" I asked him as I finished the last of my spaghetti in clam sauce.

Colin took a final bite of his osso bucco and washed it down with red wine. "Delicious. Almost as good as one I had in Rome." He removed a hint of gravy from the corner of his mouth with the tip of his napkin. "What did you ask?"

"Travel. How were you able to travel as an undergraduate? I had to work every summer to pay for books and tuition."

"Well," he began, "that's an interesting story. When I was a junior in high school, my favorite aunt broke her wrist just before her tour to Italy was about to leave." He pointed to his right hand. "I got a call from her asking if I'd go along as her companion and nurse, basically. Separate rooms and all expenses paid."

"Wow."

"I jumped on it, of course. We got along famously. I took care of the luggage, carried the passports and tickets, and made her comfortable while her wrist healed. When her cast got wet in Venice, I found a little clinic to do the bandage change. They even let her sip a cocktail while they worked."

"She must have appreciated that."

"She did. Very fond of her cocktails was my aunt. She was a widow and really didn't enjoy traveling alone. So every summer she booked a tour somewhere and invited me along. We even went to China together."

The waiter came by and whisked our empty plates away.

"Dessert?" Colin asked, when the server returned.

"Of course."

He smiled at me. "I like a woman who knows her own mind."

Despite the hour, I decided on a chocolate mousse. Colin ordered the lemon tart and an espresso.

"Does the espresso keep you awake?" I asked him.

"Not at all. I'm one of those people who get a rush of energy at night. I'm usually painting until three or four in the morning and don't get up until after noon." He picked at his tart with his fork.

"Is your aunt still traveling?" I asked with a spoon filled with mousse in my hand.

"Sadly, no." He stared over my shoulder for a moment. "She passed away a little over two years ago. A blood vessel burst in her brain."

"An aneurysm? I'm sorry."

His fingers tapped the tablecloth. "It was quick and painless, the doctors said. That was something to be thankful for."

We finished our desserts in silence.

When the bill came, I put it on my credit card, while Colin gave me his half in cash.

"I'm glad we could get together," he said, smiling at me. "Would you like to have an after-dinner drink at my studio? It's not far from here."

His invitation was blatant. How many other women in town had been offered the same late-night drink? Quite a few, I ventured. Why not? Colin was young, unattached, and perfectly free to enjoy his active social life. Just not with me.

I rose up on my tiptoes and gave him a brief kiss on his cheek. "Sorry, but I've got to work tomorrow."

His handsome face betrayed no disappointment. "Of course. So, if I don't see you before I leave, please email me. I'd love to hear how you're doing. In exchange, I'll regale you with tasty Finnish stories."

We stood inside the restaurant by the exit. "How do I get hold of you?"

Colin wrapped a cashmere muffler around his neck and answered, "Go to my website. There's a link to the Helsinki gallery show and a message board. You can browse through my sales catalog, too."

"I'd like that."

We stood for a moment blocking the exit door when Colin took my hand, drew it to his lips and said, "*Arrivederci, bella.*"

I didn't know much Italian, but I knew those words. *Until we meet again, beautiful one.*

At home I smiled to myself as I put on my nightgown. Such a fun night. Thinking about Rome and traveling, I climbed into bed. Posey's notebooks lay on the nightstand, alongside a veterinary journal and a mystery novel.

Dutifully I picked up the journal and promptly fell asleep.

Chapter Thirty-One

ONCE AGAIN, I AWOKE TO THREE DOGS LICKING MY fingers. This time I held firm. No dog bones before breakfast. I had the feeling they conducted secret meetings while I slept, coordinating their plans for getting more treats.

When I mentioned this begging to Mari, she immediately frowned.

"Desi never does that at home," she told me with a straight face.

"Really?"

"Really."

"You never give him people food?" I asked.

An indignant look was her answer.

"So, that's a yes?" I poured another cup of coffee and searched for a breakfast bar in the staff freebie basket.

Cindy interrupted us with the day's schedule. Another snowstorm was predicted for that afternoon, so she adjusted our house calls accordingly.

"You've got a recheck on that French bulldog," she said. "I made it your last appointment."

"That shouldn't take long," Mari said. "From there it's a straight shot back to the hospital."

"Good. I don't want you two driving around in the middle of a storm." She turned to leave, then added, "Daffy wants you to stop by, too."

"What?" I almost yelled in astonishment. "Those Chihuahua nails can't possibly need clipping again."

Cindy agreed. "This time it's a skin thing."

"Like when she thought a dog nipple was a tick?"

"No, it's some kind of sore." Cindy looked down at her electronic notes. "You know how anxious she gets about everything."

Mari stood up and stretched her arms over her head. "No problem. I'll bring a carrier in case he needs to come back to the hospital."

Having the always growling, uncooperative Chihuahua in the hospital during a snowstorm? What could possibly go wrong?

Daffy was in a chatty mood when we arrived. Sometimes I thought she wanted the company as much as the veterinary advice on these house calls.

Both she and her Chihuahua were resplendent in long-sleeved, hand-knit sweaters. As we walked down the hallway, our client brought up our town's two recent deaths. "Such terrible tragedies. I didn't know Sookie that well, but Posey was someone I was very fond of. She'd had a difficult life."

I immediately prompted her to continue. "What do you mean by 'a difficult life'?"

Daffy sat down at her kitchen table, Little Man on

her lap. "Posey grew up here in Oak Falls. When she was eighteen, she met a man while skiing at Belleayre Ski Resort. He was from Staten Island, I think, or New Jersey—somewhere in the city."

"What happened?" I asked, trying to speed her along.

"Well," she said through pursed lips, "they got together…and she followed him back to his parents' place. A little over a year later, she was knocked up. His family was Italian and pushed for a quick marriage. Such a handsome man, dark curly hair, white teeth."

So far, I didn't see where this was going.

"Anyway, they got married in the local Catholic church. But Posey soon discovered some terrible things about her new husband and his family. Her father-in-law worked as an illegal bookie, taking bets over the phone. Meanwhile, the husband—I can't remember his name—was unfaithful with a bevy of different girls, even while she was pregnant. Posey had a small inheritance from her grandparents, but as soon as they got married her husband stole it. She had no recourse. He told her the man controls the finances and is the boss in his home. A wife must obey her husband.

"One rainy night, with only a few weeks before the baby was to be born, Posey fled the house in a rage. While she was crossing the street, a truck ran a red light and hit her. One of the tires rolled over her abdomen."

"Oh, no," Mari said, listening over my shoulder. "Poor Posey."

Daffy nodded. "She lost the baby. Because of internal injuries, they did an emergency hysterectomy to save her life. The in-laws called her a murderer."

"This is so sad. I had no idea." I remembered Posey smiling, cheerfully ringing up my purchases at the Circle K.

"After she recovered, she came home to Oak Falls. A small insurance settlement helped pay the bills. She went back to her maiden name. The rest of her life was spent taking care of her elderly mother, working multiple jobs, and getting into one disastrous relationship after another. Such a romantic girl—but she always picked the wrong guy. One time she confided to me that she'd given some of her savings to her new boyfriend, who promised to double it on the stock market for her. Instead, he disappeared. After he left, she fell into a depression and tried to commit suicide."

"Any family left?"

"No. Posey was an only child, and I never recall her mentioning any relatives. She had a high school girlfriend here in town…"

"Linda," I said.

"That's right. Linda." Daffy absentmindedly played with a loose thread on her sweater.

"How do you know so much about Posey?" I asked. I doubted Daffy spent that much time gossiping in Circle K.

"Didn't you know?" Posey asked. "Posey cleaned houses on the side. She came here once every two weeks for the last five years to help with the heavy cleaning—floors, windows, the kitchen, and bathrooms. That's also how she knew Sookie."

Suddenly acutely alert, I questioned, "What do you mean?"

"When Sookie needed extra help with her organizing jobs, she'd hire Posey."

I stared at Mari. Another confirmation of a link between the two dead women. "Daffy, were you surprised when Posey committed suicide on New Year's Eve?"

"Surprised? I'm flabbergasted. It's obvious to me that Posey was murdered."

I took our client's murder pronouncement with a heaping spoonful of salt, since everyone knew Daffy loved drama. Although we were pressed for time, I continued to talk to her about Posey until Mari started giving me signals to cut it short.

I stood up, then realized I hadn't looked at the skin thing on Little Man. At the last two nail clippings, the tiny Chihuahua had worn doggy clothes.

"Where is his sore?" I asked my client.

"On the side of his belly, sort of," she answered, slipping off the sweater so I could get a look.

My heart sank. A red circular lesion, slightly elevated and ulcerated. I didn't like what I saw.

"He's been scratching it with his back leg," Daffy added. "That's why it looks so bad. I can't get him to stop."

When a veterinarian sees a skin tumor, a number of possibilities immediately jump to mind from previous experience. However, it's impossible to tell for certain what you are dealing with unless the growth is biopsied—which is exactly what I told Daffy.

"But I'm flying down to Florida the day after tomorrow. I even booked my Little Man a place in the cabin with me." Her worried face betrayed her fear.

Taking a trip right now presented a terrible dilemma. If this was a mast cell tumor or squamous cell carcinoma, the faster we removed it, the better his prognosis.

As if to comment, the Chihuahua began to growl, then scratched his side. A drop of blood appeared on margin of the lesion. A quick shake scattered the drop into droplets that transformed my white coat into a Jackson Pollock painting.

"Oh. Is that…blood?" Daffy started to turn pale. Mari grabbed her arm, and I helped her to a nearby chair. Little Man, still clutched in her arms, squirmed and barked, while another drop of blood rolled down his belly.

"Close your eyes and take some deep breaths," Mari said. "Everything is fine."

"Can you give Little Man to me?" I asked Daffy.

She handed the Chihuahua to me, holding him under his front legs. The eight-pound dog's brown eyes bugged out. He seemed completely confused and surprised his mommy had given him to me. The enemy. I tucked him under my arm, positioning him over the drip design on my coat, careful to give him no target to bite.

Mari handed Daffy a glass of water and a hard candy. The color began returning to her face. "Chew the candy and take a sip of water," my assistant instructed.

We watched her do just that. "Okay, I'm feeling much better," she said. "I'm so sorry. The sight of blood sometimes…" She drank a little more water. "Dr. Kate, what would you do if he were your dog?"

That was an easy question. "Honestly, Daffy? First I'd do some preliminary tests; then I'd take that thing off as soon as possible. The pathologists will let us know if we're dealing with a malignancy and will formulate a treatment plan."

"I don't know…"

"Frankly, I'm worried that Little Man will cause it to bleed again, and you'll faint and hit your head on the floor."

"And I'm all alone here."

Mari and I looked at each other. "You might end up in the hospital."

Or worse, I thought.

"We could take him with us now," Mari suggested. "Dr. Kate, how long before the pathology report will be back?"

"Biopsy results can take from two to five days."

"Can you keep him a few days with you after surgery?" Daffy said. "I'd be too nervous he'd tear a stitch out. And I'm not sure if I can give him pills."

All of this was leading up to Little Man staying at the hospital five or more days.

"How long will you be gone?" Mari asked.

"A week. I'm spending a week by the ocean with three of my girlfriends. I'm meeting Paula in New Jersey; then we fly out together from Newark. I was so looking forward to it." Her eyes drifted back to her beloved pet, still tucked under my arm.

"In seven days when you get back, Little Man will be well along with his healing, plus we'd have our diagnosis and treatment plan in place."

Mari joined in. "Dr. Kate and I will take good care of him, Daffy."

"Oh, I know that." Her voice trembled slightly. "Well, I want to do what's best for him."

"So...?"

"Can you take him with you now? It's better, I think. Before I change my mind." Her words said one thing, but her eyes said something else.

My assistant slipped her coat on and picked up Little Man's sweater.

"Mari and I will send you a picture or a video every day, if that will help." Daffy had been one of my first clients, and I knew her Chihuahua meant the world to her. Pretty sure we needed to leave before the tears started to fall, I signaled to Mari.

We began to back up toward the front door, Mari grabbing my coat and bag. "I'll send you a consent for surgery and an estimate by email. Can you print it up, sign it, and send it back ASAP?"

"Yes." Daffy was following us, petting Little Man

and murmuring assurances to him as we inched along the corridor.

"Be good," she admonished the Chihuahua, after a final kiss on the top of his hairless head. Astonished he was leaving his home, Little Man said nothing.

I lifted his front paw and we waved goodbye.

Safely in the truck, Mari took out the large hospital cat carrier. I gently slid Little Man inside. To my amazement, he didn't protest at all. He most likely was in a state of shock.

"I'm not sure if he had his dinner," Mari said, "but just in case I poured some of his dog food in a ziplock bag."

"Good thinking," I told her. "How are we doing on time?"

"A little bit behind. We should be okay." She opened her computer and began to scroll down. In the back seat, Little Man was uncharacteristically silent.

Probably plotting his revenge.

Chapter Thirty-Two

IT TOOK ABOUT TWENTY MINUTES FOR US TO GET TO our final appointment, rechecking Chloe Ramboulle's French bulldog. Just like before, we stopped at the closed gate, buzzed the main house, and announced who we were. This time, I noticed one of the cameras mounted on the empty guardhouse swivel toward us.

The metal gates swung open, and I downshifted in anticipation of climbing the hill. It didn't look like the road had been plowed since we'd been there last. A back tire slipped a bit just as we reached the crest.

"We should have taken my SUV," Mari said.

"Yep," I agreed. Mari's vehicle had huge snow tires on it and was a lot newer that the old F-150.

"Do you have chains?"

A vision of snow chains piled in the corner of my office materialized. I had meant to put them in the truck this morning. "We should be all right. The snow hasn't started yet." Ominous clouds darkened the sky off to our left. "Let's make it quick."

When we arrived, Chloe waited in the doorway, holding her Frenchie in her arms. One of the men in black stood at attention to her right. The puppy started yipping and squirming with excitement. From

the back seat, Little Man answered the yips by barking too.

"What are we going to do with him?" Mari asked.
"Can't leave him in the truck."

I swiveled in my seat to see Little Man had shoved
his snout through the bars of the carrier door. A growl
indicated he felt like his old self.

"Guess he's joining us."

Chloe and Aldo stared at the cat carrier in my hand
as we walked up the pathway to the house.

"What's that?" the bodyguard asked, his hand
moving under his coat.

"It's a tiny dog," Chloe said. Her bulldog began to
wriggle, and Little Man yowled like a soprano.

"I'm so sorry," I told them. "This is another house-
call patient, but we're admitting him to the hospital
today. He has nothing contagious, just a wart that has to
be removed." I didn't want to go into a long explanation
of Little Man's lesion.

"We can't leave him out here in the cold," Mari said.

"Of course not!" Chloe shivered and wrapped her
coat tighter. "Bring him inside. He's so cute."

As we walked past Aldo, Little Man began to growl.

"Hey, look at the tough guy," the bodyguard said. He
lifted his hand and pointed it close to the carrier.

Little Man immediately lunged, his tooth slicing
down on Aldo's index finger.

The bodyguard screamed like a little kid. "You son
of a…"

"Stop," yelled Chloe, projecting her voice loudly like the actress she was.

"Look." Aldo held up his finger, a drop of blood pooling above the nail.

"Put some snow on it," Chloe said, ushering us inside. She slammed the front door shut and locked it, leaving Aldo banging at the door cursing.

"They're going to freeze out there," I told her.

Chloe stifled a giggle.

"Come with me." Our client raced down the hallway, her dog under her arm. Toward the back of the house she flung open a door that revealed a sumptuous bedroom, with a sleek steel-and-glass fireplace filled with glowing white crystals. "Hurry up. In here."

We found ourselves inside a massive closet larger than my whole apartment. A bank of shelves displayed her vast collection of shoes and boots. Chloe reached inside a pair of red heels and pulled out a metal fob. A section of the shelving swung open, and Chloe scooted us all inside. I thought we were getting a tour of the project Sookie had worked on. A quick slam of the door and press of the fob in her hand, and we heard bolts being thrown.

"Now no one can disturb us," Chloe said with another a giggle.

Her giggle annoyed me. Our situation didn't seem that funny. I had a horrible feeling we were locked in a safe room.

"What is this?" Mari asked her.

"It's our emergency room. My husband had it built for security. See," she gestured to a mini kitchen in the far corner with a refrigerator and microwave. "It's always kept full with food."

"This is so cool," Mari said, taking in the ultra-modern room.

I fumed in silence while my assistant glanced at everything in awe. "Can you open it now, Chloe?" I asked. "I'd like to recheck Baby. We're a little pressed for time today."

The bulldog, still under her arm, pricked his ears up at his name.

"I'd love to, but it automatically locks itself for one hour. Want some juice?"

To hell with your juice! I wanted to say. This is the kind of stunt I'd expect from a ten-year-old.

"Look." Mari pointed to the wall of monitors over the control desk. We watched Aldo kick at our truck tires while a gentle snow began to fall.

The snowstorm had started. Thanks to our client's little trick, in one hour we'd be driving back to the animal hospital during a winter storm.

"Dr. Kate, why don't we do Baby's exam in here?" Mari suggested.

Chloe stared at both of us.

"Good idea." At least Mari and I would be able to leave as soon as the hour was up. "Can you put him down so I can see him walk, please?"

The actress hesitated, then gently placed the dog

on the floor, where he proceeded to dance around his owner's legs. I detected not a trace of a limp.

"He acts like he's completely recovered," I told her. "Cindy said he's still limping a little?"

Twirling around with her dog now in her arms, she avoided my gaze. "That may have been a *petite* fib. I was bored and wanted company—and you two are so nice, and so funny."

She flashed an enchanting smile at me. One, I suspect, that usually got her what she wanted.

It didn't work on me.

Chloe had lied and made us drive all the way up here because she was bored? She twirled again, expecting to be forgiven.

I looked to my assistant for some support, but she was staring at the monitor. Aldo and his friend were no longer on the screen. The snowflakes had thickened and were falling straight down, obscuring the view of the mountains.

"Shoot," Mari said. "We're going to miss the lab pickup at this rate. That means Little Man's bloods won't go out until tomorrow."

Our prankster wasn't listening. She'd opened the fridge and was peering inside. Once again Chloe asked if we'd like anything to drink.

"I'll take an orange juice if you have it," Mari politely said. "Dr. Kate?"

Frustrated and annoyed, I moved as far away from Chloe as I could. I took Little Man in his cat carrier with me.

"She'll have a water," Mari replied.

"Of course. Anything you want. You are my guests." A clink of glass and Chloe turned with two glass bottles in her hands. "These are French. I hope you like them."

I opened my Evian while Mari tried a fizzy fruit drink. Chloe, on the other hand, popped open a bottle of champagne and poured it into a fluted glass.

Little Man yipped loudly, as though saying *no one is paying attention to me.*

"Oh, you cute little sweetie pie," Chloe said in a baby-talk voice. "Why is he in this ugly carrier?"

After seeing the look on my face, Mari spoke up. "He has a tumor that must be removed."

Chloe poured another glass of champagne. "Let's drink to his health." Without waiting for us, she downed her drink like it was water.

I checked my watch. Only fifteen minutes had passed, but it felt like an hour. I watched while Chloe poured herself another flute of champagne.

"Do we have a Wi-Fi connection in here?" I asked.

"Of course," she answered imperiously. "We are not savages."

The wall phone suddenly rang, its jarring tone echoing in the locked room.

"Allo?" Chloe pressed the receiver to her ear and turned her back to us.

We both listened, but the most she said was *"Oui"* a few times, then *"Salut"* before she hung up.

"My husband is coming home tonight instead of

tomorrow." A beautiful smile lit her face. "I am so happy!" Once again, she unselfconsciously twirled around, stopping only to pour another flute of champagne. By my reckoning she'd almost finished the bottle.

"Won't he wonder how we all ended up locked in the safe room?" Mari asked.

A delightful laugh was her response. "No, he knows I can cause mischief when I'm bored. He finds it charming."

Needless to say, the charm of our situation escaped me.

At least Mari kept the conversation going. "Has he found out what happened to his Bitcoin yet?"

"No," Chloe said, "but he will. Arthur hired some computer specialists to track it. They followed the money to somewhere in the Caribbean where they lost it for a while. But they think they know where it ended up."

That at least interested me. Rainbow told me that it could be tricky following Bitcoin through the cyber world. "Any clue as to who stole his money?"

The champagne bottle poured its final glass. Chloe held it up high, draining the last drops. "Someone in Oak Falls, I believe. Whoever it is, I feel sorry for them."

Mari frowned and asked, "Why would you feel sorry for them?"

"Because," our hostess said, "my husband is very angry. He takes his finances very seriously, and—when he's angry, he is very dangerous."

The final half hour dragged, even though Mari and Chloe talked about everything from redecorating to puppies to her last movie premiere.

I'd listened to enough banter, preferring to sit on the small love seat and scroll through my emails with Little Man next to me. For now, he lay quietly, only growling a few times for effect. He'd gone from king of his house to being a prisoner of his nemesis. Little did he know at this moment we were both trapped.

Periodically, I heard bursts of laughter from Mari, my fellow captive, but for the most part I kept working. As always, there were emails to answer from clients with questions, or updates, or approving refills of medications. I'd just finished texting Cindy when a metallic clang signaled the door was finally open.

"Freedom!" Mari said in a loud voice.

I half expected a bodyguard to be standing outside with a pointed gun, but when Chloe pushed open the door the room was empty.

Before we left, Mari paused to look at the magnificent closet. Cabinet doors of glass and wood both revealed and concealed different sections. Custom drawers mixed with open shelving, and the wardrobes were organized by color. "Every woman's dream," Mari said. "Sookie did a great job."

"Yes," Chloe agreed. "Too bad she can't do the same for our co-op in Manhattan, but my husband wouldn't have hired her back anyway."

"Sookie's dead," Mari reminded her.

Chloe kissed her French bulldog on the nose. "Yes. My husband has a terrible temper."

Mari and I dropped back as Chloe wandered out into the main house. Did we just hear her accuse her husband of murder?

My assistant started to speak, but I whispered, "Later."

Little Man moved restlessly in the improvised cat carrier. Did he need to go to the bathroom, I wondered? Daffy had slipped a harness on him, which made it easy to put a leash on the little escape artist.

"Chloe," I called out to our client, who was quite a bit ahead of us, "is there a place where I can let this Chihuahua do his business?"

"Business…ah, go wee-wee. Of course, the two boys can go together."

Following her at a brisk pace, I only hoped Little Man liked dogs more than he liked people. The snow height might be tricky for our eight-pound patient, more used to spending winters inside.

Guarding the front door was Aldo, a big frown on his face and an even bigger bandage on his finger.

"Yo, Doc. Does that mutt have his shots?"

"Yes. He's healthy and completely up-to-date on his vaccinations. Including rabies. Would you like to file a bite report? Our receptionist can provide you with the information you'll need."

"You should never have stuck your finger in front of him," Chloe said, while sticking her finger in his face.

"This is a tiny doggie. He fits in a cat box. His bite can't be that bad."

Personally, I thought someone had overdone the bandage material.

"That's what you think. It hurts real bad." He held it up again to show all of us his boo-boo.

This guy wasn't as tough as he looked.

Inside the cat carrier, Little Man shifted around again.

Chloe opened the door and pointed to an unfenced area off to the left of the pathway. "Here's where my Baby goes potty." As if to demonstrate the accuracy of her statement, the Frenchie almost jumped out of her arms, eager to lift his leg on an incongruous plastic fire hydrant about ten feet away. Snow still fell. Almost two inches topped the roof of the truck.

"My husband hates our Baby going in front of the house, but he also hates wee-wee pads. Once the winter is past, he's promised to build an internal covered courtyard, with grass and flowers, for the doggy to use." Chloe stayed under the overhang as we all watched the bulldog do his business.

From the stoic look on the other bodyguard's face, I guessed one of his duties was cleaning up dog poop.

Snowy woods stretched as far as my eyes could see. "I'm not going to risk Little Man running away," I whispered to Mari, "Let's get going."

"Chloe," Mari said, "we have to leave, but I'll send you an invoice by email, if that's all right."

"Perfect," she replied. "Aldo, go put a bottle of

champagne on ice—no, two bottles. My husband is on his way home."

Her joy felt infectious. I almost forgave her until I looked up at the gray skies and felt the wind rising.

After a brief farewell, I put the truck into low gear and started down the driveway. There were two areas I felt I had to watch out for—the first hill, which was steep and ended at a curve, and the second slope shaded by overhanging tree limbs, which might be icy.

"We should have taken my SUV," Mari said for the second time.

"Chloe shouldn't have locked us up for an hour," I answered back. "Make sure you are buckled in," I reminded her, "and Little Man, too."

The truck dug in. We'd almost made it down the second incline when a black limo appeared directly in front of us.

"Hang on," I told Mari as I carefully downshifted. There'd be no slamming on breaks in this snow unless I wanted the truck to slide off the driveway.

The driver of the limo didn't get that memo. We watched as the limo skidded in slow motion, its right rear tire catching in the runoff ditch along the driveway. There was nothing we could do but watch the limo try but fail to stop the back end from sliding into the four-foot ditch.

Almost immediately, a man leaped out of the back seat. His polished leather shoes, appropriate for Wall Street but a disaster in snow, slipped on the icy sloped driveway. He landed butt first in the snow and almost cracked his head.

Mari and I jumped out of the truck and tried to help. The limo driver opened his door and pulled a gun on us. "Don't move," he said. "Put your hands over your heads."

"You've got this wrong," I said. "I'm Dr. Kate Turner, a veterinarian. This is my assistant. Chloe called us to come look at her French bulldog. We were on our way back to Oak Falls Animal Hospital." With my hands in the air, I gestured to the sign on the driver's side panel.

"Would someone help me up?" The man on the ground was in his late thirties, quite good-looking in a rough way, and obviously used to giving orders.

"Sorry, boss." The bodyguard holstered his weapon. Mari inched over and the two of them hoisted the man off the ground. I assumed we were about to meet Chloe's husband, Arthur.

Once on his feet, he looked at the limo and said, "Crap." Planting his feet carefully in one of the tire tracks, he said, "Hello. I'm Arthur Gambino. I own this mess." He turned and smiled a million-dollar bright white smile at us. "Can we hitch a ride to the house? Please?" His thick hair was lightly dusted with snow.

"Sure. Climb in," I told them.

With both men wedged into the back seat, Little Man stuffed between them, I put the truck into reverse and carefully backed up the driveway.

Arthur took his cell phone out and left someone a

verbal message. "Have the driveway in the Woodstock house completely redone. Include an area to turn around and widen the approach to the gate."

Little Man growled at having to share the back seat.

"I'm so sorry for the gun," he said as if apologizing for a restaurant seating delay. "Both my wife and I have recently been dealing with threats," Arthur explained. "There was always a possibility you were trying to kidnap me."

A remote possibility, but I couldn't blame them for being on high alert. "No worries," I said. "I'm glad we were able to help."

Arthur turned to his bodyguard. "I'd like to kill that real estate agent who promised the driveway would be no problem in the winter."

"Sure, boss," the driver said.

"It might be a while before I can get the limo towed," Arthur said. "I'm sorry if this will delay you."

"Dr. Kate," Mari said, "we really should try to get back to the office."

As we approached the house the cleared area widened. I saw Chloe ahead framed in the doorway, waving. Better to try our luck with the driveway than risk being locked up again. A glance in the rearview mirror confirmed that Arthur seemed unconcerned about our predicament.

"We'll just drop you two off," I said to our passengers. "I'm pretty sure we can squeak past your vehicle."

As soon as we stopped, the two men clambered out

of the back seat. Arthur rushed over to his wife while the bodyguard hurried them inside. In seconds everyone had vanished behind the massive front door leaving us alone in the snow.

"This day has been a disaster," I told Mari.

Little Man barked in agreement.

For the second time that day, we started down Chloe's driveway. The snow had continued to fall this whole time, adding an additional half inch on the ground. I drove slowly and carefully, and the truck performed admirably. With Mari guiding me, we moved past the stranded limo with only inches to spare.

My hands tightly clutched the steering wheel. I didn't relax until we reached the bottom of the driveway. When the gates opened, I set off for home, the road a bit slippery with new snow but sanded and drivable. Normally, it takes about fifteen minutes to get back to the animal hospital, but tonight the trip took twice as long.

Mari cheered as the hospital sign loomed ahead. Pinky had already done a quick plow of the parking lot, for which I mentally thanked him. Cindy was long gone, and I was delighted that only Mari's truck remained in our parking lot. No police cars. No suspicious vehicles, no ex-boyfriends, just a large expanse of dark asphalt under the newly fallen snow.

"Why don't you head home?" I told Mari. "I'll be marooned here all night with Little Man. We can pull bloods in the morning."

"Thanks," she said. "It's been a very long day. I wonder if Daffy will even fly out tomorrow."

"Daffy decided to leave early because of the storm," I told her. "She's staying with her girlfriend in New Jersey. I've already received an email and a text from her, asking if Little Man is okay."

"Don't forget to send a picture," Mari admonished. "I promised her." She climbed out of the truck, taking the laptop with her.

With one hand holding my medical bag and the other holding Little Man, I bade her goodnight and told her to drive carefully.

As soon as I opened my door, the three musketeers began barking and dancing with happiness, sniffing the cat carrier holding Little Man like I'd brought tonight's hors d'oeuvres.

"Go potty," I commanded them all. Once everyone finished, I shut the door and brought Little Man into the hospital. Certain that he lived the spoiled life of a tiny dog, I did the best I could and arranged a double-sized cage with blankets and a water dish. A reasonable portion of the bag of dog food Mari had brought from Daffy's place went into a second bowl.

Although I anticipated problems transferring Little Man into the cage, he remained surprisingly coopera-tive. "Good dog," I told him, closing the cage door. He stared at me in astonishment when I took his picture and emailed it to Daffy.

Looking forward to taking my boots off and sitting

down, I went back into my apartment. I think I got as far as putting a frozen dinner in the microwave before the howling started.

You would think the animal hospital was full of coyotes singing arias by the plaintiff yowls and howls originating from Little Man. Desi raised his bass voice in agreement. After ten minutes straight, and with Buddy's tenor bark joining the chorus, I suspected Little Man had won a reprieve.

Daffy's client information included her cell phone number, which I called out of desperation.

"Dr. Kate, is everything okay?" Anxiety oozed from the receiver.

"Everything is fine," I told her. "I just want to know if Little Man sleeps in a dog bed. Also, we've got dry food for him. How often does he eat?"

There was dead silence on the other end. At first I thought I had a dropped call, but later I realized Daffy was scripting her answers.

"Well, Little Man has slept with me every day of his life, since he was a puppy," she began. "He loves to cuddle. Make sure you cover him with a blanket, or put a sweater on him at all times because he tends to get cold."

The image of me cuddling with this grumpy Chihuahua was enough to provoke a nightmare.

"As far as feeding him dog food, well, that's down all the time as a snack."

What more? I wondered.

"I usually feed him some of my food. Mostly chicken

and ground beef, with a little pasta or rice. He'll eat the tops of the broccoli but not the stems. Oh, he hates peas. Before bedtime I let him have a little saucer of beer. You know, to settle his stomach."

Too astonished to say anything else, I murmured, "Okay."

Daffy chatted away, oblivious of the fact that I was contributing nothing on my end. "Let's see. When it's really cold outside, he uses his wee-wee pads. Take them up right away because he won't use it twice. He likes ice cream as a treat, and a little vanilla yogurt first thing in the morning."

"How does he like his coffee?" I asked facetiously.

"With half and half. Don't give him too much because it revs him up and I have a hard time getting him in for his afternoon nap."

This was a dog we were talking about, I almost reminded her.

Another heart-breaking yowl rang out.

"What was that?" Daffy asked.

"Nothing. Thanks for all that information," I told her. "Have a wonderful vacation."

She sighed over the phone. "I still feel a little guilty leaving him."

"It was the right decision." I hung up before the Chihuahua and friends sang an encore.

Trying to wait him out, I gave Little Man another ten minutes of yowling before admitting defeat. The

Chihuahua would be sleeping in my apartment tonight, although I vowed not to snuggle in bed with him.

Now I'd be sharing my living space with four dogs. All dudes. I'd almost forgotten why Desi had taken up temporary residency. With the identity of the mysterious strangers as bodyguards, I didn't feel I needed a trained attack dog at my command—an attack dog afraid of a Chihuahua.

As soon as I'd taken the leash off the tiny terror, he commenced barking at all the other dogs, warning them to stay away. If they ventured near him, he nipped at their heels, forcing them to scurry back to their beds.

"No," I told Little Man. "Be nice." He looked up at me as if to say *what's the problem*? I picked him up and deposited him on his comfy bed. Reluctantly, I removed one of my soft throws and threw it over him. Immediately he tunneled around and stuck his face out of the folds.

"Sit," I told him.

Since he was under a blanket, I gave him the benefit of the doubt and offered a treat.

No interest whatsoever.

I left it in front of his nose. After putting each remaining dog through basic commands, I rewarded them with a savory treat.

Little Man was studying the other dogs from under his blanket hood as if his final exam was tomorrow and he had to cram for it. Since he and Daffy lived alone, I assumed they'd fallen into predictable patterns that long ago eliminated canine commands. Owners of little dogs often carried them around, treating them more like babies, or dolls, than dogs. My veterinary continuing education seminars on behavior taught a class on little dog syndrome—the observation that small dogs are bossy or aggressive for reasons having to do with vulnerability because of their size, all the way through inadequate socialization with other dogs or people.

For now, Little Man fit in and, more importantly, wasn't yowling.

Which meant I could get some sleep.

I glanced over at my nightstand and the small pile of Posey's notebooks, still unread. I'd marked the page I stopped at in the second notebook, *True Love Blooms*. Remembering this focused on the vampire/servant girl romance, I began to read.

She longed for his bloody vampire fangs to pierce her to the brim and beyond. His hot lust was peanut butter to her jelly.

Yikes, peanut butter and jelly again. Not an image conducive to sleep. I put the notebook down and picked up a veterinary journal. Tomorrow, I promised myself. Tomorrow I'll read about horny vampire/teachers, steamy servants, and stolen golden doubloons.

Chapter Thirty-Three

AFTER TAKING CARE OF THE WHOLE CREW OF ANIMAL guests in my apartment, I corralled Little Man and brought him with me to the animal hospital treatment room. Maybe it was the surprise, but I only got a brief protesting growl out of him.

"You two look like you're getting along," Mari said. She sat at the small table in the employee lounge, sipping her coffee and reading a dog magazine.

"We're trying," I answered, opening his cage and placing him inside.

With my second cup of coffee in hand, we sat together for a few minutes and were chatting about an article Mari had read when Cindy arrived.

"Take your time, ladies," she said, holding a granola bar in her hand. "Thanks to the weather, we've had a bunch of cancelations this morning."

That didn't surprise me. Many of our clients needed their driveways plowed out before they could safely travel. Often it was easier to reschedule their vet appointment than their plowing.

"Good. That gives me more time to work on Little Man."

Cindy raised her eyebrows. "I can't believe you pried

that dog out of Daffy's hands for a week. How did you do it?"

"Serendipity." Mari and I explained her vacation trip to Florida.

"What kind of tumor do you think it is?" Cindy asked.

"Well, I can tell you what I hope it isn't, a mast cell tumor or squamous cell carcinoma. I'm going to do a needle aspirate and check it under the microscope."

"That reminds me," Mari said. "We need to draw all his lab tests this morning. Maybe I can call the lab and order an early pickup."

"Good idea," I told her. The office phone began to ring.

"Anyone heard a weather forecast?" I asked.

"Snow," Cindy said, reaching for the phone. "More snow."

Mari held him while I drew blood from Little Man, who was still being unusually cooperative. As my assistant hugged the dog tightly to her chest, I drew a small amount of fluid from the round mass on his belly.

"Keep the gauze pressed hard against it for a few minutes," I cautioned Mari. "If it's a mast cell tumor, it's going to bleed a bit."

While Mari stayed with Little Man, I prepared a slide, stained it, and took a look at the cells under the microscope. I'm no pathologist, but I didn't see any mast cells lurking in the sample. Of course, that wasn't diagnostic, since it was only a random sample, but I felt hopeful we might soon be able to rule out that type of tumor.

The day bumped along at a slower than normal pace. Given the forecast of more snow, the lab happily arrived early to pick up our samples. That meant Little Man's surgery could proceed as early as tomorrow. I had to admit I wasn't looking forward to it. There is a vast difference between doing surgery on an eighty-pound Labrador retriever versus an eight-pound Chihuahua—plus Little Man's abdominal skin was thin and particularly transparent.

"At least you'll have a map of the vessels," Mari joked.

"Right," I answered. "But let's not forget our patient only weighs eight pounds, so every drop of blood is precious."

"We've got two big donor dogs if necessary," Mari reminded me. "Desi is registered with a veterinary blood bank, typed and cross-matched."

"If it comes down to that, which I hope it doesn't," I said, "the first transfusion should be fine. But let's think positively."

Mari nodded but added, "Hope for the best but prepare for the worst."

Mr. Katt gracefully jumped down from his perch and stared at the Chihuahua. It looked like they were preparing to rumble.

"Can you check the surgical packs and make sure we sterilize some small hemostats?"

In medicine, there's a grim saying that all bleeding eventually stops. Although removing the mass on Little Man's belly was a relatively minor procedure, I agreed with Mari. Better to be overprepared.

As if adding his approval, Little Man gave out one of his otherworldly yowls.

While we went about our day, Little Man's expressive eyes caught mine at every opportunity, followed by a low yip. As part of his escape plan his front paws tried to dig their way through the stainless steel cage.

It didn't help that Mr. Katt had positioned himself directly in front of the Chihuahua's cage, taunting him.

"Leave him alone," Mari told the big fluffy cat. As if personally insulted, Mr. Katt gave us a dirty look, skillfully jumped first on the countertop then to the top of the upper cabinets, where he fastidiously groomed his paws and glowered at us.

Finished with Little Man for now, I took him out of his hospital cage and brought him back to my apartment. He greeted the other dogs then proceeded to tell them in a doggy yodel about his adventures. I retreated to my office to catch up on some paperwork. I'd been at it for about twenty minutes when Mari stuck her head in. "I've got a health certificate for travel and vaccination update in exam one."

"Be right there," I said. It used to be that traveling with a pet was pretty straightforward. Now, however, each airline sets requirements for travel. There are breed restrictions, cabin restrictions, temperature restrictions, length of time from last rabies shot—not to mention the complicated international rules, made even worse with Brexit.

Most veterinarians suggest that owners verify for themselves travel guidelines for their pet. I logged off and went to examine my patient.

When I opened the door, I got a surprise.

"Hi, Dr. Kate," Elaine said to me. "How have you been?"

"Good," I told her. I realized although I'd listened to Elaine's lectures, this was the first time I'd spoken one-on-one with Sookie's replacement. "Mari said you need a travel health certificate?" On the stainless steel exam table, an unusual dog slowly wagged its plume of a tail. Elaine was the owner of a Chinese crested dog, the hairless variety, a breed devoted to their owners. Her pet had long, white-fringed fur on its ears, feet, and tail paired with a dark-skinned, hairless body.

"What's your name, sweetheart?" I asked, letting her sniff my fingers.

Elaine came over and stroked her ears. "Her AKC name is Ling's Crested Wonder, but I call her Ling Ling. I socialized her right from a puppy, so she's very friendly."

"She's adorable and so well behaved," Mari said. "Dr. Kate, Ling Ling has normal vitals and, according to Elaine, no health issues."

"And she's how old?" I paused for the answer before putting my stethoscope to her chest.

"Only three," Elaine answered.

The exam on this interesting breed showed no health issues. Since each pure breed is prone to certain problems, I carefully looked at Ling Ling's retinas, teeth, and overall body conformation.

"She doesn't occasionally hop, or hold one leg up?" I asked, looking for the signs of a kneecap problem.

"No. She's a fast little runner."

A look at her teeth and down her throat revealed a correct scissors bite and healthy mouth. All other systems, including cardiovascular, seemed fine.

I decided to address a common problem in small dogs. "Is she house-trained?"

Elaine smiled. "Perfectly. She mostly goes inside in the winter. I put wee-wee pads down, and she never misses."

I made a mental note. If I ever had any extra money, I would buy stock in the company that makes wee-wee pads.

The small dog relished all the attention.

"Here's a suggestion," I said. "Put the wee-wee pad inside a large litter box pan. Encourage Ling Ling to step in and do her business. The pan confines the urine to one spot and makes cleanup much easier."

"Great idea," the owner said.

"So, I need to know when you are leaving, where you are going, and what airline you are using. It's a direct flight, I hope?"

"Yes. First we're driving to Virginia to visit my cousin. Then we'll be flying to LA," Elaine informed us. "I've already got her place reserved in the cabin."

"What about your pet carrier?" Mari chimed in. "There are size restrictions so it will fit under the airplane seat, if I remember correctly."

She pulled a folder from her purse, with a copy of the airline's pet policies. The company logo was prominently displayed, as was its web address. "Will this help?"

I was impressed with how thorough and organized Elaine was. Since her vaccines were all up-to-date, the only shot Ling Ling needed was her rabies booster.

"Remember to keep within the time guidelines posted by your airline," I reminded Elaine. Most animal health certificates must be issued within ten days of travel. She seemed to have benefited from her association with the late Sookie Overmann.

Mari held for the rabies vaccine, which Ling Ling barely felt. After turning the dog over to Elaine, she asked, "Does this mean you're not doing any more organizing seminars?"

"I'm finishing the last one in the contract," she confessed. "But Glenn has been such a…jerk…about everything, I decided to move and leave all the unpleasantness behind."

Since I'd seen Glenn Overmann in action, I could only imagine what Elaine had gone through. I was trying to figure out some way of asking her about the Bitcoin theft, but Mari beat me to it.

"Sookie's name came up yesterday when we visited Chloe Ramboulle. She was quite pleased with her closet renovation."

"That was all Sookie. Chloe was her private client. I didn't even get a chance to see the place." On her careful face, I caught a shade of annoyance.

"Was that part of your contract?" I asked. "You had your jobs, and she had hers?"

Elaine stroked her dog's hairless back. "My employment contract didn't exactly say much. I was hired as a general company employee only. My job was sort of to come in after the design phase and make sure everything ran smoothly."

"I think that's the hard part," Mari interjected. "Coordinating all the tradespeople. When I renovated a bathroom a couple of years ago, it was a nightmare."

"You have to have a lot of patience," Elaine said. "But don't be a pushover. Even a plumber needs a deadline."

"Don't get me started on plumbers," Mari said.

One other thing puzzled me. "Why did you choose LA?"

"Sunshine, the ocean, and an influencer opportunity I couldn't pass up."

Call me old-fashioned, but I still couldn't fathom a profession like influencer. It seemed to me the Internet was a restless thing, gobbling up the new and spitting out the old. However, Elaine seemed happy, and who was I to question her choice?

"Are you working on anything else?" Mari asked. "Something I could subscribe to?"

Elaine hesitated. "I will be cleaning online if you want to join me."

Busy filling in the travel forms, I only heard a snippet of their conversation. It didn't make any sense.

"What did you say?" I asked, pressing Print on the office laptop, which would send health certificate copies to the receptionist's printer.

"I'll be cleaning various parts of my new place for my subscription audience," she said. "The introductory price is fifteen dollars a month. That doesn't include private sessions and requests." Her smile appeared genuine, eager to launch this new endeavor.

Except for the fact I still didn't understand.

When I glanced over at Mari, she simply shrugged.

"Do you mind explaining what exactly you do for your…members? Is this some kind of seminar?" My mind still hadn't wrapped around how she made any money.

She blushed. "I'm going to be cleaning my home, online. Many people get pleasure out of watching someone clean, or they like to clean along."

"Viewers pay to watch you vacuum your rug?"

"Certainly. Of course, they pay more if you vacuum in your underwear." This time her smile was much more confident. "Sookie had an OnlyFans account with around four hundred people watching her from around the world. That generated six thousand dollars a month, minimum. I helped her run it. With special requests, like bathrooms, she easily boosted it up an additional five hundred."

A quick math calculation added up to seventy-two thousand plus a year. No wonder she wanted to dump Glenn.

Elaine seemed to warm up to her topic. "Some men like to watch a larger woman eat, or sit on a cake— You wouldn't believe how you can make money on the Internet."

This topic was making me uncomfortable. "Do you have any other questions for me?" I asked her. "Is Ling Ling a good traveler?"

"She sure is," her owner said, giving the dog a hug. "She curls up and goes right off to sleep."

"Maybe you could get Ling Ling her own show," Mari said. I thought I detected a whiff of sarcasm.

"What a great idea," Elaine said enthusiastically.

I could see the possibility of more money brighten her eyes. Cleaning house with your dog. Ling Ling shook her head, her long ear fringe reminiscent of blond hair floating in the California sea breeze.

Back in the treatment room, I asked in disbelief, "Does that sound like an odd career choice?"

Mari poured a half-cup of coffee and peeled open a granola bar. "At first I kind of got the creeps just thinking about it." She took a bite and added, "Then I began to wonder how I'd feel emptying the dishwasher in a bikini."

"Cold?"

She laughed. "Enough said."

"Agreed." Sometimes you can share too much.

―――――――

Early the next morning, the rest of Little Man's lab work came in, and everything looked good. For an older Chihuahua, he appeared in extremely good health. Mari clicked his leash onto his thin blue harness and put him on the floor. I took a few pictures to send to Daffy, and we patiently waited for him to use his wee-wee pad. I'd taken all the food up after his six o'clock dinner. Little Man yipped when I placed him in the hospital cage with no breakfast.

"Did I tell you he acted like the king of the hill last night?" I said to Mari. "Even Desi stepped back and let Little Man have his say."

"That doesn't surprise me. A lion's heart in the body of a mouse."

"If I squint my eyes a little, he sort of looks like a mouse. Pointed nose, big ears."

Mari laughed. "That's why he thinks he's the big cheese."

We had a few more clients, but the reception area cleared out by lunchtime. Dark clouds rolled in around noon, and the outside temperature took a nosedive. Once again, snow was predicted for the Hudson Valley.

Blowing winds meant unpredictable drifts of snow. At noon, a travel advisory was announced starting around three p.m. and continuing until three a.m. the next day.

"Sometimes I wonder why I don't move to Florida," Cindy said, eating yet another salad for lunch. A native of Oak Falls, she and her husband always tried to get away for two weeks in winter, either to Florida or on a cruise to the Caribbean.

"Because of our other three beautiful seasons," I reminded her. "Besides, Florida battles hurricanes and flooding and humidity."

"But they get to battle it in shorts and flip-flops," Mari added.

"Funny, Mari." Cindy took out her fork and dug in. "I can dream, can't I?"

Mari and I prepped for Little Man's surgery. Whatever the biopsy showed, I was going to make sure there were wide margins around the tumor. I didn't want the pathologists to say I needed to go back into surgery because abnormal cells extended past the margin of the sample.

Things went smoothly once our tiny Chihuahua went under anesthesia. Using electrocautery to limit bleeding, I carefully made a large incision, removing the mass and at least another inch and a half on all sides. With an eye to creating minimal scarring, I created a neat closure using my pink suture material. To protect the surgical site, we outfitted our patient with a lightweight foam collar. On his back paws were a pair of soft booties. I didn't want him to bother the incision site by swiping it with his toenails.

As soon as he was sitting up in his cage, I snapped a picture and texted it to Daffy. She'd been a wreck, she said, but was glad that the surgery was over. To prove her statement, she sent us a selfie of her and her girl-friends in matching straw hats drinking icy margaritas in front of a marina filled with sailboats.

Cindy poked her head in. "The remaining appoint-ments for this evening canceled or rescheduled," she said. "That means a shorter workday for everyone."

"Not me," I told both of them. "I'll be babysitting Little Man."

"I think this is the beginning of a beautiful friend-ship," Cindy said with a laugh.

A half hour later, all the countertops were clean, medical waste disposed of, and our surgical log updated. The surgical instruments had been washed with soap and hot water and were ready to be sterilized. A hint of lemon lingered in the treatment room air.

"Go on home, Mari," I told my assistant. "I'll finish up what's left."

"You sure?"

"Yep. Do you want to take Desi with you? I'm not sure I need him anymore." Learning that the two thugs at Elaine's lecture were Chloe's bodyguards, and not connected to dogfighting in New Jersey, made me feel silly for jumping to conclusions.

"Can I leave him here for a few more days? I didn't realize that Lucy needed a break. She's more relaxed without him always trying to distract her. Plus, I have an excuse to concentrate on her and the puppies."

"Fine with me. The more the merrier, sort of."

I walked my friends out to the reception area. Snowflakes already thickened the sky, sticking to windshields and car hoods. As Mari and Cindy drove away, I closed and locked the animal hospital and set the alarm.

With the storm moving in, I anticipated having only animal companions this evening. Since it was relatively early, maybe I'd have time to finish Posey's notebooks. I had to admit I'd started to wonder how her book ended.

And whether she knew who killed Sookie the Sorceress.

Chapter Thirty-Four

Back in my apartment, I helped Little Man crawl into the safety of his large cat carrier. Buddy lounged on his dog bed upside down. Mr. Pitt sprawled on the floor chewing his moose toy, and Desi stared up at me. I figured he'd heard Mari and assumed he'd be going home.

After a few treats and plenty of attention everyone settled, dozing comfortably. The storm slammed some overgrown branches up against the kitchen window and rattled the panes. Only Desi, still new to my apartment, paid any attention. Doc Anderson had bought a backup generator for the hospital several years ago, so I didn't worry about losing power. Food wouldn't be a problem either. I'd taken Elaine's advice from the organizing lectures and gone on a supermarket shopping spree, loading up on soups, veggies, and frozen fruit for smoothies. A small mountain of canned goods, chips, peanuts, and chocolate took up the back of the pantry.

Again, a little memory of Luke and me weathering a storm cropped up. Cuddled together on the...

Sabotaged by my own brain, I stood up, made some tea, and fished out half an oatmeal raisin cookie from my cookie stash. On the kitchen table sat two veterinary journals and an old Agatha Christie mystery. I'd already glanced at the electronic versions of my medical journals and knew the Christie mystery backwards and forward. Then I remembered Posey's notebooks. I'd promised myself I'd finish them, so I picked them up from the nightstand and made room on the kitchen table.

I'd been reading them in order and jotting down a few things as I read to help jog my memory. So far, all I had was a list of character names and the basic plot.

One thing I did find odd was how Posey added new characters. Often, they appeared with no introduction; only after several paragraphs did we learn who the new character was.

The last page read in the second notebook was easy to find. So far, the servant and the tutor/vampire were still hatching a plot to steal money from the duke. Pansy, it was revealed, had some sort of secret connection to royalty, which is why she felt entitled to her share of the gold. The tutor, Count Grazanski, taught the duke's children by day and transformed into a vampire by night. Every three pages, it seemed, Pansy and the vampire had a romantic tryst. The couple's ultimate plan was to change Pansy/Posey into a vampire and fly away into the night with a big pile of stolen gold.

Count Grazanski held my tender heart in his hands, my poor achy and perhaps breaky heart, that yearned for his caress.

Wait. Did Posey just borrow a very famous Billy Ray Cyrus lyric?

I assumed the vampire didn't actually hold her heart in his hands, only metaphorically. Trying to finish my tea before it got cold, I stopped reading, poured some more tea, and consulted my notes. I'd taken a guess and paired up the fictional characters with real people from Oak Falls. The servant Pansy stood for Posey. Count Grazanski might be Glenn, and the way the sorceress died sounded a lot like Sookie. So far, it appeared that Posey deliberately paired up the first letter of her book characters' names with the real names of the people she knew. But I didn't find any match to Elaine yet.

Unbeknownst to the powerful sorceress who brought Pansy to the duke's mountaintop castle, the servant vowed to search for the key to the golden coins. Her quest was righteous, for she knew the duke and his family to be black-hearted thieves.

I was starting to recognize more patterns in Posey's story. The mountaintop castle likely referred to Chloe Ramboulle's home up on the mountain, which real-life Posey had visited. Was the duke supposed to be Arthur, Chloe's husband? Could I make a giant leap and assume that the theft of the golden coins referred to the missing Bitcoins?

Chief Garcia would never believe any of it. I'm not sure I did either.

I kept reading, looking for clues as the story progressed. Another new character appeared on the next page. The wizard, dressed in black, asks many questions of the couple, but the servant suspects the wizard lusts over the vampire. Even some of the ladies in the court have designs on the handsome vampire teacher, who never seems to get around to teaching anyone anything academic.

Who did I know whose name started with a *W*?

I reminded myself that thinking fictional characters might stand for real people was mere speculation. Not every character represented someone in Oak Falls, so I shouldn't jump to conclusions—especially wrong conclusions.

Sipping my fresh cup of tea, I went back to the story. Many people stood in the way of true love, forcing Pansy and her vampire to fight for their love. At one point, the sorceress forbids their union. But as in fairy tales, the sorceress, who is described more as a witch, is struck to the ground, her feet left sticking out of the bushes similar to the Wicked Witch of the West in *The Wizard of Oz*.

And very much like Sookie.

I supposed imitation is the height of flattery. If so, Posey flattered plenty of authors in her notebooks. But what about outright theft? Or plagiarism? There also were similarities between Posey's couple going at it like bunnies and a certain extremely popular Netflix costume drama, also set in jolly old England.

Pansy's rounded orbs hung like clusters of purple grapes, ripe and ready to be plucked. Her vampire lover's manhood pointed the way.

That grape cluster reference didn't seem very flattering. I started the third notebook, called *The Quest for Justice*. The vampire and the servant got it on for a few pages, then finalized their plan to steal the duke's gold. In the dead of night, the vampire flies into the castle through an open turret window. The count put his magical undead skills to use by sending the doubloons soaring into the sky like a golden fountain, to rematerialize in their new home far away. The servant, Pansy, now also a vampire, is vindicated in her quest for her inheritance. After another sexy encounter using their wings in surprising ways, the lovers fly away cloaked by the darkness of the waning moon. *THE END*

I was puzzled because there were plenty of pages full of notes left in her notebook after the ending.

After flipping past a few scribbled pages, I noticed a description of the sorceress. Posey had written the words "add modern clothes," and underlined it several times. She now described the character as having a short silk robe, camouflaging a black modern suit, closed with shiny obsidian buttons. On the sorceress's feet were black snakeskin boots.

Sookie wore boots and a black suit the night she was murdered.

On the following page was a brief mention of the duke. Dark-haired, handsome, and arrogant, he wore a gold bracelet and necklace. Always surrounded by guards sworn to fight to the death to protect him, he was difficult to approach. There were more suggestions for describing the palace—soaring ceilings and buttresses, glass, and perched on a mountaintop. A bridge over a moat protected his privacy.

Except for the bridge and moat, it still sounded like Chloe Ramboulle's estate.

A funny note said "Add Aliens!!!!" with several exclamation points.

On the next-to-last page of the third notebook, Posey described the local pub where most of the characters—except the duke, of course—hung out. It had beat-up wooden tables, a large open kitchen, and a spit for roasting meat turning over a wood fire, plus endless glasses of mead. The owner of the tavern was a large woman who brandished a wooden spoon, using it to smack customers who got out of line. Jude was the woman's name, and few dared cross her.

Jude?

It wasn't a far stretch to think this was Judy, the owner of my favorite café in town. Mari and Cindy had told me many stories about Judy, who single-handedly threw some guy out who was making racist remarks during lunch. One of their tales included brandishing a wooden spoon.

I sat up.

Another character possibly based on a real person. Another character whose first name started with the real person's initial.

At seven a.m., my alarm rang. Before I even got out of bed, I received a text from Cindy.

GLENN OVERMANN HAS BEEN
ARRESTED FOR SOOKIE'S MURDER

An odd feeling of relief was my first reaction. Relief that a man like Glenn would finally be held accountable. Everyone who knew the couple knew how abusive he was. So why did I keep thinking about Posey's notebook that described the servant smiting the sorceress?

Without any goading or licking from the dogs, I slipped out of bed, pulled my boots and coat on over my pajamas, and let the big dogs out for their run. Little Man, however, made do inside with his wee-wee pad. This morning he appeared alert and feisty, his normal behavior. Since his tissue sample had gone out before the storm hit, we wouldn't have to wait too long for his results.

The three larger dogs romped in the fenced-in run, scooting in the snow and generally making a mess.

A double-tap honk sounded close by. Pinky drove down the driveway, his plow lifted up and packed with snow. A mounted shotgun rack was visible in his rear window. Most likely he'd been plowing all night. As always, he'd done a great job with the animal hospital parking lot.

In response to his honk, I raised my hand and waved. He blinked his lights as a hello just before his commercial-sized double garage door opened and he disappeared inside.

"Come on, boys," I told the dogs, who obediently came running. I checked everyone's feet and rubbed each with a towel before they went back inside.

Of course, Little Man started yapping and tried to direct traffic. The other dogs gently nudged him out of the way. Mr. Pitt sweetly licked the top of the Chihuahua's head.

When my phone pinged again, I assumed Cindy had another update for me. It was an update, all right, but not from my receptionist.

BACK IN TOWN FOR THE WEEKEND
MISS YOU. XXXXXXXX
WANT CHINESE TAKEOUT TONIGHT?
MY TREAT. LUKE

I sank into the sofa feeling like I'd been sucker punched. How many times had we eaten Chinese takeout here in my place after work? We'd laughed and argued and I'd fallen in love with him. He'd met Gramps, met my friends; I'd met his family. For a short while, our relationship was my warm blanket, my go-to place, a reliable constant.

I stared at the television's black screen.

What happened to the girl you met in school, Luke? Did

she dump you? Am I the girl on the bench being called in as
a last-minute replacement?

Cindy said Luke's a great guy, but he's not ready to commit to one person. Well, I'd found out the hard way my girlfriend was right. Strike three. Game over.

One text didn't change anything, didn't let him walk in and out of someone else's life.

> BUSY THIS WEEKEND
> I'M SURE YOU'LL FIND SOMEONE
> TO SHARE TAKEOUT WITH, BUT
> IT'S NOT GOING TO BE ME

Hitting Send felt great. In a rush of energy, I fed the dogs, took a quick shower, got ready for work, and high-fived my mirror. Later on, I expected I'd have second thoughts, but right then I felt invincible.

My happy morning greeting to Cindy and Mari caught them off-guard.

"What happened to you?" Mari asked.

"All is right with the world," I said.

A box of mixed pastries sat open on the employee lounge countertop. "My fault," Cindy said. "The hubby brought them home, and I needed them gone."

"So you dumped them here for us to eat?" Mari acted annoyed. "Well, thanks for the five extra pounds, Cindy."

Cindy showed no remorse. Mari always protested, but somehow the food all got eaten—and she never seemed to gain an ounce.

I picked out a small croissant and poured a cup of coffee. Biting into the buttery goodness, I hit an almond surprise. No complaints here.

"What do you think about the arrest this morning?" Cindy asked. Although she'd brought in the high-calorie treats, she only nibbled the broken-off tip of an apple cruller.

Mari took a sip of coffee and remarked, "Frankly, I'm astonished it didn't happen sooner."

"The chief moved forward slowly," Cindy explained, "because he had witnesses contradicting each other, and of course, Glenn, appeared to have an alibi."

"Alibi, schmalibi." Mari didn't seem impressed. "Right from the beginning, I knew it was him."

"What do you think, Kate?" Cindy looked my way. "Was offering the twenty-thousand-dollar reward a part of his cover-up?"

"Maybe." Breakfast tasted great. Life was great. I didn't care about Glenn at all.

Cindy continued. "Well, we'll have the entire length of his trial to figure things out. Now we can concentrate on other, more important things."

"Like?"

"What color uniforms we should order for the springtime?"

I was surprised Mari didn't scream out "Nooooo!"

You would think ordering hospital uniforms would be an easy task. Not here. It took six months of discussion about fabric blends and styles and pockets for us to settle on gray for our winter uniforms. Spring meant pastels. Pastels were tough. Pink, pale yellow... Mari's eyes lifted skyward while mine headed in the opposite direction.

Out in reception, I noticed our bulletin board had doubled in size.

"It's all the post-Thanksgiving and Christmas pocket pets," Cindy said. "Hamsters that don't like being held, rats that give someone a rash, and all sorts of lizards, snakes, and frogs that turn out to be too much work."

This came as no surprise. It's fun and educational for children to be exposed to some pocket pets, but often the prospective owners have no idea how much work it can be. Terrariums in particular need to be large enough to provide an enriched environment and a variety of hiding places. Some lizards, like iguanas, need a more tropical climate, while desert dwellers such as horned toads prefer a drier environment.

We tried to steer our clients toward rescue and shelters, which provide quite a bit of practical education to someone wanting to adopt or foster.

My eye perused the notices. The large color picture Colin posted of his iguana was still there. No one had taken any of the phone numbers at the bottom. The big lizard, almost four feet long, was named Masher.

Lizards and mice were not on my mind when I walked into Judy's and straight into another informal going-away party for Colin. Three tables in the back were crammed together, and at least ten people appeared to be boisterously enjoying themselves. Some of the women I recognized, but others I assumed were fellow artists who worked at the Hay Barn Gallery.

I'd just given Judy my takeout order when someone called my name.

"Kate, come join us." Colin shouted out.

Judy finished writing everything down. "Go ahead. I'll let you know when your order is done."

Although I only knew Colin and perhaps one other woman, I joined the group. In a quick series of introductions, which I promptly forgot, Colin put names to the faces. Sitting next to me, opposite Colin, a middle-aged man lifted a briefcase onto his lap and snapped it shut.

"Kate," Colin said, "this is my agent, Serghi Davinoff."

"Nice to meet you," I said. "Will you be staying long?"

"I'm actually on my way out," the man said, standing up. "From here I go to Albany for a few days, then drive back to help load Colin's work into the van and transport it to Manhattan."

"Then does it get mailed out to Finland?" I honestly had no idea how paintings or artworks were sent internationally.

A ripple of polite laughter followed my question.

"Hardly. Everything is brought to my warehouse. Then each piece will be professionally photographed and uploaded into an electronic catalog and a hard copy glossy printed."

"How old school," someone commented.

The agent shrugged his shoulders. "Somebody always wants one. Anyway, the Helsinki opening will be presented in multiple forms—virtual, streaming; the gallery owner also wants some holograms. Holograms are big in Europe."

I nodded in agreement at that statement, having no idea if it was true or not.

"Then it's up to graphics to generate our advertising and public relations products."

"Helsinki's got a few informal photos I sent, but none of the finished works," Colin added.

"When do you actually leave, Colin darling?" a dark-haired woman wearing huge silver earrings and dressed in black asked. Her voice had a Bostonian flatness. "It seems we've been saying goodbye for weeks."

Colin joined in on the subdued laughter. "Ask Serghi. He's in charge of my travel arrangements."

The agent patted down his jacket pockets. "You ladies have him for another six, maybe seven days at the most. We've got a few details to iron out, but for now he's booked on the red-eye Saturday evening from NYC on Finnair. Let's keep our fingers crossed nothing changes before then. I already had to reschedule once."

Someone said they envied the artist's life. I felt the same. Colin's life rolled along like a movie or a limited-edition television program.

"Dr. Kate…" said the good-looking young man to

my left. He wore a hand-knit sweater matched with designer jeans. "I'm Wyatt. Wyatt Cressan."

Where had I heard that name? Wait, was this Glenn Overmann's mysterious lover?

At a loss for what to say, I simply said, "Nice to meet you."

"Thanks for taking care of Babykins. Isn't she a sweetheart?" he asked. Not pausing for a response from me, he kept talking. "Glenn is such a turd about taking care of a cat. I would have volunteered, but we were going through a rough patch—what with the murder and everything." He lifted his chin up and crossed his legs as if he were talking about the weather. Around his neck, a thin cashmere muffler draped itself beautifully.

"Someone said Glenn had been arrested?" I wondered how Wyatt felt about his boyfriend going to jail.

He stroked the end of his muffler shifted his weight, and took a sip of red wine. I noticed I wasn't the only one listening carefully for Wyatt's answer.

"I'm not worried," he stated. "Glenn said he didn't do it, and I believe him, although I wouldn't blame him if he did. After Sookie wrecked our finances, I felt like bashing her in the head myself."

The woman with the silver earrings opened her eyes wide, shocked.

Wyatt simply laughed, a loud braying sound—a sound that I'd heard before. Where?

"Don't forget to pack up that final piece," Serghi reminded Colin just before he walked away. "Keep the fans on it. It should be dry by the time I get back. No last-minute touch-ups!"

"Cross my heart," Colin said. "That's the only one left to crate up." He rose to give his agent a hug. "Have a good trip."

Some of the others joined in and waved goodbye.

Colin took his seat again and said, "My one problem now is rehoming Felicia's iguana that she dumped on me. Any takers? It comes with a terrarium and a bunch of lizard stuff."

"You don't make that iguana sound very attractive," an older woman said. "What's its name and how old is it?"

For some reason Colin looked toward me. I'd barely glanced at the poster he'd given Cindy. When I shrugged my shoulders, he continued. "Its name is Masher. Felicia had him for about six years, I think. He likes women and he doesn't bark."

Wyatt laughed at the joke—a very distinctive braying laugh.

"What do you feed him, Colin?" another person at the table asked.

"Iguana food."

"You must supplement it with leafy greens, fruits, calcium sources..." I began.

"That too."

"What will you do if you can't find anyone to keep him?" someone asked.

Running his hand through his thick hair, Colin explained that the local shelter had agreed to take him, as a last resort. "Someone called last night. Maybe they'll take him," he added.

Changing topics, we talked a bit about travel, with one of the women mentioning seeing the Northern lights and sleeping in an igloo Airbnb in Norway. Someone else regaled us with stories of exploring Machu Picchu. Their adventures seemed so exotic.

Judy came over to tell me my order was ready, so I excused myself. The conversation at the table barely stopped.

"Sorry to see him go," Judy told me as she rang up my bill. "He's certainly been good for business."

"What do you mean?" I asked.

"He eats here a couple of times a week," she said. "The studio he sublet is close by, about two blocks away. And Colin's usually got company, if you get my drift."

Looking back at the group still talking to him, I saw what she meant. "Did he happen to know Sookie?" I asked her.

"Sure. They were hot and heavy for a while. There were several others, Posey too, I think, but that was short-lived. Too clingy, I'd suspect. Colin's a lot of fun, but ultimately he's not interested in a serious relationship. Which is okay."

"I suppose so..."

"It's the romantics who have a problem with someone like him. They think he's their knight in shining armor—but instead he breaks their hearts." Judy looked over my shoulder at Colin's table. "But I guess every person needs to experience one Colin in their life. As long as they survive it in one piece."

Judy's brown eyes stared up at me. Forty or so years of experience, some hard years, had lined her eyes and forehead. She ran both a restaurant and catering business and sponsored many community programs. There was no Mr. Judy in the picture.

"I think you're right," I said. "Thanks for the advice."

As I walked along Main Street toward my truck, I thought about Colin and then Luke. There were times I felt that little shards of myself were being chipped away in my relationship with Luke. Taking control and turning down his Chinese takeout offer felt as though I'd picked up a sliver of my self-respect and hot-glued it back on.

Rainbow and I officially dissolved our brief business partnership over the phone. With Glenn now a murder suspect and under arrest, the possibility of reward money vanished. An investigation into a Bitcoin theft of multiple millions was completely out of my league. I wanted to make sure Rainbow had no other schemes in mind.

"Sorry it didn't work out."

"Sure. I understand. Besides, I've got to concentrate on raising funds for my start-up. There are friends in California who want me to join them."

Rainbow sounded fearless, but I suspected much of it was an act.

"How are you getting on with Posey's journals?" she continued. "If you don't want them, maybe my mom will take them off your hands—she and Posey being best friends and all. I'll ask her."

"That's a good idea. Maybe we can have lunch before you go?" I said.

"Great. Oh, I've got a vet question for you. What do you know about iguanas?"

"Iguanas?"

Over the phone I could feel her giving me the eye roll. "Yeah. This great-looking guy is giving his iguana away, and I wanted to know how difficult it is to keep them. Do they eat mice?" She made a cringing noise over the receiver.

"No mice. They're primarily herbivores. There are several balanced commercial diets available, but it should be supplemented with a lot of greens, leaves, some fruits…and they need a temperature-controlled habitat, unless you live in Florida."

"Sounds too complicated. I'm going to be sleeping on my friend's sofa in Marina del Rey. Too bad, the guy was super hunky."

There couldn't be that many hunky men in Oak Falls hawking iguanas.

"You must mean Colin," I said.

"Yeah. You know him?"

"I've met him. We danced a few times at the New Year's party. Remember the night you caught a ride with Luke and me?"

"Wow. That's right. It feels like such a long time ago. I'm afraid I was a little out of it that night. Too much partying before the party," she laughed.

That, I could attest to. But Rainbow was right in one respect. It did seem like a long time ago—a very long time ago.

After hanging up, I got the dogs walked, situated, and bedded down. With all the daily dog chores I now handled, it felt like I was running a kennel. Even though I wanted to relax in front of the television, I picked up book number three of Posey's notes and thumbed to the last few pages. Past THE END, I continued to the last few pages of the notebook where I found more disjointed entries, full of notes and suggestions for Volume Four, *The Epilogue*.

Epilogue? Did I miss a notebook when I fished them out of the Circle K dumpster?

I picked up the black marbled notebooks again and counted what I had, clearly labeled One, Two and Three. If there was a Volume Four, it probably was long gone.

The last two pages of Volume Three had more random notes, as if Posey was gathering her thoughts, jotting ideas down for later use. *Add a dragon*, she'd written. *Green scales, forked tongue, and spitting fire. Give Sorceress a strange-looking animal she channels through. Maybe cat/dog/pony?*

At the very bottom of the page, she scrawled another cryptic note.

They hide their forbidden love along with the golden treasures, waiting for the stroke of midnight to steal away into the forgiving night before all was lost—and they die by the duke's enchanted sword. Danger lurks within.

Her story sounded like a movie script. Maybe Posey mixed fact and fiction and these notebooks meant nothing. A yawn and then another signaled time to sleep.

It was frustrating to think there was more to be revealed in Volume Four, wherever that was— probably in the middle of the landfill. A slight headache began to brew as I put the notebooks aside and turned off the light.

Stress often makes me dream. As I fell into a restless sleep, a headless knight on horseback charged toward me, hooves pounding on an asphalt parking lot. In the dream a huge book, skewered by his bloody lance, wriggled on the sharp steel like a living thing. Page after page ripped away from the binding and fell to the ground. Each page soundlessly screamed *Epilogue!*

Chapter Thirty-Five

I AWOKE TO A SURPRISE FROM MOTHER NATURE—AN impossibly bright, sunny day. Sunbeams bounced off snow, the many ice crystals sparkling with attention. But after too much of a good thing, snow everywhere started melting, dripping and, with no warning, sliding off the hospital roof.

Our office phone rang like crazy as Mari and I took time to bring Little Man into the treatment area to change his dressing. His stitches looked clean, not a lot of crusting, and the best news was that the Chihuahua was leaving the surgery site alone.

"You haven't seen him try to scratch, have you?" I asked her.

"Nope. He's even leaving his booties on."

"Hmm," I said, looking at the Chihuahua temporarily housed in an upper-level cage. "Maybe because Daffy dresses him up so much?" My instincts told me to keep him under close observation. "Here you are," I told the little dog, giving him a fairly large chew bone. I wanted to keep him busy and safe and quiet during office hours.

We were finishing up the day when Mari reminded me it was Wednesday, and tonight was the final lecture of

our home-organizing course. To tell the truth, I'd completely forgotten. I'd made a stab or two of following
through with some suggestions but quickly had slid
back to my bad habits.

"Do you want to meet us there?" Mari asked.

"I suppose so." From my voice, she knew I was less
than enthusiastic. "Six o'clock? Save me a seat?"

Since I didn't want to leave Little Man alone yowling
in the hospital, I anchored a pet gate to my bathroom
door. Surrounded by his personal belongings, the small
dog could interact with the bigger dogs on his terms
while I wasn't home. Desi took one look, grunted, and
went back to his chew toy. Little Man perched on his
bed, actively guarding his growing pile of stolen toys.
Mr. Pitt walked over, and the two dogs touched noses
with a minimum amount of growling on Little Man's
part. With canine peace established, I put on a clean
pair of jeans and a cheap pair of UGG lookalikes.
Hoisting my backpack over my shoulder, I climbed into
the truck and carefully drove to the community center.
Once again, the parking lot was full. This time I parked
in the third-row center, in line with the one functioning
camera over the main door.

I wasn't anticipating any trouble, but being seen in
the camera lens was a good thing.

People were still streaming into the auditorium as I
slipped off my coat. A quick overview of the room showed
Mari and our baking friend Henry James chatting away in
the fifth row. It looked like they'd saved a seat for me.

I picked my way along the row, dodging purses, coats, and Henry's big leather bag, to safely sit down next to Mari. The crowd sounded unusually rowdy, as if we were waiting for a rock concert instead of a lecture. "Is Chloe here?" I asked, wondering if my actress client decided to attend. Tonight, there were no bodyguards blocking the aisle. Nothing unusual caught my eye.

"Not so far," Mari answered. "I wonder how Elaine's going to tie this lecture up? The truth is no matter how organized you are, housework never ends."

Henry overheard her gloomy proclamation and went into a lecture on cleaning up as you go—a habit, he said, that helps him not lose his mind while cranking out his commercial baked goods.

I shared what a friend advised once. When your house gets too crowded with stuff, move to a bigger house.

We all snickered. On stage the crew checked the microphone for Elaine's final lecture. I noticed someone setting up a PowerPoint presentation. Usually, slideshows put me to sleep, so I told Mari to elbow me if I nodded off and started to snore. Only a short while later, the lights began to flicker, signaling the start of the presentation.

Elaine's introduction elicited effusive clapping from the audience. She blushed a little and held up her hands.

"In these last few weeks, I've bombarded you with ways to organize various parts of your homes," she began. "Some suggestions will work wonders for some of you, while others of you will never see the point in color-keying anything."

This got a good-natured laugh.

"But tonight, I want to share a success story with you. One that never would have happened without the intervention of someone you all knew, my mentor and friend, Sookie Overmann." A click of the computer keyboard brought up a picture of Sookie laughing into the camera with a double thumbs-up pose.

The image on the screen surprised me. Sookie looked much younger, her hair in a messy bun with very little makeup on. Not a power suit in sight.

With the next slide, the dates of her birth and death, printed in a plain black font, flashed across the bottom of the screen.

Elaine stood completely still. The lights in the room started to dim, along with the image on the screen. I found it to be a very dramatic moment.

After a minute of complete darkness, the lights burst back on along with a new screen image—an apartment building.

"We met by accident," Elaine said. "Sookie was renting an apartment next door to me. My wrist was in a temporary brace, and I was struggling with opening my door and carrying in the groceries. I tried to discourage her from helping, but she basically pushed past me and carried two bags of food inside. This is what she saw."

One picture after another flicked overhead. Rooms filled with stuff. Tall towers of boxes and bins lined a hallway. A living room so crammed with items that it obscured most of a large picture window.

A gasp stirred the audience.

"This was my home," Elaine said. "If you ask me how it started, I could give you a million reasons. I broke up with my boyfriend, shopping made me feel happy, I didn't like to waste anything."

The next slide revealed bulging suitcases, more plastic bins, and stacks of newspapers three rows deep.

"My parents lived in Milwaukee. They hated to fly so I always visited them. No one came to my home. No one knew my secret."

More photos followed that showed a clean kitchen, one empty recliner, a folding TV tray table, and a television, an oasis of order in a jungle of stuff.

"Do you see this small space? This is where I lived. The recliner was my bed."

Henry James leaned over and whispered, "It's brave of her to tell us this."

I nodded my agreement.

After a pause, Elaine continued. "Sookie didn't judge me. She took me under her wing, like a hen with a chick. She found me counseling, and I started on medication, since hoarding can be a mental health issue. Every Saturday morning, we would set a goal, always reminding me that by donating I'd be helping someone else—someone truly in need. Gradually I came to feel the generosity of letting go."

Another set of photographs showed the same rooms

cleared out, closets in order, and a small gathering in Elaine's living room watching a football game.

"The reason I'm sharing my story," Elaine explained, "is that there is always help out there, be it in person, in videos, on the Internet, or in book form. Stop being embarrassed by the way you live. Life is too short not to be happy."

Someone in the front row jumped up and began clapping. The rest of the audience joined in.

"Thank you so much," Elaine said. "Now, I'm going to open up the rest of our time together for questions. Remember, often you can learn from someone else's problem."

A community center volunteer walked down the aisle with a microphone. One older woman held up her hand. "I can't clean the way I used to because of my arthritis, but everyone I hire does a terrible job. What do you suggest?"

Elaine walked down the aisle toward the woman and said into her microphone, "I'm sorry to hear about your arthritis…"

"Vera," the woman in the audience replied. She nervously fingered a pearl necklace through her knobby fingers.

"Vera. Thank you for your question. But let me be frank. You will never find anyone who cleans like you used to unless you clone yourself. Make that a pre-arthritis clone."

"How about a twenty-year-old me?" the woman joked.

Elaine smiled. "We're often too polite to point out things we are dissatisfied with. I suggest you sit down with your cleaning person and explain what's most important for you."

I noticed several women around me nodding their approval.

"Start with the major issues like toilets or floors but skip the things you can finish up yourself for now. That way you'll get the most for your money, and also have the satisfaction of not feeling helpless in your own home."

"I like that," Vera said. "Thank you so much."

Elaine then showed another photo of herself, a waving Sookie, and someone with her back to the camera. All three wore green sweatshirts, the corporate logo on the back. "Here's a picture of our local team packing items for donation."

I recognized Posey's tight curls just visible in the background. More proof that Posey had worked with Sookie.

Someone stood up toward the back of the auditorium and loudly yelled out, "If you're so great at what you do, then why was Sookie going to fire you?" The tall blond woman angrily gestured toward Elaine. "You never told any of these rich clients you're working for about that, I bet. She was the brains, you jealous troll." A self-satisfied grimace contorted the anger in her face.

My eyes traveled from Elaine to the woman in the audience and back again.

"This is going to be good," said Henry. "Catfight."

The volunteer on the stage who had overseen the PowerPoint presentation a few moments ago looked like she was about to cry.

More buzzing spread through the audience. Those murmurs hushed when Elaine tapped on her microphone.

"Please, everyone. Let's remain quiet and stay in our seats." Elaine pointed at the back of the room. "Ladies and gentlemen, let me introduce Phillipa Overmann, Glenn Overmann's sister."

Immediately more whispering broke out.

"As most of you know, Glenn Overmann, Sookie's estranged husband, has been taken into police custody and charged with Sookie's murder. Phillipa, no doubt, is understandably distressed."

Once again, I was impressed with how Elaine handled yet another public confrontation.

By that time, one of the center volunteers had recruited a maintenance man and the two of them started to escort Phillipa out of the room. She pushed them aside before saying, "I'll go. Don't touch me." Before she exited, she turned toward the audience and screamed, "You killed her, Elaine. Somehow you killed Sookie, and they're blaming my brother. He was home with me that night."

As the staff members forced her through the exit door, she continued to yell vague threats and obscenities at Elaine and everyone participating in the seminar.

Mari poked me. "Who says that small towns are boring?"

During the ruckus, the moderator escorted Elaine in the opposite direction, down the aisle and toward the stage curtains. Once our moderator was safely hidden from view, the community center representative took the mic and said, "That concludes tonight's session and our organizing seminar. Please give a round of applause to our speaker. As always, there are refreshments in the main reception area."

After a smattering of confused clapping, most people picked up their coats and began to move in an orderly way toward the exit doors. From the chatter, it seemed everyone had an opinion on Phillipa's accusations. Our little group became hedged in on both sides, so we resigned ourselves to being some of the last participants to leave.

While waiting our turn, I checked the stage but didn't see Elaine anywhere. I assumed the community center management took all threats seriously.

"Do you think anyone will call the police?" I asked Henry and Mari.

"Perhaps," he said, "to cover their butts. Someone's probably posting pictures on Facebook as we speak."

A sad commentary on modern life, I thought, sad and potentially dangerous. We were in an age when TikTok stars are targeted, Internet celebrities harassed, and everyone on the planet can be a potential critic or potential victim on social media.

Once in the reception area, our little group huddled together. Henry inspected the baked goods with a professional eye while the rest of us drank decaf and discussed the evening. I didn't expect Elaine to make an appearance, but all of a sudden, a small round of applause broke out in the far right corner of the room.

Henry, who was the tallest of us at well over six feet, said, "It's Elaine. That shows guts," he added, approvingly. "Let's hear what she has to say."

Mari and I followed behind Henry James like convoy boats behind an icebreaker until we were close enough to overhear the conversation.

Someone asked if it was true about Sookie firing Elaine.

Elaine answered. "It's true that we all lost our jobs, but we weren't fired. The corporation that hired us was in the process of being dissolved. Sookie generously gave us two months' pay as severance. This chapter of her life was closed, she explained, and a new adventure awaited."

"Did she ever tell you what it was?"

"Not specifically. She hinted about leaving winters behind, though. Part of the secrecy, I believe, was to avoid additional confrontations with Glenn. He made her life miserable."

"So you weren't fired," a short, athletic-looking woman repeated.

While she spoke I got a peek at Elaine. She showed no anger in her voice or demeanor.

"Correct."

The answer came out clipped. Final.

Other audience members pushed around, curious but reluctant to speak. From behind me someone said, "When did she tell you all this?"

Waiting for Elaine's response, for the first time I saw a hint of something in her eyes. Remorse? Regret?

Her gaze flickered downward. When she looked back up, she stared directly at me. "I found out the night before she was killed."

After Elaine left, we hung around, speaking with friends and eating snacks. While we were getting ready to leave, Mari pulled me aside and whispered, "I'm following you home tonight. I miss Desi."

"Sure." I checked to make sure I had my backpack. "I guess your sister-in-law couldn't make it tonight?" Of all of us, I thought Barbara was the most tuned in to the lectures.

Taking a final bite from her cookie, Mari shook her head. "One of the kids started vomiting just before she was supposed to leave—and hubby doesn't do vomiting."

Since I knew several people who gagged at the thought of anyone around them barfing, I understood completely.

Henry stood behind me having a spirited conversation about flour with a fellow baker, an attractive woman in her thirties. With a raised finger he warned,

"Don't get me started about the British. Strong flour, self-raising, golden syrup…"

"Sorry to interrupt," I said, "but Mari and I are heading out."

"You two okay?" Henry asked. "Marilyn and I are debating the pros and cons of European milling techniques and specialty products."

"We're fine." If it had been anyone other than Henry, I'd have thought he was flirting with her.

Quite a few women were buttoning their coats and putting on hats as they drew closer to the community center exit. Each time the doors opened, a stream of frigid air slipped in. Mari and I followed suit. I figured by the time the heat was blasting in the truck, I'd be pulling into the animal hospital parking lot.

Of course, our entrance into my apartment rivaled a royal welcome, especially from Desi, who couldn't believe his good luck. Mommy was here!

The huge rottweiler turned into a puddle of mush at Mari's feet, wiggling and rolling and pushing his face up against her leg. The other dogs all vied for the same attention. Even Little Man carefully watched the celebrations.

"Everyone out," I told them, first opening my front door, then the gate to the fenced-in area. Little Man trotted along behind the other dogs, letting them create a trail in the snow.

"Little Man is turning into a real live dog," Mari joked.

The three larger dogs were tearing around the dog run area, the Chihuahua barking at their heels.

"So, what did you think of Glenn Overmann's sister's tirade?" I asked.

"Interesting. I wonder what she's been telling the police? She obviously thinks Glenn is innocent."

I pulled my coat tighter around my neck. "Of course she does. They're family. Has Cindy said anything more to you?"

"Nope. I think Chief Garcia clamped down on her sister-to-sister information hotline."

Knowing our receptionist, I predicted, "That won't last long."

Chapter Thirty-Six

AFTER OVERSLEEPING THE NEXT MORNING I HURRIED through my morning dog routines and entered the treatment room fifteen minutes before my first appointment.

"We were just getting worried about you," Mari said.

"Doggy-mom duties," I answered, plucking a granola bar from the breakfast basket.

"I've got your first appointment set up in Room 2 when you're ready. We're off and running this morning," she laughed.

At lunchtime I was checking my email and straightening up my desktop when some good news appeared. I received the veterinary pathology report stating that Little Man's growth was benign, with all the margins clear of any abnormalities.

We all needed some good news in our lives, so I immediately texted Daffy, Mari, and Cindy. It didn't take long for Mari to pop up at my office door.

"We should celebrate," she said. "I'd love a big fat brownie from Judy's."

Cindy came up behind her. "Or I can share my rice crackers with both of you," she said. "They're seaweed-flavored."

An image of Mari gobbling down seaweed made me break out in giggles. Cindy wasn't amused.

"We don't have to celebrate all the time with sweets."

She was right, but a brownie sounded awfully good.

"When I was your age, I ate whatever I wanted, and as much as I wanted," she continued. "You'll discover, as you get older, that becomes impossible. So now for me it's less chocolate, more low-fat yogurt."

Mari didn't let it rest. "So if you follow that argument to its logical conclusion, I'd better start eating like crazy while I'm still young."

I stifled my second burst of giggles in my hand. It didn't go unnoticed.

"All right," Cindy replied. "In honor of Little Man, let's make it three brownies. I'll call Judy and tell her one of you will pick up in fifteen minutes."

"I'll volunteer," I said. "I think I need some fresh air to clear my head." Before Mari could object, I took my coat and waved goodbye.

By the time I walked into Judy's, I'd decided to add a soup and her roast chicken with vegetable special to the takeout order. That took care of a lunch and dinner for me. Her place was packed, as usual, so I waited by the counter and checked my messages. Rainbow texted and reminded me that her mom wanted Posey's three notebooks.

As I waited, I looked out at the dining room, crowded with people.

Among the customers was Elaine, sitting with three young women wearing green sweatshirts. Our eyes met, and she acknowledged me with a smile.

A few tables down, Phillipa Overmann and two strangers wearing suits were obviously distressed. The volatile Phillipa was the listener, not the speaker. One of the men had a stack of papers he appeared to be going through with her. Also at the table, glumly staring at his cell phone, was Glenn's boyfriend, Wyatt Cressan.

It occurred to me that at one time or another, I'd seen everyone involved with Posey sitting in Judy's restaurant.

"Your order is ready," Judy said, placing a paper bag on the counter. "What are you looking at?"

"Oh, just thinking about how so many lives have been disrupted by Sookie's death. Her employees with the corporation dissolved, her family, her clients..."

"My business." Judy explained that Sookie's crew ate lunch at her place at least twice a week.

"How often did you see Posey with them?" I asked her.

"Some of the time. My impression was she did a lot of the scut work—the cleanup, packing, that kind of thing. Why do you want to know? Still investigating?" It was difficult to get anything past Judy.

"I'm interested," I told her, "in any links between Sookie and Posey."

Her hard brown eyes stared me down. "Because?"

How could I explain this odd feeling I had? "Posey

was writing a book. We talked a little about it one night at Circle K. Sookie might be one of…"

"Hello, ladies."

It was Elaine who interrupted me, so close I could smell a whiff of her perfume.

"Hi, Elaine. Did you need your bill? Separate checks, or all together?" Judy started to clear away some dishes from the counter.

"Together, please. My treat. I wanted to say goodbye to the last of our employees. I'll be leaving at the end of the week."

It seemed as though there was a mass exodus from Oak Falls. "You, too? I forgot to ask Judy if Colin has left."

Elaine fidgeted on her seat. "Colin? That artist? Haven't seen him in quite a while."

"Did the police resolve that incident at the community center between you and Phillipa?" I couldn't help notice they were once again in the same room, though this time peacefully.

"Oh, that. I didn't press any charges. Phillipa was reacting in the heat of the moment, I believe," she said. "Oak Falls has been good to me, but it's time to leave." Elaine removed her wallet from her purse and took out a credit card. Judy was busy taking a phone order and signaled she'd be with her in a moment.

"Did I hear you mention Posey?" she questioned. "Such a tragedy. I had no idea she was depressed."

"Me either."

"Did you say you have her notebooks? Our crew

joked that she was always scribbling away in those note-books, even at our job sites."

Finished on the phone, Judy came over with a mobile reader device and ran Elaine's credit card.

"So, you knew about the notebooks?"

"Of course. Anybody who spent any time with Posey knew she was writing some kind of historical novel. The last time I spoke to her she said she'd started on the Epilogue. I just hope she didn't write anything about me in them." Her voice sounded jokingly conversational, but tightness around her mouth and forehead betrayed her.

Elaine looked scared.

"Sorry I took so long," I blurted out to Mari and Cindy as I rushed into the employee lounge and put the bags on the table. "I decided to get dinner for myself."

Mari was busy digging through the individually wrapped food items. "Here they are," she exclaimed. Three brownies materialized in her hands.

"I think I'll have half and save the rest for tomorrow," Cindy said.

"Not me." In record speed Mari had the brownie unwrapped and missing a large corner.

Still thinking about Elaine's reaction in Judy's Café, I sat motionless, the brownie uneaten in my hand.

"What's up with you?" Mari asked. "Brownie got your tongue?"

Cindy chided her. "You can see she hasn't even tasted it. Did anything happen to you at the restaurant?"

I came out of my daydream, not sure what to say. "I keep thinking about Sookie's and Posey's deaths."

"Oh, no." Cindy rose and made her way toward the refrigerator. "I thought you dropped all that."

"I did, but I can't help I thinking I missed something. Especially now that the rats are deserting the ship."

"How so?" Mari pulled her chair closer to mine.

Trying to put my apprehension into words was proving tough. "Colin is leaving. Elaine is leaving. Rainbow is leaving. Sookie was going to leave before she was killed."

Cindy spoke first. "Colin has a gallery opening in Finland. He's been telling everyone for months about it. Didn't you meet his agent a few days ago?"

"All right, that's true," I admitted.

"Rainbow only came to visit her mom and is going back to California, I believe," Mari added. "We heard Elaine say she's leaving because Glenn and his sister are screaming at her in public."

Everything they both said was true. "So what about Sookie? Why was she leaving?"

"Get real, Kate," Cindy said. "Sookie was going through a divorce and had a new mystery boyfriend. Who can blame her?"

They made excellent points. Everything they mentioned made a lot of sense. I nodded my agreement and took a bite of brownie. But instead of enjoying the fudgy richness, my brain stayed fixated on one thought that circled around and around in my consciousness, like that tiny ball you see rolling in a roulette wheel.

You're missing something.

You're missing something.

———————

That feeling of something missed stayed with me, so on Saturday afternoon I decided to go into town and pick Judy's brain about Posey and Sookie and Glenn. I knew she'd be at the restaurant, so as soon as the office closed, I drove into town.

Parking on Saturday could be difficult, and this was one of those difficult times. I ended up parking blocks from my destination. Buttoning my coat around me, I started walking toward the restaurant.

"Kate? Is that you? Wait up."

Behind me a familiar voice said my name. When I turned I saw Colin hurrying to catch up.

"Hi," I said.

"Hi, yourself. Listen. Can you do me a big favor? I got someone to adopt the iguana, but it's not looking so good this morning. Do you think you could take a quick look at him?"

I knew Colin's studio was close by, but…

"It's only one block away in that direction," he pointed, taking me by the elbow.

"I'm on my way to Judy's," I started to explain. "I thought I'd pick something up for a friend."

We started to walk together, his arm in mine.

"She's incredibly busy this morning. One of her servers didn't show up for his shift. I tried to get coffee and the line is out the door."

It felt nice to be walking without snow or wind to contend with.

"I'm a little worried about Judy," he confided. "Someone told me the restaurant is struggling financially." He turned off abruptly onto a walkway that wound around the back of a storefront. "Here's my place." Several spaces in the building looked to be in the process of being remodeled.

Stopping at a glossy black door, he entered a series of numbers into an electronic lock. The device whirred, and then a light turned green. He held the door open for me. From the smell of solvents and paint, it was obvious it served as an artist's studio. Very modern in appearance, one wall was mostly glass. Skylights flooded the space with light. The only furnishings were a worn couch, two armchairs, and a small bistro table with four folding chairs. A large terrarium took up most of a long folding table. Tucked underneath was a green plastic bin full of food, supplements, and a half-empty bag of cedar shavings.

"I'm sorry to practically kidnap you." Colin walked over to the habitat. "The people who have been taking care of it for Felicia dumped it on me about two weeks ago. This morning I noticed he wasn't moving much."

The glass terrarium measured about seven feet long,

with a plastic cover and a light bulb rigged over part of the habitat for heat. As soon as I saw cedar chips I was concerned, since cedar isn't recommended for use in reptile enclosures due to its aromatic oils.

Inside the dirty glass box was a four-foot-long green iguana, with one branch to perch on and a pile of food on a flat plate.

"Colin, have you been giving him fresh green vegetables and fruits in addition to the dry food?" Nutrition was a big part of keeping exotic animals healthy. "What about the temperature and humidity?" I also noticed the water needed to be changed.

"I've been busy getting ready to move," he said. "Like I said, Felicia's friends dumped him on me. Each time I touch him or anything he's touched, I start to itch." As if punctuating the sentence, he began to scratch his arm.

"Well, let me at least get these cedar chips out. Do you have any newspaper I can use?"

He looked around, then opened a black garbage bag sitting next to the sofa. After pawing through it, he pulled out a bunch of newspaper pages. "These are clean," he told me.

I folded a few pages into a rough funnel and with my hands started to slide the dry cedar chips onto the paper. The big lizard didn't blink, but stayed motionless on the only branch in the habitat.

"Do you have a garbage pail I can put this in?" I asked.

"Sure." He removed a small white pail with a plastic liner in it from under the sink and held it in front of me.

"Okay. Hold it steady." I started to slowly pour, but there must have been a stray clump hidden underneath because all of a sudden there was a plop, and Colin had yucky used cedar chips on his hands, lower arms, and on his shoes.

"AGGH!"

A bunch of incomprehensible sounds poured out of his mouth, all signifying disgust.

"I'm so sorry. Go ahead and wash up," I told him. "I'll clean this mess."

He grunted an okay, tripped over the food bin and slammed into the black garbage bag on his way to the bathroom. His frustration must have maxed out because he kicked the bag, sending paper and garbage flying.

The iguana hadn't moved.

I found a broom in the kitchenette and swept up all the remaining cedar chips. Since anything iguana-related was what Colin was allergic to, I immediately tied the bag shut and put it over by the front door. I quickly washed my hands then set about picking up the rest of the trash scattered on the floor.

It looked like most of it was last-minute useless papers and magazines, with most of the yucky stuff down at the bottom. When I was down on my hands and knees picking up trash from under the sofa, I caught a glimpse of more magazines on the bottom level of his coffee table. Several gallery pamphlets were mixed in with various catalogs on garden supplies, computer parts, and European river cruises.

Colin was still grumbling and cursing in the bathroom somewhere down the hallway. Taking a quick look around, I didn't see any of his personal items at all. What I did see were several cardboard moving boxes stacked in one corner.

The iguana still hadn't moved.

I decided to see if there was something in the refrigerator the lizard would eat. The remains of a veggie salad without dressing looked like just the ticket. Picking up a pair of chopsticks from the silverware drawer, I held some Swiss chard in front of the iguana's nose. His head turned, eyes flicking. In a super-fast move, he chomped down, just missing the chopstick, and munched away. After watching how quickly he moved, I carefully offered a bowl of clean water.

When Colin returned, all the garbage had been picked up. I'd tied the black bag closed and dragged it across the floor to rest it next to the other trash bag.

"Thanks so much," Colin said as he looked around the room. He'd changed his clothes, even down to his shoes and socks, in the hopes of curtailing any skin irritation.

"I threw all the dirty stuff in my washing machine. I'm glad there isn't anything more to add."

"No. I bagged anything with cedar chips on it. You might want to wipe down some of the surfaces or have someone else clean them for you," I told him. A quick look at my watch reminded me it was after lunch. Time to talk to Judy.

"Maybe you can come visit me in Finland," he said and moved toward me.

He smelled good and looked delicious, but I backed off. "Careful—I might still have some of that cedar dust on me," I told him, holding both hands up. "I think I should probably get going. Tell the new owners to take him to a veterinarian who specializes in exotics for a checkup as soon as possible. And in my opinion, he needs a larger habitat. And a more diversified diet."

With an amused smile, Colin thanked me from afar. "It's been a real pleasure, Dr. Kate. Do you realize you've evaded my attentions time and time again?"

I threw him a kiss. "There's always Finland." I picked up my stuff, opened his door, and backed outside.

And ran smack into Elaine.

Elaine appeared at a loss for words. Her eyes wide, pupils dilated, the unflappable organization specialist appeared startled.

"Hi, Elaine," I said. "What are you doing here?" Only a few days ago Elaine implied she hadn't seen Colin recently. They certainly didn't look like strangers to me.

Her quick response mirrored what I'd seen during her lectures. "I could ask you the same question."

"I'm on a veterinary call. Colin asked me to look at the iguana," I told her. "It's getting adopted out tonight, but he thought it wasn't acting right."

From the look on her face, I didn't think Elaine was expecting an innocent explanation.

"And you're here because—?"

Colin answered, temporarily putting her out of her misery.

"I hired her to come and help me finish cleaning up the apartment," he said with a perfectly straight face. "There's still a lot to do." He gestured down the hallway in the general direction of the bedroom and painting studio.

"That's right," Elaine agreed, looking somewhat embarrassed as she hurried past me.

I decided to step back in and close the door. Neither one of them expected that.

"You know, this is the first time I've been here in this building," I said, keeping my backpack hoisted over my shoulder. "Colin, is your studio back there? How many bedrooms and bathrooms all together? I've got a friend in the city who might be interested in a weekend place."

Colin and Elaine stared at each other. Once again, it was Colin who answered my question, while Elaine retreated. She walked over to the sofa and slumped down in the corner.

"I believe this is one of two rentals in this building," Colin said, as though he also worked as a real estate rental agent. "This is a converted warehouse, with several apartments and a couple of storefronts. The owners are allowed to sublet only for one six-month period of time, which is why she offers it to artists who are connected with the Hudson Valley—that and the fantastic light at the back of the apartment."

"Oh, I'd love to see," I said, feigning interest.

"Maybe another time. At the moment, the space is filled with boxes."

"Yes, too bad." I looked around the great room once more, then for the second time headed to the front door. "Well, have fun cleaning," I said to Elaine.

Just before I shut the door, I glanced back at Colin then Elaine and mischievously added, "I'll let you two get on with it. I'm sure you'll both get your money's worth."

Chapter Thirty-Seven

I RETRACED MY STEPS AND SET OUT TO SPEAK TO JUDY.
Life throws you surprises all the time, Gramps always
reminded me, and bumping into Elaine at Colin's apartment was one of them. Elaine and Colin? Despite the
denial were they more than friends? With all the women
in his life, it's a wonder Colin had the time to paint anything. But their private lives were their own business.

Neither one had been mentioned in Posey's book.

When I walked past Judy's, the line to get in spilled
out onto the sidewalk. I overheard a party of four
decide to go somewhere else, complaining about the
wait when they walked away. I made a note to return
on a weekday.

Climbing into the truck, I remembered something
Elaine had said. That Posey had been writing the
Epilogue. When I noticed my gas tank half full, I decided
to revisit the Circle K where I'd rescued the notebooks
from the trash. Maybe I had missed something.

There were no other customers at the Circle K gas
pumps when I turned in from the main road. I took
the opportunity to fill up, then hurried inside. With no
clear plan in mind, I decided to improvise.

At the cash register, appearing more confident than

when I first observed him, stood the young man who replaced Posey. Fighting an urge for a quart of vanilla fudge swirl ice cream, I instead picked out a pack of sugar-free gum and headed to the counter.

"Is that it for today?"

The kid looked bored out of his mind. A textbook lay on the counter behind him, its pages pristine.

"Yes." Then I had a brilliant thought. "Do you have a lost and found here?" I asked with a friendly voice. "Because a friend thinks she left her notebook here and asked me to check for her." I started making up a more elaborate story in my head in case I needed it. However, even before I finished, the clerk bent down and slid a cardboard box out from under the counter. Inside was a mixed assortment of sunglasses, baby bottles, thermoses, and a baseball mitt. Piled at the top sat some single gloves and a few scarfs.

"Here's the lost and found."

"Can I look for myself?"

"Sure. There's another box in the storeroom for big stuff."

My mind blanked on what big things customers could have left behind. Trying not to disturb the contents too much, I dug to the bottom of the box. Peeking out from beneath a bright yellow scarf was a familiar black-and-white marbled notebook.

"Found it," I said, waving the notebook in the air. To make sure it was Posey's, I looked at the first page. A blue number four written on the top right corner gave me hope. Her characteristic writing on the next few pages confirmed it.

"Boy, is she going to be happy," I said as enthusiastically as I could.

The clerk stared right through me. He couldn't have cared less.

Sliding the notebook under my coat, I paid my bill and started to leave. A glance back at the register confirmed the clerk had already shoved the box back under the counter.

Our eyes met. Puzzled, he must have wondered why I'd looked back, but his training kicked in because he muttered, "Thanks for shopping at Circle K."

My mind was so occupied with finding out the contents of Posey's fourth book that I almost drove off the road. For the rest of the trip, I concentrated on getting back to the animal hospital intact.

Pinky must have plowed the parking lot while I was gone, since welcome patches of black asphalt were visible. A devoted dog dad, our neighbor made sure clients had no trouble getting in and out of their cars with their pets.

As soon as I opened the apartment door, I was greeted with the usual uncontrolled bedlam. Four dogs, or maybe three and one-quarter dogs, thought at this moment that I was the single most important, beautiful, smart, and perfect person on the planet.

And they all had to pee.

I opened the gate, and they ran inside the exercise

area, even Little Man. They romped, and peed, and peed some more. From the smile on his face, I knew Little Man was enjoying his vacation with his canine friends. I wondered how often Daffy let him play with other dogs.

After fifteen minutes, I called a halt to all the masculine frolicking.

"Come on, everyone," I yelled. "Let's go inside." Desi and Mr. Pitt stormed to the front of the line, with the two smaller dogs bringing up the rear. However, when I opened my apartment door, the first to scoot past was Little Man. I swear he would have done a victory lap if I'd let him. "You've been a good patient," I told the tiny dog, "so I'm going to take this collar off you." I removed the bulky foam cone and scratched his neck, which elicited a halfhearted growl.

Inside, I dried off everyone's feet and rewarded each dog with a chew treat. Then it was time to change the water bowls, get four dishes of food ready—making sure Desi and Little Man got their special diets—and, finally, collapse on the sofa.

As much as I wanted to lie down and take a nap, it was time to read Posey's last notebook. Knowing I'd need some help concentrating, I brewed a fresh pot of coffee and placed the fourth installment on the table. As I stood in front of the machine waiting, I wondered what I'd find. Did writers make notes when they finished a first draft of a book? Maybe plot suggestions, or lists of clues or red herrings they wanted to include?

Sounded complicated.

With the coffee finally ready, I poured a mug and sat down at the kitchen table. So this was the elusive fourth notebook, the number 4 prominent on the right-hand corner. On the following page only one word was written, "Epilogue."

If I remembered correctly an epilogue is used to finish a story or comment on the ending. Posey's epilogue began after the successful theft of the gold doubloon coins from the duke. The servant, Pansy, now was rich beyond her wildest fantasies, with the vampire busy handling all the gold.

There was a note in the margin in Posey's distinctive handwriting that said, *"Add aliens."* Those poor aliens always seemed like an afterthought.

The two lead characters paused the busy action of hiding from the duke for another sexy break. Strangely, mid-dalliance the duo was teleported into a future teeming with big-eyed aliens. Telepathically, the aliens warned Pansy that a powerful wizard was chasing them, intent on finding the stolen gold. After a brief tour of the future, with flying cars and girl aliens in miniskirts, they hurtled back in time. Separated by a black hole vortex, Pansy catches a glimpse of her vampire boyfriend through a time/space portal kissing another woman.

His was the touch that stirred her soul and loins. Let their love not prove a false love, for she had flung all her eggs into the same basket. To thine own self be true or false? Hath another stolen the key that unlocks her lover's deadly lips? She must question the aliens.

I skipped over a few more fractured Shakespearean references to continue reading.

The churning lovemaking the servant enjoyed with her vampire had a heavy price. She knew she must return the duke's gold and claim her true place on the throne.

To illustrate the scene, Posey had drawn a disjointed sketch of a vortex-like tornado, with lightning bolts flashing in all directions, hitting the ground. Floating in the sky above was a pot of sparkling gold coins.

Halfway through the fourth book, I needed to stop and take a break. Trying to keep track of all the subplots and multiple characters, some of whom showed up only once, proved exhausting. My notes resembled a scrimmage diagram with arrows and circles organizing the characters. Not knowing much about writing a book, I assumed these four notebooks were Posey's ideas more than anything else, for a bigger story she had hoped to tell.

Something had changed, though. In this final notebook Posey's fictional character had regrets. She wanted to give the duke's gold back to him.

A knock on my door resulted in an explosion of barking. "Quiet," I yelled out, which didn't do much to decrease the noise. A quick look out the window revealed a woman, bundled up in a coat and hat. When she lifted her face, I immediately recognized our Wednesday-night organizing lecturer.

What is Elaine doing here?

Although I felt very safe surrounded by the dogs, I didn't want her coming inside.

"Be right out," I said, taking my coat off the rack.

A cluster of sunrays pierced the clouds behind her, giving the illusion of warmth. The only patch of blue sky disappeared behind the pine trees. Inside, the dogs continued barking.

Elaine seemed puzzled we were meeting outside.

"Hi, Elaine. I'm sorry, but you caught me at a very busy time."

"This is a bit embarrassing." Again, I noticed the tightness in her face. Something was bothering her.

"Does it have to do with bumping into you at Colin's apartment?"

She frowned. "Maybe."

"Then it's best to get it over with." I lifted my collar up to protect my neck against the cold.

"Did Posey write anything about me in those journals of hers?"

A surprising question, almost as if she expected there would be something. "No, your name isn't mentioned anywhere." There wasn't even a character who began with the letter *E*, but I didn't tell her that.

"Are you sure?" Her voice was tinged with disbelief.

"I'm positive. Posey was writing a novel, an Edwardian romance between a servant and a vampire. Most of it consists of notes and plot ideas. It's very disjointed."

She listened quietly.

"It's not finished by any means; in fact, it's not in book form at all."

Elaine's shoulders relaxed. She put her hands in her pockets, staring at the snow. "I was so afraid she wrote about a stupid mistake I made."

"Mistake?"

Her face relaxed, tension gone. "A mistake that shall remain private. I'm sorry for disturbing you." Elaine turned but paused to ask, "What will you do with Posey's notebooks?"

"I'm giving them to a high school friend of hers here in town. As a remembrance."

Her gaze continued to be focused on the snow, thoughtful but distant. "Well, I for one will never forget Posey. Or forgive her."

"For committing suicide?"

"No, that choice was hers alone to make." Elaine took a few steps backward, as if weighing her words. "I'll never forgive her for everything else she did."

Before I could ask any more questions, she walked over to her car and drove away.

As soon as I went back inside, I hurried over to the kitchen table and picked up the last notebook intent on searching for any references about Elaine. Deciphering clues from a jumbled mess of knights and lords and Edwardian life proved tough. Relying on Posey's previous trick of using a real person's initial for her fictional character, I paged along but never found a woman character whose name began with an *E*. Obviously, author

Posey picked and chose the real people she based her characters on.

I slogged on with Pansy becoming more worried about the duke's men and being betrayed by her vampire boyfriend. It seems another younger woman had caught his eye.

Just as I was about to take a break from the final notebook, my phone rang. Caller ID said it was Rainbow. I wondered what she wanted now.

"Hello?" My voice sounded a bit gravelly. I reached for my coffee to find it turned cold and unappetizing.

"I decided to leave town tomorrow. All this snow is getting me down. Can I pick up the three notebooks for my mom?"

I'd finally become used to Rainbow's abrupt manner, but I wasn't sorry to see her go. "Sure. I need to make a copy of a few things tonight, though. Oh, and there are four notebooks now." I dumped my cold coffee into the sink and ran water to avoid a stain. "I'll be happy to leave them at the receptionist desk for you. Sorry our little detective collaboration didn't pan out." The dogs were all snoozing in their beds except for Little Man, who had decided to bed down in his cat carrier shoved next to the laundry hamper.

As I spoke on the phone, I saw Desi raise his head up, listening. The big dog's movements must have been felt by nearby Mr. Pitt, who also turned his head in the direction of the parking lot. I figured Pinky might be at his place taking a break, but I thought the dogs were used to the sound of his truck. Then I heard Desi growl.

There was nothing but silence on the line.

"Are you there?" Dropped calls were frequent in the Hudson Valley.

"Yes. Sorry. That should be okay, I guess. But there's something I need your advice on, if you don't mind." Rainbow sounded forlorn.

"Well, can we do it early tomorrow..."

"I'm right outside," Rainbow said.

By then, Desi was up and pacing, along with Mr. Pitt. Buddy let out a high yip as he also heard someone outside. Rainbow had been to my place at least two or three times, so she wasn't a complete stranger to them anymore. However, as soon as she knocked on the door all hell broke loose again. Desi was barking and growling, Mr. Pitt made deep huffing sounds, and Buddy raised the level of yapping up a notch.

When they saw Rainbow step inside, they immediately congregated around her. She tried to say something but was drowned out by the three larger dogs, all wagging their tails and asking for attention. Little Man poked his head out to see what the fuss was about, then went back into the cat carrier.

"I've got a splitting headache," she confessed. "Can you put them in the hospital? I'm not going to be here very long."

All the noise was getting to me, too, so I guided the pack through the connecting door into the hospital hallway. "Stay," I said as I made sure all the other office doors were closed. "Quiet." I still had a few chew treats in my pocket, so I handed them out. Desi let his treat drop to the floor.

"Be right back, guys," I told them. "Be good." Then I closed the door.

Rainbow stood over by my front door, her back to me. She looked over her shoulder as I began walking toward her. Then she backed away.

"So, what do you want to talk about?" I asked.

The wheels on the bus had nothing on her as I watched her brain shift into high gear trying to spin a story I would swallow. In a way it was comical. I assumed she was about to ask for money to get back to California.

Instead of answering, she moved to my front door and opened it wide. In strolled Colin.

"Dogs put away?" he asked Rainbow, before nodding in my direction.

"Yes. They're in the hospital." She made a movement with her shoulder to indicate the direction of the connecting door.

"Hello, Colin." I could see shadows of dog feet moving back and forth in the gap between the door and the floor. *Why is Colin here?* I hoped it wasn't about the iguana again.

"Hi, Kate," he said in a perfectly normal voice. "I know you planned on giving Rainbow those notebooks tomorrow, but I need to take them tonight. There are some terribly damaging words in those things. Before she died, Posey swore to me she'd destroyed them."

Colin and Posey.

Colin and Rainbow.

I had missed something. Posey's notebooks said it all, but I hadn't looked hard enough. She'd written her part as the poor servant, while the sexy teacher/vampire was Colin. The fictional vampire Count Grazanski was based on Colin, not Glenn. She used the C in Count to identify her real lover.

"Okay. I got you inside," said Rainbow. "Give me my money, Colin."

Colin ignored her.

"Posey told you she'd destroyed her notebooks before she committed suicide?" I asked him.

He rearranged his face to look concerned. "Yes, she did. You see, she was fantasizing about me, and writing it down. All lies. A terrible invasion of privacy."

An image of Posey standing behind the counter at Circle K crept into my consciousness. *Knowledge is power. Power is money.*

I said to Colin, "So these stories were all fantasy on her part? Is that what you want everyone to believe?" I moved slightly toward the door between the hospital and my apartment. "I don't buy it. You're single. She was single. What did it matter if it was real or not?"

His response sounded one hundred percent sincere. "It matters to me. Posey was sweet but very disturbed. Surely you realized that when you read her notebooks?"

Was that what was bothering him? He didn't want his arty friends to know about his relationship with the Circle K clerk.

"If that's the case, then why are you resorting to this...ambush?" I looked at both of them. Rainbow couldn't meet my eyes, and Colin—well, Colin could lie to Saint Peter, while trying to slip through the pearly gates.

Predictably, it was Colin who answered. "Maybe this was a little dramatic, Kate. But I don't want any copies of Posey's notebooks in circulation. Rainbow agreed to get you to open your door, so I could reason with you. I'll read through them, delete what is offensive, and then give them to Rainbow's mom."

"He paid me," Rainbow stated.

"You could have asked." I backed up again. My internal alarms were going off. There was something wrong here.

"He didn't think you'd do it," Rainbow blurted out.

Colin meanwhile was looking around the apartment. "I see them," he said and walked over to my kitchen table. There were the four notebooks, stacked neatly for the taking. Colin picked Posey's notebooks up and shoved them and my notes into his leather bag.

My Gramps had been right. Follow the money. I couldn't let it rest. "When did you figure out Posey took the ledger with Bitcoin numbers from Chloe's house?"

Rainbow looked like a kid caught with her hand in the cookie jar. Colin's expression didn't change.

"Very clever of you, Kate. You see, Posey and I had an arrangement of sorts. She ran errands for me, did my laundry, and I provided her with my services twice a week."

"Paint costs money," Rainbow chimed in.

"When Posey confided her theft of the Bitcoin ledger to me, I immediately told her to give herself up to the police."

His statement sounded reasonable, but I didn't believe a word of it.

It was right there in her unfinished book. Posey had fallen madly in love with Colin, the romantic hero of her story. To keep him close, she turned over the only valuable item she had, the only thing he truly wanted. Money, crypto currency in the form of Arthur's Bitcoins. But then she changed her mind.

"Don't you believe me, Kate?" Colin said.

"It wasn't stealing," blurted Rainbow. "Posey's ex-husband owed her that much and more. His family cheated her out of a lot of money that she loaned him a long time ago. That rich guy, Arthur Gambino, is Posey's nephew. The family is worth almost a billion dollars."

"Honey, you don't have to explain." Colin watched me process her words.

"And, Colin, you get the Bitcoin because...?"

Rainbow interrupted. "Posey wanted to support Colin's work. She was going to split it with him. Now he's her heir."

It was obvious that Rainbow believed what she'd been told. For a smart girl, she'd made a dumb decision. Or she chose to believe his lies.

Behind the closed door one of the dogs began to whine.

"If all this is true," I said, "why did Posey commit suicide?"

"She regretted killing Sookie," Colin smoothly answered in his charming voice. "I believe her decision to jump that night was an impulsive desire to make things right."

"Make things right?" I wondered how that worked.

"Yes." His face took on a sad cast. "With her death, she made things right again in the Universe."

I couldn't stop laughing at this pretentious answer. "She made things right, but you keep the money."

Colin's eyes darkened. He didn't like being laughed at.

"You could return the money and keep the finder's reward," I told him.

"I suppose I could," he replied. "But why would I do that?"

"I'm done," Rainbow said, sliding her purse over her shoulder. "You guys figure it out."

I glanced over at Colin. He raised his eyebrows and smiled. Not a nice smile.

"I'm afraid it's gone a little too far for that, sweetie," he said, making his voice soft and compelling. I watched as Colin slipped off his soft leather gloves, revealing a pair of exam-style gloves underneath.

I froze in place.

"Wait a minute," the girl said. "You can't do this."

He removed a gun from his pocket. "You're correct, Rainbow. You have to shoot her."

My survival instincts went on high alert. As they argued I stared at the hand holding the gun.

"What? Are you crazy?" Rainbows eyes widened. She looked at me and then Colin with a panicked expression. "You said we were just going to get the notebooks back from her."

His hand languidly caressed her shoulder. "She's figured it all out. Now she's standing in our way."

It sounded like an excerpt from Posey's book.

"He's lying," I told her. "There are a lot more people standing in your way than me. Chloe Ramboulle told me her husband has an IT team working on finding his money. They've already traced it to the Bahamas. Believe me, they won't stop until they recover it. They're already focused on Posey and the people she knew."

Rainbow looked like she had short-circuited. Her eyes glazed, withdrew, not seeing anything.

Taking a step back, I appealed to the handsome artist who'd danced so beautifully with me. "You can stop it here, Colin. Don't derail this young girl's life."

His eyes held no pity. No remorse.

My words meant nothing to this version of Colin. The money, millions and millions of dollars, eclipsed everything.

I tried again. "Why did you have to choose Rainbow out of everyone you know to help you tonight?"

"Because I could."

His handsome face hid his true nature. The evil vampire who was Colin emerged from his lovely disguise.

Arguing with him was futile. I appealed to the quirky young girl I knew. "Rainbow, I think Colin killed Posey.

Don't throw your life away on someone who doesn't love you. Someone selfish and…"

"Shut up!" Colin roared. He slapped me in the face and shoved me against the wall.

I tasted metal in the corner of my mouth. "Classy move, Colin," I told him.

"You look beautiful when you're bleeding."

"Don't get any of it on that expensive cashmere coat." I added "sadistic" to the artist's resume. "See what he did?" I said to Rainbow, turning my face to show her the angry mark on my cheek, my cut and swollen lip. "Take a good look because you're next."

Colin started to pace, the gun still in his hand. Meanwhile, the dogs began barking at full force. One of them, Desi probably, started slamming his body against the connecting door.

"Enough of this," Colin shouted. He strode over to Rainbow and shook her. "If you love me, you'll shoot her, now. Our future is in your hands, sweetheart." His gloved hands caressed her throat, her face.

I understood Colin's plan. There would be no evidence linking him to my murder. The blame would fall on "crazy" Rainbow, who committed this senseless murder-suicide.

With eyes wide, all bravura gone, Rainbow answered robotically, "Colin didn't kill either of them, Kate. Posey killed Sookie."

"Then why is he handing you a gun?"

I thought for an instant Colin was going to slap me

again, but instead he put his arm around Rainbow, pressing her closely to his chest. I used that moment to sprint toward the connecting door to the hospital.

"Stop right there," he yelled at me, the gun pointed at my heart.

The gray exam gloves over his hands resembled old, wrinkled skin. *Did he come here with any sort of plan in place?* He must have known he couldn't depend on someone like Rainbow to keep a secret.

Then it all made terrible sense. "Rainbow, don't touch that gun. He wants the evidence on your hands. After you shoot me, he's going to kill you."

"No. We love each other," she said. "Right, Colin?"

"That's right." He guided her hand up and around the gun, taking care to place her finger on the trigger. "We'll drive to the airport tonight. Take a late flight and disappear. We'll get married. That luscious money will smooth our way."

"Don't listen…"

Colin pivoted Rainbow toward me. The frightened girl held the gun loosely, her hand shaking. All the self-defense lessons my Gramps made me take kicked in. I'd dive and drop-kick Rainbow and in the confusion grab the gun. Maybe Colin would back down if I was armed. Maybe.

Rainbow started to whimper. With a look of disgust, Colin covered her fingers with his. He meant to force her to pull the trigger. Trace evidence would show she fired the gun.

My mind felt icy sharp. Concentrated. No time left.

A piercing scream changed everything.

"Damn it." Colin howled in pain, shaking his leg, trying to get something off.

Rainbow turned, distracted, the gun dangling from her hand.

I shoved my palm up under Rainbow's jaw. She collapsed like a soufflé. The gun clattered to the floor. With my adrenaline pumping it only took a second to pick it up. Colin was still screaming and hopping around, batting at something with his hands. I had no idea why until I stared at his leg. With all four feet off the ground, clinging on for dear life, Little Man had come to my rescue. The Chihuahua had bitten deep down into Colin's flesh just above his boot. Truly, a lion's heart beat in the body of a mouse.

Behind me, a hundred-pound rottweiler rammed his body into the connecting door. Keeping Colin in my sight, I flung open the door and called out Desi's attack command. Three dogs streamed in, Desi in the lead. He leaped at Colin's arm in a classic Shutzhund attack move, his jaws biting through the cashmere coat. Mr. Pitt tried to help his Chihuahua friend by clamping down on Colin's other leg.

Colin pounded his fist on Desi's head and yelled, "Get him off me," as the rottweiler pulled him down toward the ground. "Kill her!" he yelled at Rainbow. "Kill her!" Crumpled on the floor, the girl rocked back and forth, eyes closed. I gave Desi the stand-down command. The big dog immediately let go, his deep brown eyes anxiously searching the room. Short black hairs along his spine stood straight up.

Despite his arm bleeding, Colin stared at me with wild eyes—a desperate man, willing to do anything to keep all that money.

"Get up," he ordered Rainbow. "Get up. There's two of us, and only one of her. We can rush her. She's a veterinarian. There's no way she's going to shoot us."

His accomplice opened her eyes but didn't move. The rocking became faster.

He tried a different tack. "I love you, sweetheart. We can still be together. The gun was a bad idea, I admit it. Let's just tie her up."

It was pathetic to see her young face light up.

Time to put an end to this.

With both individuals in clear sight, I adopted a two-handed shooter stance. "My Gramps taught me how to shoot nice and straight," I advised them. "Rainbow, stay where you are."

Colin shifted his weight slightly.

"As for you, Picasso," I said, "this rottweiler is attack trained. One more move, and I'll command him to go for your lying throat."

Desi growled deep in his chest and fixed his eyes on Colin. Mr. Pitt bared his teeth and stood in front of Little Man, guarding his tiny buddy.

The rumbling of a truck engine in the parking lot made all eyes turn. Bright headlights swung by, lighting up the living room. A sudden knock on the door elicited another round of barking. Desi stood his ground, his eyes never leaving Colin.

A familiar voice called out. "Dr. Kate, are you all right?"

"Come in, Pinky," I yelled to my neighbor.

Pinky stood in the doorframe blocking the exit. In his hands was a shotgun. "Was checking your parking lot and heard the dogs barking like crazy," he said. "Thought there might be something wrong."

At the sound of his voice, all the dogs wagged their tails. Everyone knew Pinky.

His eyes rested on my bloody swollen lip. "Did this guy hurt you?" He racked in a shell and glowered at Colin.

"Only temporarily."

A sob came from Rainbow now sitting quietly on the floor, my dog Buddy cradled in her lap.

"Seems like you've got things under control," he said. "Hey, this guy looks like he wants to bolt. How about we discourage that." His shotgun pointed to Colin.

"I was thinking the exact same thing. I've got duct tape in my pantry."

"Always got some in my truck. Want me to call 911?"

"Give me ten minutes," I told him.

With Pinky watching, I checked Colin's bite wounds. None of them were life-threatening, so I secured his hands behind his back, then for good measure taped his ankles together. He tried to wriggle away from me so I double-wrapped him.

Rainbow stopped sobbing and tried to explain. "Colin said he'd pay me five hundred bucks and take me to Helsinki if I could get the notebooks from you. That was all…"

"Shut up," Colin threatened. "Don't say another word."

I ripped off a good-sized piece of duct tape and stretched it across his mouth. "It's not polite to say shut up."

Pinky stood guard as I approached Rainbow, huddled on the floor still cuddling my dog, Buddy. "Now"—I bent down to her level—"what were you saying?"

With my phone videotaping everything Rainbow said, and Pinky witnessing it, we both heard the details of Colin's scheme. It began when Sookie and Posey worked on the expensive organizing job for Chloe. The security cameras were being repositioned as part of the job, so Posey started nosing around. She found the green Bitcoin ledger in Chloe's husband's nightstand. At first Posey had no idea what she'd stolen until they were questioned a few days later by the bodyguards at the house.

Luck was temporarily on her side because Chloe's husband didn't remember where he'd left it—at their apartment in the city, their house in Malibu, in one of the limos, his office, or their country home near Oak Falls.

But Sookie figured it out right away. She demanded half of the proceeds or she'd go to the police. Desperate for some guidance, Posey confided it all to her good-looking lover, Colin.

"Posey wanted all the money for her and Colin, so she killed Sookie," Rainbow added.

"Are you sure Colin didn't kill Sookie?" I asked the girl.

A blank look was her only answer.

The rest was easy to figure out from Posey's notebooks. She'd fallen madly in love with the handsome artist. They hatched a scheme, led by Colin, to remove the Bitcoins from their electronic storage "wallets" then send them to an offshore crypto-currency exchange, to be tumbled. Tumbling would take their stolen Bitcoins and mix them with similar coins from many different sources, making them harder to identify—sort of virtual money laundering.

Posey made the mistake of giving Colin the ledger. Did he return the favor by throwing her off the catwalk of the Hay Barn Gallery to her death? I suspect she was unconscious before he dropped her. I wondered how the police would prove it.

When I questioned Rainbow, she equivocated.

"I don't know if he killed her," Rainbow told us. "I did see him up on the catwalk just before midnight with Posey." She admitted trying to keep an eye on him so they could hook up for a New Year's kiss.

On the floor, Colin slammed his legs on the ground, in a futile attempt to silence the girl. Looming over him, Desi growled a warning.

Eyes blank once again, Rainbow said, "I'll probably never get to Helsinki."

Pinky used his cell and called 911.

I was certain Colin would deny everything to the police and then lawyer up—with or without poor Rainbow.

Chapter Thirty-Eight

THE MEDIA JUMPED ON THE STORY BREAKING IN Upstate New York. Two gruesome murders, millions of dollars in stolen Bitcoins—and in police custody, a photogenic artist who'd had affairs with both of the victims. The interest fired up into a frenzy when someone revealed the stolen Bitcoins belonged to Chloe Ramboulle, the beautiful young French actress, and her husband, tech billionaire Arthur Gambino. Oak Falls became number one in the news for four days. The tabloids descended, eager to film Colin's studio, the Hay Barn Gallery's catwalk, and the community center parking lot. Released from jail, Glenn Overmann gave interviews to anyone who asked, basking in the attention. Chloe Ramboulle issued a statement through her publicity team, deploring violence and plugging her upcoming Broadway debut—tickets available at the box office or through Ticketmaster.

Judy's kitchen did a whopping business from all the hungry reporters, cameramen, and gawkers flocking into town. A *New York Times* food critic wrote her a glowing review, and the Food Network pitched her a spot on one of its shows.

A safe deposit key was found by Babykins's new

owner, much to the joy of Glenn and his boyfriend, Wyatt. Sookie had stashed it inside the shocking-pink pillow of her beloved kitty's cat bed.

Cindy turned down any and all requests to interview me. The police minimized the role Pinky and I played in the capture, but the basic facts soon became common knowledge. Pinky posted a NO TRESPASSING sign at the top of his driveway and didn't open his door for anyone he didn't know.

Luke texted me asking if I wanted him to come by. Twice. I texted back "No."

A ghostwriter turned Posey's book, now titled *Aliens, Vampires, and the Servant Girl*, into a screenplay. Netflix quickly optioned it as a limited five-part series. Rainbow's mother, Linda, was listed as an associate producer.

Rainbow shut down from all the attention. A famous tech celebrity, public about his own Asperger's diagnosis, sent a slew of high-powered lawyers to her aid. A week later, tabloids published pictures of them holding hands on a secluded beach.

With all the publicity centered on the town, Cindy and the shelter doubled up on trying to find Mr. Pitt's owner. Success hit soon after the crowds began to disperse, and the media moved on to the next big story. After a Zoom call confirmed the silver dog had been stolen from a loving home, his anxious family piled into their SUV to pick him up.

Mr. Pitt was going home.

Mari, Cindy, and I waited in the reception area of the hospital. I clicked a leash on Mr. Pitt, who sat quietly by my side. His coat shone and he'd put on fifteen pounds of muscle. Such a change from the first time I'd laid eyes on him wrapped in an old blanket, shivering by the dumpster.

His wounds had healed, but his chewed-up ears gave testament to what he'd lived through. The ever-present scruffy moose toy hung from his mouth.

"Do you think he'll recognize them?" Cindy asked.

"Of course," I said. "He'll recognize their love."

A dark blue SUV pulled into the parking lot and a youngish couple emerged, the woman six or seven months pregnant. Steadying her as they walked down our sidewalk, the husband held his wife close. They rang the doorbell and peered through the door before coming inside.

Mr. Pitt looked up.

"Mouse!" the woman cried out. "Mousie, is that you?"

I'm not sure what I expected. Jumping, twirling, even slobbering. Instead, he walked over to her, tail wagging furiously, and leaned his big head against her belly. Protective. His mommy was here.

The husband knelt down and rubbed the big dog's

face, tears in his eyes. When his fingers felt the scar tissue above his eye, he frowned and looked at me.

"He'll be fine," I told him. "He'll be fine now."

Tears flowed, and we heard all about our pit bull's past. The couple stayed for almost an hour, showing us photos of Mr. Pitt/Mouse as a puppy. He'd been their baby for two years before he'd been stolen out of their backyard the day they moved. Despite posters and postings on social media about their dog's disappearance, he remained lost. When they moved again eight months later, they'd forgotten to update the microchip information.

During our reunion meeting, Mr. Pitt stayed close to his family, even sitting on his dad's foot. When they were ready to go, the woman dug into her large purse and retrieved a frayed toy mouse. "Here's Squeaky," she said. "Want to play with Squeaky?"

The big dog looked over at us, the brown moose firmly in his mouth.

"Go ahead," I said to him. "It's okay."

He dropped the moose on the reception floor and delicately plucked his mouse toy from her fingers.

"Guess we'll be going," the husband said. "We can't thank you enough for all you did for him."

Cindy, Mari, and I knelt down on the floor to say our goodbyes. Mr. Pitt's light green eyes appeared happy and calm. I gave him a kiss on his forehead and stood up.

After final farewells, the husband picked up Mr. Pitt/

Mouse's leash. The big pit bull swiveled his head back toward me, then stopped to pick the brown moose up from the floor. His mouth now full of toys, he looked back for the final time, then followed his family out to their car.

"I love a happy ending," said Mari, blotting her eye with a tissue.

"Me, too. Do you have another one of those?" I asked.

The three of us stood and watched the SUV leave our parking lot and turn onto the main road.

"Well, that's that," Mari commented. She swiped a ChapStick across her lips.

Staring out at the window, I reviewed in my mind the events of the last month. So much had happened since we'd found Mr. Pitt and said goodbye today to Mighty Mouse. "Back to normal life," I told my friends.

"Don't remind me," Cindy said.

Another dog was also being reunited with his owner, with little or no fanfare at all. Daffy had returned from Florida exhausted, suffering from jet lag. Since Little Man's surgical site had healed well, and we expected no problems for our brave little dog, Mari and I volunteered to drop the Chihuahua off at her place that afternoon.

"Where's Little Man?" Mari asked me. "He's not in any of the hospital cages."

"Oh, he's at my place," I casually noted, "saying goodbye to Buddy."

"Do you want me to get him?" she asked, grabbing her coat.

"No, that's okay. Why don't you go warm up the truck?" I suggested. "I'll bring him right out."

Little Man lounged on my bed, half-covered in a soft blue blanket. He lifted his bald head then stretched out his stick-like legs. The skin of his bat ears was so translucent you could read through them.

We'd cuddled together in bed the night before.

He'd eaten shredded rotisserie chicken and only the tops off the broccoli.

No beer to settle his stomach.

No coffee this morning—just a few licks of vanilla ice cream.

I stroked the thin fur above his bulging brown eyes as I prepared to pick him up.

"Don't tell anyone," I said to the Chihuahua.

Little Man smiled at me and growled.

THE END

If you enjoyed *Last But Not Leashed*, don't miss the following excerpt from *Saddled with Murder*, another Dr. Kate Vet Mystery available from Poisoned Pen Press.

Prologue

A WISH CAN BE MANY THINGS: OPTIMISTIC, GREEDY, or a simple request for a favor from the vast unknown. We look up to the heavens when we wish.

Some of us look down.

Three wishes made in jest might bring three presents to Dr. Kate Turner, a bit of cheer during the holiday season. Of course, you can't wrap dead bodies in red and gold Christmas paper and shove them under the tree—but it's the thought that counts.

A simple card would have to do.

Gossip will run rampant if the wishes come true. So easy to drop a hint here, a confusing lie there—sprinkling suspicion in the streets of Oak Falls like dirty snowflakes.

Always show the world a normal face, but under the surface something dark lurked, tightly tied and bound by societal expectations. Kept in check.

Time to set it free.

Chapter One

"WHO WANTS A SLICE OF LITTER BOX CAKE?"

With that provocative question the Oak Falls Animal Hospital Christmas party shifted into overdrive. It was Friday afternoon, the weekend awaited, and bonuses were being given out along with presents from a Secret Santa. The staff laughed and noisily lined up for a taste of this ever-popular veterinary and/or Halloween treat.

Only weeks before Christmas, and outside the Hudson Valley glimmered with a soft layer of snow. The blue-gray mountains, their dark green pine trees dusted in white, resembled greeting cards, and the village of Oak Falls took advantage of it. Lushly festive decorations evoked a storybook feeling meant to entice tourists to enter the stores and buy buy buy. It was impossible to escape the relentless cheeriness.

This time of the year I morphed from Dr. Kate Turner, friendly veterinarian, to grumpy Dr. Kate Scrooge. The music, the decorations brought back difficult memories. Just before Christmas, the year I turned fifteen, my mom and brother, Jimmy, were killed in a hit-and-run accident. My father and I didn't deal well with our tragedy. I embraced anger, and he embraced another woman. The Christmas tree stayed in the house, all the presents wrapped but untouched, until February, the following year, when Gramps came and took it down.

"Come on, Dr. Kate," my cheery office manager/ receptionist Cindy said, waving a red paper plate. "Dig in. You know you're dying to try it."

Putting away my own thoughts and knowing that tasting this mess was inevitable, I plastered a smile on my face and stood up. The treatment room, the hub of the animal hospital, glittered and glowed with twinkling Christmas lights shaped like dogs and cats. A silver garland composed of hundreds of tiny reindeers draped over the IV stands and hung pushpinned around the windows. Jolly holly Christmas music poured out of the hospital sound system inviting all to sing along.

The infamous litter box cake rested on a Santa-and-his-elves-themed tablecloth, which covered our stainless-steel table, making it as festive as stainless steel can be. The baker, my technician, Mari, had strived for realism—succeeding beyond her wildest nightmares. Tootsie Rolls and Baby Ruth bars starred as the cat poop, while some kind of granular sugar/graham cracker mix stood in for the litter. A partially melted piece of chocolate artistically draped over the side of the litter box represented the kitty that—"oops"—had missed the mark.

And, yes, she had transferred the "cake" into a real litter box, complete with plastic liner, uncomfortably close to the ones we actually used.

"You've outdone yourself," I told Mari. "Now, if only you had buried a tiny Santa Claus surprise in the middle of this…masterpiece."

Cindy raised a carefully enhanced eyebrow while she thought about that comment but proceeded to cut the cake to the delight of the group and present me with the first piece. "To your first Christmas in Oak Falls, Dr. Kate. Ice cream?"

"Why not?" I slid the red paper plate with my generous portion toward her. "What flavors do you have?"

"Only one. I made it myself in our ice cream machine."

When she paused I knew something was up.

Wondering how you top a litter box cake, I asked, "What flavor did you make?"

"Reindeer Crunch."

Score one for Cindy. Medical humor across the board is pretty strange to outsiders, but it helps defuse what can often be a stressful job. "I hope no reindeer were injured in the making of this ice cream."

Mari, busy capturing the fun with her phone, said, "All reindeer are present and accounted for. It's a blend of milk chocolate, which stands for their coats, with vanilla-and-dark-chocolate-covered wafers mixed in to resemble their hooves. Oh, and a couple of Red Hots. They help blast you to the North Pole."

"They sure do," chimed in our kennel helper Tony, always ready with a comment.

"Are the Red Hots an homage to Rudolph's nose?"

"You've got it, Doc."

As soon as I returned to my seat, I tasted an over-loaded forkful of litter box cake topped with melted Tootsie Rolls and Reindeer Crunch.

It was delicious.

———

Thirty minutes later with everyone well fed, the party started winding down. Cindy updated me on two angry clients, one of whom refused to pay his bill. Mari and Greta, the shy intern, were comparing notes while Tony explained something, complete with hand gestures, to the new kennel worker. At the back of the room next to a bank of cages sat our next-door neighbor and snow-plow guy, Pinky Anderson. Pinky had brought his senior citizen dog Princess in to see me several times, but today he'd come in to talk about the holiday plowing sched-ule. Cindy insisted he stay for the party. Our hospital cat, Mr. Cat, meanwhile, managed to dislodge the red bow scotch-taped to his collar. No attempt to dress him up withstood the power of his claws. Terribly annoyed, he parked himself under an IV stand festooned with a loop of sparkly garland and vigorously began to groom his fluffy tail.

I jumped up and stashed the bow in my pocket just as Cindy announced it was Secret Santa time.

Blond-haired, blue-eyed Cindy had been a cheer-leader in high school, and you could tell. Her genuine upbeat attitude made her popular with both clients and staff. Today she wore what she called her traditional ugly Christmas sweater, an explosion of badly knit reindeer and lumpy trees with an unintentionally evil-looking Santa suggestively nestled over her chest.

Almost all the staff were here, including our perennial student, Tony Papadapolis, along with a new part-time kennel helper, Aaron Keenan, and college intern, Greta Weber.

Mari scrambled up to the front to help clear the empty pizza boxes, jingling as she walked, thanks to the two dog collars she'd woven around her neck. She shot an evil eye at her personal nemesis, Tony, who merely turned his back.

I'd forgotten what they were feuding about at the moment.

Before exchanging the presents, Cindy insisted on playing a holiday game. "Well, it's not exactly a game," she said, qualifying her statement. "There's no prize." She clapped her hands to get our attention. "Everyone has to reveal their secret selfish holiday wish." Mari raised her hand with the inevitable question that went ignored.

"And no peace on earth or anything like that. Your wish has to be down and dirty, and it has to involve the animal hospital."

"What if you don't have one?" asked the somewhat shy Greta, sounding worried she might offend someone.

Cindy smoothed down the front of her sweater,

inadvertently rubbing Santa the wrong way. "Just try. It will be fun."

"We all have selfish wishes," good-looking Tony piped up. "I'll go first if you want."

Dead silence confirmed that no one else wanted to start.

"Okay. I wish that all the dogs in the kennel," he paused dramatically, confident in front of the group, "took self-cleaning poops that smelled like roses."

A round of cheers greeted his statement, since everyone knew how often he complained about his cleaning duties.

"Good one," acknowledged Mari. "Next? Cindy? Come on, you started this."

Cindy immediately accepted the challenge. "I know it's selfish, but I wish the parking space next to the front door had my name on it." With that she covered her face with her hands, embarrassed.

"Maybe we can arrange that," I announced and stood up. "Presto." I waved a pretend magic wand. "The first space to the left along the sidewalk will be reserved for Cindy."

Everyone clapped.

"What about you, Dr. Turner?" our pre-vet student asked.

"Yeah," seconded Tony.

"Wait a minute. Let me record this for posterity." My assistant stood up and began to scan the room with her phone.

"Well," I began, definitely feeling on a sugar high, between the cake and the ice cream. "Since I have my magic wand out already," I lifted my finger in the air, "I wish that two dissatisfied clients of mine…who will remain anonymous…"

Mari loudly interrupted by shouting out, "Frank Martindale and Eloise Rieven."

"And Raeleen Lassitor," added a voice from the back of the room.

I should have stopped there, but I didn't. Instead, with arm raised and magic index finger pointed, I continued. "I wish that my Secret Selfish Santa would make them all…disappear." With that I drew a few circles in the air and cried, "Abracadabra, poof. They're gone."

Cindy clapped her hands, and Mari called out loud to me, "Well, we can all dream, can't we?"

———

Party over, Mari and I stayed to clean up and do treatments on Goober, a diabetic dog, and Fluffernutter, a rabbit whose nails and teeth we'd trimmed. Both were being discharged in the next half hour, leaving me with an empty hospital. After checking Goober's blood sugar, we fed him an early dinner, then administered his adjusted insulin dose.

"You surprised me today," Mari confessed as she cleaned the gray laminate countertops.

"What do you mean?" I was busy entering Goober's latest values into his chart and writing up instructions for his owners.

"Your wish."

My fingers paused over the keyboard. "I surprised myself, and not in a good way. Honestly, I don't know what or who possessed me. Maybe I should wish that wish would go away."

"It was a joke," Mari said. "Everyone knew it. You almost never complain about clients, so the universe owes you one."

"Two. Make that three, thanks to Pinky. What exactly was he doing here, do you know?"

She put the plastic covers over the microscopes. "He dropped by to talk about plowing schedules and some hole in the parking lot. Cindy felt sorry for him and invited him to stay for pizza and the cake. I mean he lives right next door."

"True."

"You know, Doc Anderson used to complain every week that his clients were driving him crazy."

"That's probably why he hired me and went on a round-the-world cruise." I finished up my notes and logged out.

"Well," Mari said. "I'm glad he did. If he hadn't, we wouldn't have met you."

"Ahhh. That's so nice. Thank you." A tiny piece of that icy grumpiness I secretly carried around started to melt. "Okay." I stood up next to the computer station.

"That does it." Raising my hand, I enthusiastically swirled it around in the air then pointed my finger at my tech. "Abracadabra. I wish everything would go back to normal. There. My magic wand is hereby officially retired."

Acknowledgments

I found 2021 one heck of a year to be writing a book. It took all my discipline to close off the universe and dive into the world of Kate Turner. But dive I did and found myself adding more and more humor into the story because, quite frankly, I needed it, and I suspect my readers do too.

My thanks to everyone who worked so hard to bring this book to publication. A shout-out to the staff at Sourcebooks, my editors Diane DiBiase and Beth Deveny, and the folks at Poisoned Pen. I owe an immense debt of gratitude to the members of my critique group, Betty Webb, Arthur Kerns, Charlie Pyeatte, Sharon Magee, Ruth Barmore, and Donis Casey, for their guidance and helpful suggestions. Thanks to fellow author Rosemary Simpson for brainstorming the rough spots with me, and to Dr. John Hynes, whose enthusiasm for Dr. Kate never wavers. Last, but never least, I owe so much to my husband, Dr. Jonathan Grant, whose calm support of my crazy late-night writing marathons before deadline is forever appreciated.

Finally, we inhabit this world with many other living beings. Don't forget to be kind to the creatures that share our air, our oceans, our soil, and our forests. This fragile planet that circles our sun is on an unknown adventure. We are all just here for the ride.

About the Author

A practicing veterinarian for more than twenty years, Eileen Brady lives in Arizona with her husband, two daughters, and an assortment of furry friends.